THE PALACE OF
THE WHITE SKUNKS

THE

PALACE

OF THE

WHITE

SKUNKS

REINALDO ARENAS

TRANSLATED BY
ANDREW HURLEY

VIKING

VIKING

Published by the Penguin Group
Viking Penguin, a division of Penguin Books USA Inc.,
375 Hudson Street, New York, New York 10014, U.S.A.
Penguin Books Ltd, 27 Wrights Lane,
London W8 5TZ, England
Penguin Books Australia Ltd, Ringwood,
Victoria, Australia
Penguin Books Canada Ltd, 2801 John Street,
Markham, Ontario, Canada L3R 1B4
Penguin Books (N.Z.) Ltd, 182–190 Wairau Road,
Auckland 10, New Zealand

Penguin Books Ltd, Registered Offices:
Hardmonsworth, Middlesex, England

First published in 1990 by Viking Penguin,
a division of Penguin Books USA Inc.

1 3 5 7 9 10 8 6 4 2

Translation copyright © Reinaldo Arenas and Andrew Hurley, 1990
All rights reserved

Originally published in Spain by Editorial Argos Vergara, S.A. as
El palacio de las blanquísimas mofetas. Copyright © Reinaldo Arenas, 1982.

LIBRARY OF CONGRESS CATALOGING IN PUBLICATION DATA
Arenas, Reinaldo, 1943–
[Palacio de las blanquísimas mofetas. English]
The palace of the white skunks / Reinaldo Arenas;
translated by Andrew Hurley.
p.   cm.
Translation of: El palacio de las blanquísimas mofetas.
ISBN 0–670–81510–1
I. Title.
PQ7390.A72P3413   1990
863—dc20   89–40688

Printed in the United States of America
Set in Trump Medieval
Designed by Ann Gold

C O N T E N T S

PART ONE

PROLOGUE AND EPILOGUE

Death is out there in the backyard, playing with the wheel off a bicycle. There was a time when that bicycle was mine. There was a time when that wheel without a tire was a new bicycle. And I would ride it all the way up the street, up to the top of the red dirt hill. And sometimes I'd be going so fast it would make your head spin, and I would skid and fall off that bicycle and it's a wonder I didn't break my neck. And my knees would be all scratched up and scabby, and I'd keep them covered so nobody would see them. I'd plaster them with mud so people would think what I had was dirty knees, not scabby ones. There was a time when that bicycle had both wheels and every kid in the neighborhood wanted to ride it.

But I told every one of them no.

I was the only one that could ride it.

Mama would run out and yell and call me in to eat. But I'd act like I didn't even hear her, I'd just keep on riding that bicycle—up the street, up to the top of the red dirt hill. And then down the red dirt hill. And sometimes I'd pull out all the stops, I'd take a deep breath and ride right down onto the highway and everything. I'll tell you the truth, I don't know how in the world I didn't get myself run over on that bicycle. Hey, look, look at me, look at me here, riding this bicycle. And the cars and trucks whooshing past *that* close. *Young man. Young man!* There was a time when all in the world I ever thought about was being able to have a bicycle.

And I did have one.

My mother, I don't know how she managed to save up the money and buy it. But she did. And I don't know what I felt when

I saw that bicycle. And they said, Get on. I can't even tell you what I felt. I rode that bicycle on the roof of the house. And sometimes even up above the roof. There was a time when that piece of rubber there with two or three stripes on it was a bicycle. And I would ride along the very edge of the wooden bridge that creaked whenever anybody crossed it. And I would cross that bridge and just about be riding through the air. But I never fell off. I never . . . And there were some times when I'd ride through Calixto García Park. Right through the middle of the park without putting my feet on the pedals or anything. I'm rolling right through the middle of the park sticking my tongue out at Calixto García with my feet on the handlebars. Look, look, watch this! I'm the only one that knows how to do this! Watch this, watch this! There was a time. There was a time . . . Death is out there in the backyard playing with the rusty hoop of the wheel of my bicycle, or rather with the rusty wheel of what *used* to be my bicycle. He's out there day and night, and he never leaves the yard, and he never stops to rest a single instant. He'll pick up the wheel, start it rolling, and then he rolls it around and around with a stick. And all day and all night and all of what's not day or night either, Death just trots around the yard with that stick and that wheel. Around and around the backyard. The first one to see him was my grandmother. When, I don't know. She went outside one night to go to the bathroom, because she's one of those people that always have the runs and cramps and everything all night. So she went outside. She gave a shriek. And she ran back in and threw herself down on her knees in front of the wood cookstove. Around that time I had taken to hunting bats with a mosquito net, and I heard the scream from up on the ridgepole because I had climbed up there after a bat, to teach it how to smoke. I heard the scream and I don't know why but I knew what had happened. Because it had to be what it was, more or less, for my grandmother to yell that way. Because as old as she was, what in the world would make her jump if it wasn't Death? So then everybody quit sleeping or whatever they were doing and ran in to see what had happened to my grandmother. And all she would say was, Out there, out there. And point out to the backyard. The second one to see him was my grandfather. He looked out the back door. He stuck his head out the door, and his head was as bald as a buzzard's, and he pulled it back in again without saying a word. Not a peep. Then he went into the front room and turned on the radio. But the radio didn't talk or play music or anything, nothing came out of the radio because it was real real early in the morning and there weren't any stations running. My mother and Adolfina and Digna all stuck their heads out at the same time. And the minute they saw him, they every one of them started to dance. And dance. And dance. And they're still dancing, to this day . . . *Young man. Young man, you're going to bust your mouth on that bicycle* . . . My cousins Tico and Anisia, they saw him too. And they even called him. But I don't think he paid them the slightest bit of attention because he just kept on with that bicycle wheel—around and around, around and around, all around the backyard. I was up on the ridgepole on the roof of the house, and I watched him and watched him. And I forgot all about the bats, I just grabbed the mosquito net and threw it at Death.

The mosquito net fell right on top of him and he got his arms and head all tangled up in it. And for a second there the bicycle wheel rolled away and he couldn't guide it or anything with the stick. The wheel rolled all the way over almost to the kitchen door while he was flailing around trying to get out of the mosquito net. Until he finally did get loose. And then he walked, very slowly and calmly, over to the kitchen door, and he was sputtering sparks all over the place. And he picked up the wheel. And he started rolling that wheel around and around the yard again. *Young man. Young man!* . . . The old man's sitting in the porch swing and the old woman's on her knees in the front room. The old man stares at Death and the old woman prays. Tico and Anisia relax a little bit and they start asking each other riddles. *What am I thinking now, tell me what I'm thinking about.* The old man won't talk because he just flat doesn't feel like it. Why won't the old man talk? Why won't Grandpa talk? *Guess, tell me what I'm thinking about. About a box turtle with eight legs. You got part of it, but you missed some—eight legs and one gold tooth.*

You got part of it, but not all of it.

With eight legs, one gold tooth, and a big nose on his tail. The old man's fallen off to sleep. The old woman gets tired of praying, so she goes and lies down. *You missed, you missed—I was thinking of a box turtle with eight legs, one gold tooth, a big nose on his tail, and a stake hammered through the middle of his shell. Good lord, the things you think of. Okay, though, now it's your turn to guess.* Adolfina goes in the bathroom and bars the door. In the bathroom is the bottle of alcohol. Adolfina, who never forgets a thing, is carrying a box of matches between her breasts. *I don't know what to do with my life anymore. I tell you, I just do not know what to do with my life anymore.* "Dear son, It's my dearest wish that this letter finds you well." Adolfina takes off her clothes and steps into the bathtub. Adolfina looks at herself in the mirror and shrieks. She doesn't shriek, but she shrieks all the same. What can you expect from a family of island country hicks? What can you expect from people that live with beasts? Nothing. You can't expect a thing. Everything. You can expect just about everything. Adolfina starts dancing naked in the bathtub. *What do you see? What do you see? I see a spider drowning in a dry bathtub. Don't be so silly, tell me the truth— what do you see? I see a witch playing with a spider in a bathtub. You goose, you're always telling me fibs and stories.*

I go out earlier today than ever, out to where the spiny wild coffee bushes grow all in a clump, and there is Misael naked under a wild coffee bush, waiting for me.

Misael naked.

My god. Son of a bitch. My god. God. I don't believe in you. In fact, you're a fake. I'll tell you what—if you exist, why don't you just come over here? Step over here, you prick, and I'll smash your face in for you.

I go out early on my bicycle and the first thing that happens to me is I get my feet all tangled up in the bicycle chain and I go headfirst into a mudhole. *You just come here, God, and I'll take a stick to you.* Since the hunger is so bad here, we've started eating each other. Death keeps going around the yard, around and around with that bicycle wheel, and it looks to me like sometimes he lets it roll just a little too close for comfort over by the door where we're all watching him, imagining him. And meanwhile I try to figure out a way to leave home, because I can't take any more of this living with a bunch of women and one old man who won't utter a word because he just flat doesn't feel like it. And meanwhile, Death is out there with that bicycle wheel. Round and around. And meanwhile, my mother is fixing up the papers—after a thousand years of back and forth from one consulate to another to finally get to go to New York. To work like a dog. To die of cold and loneliness. To wipe squawling babies' asses. To live like an animal. To earn some money. To bring up children that aren't her own so her own children won't starve.

The moon is terrible. She slips in through the windows and hits me and beats me up. The moon can't hit me, because I go crazy if she does. My mother knows I go crazy when the moon hits me. But she doesn't dare close the window, either, because if she goes over to close it she'll see Death out there playing with that bicycle wheel in the backyard. She sees him, she sees him. Now nobody dares to leave the house. Or even to look out the window. We're scared to death in here inside the house, all closed up, and not daring to even peek outside for fear we'll see Death. But since I can't stand that big huge moon anymore, I finally stand up on the bed and try to close the blinds. I'm scared to death, it's the truth, but even though I tell myself *I won't open my eyes, I won't open my eyes*, I open my eyes.

And I see him, shining in the moonlight, on the other side of the window. Death, dying laughing, doing somersaults and showing off and doing tricks and making faces at me on the other side of the window. I run wrap myself up in the sheets as tight as I can. But I might as well still be standing at the window—I can still see Death dying laughing, making faces and acting like a clown. The moon is still sneaking in through the blinds. Sooner or later I'll have to start howling. Sooner or later I'll have to run out into the street and start yelling. Sooner or later I'll have to cut my throat. What can you expect, what can you expect from somebody that lives with wild beasts? Everything, they said. Nothing, they said. I'm standing out in front of the house carrying the two kids and the tied-up bundle of clothes on my head and wishing the ground would open and swallow me up. He's left me. And now I'll never have the pleasure of being in bed with a man again. Ground—open and swallow me.

Ground—open and swallow me up. *Tell me what I'm seeing now. A real old little man out in the backyard playing with the wheel off Fortunato's bicycle. You got it, you got it, almost . . .*

Now me. Tico and Anisia smash all the plates to smithereens. My dead daughter is like a plate smashed to smithereens. And I try to pick up all the little tiny pieces and put the plate back together again. But there are so many little pieces . . . I pick up one piece and I drop ten, and so on and so on and so on.

My dead daughter. I have a dead daughter. Oh, happy me, I have a dead daughter. Isn't it odd that in spite of her being dead, I can still say, I *have*? Oh, happy me. At least I can say, This is my sad fate. I can point to it and display it, I can. I can savor it. Ah. Tico and Anisia. What will become of Tico and Anisia?

The factory where I used to pick up a little money now and again closes. The factory opens, and the noise of the factory drives us crazy. The noise and the smell of rotten guavas. But thank goodness we've got that factory in this neighborhood. Right here, in the backyard of this house. Because if we didn't, what would we live on? Tomasico's factory is "the lifeblood of the neighborhood." I go out on the bicycle and the kids say, Let us play with it a minute. And I say no. But they want me to let them ride it anyway. But there's no way in the world I'm going to let them ride it, so I take off at a mile a minute, pedaling like crazy. Pedaling like crazy. The kids run after me and throw rocks. But none of the rocks cracks *my* skull. My head is harder than an acorn, so my grandmother says. And even if I don't know what an acorn is, I suspect my grandmother's right. The rocks hit me in the head.

And bounce off. And run away as fast as they can. I'm on my bicycle and I ride off down the highway and disappear. Cars and trucks whistle by and drivers yell, You little ninny, keep to the right, keep to the right. But do I give a hoot, I don't know which way is the right, or what that means, keep to it. Buses pass me and go *Fzzz* and drag this blast of wind behind them that practically shoves me in the ditch. Keep to the right. Keep to the right. Little asshole, I'm gonna have a wreck on your account! . . . Any day now you're going to turn up dead on the highway, says my grandmother. Any day now . . . So I ride out as fast as I can onto the highway. My mother, before she left she told me, Don't worry, I'm going to send for you just as soon as I can. My mother . . . I've never seen the ocean and I'd like to see it. It's hard to believe, as close as Gíbara is to where I live and me never to have seen the ocean. But that's nothing, because I'm young and I can see it someday. What's sad is my aunt Emerita the Obnoxious, because she'll be fifty years old right around the corner and she still has never seen it. The other day my aunt Emerita comes in, the Obnoxious One, crying. She comes into my house, or rather my grandpa's house, which by the way she never just *visits*, and she's crying so hard she has to lean on the cabinet we keep the water jug in. For hours. You should have heard her. Such carrying on. And when my grandmother finally asked her what she was crying about, she, the Obnoxious One, she said, "Do you know what it is that any day now I'll die an old lady and I still haven't seen the ocean?" The wheel goes around and around and around. And the moon is furious and she comes down right to the roof of the house and hits me again. The doves whirr off flying and I know that now they'll never come back again.

So now I think I better take up something else.

I know—I'll manufacture wine, I'll take up manufacturing wine, and I'll hide in the bathroom every day with four or five bottles. The bicycle wheel sparkles, and shines—some of the time it's like it was crying. *Your abandoned daughter's out there, and she's dragging her two kids along behind her. Go out there and kill that son of a bitch of a husband of hers. Get on out there and at least kill him. Get out there, you old rooster. Go.* Bottles full of spoiled wine explode under the bed, and drunk cockroaches start climbing up the bedposts. It's terrible, knowing that you're a prisoner in a place where you can never solve anything by opening a door and walking out in the street. It's terrible. Grandma cries and says, "I thought he was asleep. I just thought he overslept."

It's terrible.

I slowly drag myself across the floor till I get to the bed where the old man and the old woman do their filthy acts. That's where the cigár box with the money in it is. I slowly slip under the bed and start cramming coins in my pockets. While the old man and the old woman collapse snorting and wheezing up on top of the bed, underneath it I'm sacking all their loot. As long as they keep leaving the cigar box with the money in it under the bed, I'll be all right. The bathroom lights up. The bathroom has caught fire.

The ball of fire comes running out of the bathroom. *Ay, ay,* says the fireball. Dear son, dear son, dear son, dear son.

Dear son.

Things are getting worse every day. Sales in the vegetable stand are worse every day. The whole thing is worse every day.

My daughter doesn't write me anymore. My daughter doesn't even remember me anymore. Ay, what it is to be a parent—you bring up children to gouge out your eyes. Ay, parents . . . And this is what life is. *Hello, don Polo. How are you? Thinking. I see. Ay, don Polo, life* . . . Now it's always night. My grandfather won't talk and the factory's closed.

We're dying of hunger.

The grandmother prays and god-damns Tico, the saints, and sometimes God Himself, but then she begs His pardon. We ate my daughter yesterday, but that's water under the bridge—no use crying over spilled milk *now* . . . But I'm young, and I'm sure someday I'll see the ocean. Keep to the right, the ocean. Keep to the right, the ocean. Keep to the right, the ocean. If I go on straight ahead, I'll get to the ocean. If I keep on down this way, I'll get to the ocean. I'll get to the ocean no matter what road I take. The ocean. Keep to the right, idiot! And I will get there. *I bet you can't guess what I'm thinking. A she-mule dressed in white.* The ocean. *You almost got it, but it wasn't white, it was lilac. Fibber, what it is is, you change things around the minute I guess them.* While I sweat, cough, and shoo away the mosquitoes, I write. While I cough and cough and cough, while I sweat and sweat and fan the air, I write. I don't know how I managed to get my hands on a typewriting machine, but I've run the old man out of all the paper he had in the shop. The old man doesn't say anything, because he won't talk, but he's about to pop. And Grandma wants to kill me, she's so furious when she sees that the old man has to send goods home with the people carrying them in their bare hands. While the old woman scolds and fights with me, I write and write and write. And I don't sleep. Or eat. Until finally I get over the urge to write and I throw all the paper down the hole in the outhouse. The old woman catches me and throws a fit. Tico and Anisia pretend they don't touch the ground. The old man doesn't talk. Dear son. Adolfina sets herself afire. Life is hard.

Espadrilles. As far as I'm concerned, there's nothing in the world like espadrilles. A pair of espadrilles. That's where the urges start. *Stinky-ass. Stinky-ass.* I'm going to run out in the street naked. *Hail Mary, full of grace, the Lord is with thee . . .* I dare you to stand in the front door and say Balls. I dare you. I double-dare you. *Balls. Balls!* Good lord, he took the dare. Now they'll carry him off to jail. If you ask me, that boy's not quite all there, now he's taken to frying slugs and eating them with bread. Yuck, how disgusting . . . Now it's always night and Digna sings on the porch without opening her mouth. Poor Digna— raising two kids all by herself. Poor kids. Poor Adolfina. Poor Grandma. I mean, poor Grandpa. I mean, poor Mama. I mean, poor me. Which is, poor Digna.

The vegetable stand closes because the factory closes and now nobody has even one centavo to spare—I mean even if it's cracked and has a hole through the middle of it. The vegetable stand fails. The old man tries to hang himself but he has no luck at it. The old woman stops believing in God and prays to the plate-glass window. I've finally seen the ocean. It was no big deal. It wasn't what I wanted it to be, and it didn't live up to what it had always meant to me. Just water and more water. I wish I'd never seen it. The ocean . . . Adolfina in the bathroom. And my mother writing me and writing me and writing me.

One day soon Tico and Anisia will be grown-ups. The vegetable stand fails. I get bored. I think the best thing I can do is go with the rebels. There's people gone with the rebels. There's people gone with the rebels everywhere. To the mountains. The whole town is dark. The vegetable stand has failed. Dear son, Don't get into any trouble. Death plays and plays and plays out in the yard with the wheel. Death spends his whole life now out there, out in the backyard. Esther, Esther. Where's Celia? Over there, talking to the angels and the demons. My cousin Esther and my aunt Celia. Tonight I saw Esther talking to Death in the middle of the yard. Tonight, when I got up to close the window again, I saw Esther talking to Death and she was offering him lord knows what. Death's head going up and down like he's saying Uh-huh, uh-huh. And then Esther finally started dancing. Death looked over at her, quick, and then he stood there with his head hanging down on his chest. Esther went on dancing and disap-

peared above the roof. Esther is my dead cousin. Celia was crying very softly, and finally she closed the kitchen door and went out onto the porch and started talking to the demons and the angels
and the elves
and the beasts.
I'm going with the rebels.
It's so very very hot. Terrible. It's always hot. I've had it up to here. Good lord, good lord. The buses shoot by like rockets. I can't take any more. The old woman shrieks as she prays to the plate-glass window. Dear son. I'm going with the rebels. I've had it up to here. You ninny. You ninny. You ninny. You ninny. I'm going with the rebels. There are rebels everywhere. The whole town is left in the dark. Even Eufrasia's Ball Room is closed. The whores that work there have gone off to the mountains or just somewhere else. I'm going up into the mountains. I don't even feel like jerking off. I'm going with the rebels. Ah, but you've got no weapon, so what's the use? You've got to have a weapon. A long arm, a rifle. *Ak-ak-ak-ak-ak, ak, ak*. In this house nobody dares to go outside for fear of running into Death in the middle of the yard, and meanwhile we're starving here inside. And Death

I am a girl thirteen years old and I am more bored and tired than I have ever been before. All Mama knows how to do is embarrass me in front of people . . . And Baudilio didn't look at me once all night long. Somebody told me he was already engaged to be married. And as though that weren't enough, my slip is showing and Digna's kids are screaming their heads off. I'd swallow a bottle of strychnine and go to bed right here if it weren't that I'd already taken the strychnine and was in bed already.

out there outside, like nothing was going on, as pretty as you please. But I've got to get out, I've got to get out. The wheel turns, and turns, and turns. Dear son. Esther, Esther. What a terrible moon. If only we lived like we did before, up there, up on the mountain in the country. I still have the memory. It's like I'm still that boy who disappears into the tall guinea-grass and plays hide-and-seek behind the coconut palms. It's still . . . It's still like I'm bathing in the river. And the water comes up over me and comes up over me again, and all the plants say *Brr, brr* to me, like that time, remember? Uh-huh, I know you remember. I know you can't say you don't remember. Because what you're living on now is the things that you didn't realize were part of the deepest part of you. Because there you are, opening the door of night itself, in the big wide long breezeway, under the shower-of-gold plant, with the *Grr, grr, grr* of the bullfrogs and the glow that comes from who knows where. Such a night. Such a night. I go out, up to the mountain, and all I hear is thousands of different sounds. Such a night. I bathe in the water that's fallen from the fans of the palm trees, and I scrub myself in it, and I am still bathing myself. And I run off, over to the pasture, and I lie in the grass, and I see a million sparks falling. Such a night, young man, such a night. And you there, lying there, savoring it. And you there, lying in the grass and the transparent fog. Lying on your back on top of the world, while night comes and leaves you white and wet. And there you are, growing sleepier and sleepier, until the elves come. Such a night, such a night. It's almost as though you were dreaming.

"Young man, what are you doing lying there? The chiggers will eat you alive."

But things change. Things aren't like you think they used to be, once upon a time. Things are just things you imagine to yourself so you can get by. So you can live and later on say, Back then, back then. So someday Now will be Back then. Because now, Now is nothing. But then it will be Back then. And Back then *is* something. So many things . . . The old woman grumbles and scolds and fights with everybody and says there's not a thing to eat. Adolfina won't come out of the bathroom. Celia is crying about her dead daughter and says she doesn't even remember what she looked like anymore. Digna is singing with her mouth closed. The old man spends every waking minute with the bug-spray pump, shooting down imaginary mosquitoes. And you. And you, and you . . . I went to Eufrasia's Ball Room, and it was closed. I'm going to go off with the rebels. Tonight. This is my night. The old man grabs the bug spray and starts spraying Flit all over the house. The old woman gags and coughs and stumbles into a stool. She shrieks, *I'd rather be eaten alive by mosquitoes than die of bug-spray poisoning!*

Everyone's in bed.

The old man puts the bug-spray pump under his pillow. The

old woman can barely breathe. The old man can't go to sleep. The old woman coughs and chokes. The old man grabs the bug spray every time he thinks he hears a mosquito anywhere near the bed and he goes *Psshh psshh* and sprays Flit in the air and in the old woman's face. The old woman sticks her head underneath the sheet and starts gasping and panting. The old man puts away the bug spray again. The old woman sticks her head out and with one foot she tickles the old man's foot. The old man puts one leg across the old woman's leg. A mosquito goes *Yeeeeee* and flies across the bed. But neither one of them hears it, neither the old man nor the old woman either. Outside there is a burst of gunfire. Outside there is a big huge moon that wants to scare me stiff, that wants to smash me to smithereens. You ought to close the window. You ought to run out in the street and join the rebels. The rebels are going to win any day now, and you're still all locked up in that house, like you were hiding. What are you doing in bed with things the way they are now? You ninny, locked up like a woman. You simpleton, you lazy good-for-nothing lout, you goose, you faggot. While other people risk their lives, you lie there stupid, wasting it, losing it, without risking it. Go. Anyway, the way you're living it's the same as though you weren't living at all. The other way, maybe . . . The other way. *Dear son.* The other way. I can't take any more. *Cock a doodle doo.* The old man won't talk. *Don't spray so much goddamn bug spray, goddammit, you're gonna poison me.* Ave María purísima, in this house all you hear is filth and indecency. Tico and Anisia. Anisia and Tico. Such children. Fortunato's taken to eating lizards now . . . Fire, fire! Listen to that gunfire. The bottles of wine explode under the bed. Cockroaches run all over the place. The moon slips through the blinds again and hits you and sticks out her tongue at you. You try to grab her and smack her one, but the sly cunning vixen runs away. But as soon as you fall asleep, the moon slips through the blinds again and hits you and sticks out her tongue at you again. You try to grab her, but the sly vixen gets away. And you can't even shut your eyes. You can't stand this anymore. Such gunshots.

Every night the same thing. The same thing. And the dogs barking and barking and barking and barking and barking.

The old woman and the old man are snoring. The cockroaches

run up the mosquito net. Life is pig swill. What will have become of me in ten years? No, I mustn't think about that. I stick my head outside the mosquito net. The moon stares coldly, furiously at me—she is high, high up and terribly cruel on the other side of the window. You're going to run off with the rebels. *Dear son.* On the farm it is almost dawn. A million elves and fairies run all about, in and out between your legs, and run and scramble to their hiding places. Where are you going with those lizards! Such a night, such a night. I'm going off with the rebels this very minute.

You go.

You get to the back door. And you open it. Death is out there in the backyard, playing with the wheel off a bicycle. Playing and playing. I open the door as wide as I can. One of these days you're going to bust your mouth . . . The moon bathes Death in a light that makes him look like a white star twinkling in the middle of the backyard. The wheel turns and turns and turns, rolled along by the stick Death is carrying. The door is wide open. The backyard glows and sparkles and the moon comes lower and lower. The doves up on the roof go *Brrr brrr.* The moon comes lower and lower. The moon glows and sparkles. Dear son . . . Death lets the wheel roll off on its own, for the first time. The wheel comes right to my hands. Death raises his arms and the moon laughs so hard she almost bursts. The house starts glowing and sparkling. Death raises his arms higher and higher, in a sign of total liberation. Like a man who's just finished serving out his punishment. Like a man who's just gotten rid of some terrible unbearable responsibility. The doves go *Brrr brrr brrr.* Dear son . . . I catch the wheel and start rolling it around in the middle of the backyard. The wheel goes *Brrr brrr brrr.* Death goes *Brrr brrr brrr.* Everything goes *Brrr brrr brrr.*

Tico and Anisia peek out the door and start laughing so hard you'd think they were the moon.

THE FLY—I

The fly has six gray legs, small nervous appendages like tiny grappling hooks constantly in motion, sensing. The eyes of the fly, comprised of millions of microscopic eyes, lack eyelids. With its short neck, its stubby wings, its six grappling-hook-like legs which in turn branch into infinite micro-grappling hooks, its quick, hoplike flights, and its indifference to words, the fly has managed to adapt to a great range of temperatures, to heat, to cold, to humidity, to darkness, to abrupt changes in its environment, and to continual ravages of hunger. But seen from below, the fly offers an even more desolate and dispiriting spectacle: millions of membranes, hairs, tiny barbs, rocky pink wet suppurating fetid apertures quiver and tremble all across the bristling armor of its breastplate, like a pulsing leech. The fly reproduces at a rapid and unstoppable pace. One fly may lay more than two hundred eggs per day. Moreover, it is still unproven that, as many claim, its life is limited to only twenty-four hours. Its existence has two meanings, two instincts only: to poke about in carrion, and to fornicate.

PART TWO

THE CREATURES UTTER THEIR COMPLAINTS

There was a house. And in the house, someone was dying. There was always someone dying in those wretched and miserable houses. *We are all always dying in these wretched and miserable houses.* There was also the wind, always the wind, coming in through the broken and ramshackle walls, through the gaps so big that one might think they were doors. A house, someone dying, and the earth dried out, arid, unresponsive to dreams. The land dirty and dried out, salty and dried out, forcing a man to bend, calling only to humiliate, and bearing up under all. The land . . . The boy—and back then he really *was* a boy, though now that seems incredible, ironic, and perhaps offensive even to him himself—came in from the land, the wind, and he saw, once more, his mother in her last agony of death—*always in the throes of death.* He went over to her, bent over her, and buried his teeth in her earlobe. For the first time, his mother did not cry out. It was true, then, there was no doubt this time—this time she was really and truly dying. They had to make a hole, quick, there was something else to put in that ground. They had to cover it up, quick, so they could go on scratching at the earth. But even quicker, they had to get out, get away, leave, had to leave those damned blasted rocks and boulders, that place made for turning people into stooped and hump-backed dwarves. He went in, and he turned around and left. *Here, the plot of my native land, here, the hell.* But out there, beyond, the ocean, the undulating, sparkling ocean. The swollen smooth waters of the Atlantic seemed to offer to take him off to Africa, to Australia, or to that Island where, they say, you never have to carry water to water the flowers and garden with—where, so they say, you can live by just digging a little hole in the ground and trusting to the clouds. Could it be true? Was it possible that a paradisal place such as that existed, where a man who worked from sun to sun might eat twice a day, and even take a drink of water whenever he felt like it? Such a place did exist. Many of his friends (or acquaintances, rather, since friendship implied a certain luxury, a certain right at least to time which he did not possess) had gone away—and if it was true that he had never again heard from them, that was precisely the proof that they had triumphed: they were eating every day. Only failures returned. Or never left . . . Out there was the sea, smooth and sparkling, always flowing . . . He went in, and he came out—and he saw the dried-out place he was in. The few stunted, withered trees were patent proof of the failure inherent in immobility. And the ground more and more cracked and broken. And everyone fleeing, everyone succeeding—who knew where. On that Island, surely, where you could throw down a seed and watch a tree spring up, in that place where you could cup water up in your hands. . . . At last his mother was dying. That hard face of a rough woman from the Canaries was simply disappearing, and also disappearing were the harsh hands of a rough island woman. And the body—the poor man's only treasure—the body was stiffening, swelling, beginning to exhibit a serenity—or a wry grin, at least—which in life it never had the time or talent to feel or to put on. The body which had scrabbled at the earth, which had made windrows out of the earth, the body which had forever been obliged to work the land, scrabble hurriedly over the earth, now was returning, deformed and stinking, to the earth. And the earth which had never gratified that body with fruit, with water, or with anything palpable or useful at all, which had never smiled upon the body that had been consecrated to its service, now suddenly showed an unheard-of interest in that filth and garbage—it swallowed it, ground it up and liquefied it, reduced it to *stuff* for its own loathsome ends. The land . . . And out there, beyond, the ocean, like an immense plain to glide across. The sea, the only alternative for a man who suffers from the mortal illness of islands. And quickly the boy went inside, saw his mother in the last throes of death (at last, his mother in her dying agony!), and ran into the kitchen, grabbed the conch shell, ran out, and climbed the withered tree out in the yard. And he began to blow the conch, announcing, even if it were not quite time yet, that his mother had died. The first to arrive were the cows, the few surprised cows, because the boy always blew that dirge at nightfall, calling them in to sleep, though the afternoon had barely begun. . . . And that same day Polo fled the place. (Inside the house, old women with rock-hewn faces took charge of the washing of the dead.) And that same day he came to the sea. And that same day he caught (by some miracle) one of the pirate boats (whose legal name was "emigrant frigates") that sailed away—full of Chinamen, Macaos, Negroes, Russians, Italians, Portuguese, all, like him, hungry fierce men, hungry fugitives, hungry dreamers, men who for the dream of fleeing their land grabbed up the only possessions they had, their bodies, and for the dream of escaping slavery sold themselves legally into slavery. . . . That same day he found out where the boat was going (for he hadn't cared)—the boat (the whirl of smells and noises was still unbearable to him) was bound for that Island of Great Trees, the reception center for all emigrants, bound for the Green Land Over There where, though it still sounded barely believable to him, you could cup water in your hands. But a month later, the old man (at the time but a boy) jumped off the boat onto the island of Cuba (they arrived in Oriente Province) and he saw for himself, at once, that at least that part about the water was true enough. And he promised himself, as he drank water from his cupped hands, that he would never return to the loathed, hated, and despised Canaries as long as he lived.

The stars squeal when I poke them with the sharp end of the prod. Poor stars. Every time I hear them squeak like that I get goosebumps.
But we're almost finished.
There are just two of the Seven Sisters left in the Pleiades.

And that's because we couldn't reach them. But just let us get hold of a longer prod, and they'll see. There's just one left in the Southern Cross. And we've popped every single one in the Plow.

When we finish picking up the stars we knocked down, we'll take up hunting quail and then we'll fish for eels and then we'll rope the moon. And then.

Ga-ga-*boom*, ga-ga-*boom*, ga-ga-*boom*. Tell me, ladies and gentlemen, if that's not enough to drive a woman crazy.

What will we do then?

There comes your abandoned daughter.
Shush.
There comes your half-mad daughter.
Shush.
There comes your banished daughter.
Shush.
There comes your spinster daughter.
Shush.
There, in other words, standing right there before you at this very instant, is Adolfina.
Shush.

Tall, skinny, and imperious (or as some said, *bossy*). She had heard those three words several times, always repeated "in her honor," and spoken invariably so she could hear them. *Tall, skinny, bossy*—and now *abandoned*. Because she also heard from time to time the whispering of her parents. Him, especially. Saying, With her, I'm telling you, there's nobody born that can live with her. Or, Now on top of everything we've got an abandoned daughter. Or, That's all we needed. But every week she took a sack and went off to the white-clay dirt pasture. And she scrabbled in the ground. Filled the sack. Walked home again. And scoured the front-room floor. ("Parlor," she called it.) And then, with the broom, she brushed the white dirt over the floor. And then, with the palms of her hands, she in a way paved the parlor floor white, covering the whole floor with that white paste. So when "they" arrived and with their firm tread trod that fine, crisp crust of white clay, that "coating" that crunched and crackled and crazed, they (sometimes) begged pardon, and even (sometimes) praised the labor, being told then that it was she who had performed that "wonder." That fact might help them decide. . . . *Tall, skinny, imperious* and the eldest to boot, the eldest daughter, to whose lot it fell of course, as always happens in these cases, to raise her brothers and sisters. If she had had brothers. And so who, of course, was therefore no longer considered by them a sister at all but rather a kind of second mother, something useful, that is to say, and worthy of their hatred—false, like all substitutes. As she was the eldest, she could be left alone in the house while the parents went to the fields to weed—she would cook, she would do everything. And besides the cooking, dishwashing, childrearing, herding the animals from one pasture to another, and carrying the water, kindling, firewood, and dried-out palm branches to feed the animals with (the lightest work, according to her mother), she also found time to fill all the surrounding grounds of the house with bright-leaved plants, with tall perfumed thin-leaved grasses, which (even if it was true that they produced nothing useful, as the old man quite rightly noted) at least covered the palm-leaf walls and even the holes the animals (pigs, hens, goats, turkeys, and even calves) had rooted, scratched, butted, and pawed through the walls. And also there was the fact that when spring came, the porch and breezeway were so pretty, so filled with flowers and bright-colored leaves, that it was worth the trouble to put yourself out. And the young men who stopped by to visit the house also praised those plants, or at random plucked off a leaf and raised it to their lips. And it was she, *she* who'd planted them all . . . She who was so grateful that she was almost abashed by the kind words. *Tall, skinny, imperious.* Imperious (*bossy*), but not with them, not with the young men who came by the house, treading the floor which she herself, with the palms of her own hands, had polished. Not with the young men who picked a leaf off the plants which she, with infinite pains (because there were goats everywhere), had watered and protected. . . . But besides these achievements—plus her incessant trips to the pasture for white-clay dirt, and the herding the animals from one grazing place to another—she also learned to sew. You had to be far-sighted—a man was always apt to be more interested in a woman who knew how to sew. So she learned. But *tall, skinny, bossy*—the men came, trod her floor, plucked off her leaves and flowers, some even hiring her to make a pair of pants for them, and then wound up falling in love with her sisters, who didn't know how to boil water. And she (*tall*) was the first to make them out coming across the fields, and she (*skinny*) was the first to slip outside and receive them on the porch steps, and she (*bossy*) told them to sit on the sofa (she took the rocking chair) and she entertained the suitors while the old man grumbled and growled out in the backyard and the old woman, making a batch of candy, prayed and cursed over the wood-fired cookstove. But she went on making trips out to the pasture and watering the flowers, she never stopped that. One morning she tiled each end of the breezeway with the heels of green bottles (stolen out of neighboring yards). She half-buried them around all the tree trunks, too. And you had to admit the contrast of white dirt and green glass looked nice, especially with the line of elephant ears and ivy and coleus and aralias behind them. And the men, of course, praised that piece of work too, but they sat down as always beside her sisters. And so then she took it in her head to fill the house with paper of all kinds, to paper the ramshackle cracked and rent walls with postcards, magazine covers, and fancy wrappings that she begged or stole with infinite pains from the houses of her girlfriends. She replaced the clear glass chimney of the kerosene lantern with a pink-colored one. She figured out a way to make curtains out of matchboxes. She bought a battery radio, and she let her hair down so it fell to her waist. But they, the young men, came to the house smiling, perfumed, buffed and shining, tied their horses to the rainspout or to one of the sturdy plants in the flowerbeds (and some of the horses ate the verbenas), and sat down next to her sisters. Finally, one carried Celia away. That was when Adolfina gathered up her hair, which by now reached almost to her ankles, and plaited two immense braids which she wound around and around on each side of her head so they projected forward like two menacing ram's horns, ready to butt. (In the boxes of photographs taken at the time, there is a snapshot of her during this period.) With infinite sacrifice she painted the entire house, the picket fencing of the garden, and even the tallest chinaberry-tree and fruit-tree trunks in the nearby orchard. It was around that time that another of the "prospects" began to take Onerica out courting behind the stand of prickly wild pineapples. So Adolfina made Polo fix up the roof of the house, while she herself tore down the palm-leaf-thatched walls and almost single-handedly (as the old woman cursed) rewove the walls with new palm fronds. The night the construction was finished at last, she hung ribbons from the roof and made a great batch of candy. That same night, or early the next morning, one of the perfumed suitors made off with Digna. The next day Adolfina planted the great shower-of-gold plant that in succeeding months came to twine all over the corner of the breezeway. She had a well dug and a wellhead built near the house, and she told her mother not to show her face in the parlor again when there was a visitor. Jacinta cursed her and even started to throw the mortar and pestle for the spices at her head, but by then Adolfina had learned how to wield her sewing scissors with wonderful dexterity, so the old woman thought better of it. And at any rate, there were very few young men who from then on came by to visit the house. And when someone did stop by, it was one of the ones who had not been by in a long while and only did so to ask after the sisters. But Adolfina was always ready to receive them, even when they came by mistake. But with her great ram's horns, in her best dress and her high-heeled shoes, and with her face utterly powdered and painted, she was, in truth, a sight to scare off anyone. . . . They stood, then, at the door, smiling but skittish and mistrustful. And she would laugh, talk, gesture endlessly to demonstrate her aspirations—without ever, for all of that, falling into any imposture, of course. . . . Simulating naïveté, she shrieked in a strangled voice at any silly witticism. Meanwhile, Jacinta would come into the front room ("parlor," Adolfina would insist in dismay), just to fret her, with one hand shading her eyes to see who the visitor was and the other scratching her backside. Sometimes she spat or marched out muttering imprecations to herself. Adolfina would go on laughing, shrieking, performing complicated arabesques with her arms. (She considered herself elegant.) Some of the young men even came inside. Showing them the family photographs, she behaved like a girl, and she was at those times extremely ridiculous. Speaking of marriage ("matrimony," she would enounce) she would grow serious, reasonable, judicious; she would take on a certain air of bewilderment and insult, and she was at those times frankly unbearable. When it came time to bring in the coffee, she always apologized—such an old cup, practically the only saucer that isn't chipped, oh the coffee's gotten cold, how weak this coffee is, oh dear—and always with the air of the well-born señorita, which made her truly absurd. And the young men, shining and pomaded, but straight-faced, serious, and unsmiling now, would pull off some leaf at random, and would ride away . . . And then there began to arrive her now-abandoned sisters, but this time with children, with memories, with something to cling to so they did not simply burst—and with someone in their memory they could hate. That was when she grew hard and unyielding with the young men (young men who moreover no longer existed). She grew extremely scrupulous and picky, extremely moralistic, extremely chaste and upright, a stiff-necked old maid. She was the exemplar of the family. When she went into town and some man, at random, glanced at her, she colored in rage. If one of them spoke to her, no doubt to ask after her family, she would fill with modesty and turn her face away or answer in monosyllables. And so, little by little, she forgot about the garden (the shower-of-gold stayed alive by virtue of its own inner vitality), about the parlor floor, the roof, her hair. And dedicated herself to raising her sisters' children, to sewing, and to squabbling. To bringing up and educating those children the way children should be brought up and educated, so they wouldn't be burros, she would say. And that was when Moisés came on the scene, with the notion of selling the farm. That was when he discovered, or thought he had discovered, that it was not too late to start over, that if men were no better than mules in the country (his very words), if they couldn't see his worth, his merits, it would certainly be different in the city. That was when he started preparing Polo for the idea of selling. That was when she moved to Holguín with her parents, sisters, and nieces and nephews, and devoted herself to sewing for pay, to visiting the parks, to sitting on the porch and waiting. That was when Celia's daughter committed suicide. And Adolfina promised herself that she would never come to that. She told herself there had to be another way. And at last, desperate, she made up her mind to do something. So one night (there was, as always, a war going on) she ran out into the street dressed in all her finery to find a man who even if only for a few minutes might justify her existence. So she ran out into the street. And she hunted. And she came back. And then . . .

I don't know what to do with my life anymore. I just don't anymore know what to do with my life.

I twist it and turn it, I hold it upside down, I smash it on the floor. I chop it up and mince it, I chew it. I bust it to bits, and then I chop it up some more. I pick up the shards and powder, and I rub it between my fingers like this and I smell it. But I still don't know what to do with my life anymore. I hang it on the clothesline in the yard, in the sun. I carry it up on the roof, I throw it in the toilet and flush it. I sprinkle salt and lemon on it and try to swallow it down in a gulp. And nothing. I vomit it up. And nothing. I mix it with hot water and serve it to myself in a big bowl. But nothing. I knead it up and pat it into balls and stuff them in my ears. But nothing. I beat it and I spit on it. And nothing. So I go in the bathroom. And I think, I think. And I start taking off my clothes. To get stark naked as quick as I can. Before somebody gets the urge to shit. Because that's all anybody does around here. As though there were so much food you had to be dumping out your insides every few minutes. As if we weren't all dying of hunger, to be emptying themselves out like that. My God, we aren't starving. Can you imagine me saying that, my God. But what am I doing talking about God, for God's sake. God can go to hell for all I care. I'm bored and tired. My life is thoroughly bedeviled and damned to hell.

I'm alone and I'm an old woman.

Life has gradually stripped off my leaves and branches, one by one, like I was a grapefruit tree that's borne too many grapefruits and just can't put out any more. Worse than a grapefruit tree, because I never bore any fruit at all. Because my buds fell off without my realizing it. All alone and skinnier than a stick to shoo cats with. All alone and like the whore on the corner, sewing for free and throwing in the thread for good measure. And having to bear Mama's gobbledygook—half the time she damns God to hell and the other half she just half-prays. All alone and having to stand those kids of Digna's that don't shut their traps even when they're in bed. Alone and condemned to live with this close-mouthed old man. With this lazy old rat of an old man that doesn't talk because he just doesn't feel like it. With this old man that by some terrible fate turned out to be my father. My father, that old man. And he uses the argument that he's my father so he can slap me every now and then. But those days are over. If I have to keep living with him and the rest of these people, if I have to spend my life swallowing my crazy sister and her crazinesses and my dotty mother and her prayers and my high-strung nephew and his imaginings and that goddamned factory and its banging and whinnying and carrying on, and all the rest of it, if I have to take all that, and what's worse stand myself to boot, then that old man's slaps you can just forget about. I won't stand for that. That's where I put my foot down. What the hell does . . .

"My God, woman, don't you ever plan to come out of that bathroom?"

There's the old lady calling me. Trying to find a way to irritate me and put me out. What a mother I'm saddled with. But she can chase me from now to doomsday for all I care. Blasted old witch. I tell you she does it on purpose. If I go in the kitchen, she stands there watching me like a dog watching a person eat. And all of a sudden this feeling will come over me, I get so squirmy and squeamish that I feel like throwing the washbowl at her head. If I go in the bedroom, she asks me what I'm looking for, if I've lost something. She asks me just like that, like I was a cat she was cozzening. Old bitch, as though I didn't have enough to put up with, she watches me too. Do they think I'm going to run off with some man? I wish. But I don't know who'd have me, if I'm so old the scissors grinder won't even flirt with me anymore—and before, he used to talk to me and smile at me and everything. Although I'd rather be dead than married to a scissors grinder. But that's all gone by the wayside anyway—he doesn't even look at me anymore. And the ice-cream man, I bet it's been a hundred years since he's even come down this street. He was another of my suitors . . .

In the mornings in the country the girls would get up and go off to Macial's guava trees to pick up guavas off the ground. With those guavas (at five centavos a gallon canful) they could buy themselves a dress. So the four of them, young, barefoot, giggling, would jump the fence into the next farm. They would shake the trees. And the guavas would rain down. And they not only filled their cans but even ate a few, the sweetest ones, and carried home a hundred or so to Jacinta to make candy with. That way at night there would be something to offer the young men who dropped by.

"But don't you *ever* plan to come out of there? I'm about to burst out here, woman."

Just hold your horses, hold your horses. What a fate, my lord. But just let her hold on. Or let her bust, let the damned old biddy bust. Because right now I'm going to dance, dance right here in this bathtub. And when I get through dancing I'm going to do two or three exercises I read about in the last beauty magazine I saw. I wouldn't advise her to even *think* I'm going to come out any time soon. Not even *think* it . . . Now let's see, how was that first movement? I think you put your arms down like this. Uh-huh, you put your arms down like this and touch the tips of your toes. Let's see. Let's see.

"Woman, woman."

Oh, lord. Not even *think* it. I can't do this. The tips of my toes, nothing, I can't even touch the tips of my *knees*. I'm practically crippled. How could I not be, spending all day long like I do over that sewing machine? How am I not going to be practically crippled, unless I was going to be dead? Oh lord, I'm not even going to try again, because for all I know I might even throw some bone out of joint. And with Mama making all that racket out there, I can't even concentrate. Ay, old woman, old woman, one of these days I'm going to give you a snip with my sewing scissors and cut out your tripes so you won't have to shit *at all* anymore. . . . But anyway, I'm going to dance in the bathtub. And I'm not going to stop dancing, either, not till I fall over dead of exhaustion, not till I'm suffocated from the heat and sweat I work up, not till I can't even breathe anymore. And Mama can just scream as loud as she pleases, and she can shit in the hall for all I care, because I'm bored with it all and I don't give *that* for the whole world and all. . . . Dance. Dance. Dance.

Whew. It's hot. If I could just open that window . . . But then people could see me. But it's all right. I'm going to dance anyway. Even if I'm so tired I can't move, I'm going to dance. Even if I can't dance anymore, I'm going to dance. Watch me dance here in this bathtub. Look at how nice I dance. Look. Look. Look.

This is me. This piece of flesh here jumping up and down, this is me. Me. Take my mirror away. Take my eyes. I am this. Me, this. Me. How awful.

Look at me, look at me. A woman alone. A woman alone with pimples all over her face. A woman tired and bored sick with the world. A woman damned. A woman that's an old-maid seamstress. Ay, a woman as good as dead. . . . Look at me dance, ladies and gentlemen. Before long I'll probably step on the bar of soap and crack my head. Step on it. Step on it. I'm dancing. Look at me—I'm dancing. Dancing.

Good lord, can it be that Adolfina never plans to come out of that bathroom? Can it be that I'm going to have to ask some neighbor to let me use the bathroom? My God, if I told people this, nobody would believe it. This could only happen in this house. In this accursed house. O my God, in this house where I'm the only person that has a thought of You. In this house where I'm the only person that sacrifices herself, and climbs the Hill of the Cross for You barefoot. But did I say sacrifice? Oh no, sweet Virgin, Holy Virgin, you know that that's no sacrifice for me. You know, o my God, that if I don't climb the hill more often, barefoot and on my knees, it's because my kidneys are just barely there at all, and I can't make that kind of sacrifice. O my God, I said sacrifice again. But You know, You and the Holy

Virgin know, that if it weren't for these goddamned kidneys of mine, I'd spend my whole life going up and down that hill. Up and down the Hill of the Cross. Up and down. Up and down. Up and down.

I'm through dancing. But I'm not satisfied. This bathtub is so little that I can barely do two hops in it. If I had a bigger bathtub . . . If this were like one of those swimming pools that people that know how to swim swim in. Like one of those swimming pools, but without any water. Dry. And me in it, dancing and dancing and dancing. Oh, how lovely. Me, young and naked. Me naked. And young. Young.

Did I say young? Did I say young? Maybe. But I'm not sure. And besides, if I did say it, nobody heard me say it and so it's like I never said it. Young. . . . I deserve to laugh myself to death. What if I sat down right this minute on the toilet and I started to laugh, and laugh, and laugh . . . And I never stopped. . . .

Young.

"Adolfina. Adolfina!" Father in heaven, how long? What a sad fate is mine. What a wretched, sad old age I have to live. Oh, forgive me, God. Forgive me my blasphemies. But so many times I just don't see any way out of it. My God, make that woman come out of that bathroom. Make that woman finish whatever she's doing in there. And come out.

Now the first dance will be all for me. Yes, for you, Adolfina. Adolfina the abandoned. Adolfina the starved to death. Adolfina the seamstress. Adolfina the never-married, Adolfina the never-became-a-teacher. Uh-huh, because I was going to be a teacher. That was my fondest wish. And I could have been one, too, because it wasn't for lack of intelligence. Who made all the lists and things when the old man went into town? Who kept track of the pregnant cows? . . . But good lord, with parents like mine how was I ever going to be a teacher? How were they ever going to let their daughter "go off to town and be perverted"? Let her stay home, let her carry water and firewood and chase after the hens. Let the sun roast the damned girl-with-no-hopes-of-ever-finding-a-man-that's-worth-a-damn. Blasted old goats, what I'll never forgive them for is not that they brought me into the world but that they made me stay in it.

Can it be that I'm going to have to call Polo to get that woman out of the bathroom? But that old horse of a husband of mine, it's all the same to him whether I bust or not. And he won't pay any attention to me, even if I ask him, because it's been more than a year since he's said a word. If you ask me, somebody's put a spell on him, because nobody just stops talking, just like that, just because they feel like it. But I don't dare say that to him—as savage and wild as he is, he's capable of busting a bunch of bananas on my head if I so much as mention the word "spell." What a husband you've supplied me with, God. He doesn't believe in anything, not even the mother that bore him. If he's gone to bed with me and kept on doing it, it's because it was his only outlet, because if not . . . And the proof is that when we sold the farm and moved to this infernal town, he never so much as looked at me as long as he had a five-centavo piece in his pocket. And even if I didn't care very much one way or the other, since I'm pretty old to be worrying about such things, the truth is that I'm still insulted that he never even looked at me during all that time. We should never have sold the farm, but he got it into his head to sell. Who ever saw hicks like us living in a town, I said to him. But he got the idea stuck in his head. What do you know about living in a town, I said to him. But he had the idea lodged in his head. And me trying to change his mind: My great-great-grandparents were born here, I said, my great-grandparents, my grandparents, and my parents—and here they died, and we ought to die here too. But no, he kept on with his idea. He was never anything but an adventurer and a rolling stone. And me, who's always foreseen misfortune coming, I foresaw this one. I foresaw that we'd be left with no more than ten centavos and making signs with our hands to beg for water. I foresaw this damned misfortune of watching time pass and dying by inches, praying for things we'll never be granted, unless we were to pray for more misery. But I've never prayed for miseries—they come of their own accord, all on their own, and then there's not a soul alive to shoo them off again.

I foresaw all of these misfortunes. And I foresaw the ones to come, too. They haven't come yet. But they will.

*One morning when the old man stormed out,
like he always does, headed for the mountain, he
came across Fortunato scribbling on the trunk
of a tree. Wretched child, he said to him, and
he twisted his ear. And then he went on
up toward the mountain.*

THE FIRST
AGONY

There was a ragged burst of sound. A flock of birds whirred into the air and he looked up at them, their wings glinting as they climbed up and up into the sky, just at the moment he felt a burning, stinging sensation piercing his skin, taking possession of his flesh, penetrating the deepest and most secret regions of his body, burning him, stinging him, and he knew that those scintillating flashes—as unseizable, unstoppable as bright birds—had traced through the air and found him. *At last, at last,* he whispered to himself. The burst of gunfire had got him; he was going to die. *But if you can just, if you can just, listen to me, just make it over there, over there where the fence starts and the road ends and there's a field and then a little hollow* . . . Because they wouldn't follow him, they were sure they'd got him, they'd just watch to see where he fell and let it go. And so for the first time he was free—he could run. Now nobody cared about what he wanted or sought anymore, his crazy ideas. As he stumbled and fell, he discovered for the first time in the contact with the earth and the grass a new relation, a complicity between him and the land, and even a different smell. And as he leaned on his hands to push himself up, he felt from the earth a new kind of throbbing, a new kind of thrill, a breath, a warmth. And for the first time, now on his feet once again, he perceived in the light that streamed about him that thing which enriches us as it floods over us, and he saw new hues in its glow, and just at that moment he also made out new resonances in the air, new tones, new distant voices and new whispers, new revelations far beyond those which, for a long time now, he had been sensing. For it was not events that happened, but rather sensations, inside him.

What events could occur in that remote place with its ravine that dried up every year, the house forever about to fall down? And in a family that still carried out its plantings by divinations— what kind of weather there was in the first eighteen days of January—or that declared that July had come when the feast of San Juan was celebrated, even though instead of in June they celebrated it some years in August, or not at all? . . . What could happen to a restless, perplexed, poor young man who yearned for something more, set down to live in a quadrilateral, commercial town of symmetrical streets and townsfolk inalterably practical? Oh God, sensations, sensations—sensations were the only thing that could ever happen to him. Oh God . . . and that was precisely his first memorable (unbearable) sensation—the discovery that God did not exist, or existed solely in the deception, the constant confidence game that others practiced on him in His name. God, or other people. God—sweet, distant, with His impossible prom- ises, His improbable presence. Other people—close and crowd- ing, angry and aggressive, with their palpable sweaty bodies, their shrieking and therefore likewise virtually palpable voices. God— forever forgetful, neglectful of the most anguished prayers and petitions; other people—always carrying out to the letter even their slightest threats. God—running and hiding whenever some imprecation was hurled at Him; other people—popping up in- stantly to tell you to shut your mouth. God, or other people. That then was, perhaps, the first dilemma, even agony, which life set him, and made him suffer. . . . At least once upon a time, back then, to console him for the frustration of not being able (by selling guinea eggs) to get and save up the six shining ten-centavo pieces to buy the things on his Christmas list, there was God. To quell his fears of the night-terrors in his room, there was God. To accompany him on the trip through the dark to the tamarind tree, because somebody (one of his cousins) said, "Double-dare you," there was God. For the nighttime fears and panic, there was God . . . There had been a party. The big party at New Year's. And for days before it, he had already been sensing in the air the changes that announced this great event—as the day approached, the wild pineapples covered with flowers like little bells, the greenish, still bottom of the well, the unheard-of flowering of the crepe myrtles in wintertime heralded that culmination. That morning he had gone walking through the country. He had gathered grass-stalks, flowers, leaves, and small stones, and had placed them all on the dresser before the frame that held the faded yet still divine linotypes. That night, when the house was full of his distant relatives, when everyone was drinking, eating, dancing (for somebody had brought a radio), and someone started to sing, some drunken voice shouted, "I want to die, but I don't want to be buried," he slipped out, down to the woods, and there under the splendor of the sky, in the dark shelter of the great solitary trees, he watched, he listened, he closed his eyes and heard. The big house full of noise, voices, singing. The immense house (for it was made of three old houses hammered together) built of palm-leaf husks and fronds and boards, bursting with shouts, people eating, figures passing back and forth among the scrub in the yard. God, God, and there he was under the trees, hearing that racket, that dancing, dancing, dancing. Somebody, one of the cousins, had brought a bicycle, and he had taken that bicycle and ridden out to the pen where the cows were, and he had shot down the hill like a falling star; and now he had the sensation, a new sort of ecstasy, that second rush of joy, that he was rushing, gliding with his eyes closed down through the racket and shouting, down, down, down, to where the music was born. . . . God, God, how was he to conceive back then that You did not exist, that all of that was nothing but a feigning of reality, a spell, an ephemeral and fugitive improvisation which, precisely for so being, time would later halo with the glow of enchantment? . . . On foot, talking and laughing all the way, along the broad red-clay roads, on prancing, rearing horses, and even on a truck which by some miracle managed to drive all the way down through the forest of tree stumps, the families arrived. And there was the array of baskets filled with nougats and caramels stirred to dark thick richness; there were the aunts bearing boxes of raisins, shrilly calling greetings; there were the splendid tall men whose arms became vises of affection. And the ones like him, the children, like ants, everywhere, at the big table, in the midst of the racket of the chopping block in the kitchen, hanging over the picket fence waving at the newcomers, out in the breezeway, jumping up and down, managing at last with their voices to overpower even the unceasing barking of the dogs. They kept arriving, and kept arriving still. One uncle had brought a barrel-thing you made ice cream in, and over at one corner of the house, under the rain spout, he was cranking the handle while the rosy cream bubbled. The oldest of the daughters, the head aunt, was having a wide-ranging, impassioned argument with twenty people at once about how to eat cassava—dry, wet, or with a little oil sprinkled on it; a group of his younger cousins were collecting empty bottles to smash against the trunk of the ceiba tree. And he was watching, listening, sensing, rolling over and over down the hill—reveling in the party, taking the noise and the laughter, the aunts and the cousins, the excitement of it all, and turning it this way and that, holding it up and looking at it, stretching it and twisting it, moving the figures here and there, blowing it up to grand dimensions. Inventing, imagining those figures. Sensations, sensations . . . Nothing but sensations. Because the truth is that there had never been parties of such grand proportions in that house. Because the truth is that reality was always *other*. He was always in *another* reality, in another reality which was not precisely theirs, the one they called the *real* one. The only one they knew. Sensations, only sensations occurred, inside him. At times, above all in that exclusive, brief season that came before the rains, he felt the certainty that someone—a traveler, a walker come from who knew where—would stop somewhere in the country about there and ask him—*him*—to be his interpreter and guide for a while. And for a time he would go everywhere with the visitor, protect him, show him paths, places, and even events inconceivable to the others. But other times he had the sense that the visitor would abandon him, walk away suddenly without a word of explanation, and without saying whether he would ever return. So he would stand behind the dusty barbed-wire fence, and just looking at the breezeway or the tamarind tree would be enough to make him feel that the world, and he with it, was slowly rotting, rotting. There would come then the useless, interminable days when not even a decisive horror would show itself, even if only to fill him with the passion of revulsion. Days all alike—long, suffocating days when the wind would batter the palm-thatch walls, and he would discover the necessity, the urgent, throbbing, latent desire we all feel, to die. It was at those times that he began to celebrate his first private sessions of weeping. It was at those times that he would hide behind the cornpress and imitate Adolfina, or make his voice low and husky and grumble and scold like Grandpa, or scold and squabble in the pinched furious voice of his grandmother. One day he picked up a withe of dried palm leaf and put it up his ass just, perhaps, to feel a new kind of pain. That time he cried like Adolfina. . . . But the soldier with the flashlight was still coming after him with the shaky unquiet light that sometimes leapt ahead, stretched out ahead of him, flickering, brief, as though pointing out which way he should run . . . Horses. Now he wanted to see only horses. Tall, spirited, sleek horses, breaking the line of the horizon. Enormous horses as ungraspable as great fish, horses with sleek sweat-flecked skin, with tense irrefutable virility, galloping along. And on the instant a shining herd broke into a trot across the field across which he, bleeding, ran . . . His mother would try, at first, to console him. She would look at him a little dismayed, a little frightened, and run her hand across his head. It was so frightening, so strange for her, that a boy less than eight years old would scream that he wanted to die. . . . Sunday was without a doubt the most terrible day. On Sunday he would have to go to the ball game in the center of town, or his aunts' "boyfriends" would come and he would have to dress up clean and stay out of the dirt, and he couldn't climb any trees and hang upside down all day. . . . He grew. And in order to survive he had to construct other refuges, he had to set himself and then meet the challenge of reinventing, of touching with mystery, of setting the halo of enchantment upon some hole, some place made dear to him by its coolness, by its shade. There was a vine. There was a shower-of-gold plant, planted by Adolfina in a corner of the garden. Up in the pasture there was the crevice in the steep ground inhabited by quail, and in the first big outbuilding, there was the corner where the doodlebugs ("ant-lions" somebody later had told him they were) built their little conical traps of dirt sifted and refined by their own legs and mouths. And at night, when the rain clattered on the zinc roof of the breezeway and everyone was asleep, there would be the constant rush of hooded horsemen, riding through the lily-bed, splashing through the puddle the begonias, marigolds, and larkspurs floated in. . . . At times, a feeling of hatred, or of strange fury, or of death, would burst up suddenly.

And he would sweep away all the little parapets the doodlebugs lived within, heave cats or just rocks into the air, and dig holes in the backyard and cover them with dirt and straw so somebody in the family would fall in and break a leg. And he would howl. But other times, he would sing. Yes, sometimes, in the morning usually, or just at nightfall, he would go out to the scrubby field by the woods and start to sing a song made up by him on the spot, a song that talked about everything, a song that said it all, a song that might be two or three hours long and that varied according to the wind, the temperature, or the stretch of road he was walking at the moment. The song would always begin with the same words and the same notes, but then it would make its own way, turn, take new hues and arguments totally distinct each time, until at last it would end in an echo utterly out of proportion to the little body that produced it. Fortunato would be enraptured, drunk, imagining waves and torrents of applause, and he would roll around on the ground, still singing though nearing the song's end now, and roll on across the field, through the goat droppings. . . . Those infinite hallucinatory songs, sung to the wind and utterly irrecoverable of course, were the only real creation (and he knew it) that he would achieve his whole life long. . . . One afternoon, as he lay under the shower-of-gold plant, he discovered another sensation, the pleasure of taking his sex in his hands. He discovered it all by himself, accidentally, without anyone's telling him what that was or how or why to do it. Terrified after that first experience, he ran to the outhouse. There he repeated it seven times, one after another. And he grew so weak and slack-limbed that he thought what he had just done was monstrous, a thing so dreadful that no one else in the world could know about it. He deduced that, therefore, he might drop dead from one minute to the next. Later, as he saw that he wasn't dying, what most terrified him was the idea that God had surely found out about what he'd done. And then, the next Friday, in the "temple" of Arcadio Reyes, where his mother took him every week, one of the mediums fell to the floor possessed as she was passing her hands over him to cleanse his spirit, and he thought that God was about to speak, to tell right then and there, before three hundred people (and almost every one of them a friend or neighbor), what he had dared to do out in the privy and under the shower-of-gold plant. It was around that time that he began to be jealous of his grandfather for his mother's affection (such as it was), and his hatred for the old man grew so hot that one day he decided to kill him. He went out to the last outbuilding, out where the dry firewood was stacked, and he picked up the hatchet. As on many other afternoons, after his grandfather had gotten up the cows he was pouring a few buckets of water over himself for his bath, out by the well. Fortunato hefted the hatchet and sneaked out and hid for a few moments behind the ceiba tree. He could hear the splashing and slapping of the water and the old man's snorts. He crept a little closer. He came to the wellhead and he contemplated his grandfather's immense hairy body. As his grandfather turned around, Fortunato saw his huge sex, swaying in a cradle of two twisted and tangled flaps of skin (Fortunato did not know that his grandfather was gelded). And he looked no more—he threw down the hatchet and ran. . . . He ran terrified, while that immense hairy figure, that terror that he himself had just invented (and yet which he could not swear was not real), chased him, caught up to him, and planted itself before him, right in his path. But it was after his mother, after Fortunato's mother, after *her* that the immense figure was running pell-mell. And he watched as that huge instrument reached out after her, caught her, tumbled her, and entered her. And she never said a word, or cried, or whimpered even. She almost laughed. She allowed that attack, while he stood there transfixed, unable to move, watching. What was that? What new sensation, what new God, what new manner of love was that? Because there was no doubt that such jealousy and fury could only be the consequence of some monstrous sort of love—a love so strong that it perhaps had never been felt before—the consequence of a violent, irrepressible, and irresistible desire to possess his mother, exactly as in his imagination she was being possessed by his grandfather right over there, at one end of the field across which he, bleeding, was running. And so it was at that precise moment that he realized—or perhaps he had always known but it was only at that decisive, telling instant that he dared to accept the knowledge—that *there* was his redemption, as it had been his curse and damnation as well. There, and not in the desires and ambitions that had led him to this ridiculous bullet hole in him. There, and not in the sensation of burning, stinging which pricked and drilled at his back. There, in the figure always drilled (in a sense) by another, not by him—*and it should be him*—there was the origin of his true hell, and there was his last, definitive goal. And so now, utterly certain, he ran toward her. But something stood suddenly between; something grotesquely huge, buzzing, blue, and hairy covered his sight. Something, a wet beast of some sort, purring, leapt before him, trying doubtless to block his path, to keep him from his goal. It was a fly. A blue fly, young, no doubt, for it ignored the blood—it had gotten the capricious notion of lighting on the end of his nose. . . . It fluttered up, flew away through the air sliced by another flash of luminosity. The spotlight—every time he tried so desperately to evade it, make it go away. But then the fly came back—blue, persistent, impertinent—to light on the place it had claimed for its own.

The Life of the Dead

I come with my head under my arm to walk these roads. To see how many custard-apple trees have dried up and how many are yet to dry up. With my head under my arm. I who was never man nor boy. Walking about over the things that once upon a time I wished would be eternal. Silly goose that I was. The only eternal thing was me, you . . . The world is drying up. The well is crumbling into itself and the maidenhair ferns are choking it. Every few minutes a spirit flies out and runs away. But I must stay, to bid goodbye to those that flee. To those whose stay has at last come to an end. "Poor boy," and some of them look for you. Look for me. Look for you, "poor boy." "Poor boy." Listen, listen to how they scream and cry. It still seems to me I hear those voices through the gabble and screech of the music, and the long burst of gunfire. How stupid, to die like that, so young, when I never even had time to come to fear death. Or life either, poor boy. Poor boy. Poor boy.

"Adolfina, for the love of God!"

Then came the moment when he had to confront the terrible disjunction between on the one hand what he desired and reality on the other. There was the earth, fertile and penetrable (not like the dry hard ground he had fled), there were his hands, and his ambitions. But covering all the land, and his hands, a weight atop his dreams, were the Others—and the Others made the laws, the Others ordered and disposed. They were the owners. The lords. They had, over and above the deeds and titles that accredited them as proprietors, that air, that something, those gestures, those voices, the looks and acts of proprietors, of gentlemen. They had that way of *being* (more than a way of acting), of being *placed*, as though they had been born (elected, selected, *chosen*) to order and to be obeyed. And he was a scared, clumsy, dull-headed young man, with a fear that changed quickly into violence—though the fear never left him, either. Brutish, rude, uncouth—call it what one would—and without the paper that would testify to his lineage, that might say for him, "This is he." What could he do against those self-assured gestures, against those well-placed figures? He began to work. The owners of the boat that had brought him to the Island were the ones who found him work. There was always something heavy to lift, to move, there was always a boat to load, a boat to unload, a crate, a bundle, a bale, an iron pig, a sack—something big, heavy, stinking, *foreign*, that he had to throw over his shoulder and stagger under. That was all day. But sometimes at night and into the early morning, too, Polo would have to stay on the pier, keep loading, unloading, always running with something big and valuable slung across his back. At the end of the week (or sometimes the day), the boat owners would collect his pay and keep it, as part payment ("amortization," they called it) for the cost of his trip. Although one thing he had to admit—he was never hungry. There were enormous amounts of *mabinga* ("salt beef" is what he'd first known it as) to be sent to the blacks who'd been brought to the Island for the coffee plantations, and he could eat all he wanted. And his hands, when he had a little time, could actually scoop up water, though he had not a single plant he could water with it—not to mention that where he was, the water was salty. So he left. He grabbed up a gunnysack, filled it with that nauseating salt beef, and he took off. He left the city of stinking Negroes and stinking proud red and yellow "white" men and of other men, stinking, neither black nor white, a mixture of all races—mongrels who for that very reason thought they had the right to take on every imaginable custom from every land and to badmouth everybody. He left that fevered city where everyone (*everyone*) danced, shrieked, cursed, and somehow always managed to stick *you* (him) with the nastiest, hardest jobs, while they did nothing. He headed for the country, out by the garbage dumps that glittered in the sun like the ocean. And he set himself up in a settlement of Free Chinese. Those Chinamen called themselves an "independent territory," although they would never be able to leave the Island. Nor did they have so much as a paper to identify themselves by, because they had quit the Company that had brought them to the Island and had gone off to work on their own, not paying back the debts they had incurred for the passage—exactly what he proposed to do. . . . And during that time (he remembers now) they were so poor, so miserable that they were, truly, free. They had no women to tie them down and make demands; they had no children to frustrate and hold them back; they had no property to enslave them and grind them down; they had just their hands, and so who could make claims or demands, who could swindle them, what passion (save the elemental urge to eat and sleep) could torment them? . . . Those men rose at dawn and set about planting, hoeing, weeding, watering, bringing in the produce (and he would be right alongside them), so that by the time the sun was up, all of them (and he would be right alongside them) would flood the little towns and settlements around, selling every sort of vegetable imaginable. Out of the proceeds of those sales, the Chinamen made an untouchable common fund which slowly but daily grew. For anyone but Polo, for anyone who did not live with them, it might perhaps have been moving (or "edifying") to see how those poor wretches managed on practically nothing. A piece of cloth tied around their waist, a hat plucked out of some garbage can, two pieces of wood tied with knots of hemp rope to their feet—that was their clothing. A cavelike dwelling built out of pieces of tin or zinc, planks, and cardboard constituted a house. All the income from the produce was laboriously counted each night and placed in the hands of the treasurer who was, quite rightly, of course, respected and trusted like a god. This was the man in charge of the dream that someday, when the necessary sum had been accumulated, they could all sit down with the Company and negotiate their passage home—to that other hell. But Polo knew (as well as the Chinamen did, of course) that no matter how hard they worked they would never be able by selling greens and truck to scrape together enough money for the return voyage. One night Polo began painstakingly calculating the length of time a Chinaman would have to work in order to save enough money to pay for his ticket back to China. "Two hundred years, exactly," he said aloud the next morning. . . . And most of them were old, they were sick, they would soon be dead; this was absurd. But he was young. He could afford to dream. He was young (a boy still), he had years and years ahead of him, and he could give himself the satisfaction of risking all those years at once rather than wasting them, dribbling them away in monotony, futility, and humiliation. He was young. He could dare, he could dream, he could gamble. He was young . . . and so he was bold, cruel, selfish, criminal—utterly human. That night he went into the treasurer's shack. He strangled him. He seized the treasure (a can containing hundreds of ten-centavo pieces with an occasional twenty-five-centavo one from a big sale) and forever fled that huge garbage dump which under a full moon would seem to roll and swell and sparkle like the sea. . . . It was then, in flight, that there came into his memory the image of his father, hanging from the shriveled tree in the yard of his house there, on that other hellish island. And it was perhaps because he was fleeing, perhaps because at any moment he might find himself in the same situation, that for the first time he felt no hatred at the vision of that skinny old man with a wild beard, his tongue black and swollen, hanging there swinging slowly.

"Adolfina! Adolfina! What in the world's come over you!"

He was young. He could run. He could gamble. He fled. He came to the other end of the province, and there he decided to settle. The truth was, that can full of coins held very little money to buy land with. But those were the times when a horse, even a long-toothed horse, might buy you sixty or eighty acres of black, thick land—the best. But he didn't have the horse. And it was not easy to steal one—you couldn't just throw it in a sack. But he did have the coins, and he traded them for eleven *rosas* of harsh rocky land (some ninety flinty acres as he, a Canary Islander, figured it) in the northern part of the province of Oriente. He handed over every penny of the money, fenced his land, and there he settled. The place went by the name of Perronales, which we might hear as Dogfight, but so far as he was concerned, it ought to be called Terronales, which might be rendered Clodscape. Probably, he thought, that was its real name and these stupid people had twisted their tongue around it for so long that they'd finally got it completely twisted. Though the reality of the place was pretty much the same in either case. As soon as he settled in, got the land plowed and his *bohio* thatched tight and straight, Polo went about finding a wife. The country was so harsh and mean, and everyone was so poor, that Polo, for his few acres of gravel, was considered one of the most well-to-do men (for now he was a man) in all the country around. And so it was easy to find a wife. In less than a week he was married to Jacinta, and in less than another week he had begun to hate her, to despise her. In still another week he gave her her first beating and got their first child on her— which turned out not even to be a boy, but a girl. And since he had secretly wanted to name the baby Adolfo if it was a boy, he decided the girl would be named Adolfina. Immediately after Jacinta gave birth to Adolfina, Polo said, "One whore the more," and so that night he tried again to make a boy. But he had to wait several days, since Jacinta, screaming and kicking, rejected his advances. Still, that same year they had another child, which turned out to be another girl, and this time Jacinta, whose ingrained piety had been offended by calling the first child Adolfina, insisted the church calendar lend a name to this one. The child was called, therefore, Onerica. But this time Polo, enraged by this second failure to get a son, was not to be deterred by his wife's kicking and screaming, and by the next day he had got another child, which also turned out to be a girl, and to which Jacinta gave the name Celia, in honor of her great-grandmother—"killed by an Indian with a wily arrow through the throat," said Jacinta, not without pride. Polo, who'd had enough of females, went off to the mountain and left Jacinta to work things out as best she could herself (for he had never consented to have a midwife in the house), but a week later he returned, lusty and inflamed, and with one discharge engendered Digna, whose birth produced an outburst of fury that had been brewing from generation to generation, so to speak, from birth to birth, and that was growing more uncontainable every day— in step with the advance, apparently now inevitable, of doom. He was tired of working the land alone, that land that wouldn't wait for him to get the weeds out of one corner before it started pushing up weeds in the other. And his hopes were tied to the birth of a son (even *one* son), who could help him, whom he could enslave, use, pass on his fury to, make see the horror which hangs unmoving, eternal, over the poor and miserable of the earth. (Of the other sort of person he knew nothing.) But lo, the devil, who to all appearances was taking great interest in Polo and his concerns, would only send him daughters—"Whores!" he cried. Lo, the devil (for long ago Polo had damned God to hell—even if to all intents and purposes God had beat him to it and damned Polo to hell first)—the devil was bound and determined to humiliate, vex, and mock him. And he was doing it, too, he was doing it. God or the devil, the devil or God (which obviously, so far as doom, misfortune, and impotence were concerned, were the same being) laughed. Polo's ambitions were risible. . . . When he saw this latest get of his, this daughter, this whore, he beat Jacinta. She defended herself by giving him one or two quick sharp kicks and throwing a bedpan full of dark blood at his head. He knocked over a table (the only one in the house) and smashed it, smashed what few dishes there were in the kitchen, killed the dog with one kick in the ribs, and stormed out of the house, to the accompaniment of the shrieking and screaming of his daughters, and headed once more for the mountain. But he didn't dare do what he'd planned, what he'd desperately desired, he didn't dare kill them (smashing himself furiously in the testicles), kill the four women that he had brought into the world, this hell (smashing himself again in the balls). . . . Finally, when he stopped, he stretched out in pain in the grass and he even broke down and cried. A tiredness, a heaviness he had never known before possessed him. He had run so far he had come to the coast.

Bananas at two for five centavos.

Plantains at two for ten centavos.

Oranges at four for twenty-five. Expensive, but what can I do? I've got to take advantage of the shortage this time of year, since when the season comes I won't be able to give 'em away.

Tomatoes at seven for a peso. The best ones, though, let me put 'em away for Tomasico, since he's the only person that ever pays cash.

Cigarettes and matches I can't raise the price on. Or sugar, or rice. . . . Oh well, I'll get that back in the weighing. An ounce less, almost nobody ever notices. Although this is the most starved-to-death neighborhood in the whole town. In the whole world. People fight over a half-ripe mango that falls out of the tree . . . This year they haven't brought me any firecrackers to sell yet, and it's almost Christmas already.

This candy here at three pieces for five centavos if they want five centavos' worth or twenty for twenty-five if they buy twenty-five centavos' worth. Boy, all this going over the prices all the time, when all I ever sell here anyway is hundred-proof. And by the way, that last batch they brought in tasted like diesel oil. But what the heck, people drink that stuff like it was camomile tea. Let me taste it. . . . Ah.

"Old man! I'm leaving this piece of trash of yours out here for you."

"Virgen santísima, what are you doing here with my daughter

and those children and that bundle of clothes at high noon with the sun so hot it'd split rocks?"

"Tell Polo I'm leaving this piece of trash of his out here."

"You goddamn animal! If I were a man you wouldn't say that to me. But you just hold on there, I'm going in the house and call Polo."

Bananas at two for five centavos. Right. But if they're pretty rotten I'll give 'em three. The rats'll get 'em anyway if I don't. But give 'em away, oh no, not on your life. A businessman can't be giving away his stock. If it spoils, you throw it out; if you can't sell it, you send it back; if the business goes to the dogs, you store it somewhere. But give it away? Never.

"Polo! Do you mean to tell me you're sitting here and you didn't hear what that man said? He brings Digna back home with the two kids, dumps 'em in the middle of the road, and says he never wants to see 'em again. And he insults me to my face, to boot. Get out there right now and bust his face for him. You go out there and crack his skull to teach him some manners!"

Bananas at two for five centavos. . . . I always figured it was going to come out this way. Three for twenty-five centavos the plantains. Uh-huh, three for twenty-five, because by now they've gotten hard to find.

"Go out there and smash his face! Or aren't you man enough to do it?"

What does this woman know what it means to be a man. . . . Sweet peppers two for five pesos. Four for ten centavos the sweet potatoes a pound. Ach, that goddamned woman's got me all thrown off.

"You pansy! You old pansy! I don't have a *husband*. What I've got is a piece of meat with eyes in it. Your own daughter out there abandoned, *left*, do you hear, *in the middle of the road!* Three more mouths to feed. Three more mouths to feed and the shame and embarrassment of it. Oh, the shame of what people will be saying now. My God, what will people say. . . ?"

If you think I'm going to answer you, you old crone, you've got another think coming. You can stand there and cackle like an old hen all day for all I care, I'm just gonna sit here counting . . . Pears . . . But *pears* . . . I don't have any more pears than I've got polar bears. That old biddy's got me all messed up again. The coconuts, if they're ripe, for twenty-five centavos, if they're middling or milky, twenty-five pesos. You can just march right out of here again, because I'm not going to look at you.

"You ought to be *ashamed* of yourself. You ought to take some pity. You ought to go out there . . . If you were a man . . ."

There she goes with that "man" again. Naturally—she knows that's one of the things that's the quickest to get my goat. Or that *used* to get my goat, anyway. But I proved I was a man plenty of times. Too many!

"If you don't do something, even if it's just throwing rocks at him, I'm going to call the neighbors."

Talking about rocks, damned old harpy—she thinks she's still living up on the mountain.

"O my God! O my God! What sad fate is this lot You have given me! What a sad fate!"

God. God. If You'd ever existed, You'd have died by now of having to listen to all the complaints from these people that believe in You. Pears . . . There I go again with that nonsense about pears. Mangos at fifteen for ten centavos. Cheap, but what can I do. The vegetable carts that go down the streets are ruining my business—I don't know how they manage to always sell cheaper than an established businessman with his own vegetable stand.

The old man was putting prices on the "merchandise" in his vegetable stand with that apparent tranquility conferred by constant failure, when a sort of fog descended and he heard voices, though he imagined himself to be deaf. "I'm leaving this piece of trash of yours out here for you." But the fog went on thickening and the voices gave him several slaps in the face. "Your daughter has been *abandoned*. He's left your daughter." The old man had promised himself to remain mute until he didn't have to promise himself that anymore. But this agony was endlessly drawn out; it seemed it would never end. "If you were a man . . ." Bananas turned into pears, and the prices rose and fell as though an imp were playing tricks on his mind. He heard a shout and he kept on counting. You can pop for all I care, and I won't say a word. Not a peep. He saw several beasts walk across his scales and begin to wallow in the sugar. And then the same screaming and shouting. That old crone; but I won't answer her. "Imbecile. Imbecile. Imbecile." The beasts gave him little pats on the cheek and then broke into gales of laughter and ran off, across the paving stones of avocado, leaving everything in their wake topsy-turvy. Always up to now I've done what I goddamn well pleased. Liar, said one of the beasts, and the old man became so angry he almost spoke. He thought about shying a half-ripe plantain at its head, but he immediately realized that he'd lose money on the exchange, so he controlled himself. Then came the idea of hanging himself. *If my father did it, why not me?* But immediately he discarded that idea and went on thinking. "What you are is a lazy good-for-nothing old fool." His father was hanging from the hook in the dining room he hung his hammock on. Hanging from the same rope he used for the hammock. He saw him sway and he immediately thought of the hammock now lost. "That is your daughter out there! Three more mouths to feed!" "Get out there and kill that son of a bitch. Go on. Act like a man even if it's only once in your life." Sausages at two for a peso. . . . But it was too early to wake up his mother and give her the bad news about the loss of the hammock. That was why he didn't do what he had been going to do, and so when he could hold it no longer, he urinated in his bed. And when he could hold back the news no longer, he touched his mother's earlobe and whispered, "Mama, Papa's in the dining room, hanged."

"Well, I thought the day would never come!"

How sweet it is to touch my mother's earlobe. No matter if the weather's so hot you'd think you were in an oven, her ears are always cold. They remind you of big pieces of hailstones like the ones that only fall on the days the clouds get furious and black and angry and throw down lightning bolts and thunder and water and anything else they can get their hands on. How nice it is to touch one of my mother's ears. As soon as she starts nodding off to sleep, I get up beside her and start to touch it. At first just with the tip of my finger, and then with two, and pretty soon I grab the whole ear real tight in my whole hand, and I hang on, like baby chameleons do when it thunders. And there I am, squeezing that cold ear until she wakes up and whacks me two or three times anywhere she can reach. "If you don't go out there and crack his skull for him, then *I'm* going to do something, even if it's just throw a rock at him!" How nice . . . Bananas at ten a half-peso, and the soursops I'll throw in for free, since they're rotten anyway. These sugar cookies at two for a half-peso the big ones, and the other ones . . . Damned child! Hanging on my ear again. Do you think you're a chameleon? I haven't been able to close my eyes all night because of you! You halfwit!

Grapes . . . But what am I talking about, grapes? "Your daughter abandoned in the middle of the road, you old piece of meat with eyes in it. Your daughter out there, in the middle of the road, that you could just cry to see her. . . ."

> Then she goes into the kitchen. Looking around to make sure Jacinta doesn't see her, she reaches for the alcohol lamp. She empties the alcohol into a bottle. She picks up the matches, hides the box between her breasts, and goes back into the bathroom.

I'm a washbasin, I'm the cabinet for the water jugs. I'm the first thing that comes into my mind. I'm a damned dark outdoor privy, where you can't see the shit, but it's down there, looking up at you. But that's it—the deed is done. This will be the last time I take my clothes off in the bathroom. This will be my last dance. I'm going to fly away. I'm going to be finished when I get good and ready to be finished and say When when I feel like saying When. And say, To hell with it. All this time, and the only thing I've managed to do is put off the day of reckoning. But I knew the day had to come. And here it is. I've been wanting it to come for a good while now; and if it doesn't come, why I'll give it a little push and nudge it through the door. Now to give myself a good beating—I'm going to roll around on the floor without yelling or screaming or maybe just screaming real real low, so that damned old woman out there standing by the door won't start raising Cain again the way she's always raising Cain. I'm going to rip off my skin and do somersaults and tricks. I'm going to moo, and bellow, and whinny. And then I'll walk on my hands and tickle myself behind the knees. And then I'll bite the toilet bowl. And then I'll break out meowing. And then I'll cry for Fortunato. And then I'll pull out my hair. I'm already pulling it out, I'm pulling it out already. Now I'll cut off one of my ears and eat it. I'm going to bite myself all over. Miserable woman. Take that. Take that. Damned, damned woman. Ugh, take that. I'm going to rip you to bits. If I had a knife in here I'd chop you into mincemeat. Oh, I know—I'll bang my head against the wall a hundred times. That's what I'll do. One . . .

> In the bathroom there are two pails (one leaks), a plunger for unclogging the toilet, a few nails in the wall to hang clothes on, and up high a little window—out of which, had it not been for the smoke from the factory, one might have been able to see the sky.

Damned, old, boring, mulish, stupid woman. Fool. And still you allow yourself dreams. Five. Whore that never got a good taste of a man. Six. A whore with second thoughts about it. Seven. A frustrated whore. Eight. A whore without even a whorehouse to go to. Nine. A whore for one lousy night. Ten. Remember, whore? Eleven.

> There is also, in the bathroom, a little "repertory" (as everyone in the house has somehow come to call it) nailed to the wall, a mere wooden medicine chest. In it are kept bars of soap, shaving brushes, tubes of deodorant, that sort of thing. Its tin door, highly polished, serves as a mirror.

Whore. Twenty-nine. Just remember that if you wound up an old woman with your honor, so to speak, intact, it was just because no man wanted to bed you down. Just remember that. I do, I do remember. I am conscious of that day and night. Ay, day and night. Thirty. Thirty-one. Thirty-two. Thirty-three.

> There is no bathtub. Even if Digna says there is, even if she thinks she is dancing in it. There is not one. The water simply falls onto the floor and drains down an open drain. That is why the soap often is lost in the bowels of the plumbing. And it was down that drain, says Fortunato, that he once lost a ring.

Sixty-four! . . . Hard-head! Spawn of mules and donkeys and asses! Stupid hick countrywoman. Sixty-five! A *teacher*? I ask you, a teacher? Don't make me laugh. So the whore wanted to be a teacher. Sixty-six! . . . But who did that barefoot mountain girl think she was? Good lord. Can you beat that? A teacher. Sixty-seven, sixty-eight.

"Come on. Let's peek in the hole in the bathroom wall, to see what Adolfina's doing."

"Me first."

"Get away, it was my idea."

"I'm going first!"

"Get away, I said. I'll look and tell you what I see."

"If you don't let me go first, I'll tell Grandma."

"Tell anybody you feel like. Grandma likes me better than you. She told me so herself."

"Liar, the one she really likes is me. She told me so."

"Shhh, here she comes."

"You wretched children! What mischief are you up to, climbing up on that stool like that? You better not fall and break the seat, I'll tell you. You both ought to fall and crack your heads wide open on the floor. Little urchins! What a sad fate is mine! Look at me, an old woman like me, and to have to take this mess of youngsters, too. What a miserable excuse for a life. It'd have been better if you'd both died. Ay, and that blasted woman, is she *never* coming out of there! *Ay, virgen!"*

Naturally, when a great deal of water falls, the drain clogs. And the floor of the bathroom, which is lower than the yard outside, floods. That area underwater is what they call the "bathtub."

Eighty-one!
Eighty-two!
Eighty-three! . . . There comes the abandoned wife. Oh lord, it's the truth—Polo didn't have much luck with his daughters. One abandoned, another one unhusbanded, the other one abandoned with a dead daughter. And the other one? Well, the other one, *you* tell *me*—also without a husband and with a halfwit child. Ave María purísima! This family's luck! That's why I always say that a poor man can't afford to have daughters. Why, if I had a female daughter, I'd take her by the neck and drown her in the toilet. That's the best thing for it. It's the only thing you can do . . . They'd have done me a favor, I'll tell you. Eighty-four! and hard, for not setting the house afire long ago. Eighty-five! and harder yet for not setting myself afire even sooner. Eighty-six, eighty-seven, eighty-eight! . . .

"Ay, Adolfina, I beg you. If you have any spark of humanity left in you, open this door and let me in."

Will you listen to that—"any spark of humanity"! What cheap novel did she get *that* little tidbit out of? Spark of humanity. But shit! I lost count. Now I'll have to start all over again . . . One . . .

At first Celia also had her can for picking up guavas in, and her new dress, and a man. And she even had a daughter by that man. Then, as always happens, the dress started to fade and it "got all baggy." And the man ran off. But she still had her daughter, and the almond tree, here (because by now they had moved) in the very center of the yard. And she and her daughter could sit under the almond tree, and even if she couldn't get away from the ga-ga-*boom* of the guava-paste factory, it was different hearing it that way, under the tree. It sounded different when she heard it sitting under the leaves, in the shade, beside her daughter. But as that which we most desire is always that which we lose (or that which we never manage to possess), Esther, her daughter, somehow got poisoned and died, apparently because she was loved so much. And so then all that was left her was the almond tree, which still transformed the ga-ga-*boom*, and which allowed her to reminisce. But (and this, too, often occurs among the poor and wretched) the tree was cut down, and she was left alone with the rotting, decomposing tree trunk, on which, at this very moment, she is sitting.

Every time I see this dried-up trunk of the almond tree lying here in the middle of the yard, I feel like I was looking at my own soul. My very own soul cut down and knocked over lying there in the rocks and weeds in the backyard. In the garbage heap. Breeding more slimy slugs every day.

My own soul rotting out in the middle of the yard, while Tico and Anisia jump around and play all over it and Mama pulls off a twig she needs for kindling.

Every time I see that tree trunk lying there, rain falling on it, I get so angry and so sad inside that I, even *I*, am a little scared by the size of that sadness and that anger. I get sad inside because I know we're never going to have even one almond tree out in the backyard again, and from now on the heat and the noise and the loneliness will get worse and worse and worse every day. Worse every day, until we can't take any more of it, and we melt. I get this unbearable anger inside, too, because I think if it weren't for this miserable bunch of people I have to live with, that tree trunk would still be standing. Covered with leaves. And I could talk to it, like before. And, like before, I could open my bedroom window and see—way up there on the very top of the tree where the new sprouts sprout—see my daughter Esther, dancing on the very topmost limbs. Calling me as loud as she could. My daughter Esther. . . . Who I haven't seen again since these people got it in their heads to cut down this almond tree. And I'm afraid I never *will* see her again, either. I'm afraid she'll never appear again. And that then I'll have to get used to looking at her up there nailed to the wall behind a piece of glass with cobwebs all inside it, because the spiders in this house never give a person a minute's rest. . . . What a terrible dislike these people took to that poor almond tree. What harm did that poor little tree ever do to them? But all they had to do was see that I loved that tree, and the damned pack of animals practically pulled it up by the roots. "It drops all these leaves," they said. "It drops all these leaves, and we're not going to spend the livelong day with the broom, sweeping up those leaves." "It drops all these leaves," they said. So I would sit up day and night, watching for a leaf to fall so I could run out and catch it in my hands so it would never even hit the ground. So they couldn't say that's what they were cutting it down for.

"It raises up the house. That tree is lifting the house right up off its foundations with its roots." What foundations, I'd like to know. And it was a lie anyway. Roots go down, and the house is stuck right to the ground, I'd tell them. "It raises up the house." So I bought cement and sand and rocks, and I paved the whole yard, I just left a little hole with soil in the middle around the trunk so you could at least dump a pail of water down it so the poor tree wouldn't dry up and die of thirst.

But nothing worked—beasts are terrible things.

Do you know, ladies and gentlemen, do you know what it is to live in a house where you have to step over beasts day and night, and they're always getting in your way? Where wild beasts stick out their tongues at you wherever you look, and even every once in a while throw a knife at you, or a stick of burning kindling? If you don't know, I wish you'd just come spend a day with me, and you'd see something serious.

And so the almond tree got cut down.

They carried on about it for so long that finally one day I just picked up the hatchet myself and started whacking at it. Slow. Like this, slow. And every time I whacked it, it felt like I was chopping at my own soul. And every time I whacked it, my eyes would shoot out sparks from the fury I was in, and from the tears.

And the beasts laughing and laughing and laughing, as they looked out the dining-room window. Laughing and laughing and laughing.

"It's a spirit. That tree's got the demon in its limbs," they said.

"The demon."

"The demon."

And me whacking and whacking away at it. Until it started to lean a little. And then all of a sudden it fell over. So quick I barely had time to jump out of the way. One of the limbs even caught me on the shoulder. So now I'm like this, like what you see here before you—with one shoulder up and the other down. I look like a bent-out-of-shape clothes hanger. That limb just fell on me. *Thwack*. And those beasts laughed and laughed and laughed. And I gave such a scream, from the pain that limb gave me when it smashed my shoulderbone into little pieces. And the animals almost split their sides laughing.

And so now there's my soul, lying out there in the backyard. And now my daughter, God knows where she is. . . . It's so hard to have any control over dead people. They come when they please and when they please they're gone again. And a person sits trembling and quaking to think that might be their last visit. And a person doesn't know what to do, but everything else just stays the same. The big wall clock goes *Tloc tloc tloc*. And the beasts when they snore go *Nrrr, nrrr, nrrr*. And me, peering out the holes in the walls, looking and looking and looking. And not seeing a thing.

Looking at that dried-up tree trunk out there lying in the middle of the yard. That dried-up rotten tree trunk that's actually beginning to look more and more like my face.

(One might assume, perfectly logically, that that tree trunk will one day also have disappeared off the face of the earth.)

"Adolfina! Adolfina!"

He worked. He would get up before daybreak, and long after the day was done he would come in from the fields. He scrabbled, hoed, plowed, weeded, planted. Jacinta would help him at all his labors; later, so would the girls. But always, he was the only man of the house. And they, the women, no matter how much he made them work (and he did make them work), they never produced very much; in fact, often enough what they did was just create upset, not benefits. They would get tired almost before they started, they would step into plots of seedlings, they would hoe up a whole row of sprouts— maybe even on purpose. And however much he beat them and hit them and forced them (all of which he most certainly did), it was never as though they were men, they never learned to do things the way a man would do them. And then there was the crying, which was what irritated him more than anything. That was what he reaped when he sowed advice, or a slap, or an order—weeping, wailing, sniveling, the unfailing justification they offered for their always-useless efforts. Efforts that he had to come along after them to set right. . . . He worked, he kept scratching away at the earth; he planted and hoed. But the earth, like a woman, is cruel with those who don't know how to dominate her. The earth only obeys the man who strikes her, who knows how to control her, who knows how to sweep her up in his arms and beget fruits upon her. A man had to get rid of the rocks, the scrub, the weeds, the trees, and leave the earth clean, fresh, and fertile. . . . And his daughters grew, to boot. So after a while they didn't worry themselves overmuch about helping him out with the weeding or with gathering tomatoes; what filled their minds was painting their faces, keeping the front room swept and the floor powdered, and planting half a jillion useless flowers and such around the house, just to make it "look pretty." If that would at least help them find a good man, he thought bitterly. . . . Somebody who knew how to till the land, not one of those useless boys there were these days that just knew how to slick their hair down and make a horse rear. So he went on working, in the company of the old woman (for by now he was an old man), staring gruffly from the field at the parade of young men looking spirited as they passed on their horses, and who obviously had no interest in anything that had to do with the land, and who sometimes did not even deign to greet him. So things went, of course, from bad to worse. And the old woman became a worse scold every day. And his daughters got messed up with those "good-for-nothing idlers" who almost to a man immediately brought the daughters back home big-bellied. And one of those idlers somehow put the idea into Polo's head to sell the farm.

I go out just as the day is breaking to milk the cows and this blankety-blank wife of mine is already nagging at me. I can't even have a little peace while I drink the cup of sweet coffee she brings me. As though I didn't know she makes it so sweet on purpose, just to spite me, just to get my goat—because after all these years you'd think she knew I don't like sugar in it. Has anybody ever seen such a fate as this one I've been saddled with! My son-in-law's right—what we've got to do is sell the farm and move to town. We're too old to be up here on the mountain anymore, pushing and hauling with all these animals and working our fingers to the bone. I tell you, I'd *give* the farm away, just to shut Jacinta's mouth. But what would just kill you is, the stupid woman doesn't want to sell, and without the wife's signature a man can't even get rid of what belongs to him. They've decided that a woman is a man's equal. What we need is to clean all those pretty boys and pansies out of the government, and put things back to rights again. It's got to where you don't even know who's wearing the pants in the family anymore. But nobody jumps up astraddle me! She's not getting on top of *me*, she's not. I'm selling!

"If you sell, I'm putting a rope around my neck."
"Then I'm selling tomorrow."
"You miserable old coot!"
"Listen, woman, you better hush if you don't want me to take a board to you."
"You wild heathen! You're an animal. I'm going to call my daughters right this minute and tell them what you said to me! You animal! I should've hanged myself before I let myself marry you."

"Nobody was holding you back."

"You shut up!"

"I'll shut up when I good and feel like it."

"My God! I'm telling my daughters right now."

"Go to blazes!" . . . Did you hear that foolishness—they think they can get up astraddle me. We'll see who gets on top of who. I'm selling!

She would stop—midday exploding, the noontime glare devouring the whole countryside around—at the window in the hall. And there, her elbows leaning on the sill, the noontime bursting, its blinding deafening glare flooding her face with utter clarity, she would stand and listen to the noise, that untiring, unceasing shriek and squeal of belts and wheels. Baudilio had left her. Somebody had seen him dancing with a whore at Eufrasia's Ball Room. But was that enough to make everything look so hopeless to her? Was that all it took to make her decide to "disappear," as she put it to herself? Oh, there was more. There was something else, which she herself could not quite figure out but which was there, gnawing, throbbing, slapping her in the face. There was the getting out of bed and opening her eyes, and seeing that glare already bursting in through the window, coming in. There were all the hours of the day, lined up straight and stiff—trifling, tedious, useless, and utterly invariable. There was the walking from one wall to the other, waiting (hoping). But even when everything turned out the way she wanted it to (here began the pain, that sensation of cringing recoil in a place she could not quite identify), so what? What could a person do in the face of that glare, in the face of that sense of terror, against that sense of *So what, so what?*, and what could a person do with the unbearable sadness, totally inexplicable (like all authentic things), brought on at times by simply looking at the dusty-green, motionless leaves on the plumbago plant? Even when she got married (she was thirteen now) and had children, and a house, and silence (things distant even at best), so what? For in the midst of that glare that blindingly flooded the world about, in the midst of that terrible heat, that racket, that pack of shrill shrieking people, she would still be able to reach out and touch the outlines of another glare, equally terrifying, other deafening sounds—that glare, those sounds truly inescapable. What could it be, what could that thing be? . . . And August came, with its rains. And the rain dinned and cracked on the thin fiber-cement roof. And the water ran along the rain gutters, soaked the ground, ran in rivers down the streets. There were children throwing bits of paper and orange rind into the currents. And that unbearable sensation grew. . . . And then again the sun, the dust, the coming of Christmas, as though to lend an excuse so that somebody, everybody sometimes, sometimes she herself, could get drunk, and then cry, and hurl insults at the world. . . . And then August coming around again, and once again the great spreading brightness that poured down from the sky. Yes, even when she got married. Even when she had a house, and children, and silence (which were at best remote), what would be the good of all that, what would all that serve, what would she ever be able to do in the face of that sky, in the face of such a flood of light, what would she ever be able to do so that everything, including her herself—so white, so graceful, so from somewhere else, not here—would not end up rotting, would not end up constantly and inexorably rotting away? What could she do in the face of all the supposed happiness in the world, in the face of that constant, unending sensation, that sensation of dissatisfaction, of being lied to and betrayed, in the face of the shriek (never to be muffled or to go unheard) of the unwinking, unwavering bright-glowing weather, the unalterable time, set down and fixed just beyond that other, daily glare, this other, daily ga-ga-*boom!*

You'll say she's not. You'll say she's not, but if you ask me, Celia's daughter is awful sick. Her face is as white as a piece of paper, and she doesn't even talk; and she spends the whole day as if she were in a dream or something, half asleep and half awake. Why, yesterday I put my hand on her forehead like this, and she was burning up. And you'd just finished sprinkling holy water on her to shoo the spirits away. That old man is the one to blame for all this—he doesn't believe in anything, not even so much as the mother that bore him. We've got to pray, we've got to ask

God to help. That child is not well. Tomorrow first thing in the morning I'm going to go out and find me some ironweed leaves and some rue to work against the spell, and make her a bath to sit in. She's thirteen, and that's a dangerous, dangerous age. I'll tell you, she might be going to turn out to be a medium. But anyway—this is a hard test, a test of what's yet in store for her to bear. These days she spends the livelong day, her whole life, you might say, looking out the hall window. Like there was something to see out that window—and you can't even see the street . . . But I tell you, the devil himself is in this house. Tell me the truth—do you pray every night? Well, then, from now on you better not sleep so much. Look at that face and tell me it doesn't look like the face of the dead . . . May God forgive me for what I've said, and for what I didn't say, too, and ought to have. You've got to fight it. My advice to you would be for you all to move out of this house. I believe there's some evil or something buried here. . . . Some evil, or an evil eye, or some kind of hex or other. Her bed might be right on top of where it's buried, that might be what it is. Move her bed, or at least make her sleep with her head down at the foot. Look at that face, what does it look like to you? . . . Give her lots of spiritual waters to drink. A little bottle of Turn-the-tables. I'll come first thing in the morning and take her to Requene's temple and try to wash it away. I'll do a cleansing. I'll wash away whatever she's got . . . But I'd still advise you to move out of this house as soon as you can. Oh, don't tell *me*—that thick-skulled old goat of a mountain man, there's no convincing *him*. But anyway, you ought to take more care for that girl. It breaks your heart to see her face so thin. She's almost a woman, will be any day, and she's not going to find the man to look at her a second time. And I know what that is . . .

But really it was June that was the month of flowers. June, not April as people sometimes claimed. Nor May, which was actually called "the month of flowers." June. To die in June. To die in the season when everything blossoms and bursts and shines, and out in the country there are sweet smells and leaves. To die in June, in the season when anyone can walk along and pick dozens and dozens of carnations to toss onto the casket. To enter the ground in June . . . And to feel (assuming one feels anything) one's bones transforming into stalks and leaves and buds, and blooming. . . . To escape in June, before the days of terrible glare come around again, the days when one has no strength or will even to complain. The days when wherever a person sits, or goes, or stands, or walks, or tries to settle, a person is forever, no matter what, in the way. No, but June, now . . . And all those flowers all over her body. And everyone walking along in a line behind her, and her covered with flowers. And her among the flowers, this time laughing at everyone. Her for the first time become the center of attraction for every eye, riding along beneath the flowers like a woman of respectability. Her laughing at them all. . . . But she had to hurry. In all her wavering and vacillation she had already lost the best days of the month. There was barely a week to go before June would be over.

I told myself, It can't be, but these stubborn people kept insisting, Oh yes, it was true. I went out into the backyard and threw a fit and kicked all those bottles, which had nothing to do with what those people were saying. I just had to kick somebody. And I told myself, *It can't be, it can't be.* And I didn't even know what that meant, "It can't be." But I wasn't about to admit that to anybody. Those people, they are so stubborn, they're always saying the opposite, just to be contrary. If I say, It can't be, it's because I know for a fact that it can't be. Ay, it can't be, no, I tell you,
no,
no!

June. People came. They stepped closer. They looked at her. The same poor, wretched people as always. And her in the great black catafalque. Was there a bee in among the flowers? No, it was a fly. A slow, ceremonious blue fly buzzing from wreath to wreath, flying sometimes into the glass window and then even getting in behind it, where it then rested, alert. And then it buzzed desperately, trying to escape, a prisoner within the bounds of the casket. Until someone came and shooed it away . . . Oh, if only there had been great banks of drapery. If only instead of being in that little bedroom she had been able to lie in state in some immense carpeted hall with magnificent windows opening onto a peaceful garden, and a lovely landscape beyond . . . Where had she seen that? How could she imagine such impossible things all by herself? . . . But in spite of everything, there *were* the flowers, and the murmur of the people grew to a great hum in the evening. And with the odor of flowers and the hum, out beyond the glare, another kind of light, washing, flooding the room. It was June, it was June entering that miserable room, too, the miserable room in which she lay. It was June, scattering its last remnants of opulence over those wet-combed heads, over the thin, clumsy, prematurely aged hands forever assaulted by the world, forever bashful, and over all those people come together there (all wearing their starched Sunday clothes) to pay homage to her, the dead.

I tell myself, It can't be. But these stubborn people take me by the hand, as though I didn't know that it can't be. And these stubborn people take me to her bedroom . . . And there she is, shining in all those candles, and whiter than ever in all the white flowers. Whiter than the fog, than life itself, which is white from being so empty. White, and everything shining. And me, so ugly and dirty, how was I going to touch her? Me, crying for no reason. Going up close and then running out as fast as I could, breaking bottles and throwing a fit. Saying, *It can't be.* And the bottles turned to little pieces, and cried. And those stubborn hard-headed people coming out again and taking me by both hands and taking me in to where she was all white, because it was time, they said, to take her away . . . And I was saying, It can't be, it can't be. And it broke my own heart to see myself in among all that whiteness. Me, so brown and rough I look like a stick of burning firewood somebody threw a bucket of water on. So brown-skinned I was embarrassed to stand next to her and practically touch her if it hadn't been for somebody, I don't know who, that had very intelligently put a piece of glass over the coffin between us. A little thin piece of glass, but it didn't keep me from kissing her real quick, and not getting her brown at all. A little window.

She was now lying in the center of the front room, as the bedroom had grown too small for so many wreaths, and the house was one great buzzing and a constant, varied odor of flowers. And all the people came in and looked down at her still-young face, and crossed themselves very gravely. And she lay behind the glass, thinking (for she could think), *This is how they will always see me—young, and with flowers all around.* And the young men came, too, and just stood there. And the women, amongst all the wreaths of flowers, whispered to each other as they drank their coffee. "What a pity, so pretty." And she was triumphant: *This is the way I will be forever. . . .* And there, far off, the ground open and smelling sweetly of earth, awaiting her . . . She felt them lifting her, four men picking her up by the four corners, and she was high, and covered with flowers (the fly buzzing among the lilies), and she began to glide triumphantly over the people's heads. June, June. She had managed all this in June.

And so—high, triumphant, covered with flowers—she went out into June.

"What do you see, what can you see now?"
"I see a drowned cockroach floating in the bathtub."
"You've got that bathtub on the brain. Don't be such a goose, let me see too."
"You peep in here and see if it's not the truth."
"Let me see."
"See?"
"What a numbskull you are—who told you that was a cockroach? And what's more, it's not floating either."

The place known as Perronales is a *cuartón* (or some thousand acres of land) which belongs to the *barrio* (some ten thousand acres) of Sao Arriba, which might be thought of as the Upland Meadow. Perronales is a plain which does not meet the sea. It is a featureless place where there are no hills, though where nothing is exactly level, either. Situated to the north of the town of Holguín, it is gravelly, shingly land, a rocky, arid region in which the coming of the rains is always unpredictable, as is their end. There are no major rivers in Perronales, just a multitude of ephemeral creeks which in the windy season, when there is a great deal of water, flood the lands, and in the season of drought, when only the strongest current still flows, disappear altogether. There are no great trees in Perronales, even though its inhabitants might say there are. There may have been trees at one time, when the Island was a myth and anything at all might occur, and everything was "marvelous" (farther north the great Admiral Columbus landed), but now there are only trees of very dimmed splendor and much reduced green, trees which do not serve to protect one from the fires of the sun, though they constantly seem to be inducing one to bump into them and, if one lacks prudence, knock one's brains loose. . . . There are no major roads, although there are, it is true, innumerable paths, trails, tracks which lead nowhere in particular. There are, naturally, no towns or cities in Perronales, no housing developments or grand establishments, though anywhere one looks, even in the most unexpected places, there may be a *bohio* of ratty, molting palm thatch inhabited by poor wretched country-people who are curious yet untrusting and suspicious, always peering out the door (or a crack in the walls), to keep one from relieving oneself behind a nearby shrub or from stealing the neighbor's chickens. They are a sniping, critical, back-biting people, spiteful, envious; thcy are a people who must be hailed and greeted daily, who come to visit only for the coffee, and who await the slightest stumble in order to pounce. . . . Jacinta feels an unconscious love (like all true loves) for this out-of-the-way, suffocatingly hot place. This is the only place Jacinta knows, of course, but she has a presentiment (perhaps not ill-founded) that there are worse places, and that it is almost a blessing, a privilege, a pardon, a benediction of divine grace, to be here and not there. Though at times she kicks at it and curses it, Jacinta loves this niggardly rickets-ridden land; and although she generally cuts them down with a machete (or with the hatchet if they are thicker), Jacinta loves those trees with their gnarled and twisted trunks, their leathery leaves, their grudging (or utterly withheld) fruit. And although she constantly mutters curses against the aridness and sterility of this place, Jacinta has gone out this morning, like all mornings, to the mountain. She has picked a weed at random, and sighing as the dew, the quickly evaporating dew of this region, has moistened her thighs. And has gone on alone. And has peed standing up, talking to herself. And, "owner of all she surveys," owner and utterly sure of herself, has cursed. And knelt on the very highest spot of the wide upland meadow, and . . .

I'm just going to kneel down right here, under this arbor vitae tree, to ask You, dear God, to keep this damned old man that fate doomed me to have for a husband from selling the farm. Enlighten him, God—don't let him sell. Take these desires from him, or set something in his way to stop him. We've lived here all our lives, and we ought to keep living here. Don't let him sell. Because You know I have a sixth sense for bad luck, and I see terrible things . . . What will become of us down there in that town, where a person doesn't know the people that live right next door, or even know who they are? Our Father, Who art in heaven, don't let him sell, drive away this demon that won't let him believe in You, and drive away Moisés, too, who's the one that put the idea in the old man's head in the first place. God, there is nothing *I* can do, because there are twenty tricks and wiles, and I know it (and the old man knows it, too), that the old turkey buzzard can use to sell the farm without my being able to do a single thing to stop him. Oh, God, God only knows what mischief he's planning at this very minute. . . . Clarify his mind, God. What will we be down there in that town if we are what we are up here? What will we be, o God? . . . Don't let him sell. Make those devils go away, or make him die. Oh forgive me, God. But I'd almost rather. There's no reason for me to try to hide what I think from You, because You know anyway. And You can't punish me if I am what You made me be, and You're the one that's given me these ideas. And so, You want him to end his days . . . Because that's what I want. O God, and Thy will be done. Deliver us from evil. Holy Mary, let the old man die, but just don't let him sell. Mother of God, protect us, enlighten us. Holy Mary . . . Goddamn ants, they're climbing all the way up my legs. This goddamned tree is always covered with red ants. Protect us, o Lord. Shit. Goddamned ants. Amen.

They sold the farm. Moisés, Digna knew, kept the greatest part of the money. The old man and old woman set up a vegetable and fruit stand and bought a house made of fiber cement; it was built on purpose, it seemed, to keep in the heat, cockroaches, and the nastiest smells. The house they bought, under Moisés' constant advice, was located next door to a guava-paste factory, so they might count on higher sales of vegetables and the other minor items the old man would sell. The old man bought that idea. But *they*—Digna, Moisés, and their children—bought a better house (built of wood, with a zinc roof and a concrete floor) at the other end of the neighborhood, as far away as possible from that ga-ga-*boom* ga-ga-*boom* ga-ga-*boom* which Digna found utterly unbearable (even if she only heard it when she went to visit her family on Sunday afternoons). At first, and at Digna's insistence ("A little business is always a hedge against reverses"), they set up a sugarcane-juice-squeezing machine in the living room, to make *guarapo* to sell cold to the neighbors. At first Moisés would help out, even; he would peel the cane, grind it through the wringers, and even bottle the juice. At first Moisés would even pinch her playfully on the rear as she served out the *guarapo*. And she would smile, and go on waiting on the customers. . . . This part she may not remember, but that was how it was. . . . At first she would even allow herself (showing her almost-newlywed pride) to scold Moisés when he left a piece of sugarcane badly peeled or didn't start up the machinery as promptly as he should have. Once she even had the audacity to suggest, pleasantly of course, that *she* was the one the press belonged to, since it was her father that had given them the money. . . . But then Moisés began to come in late (though he had to go out only once a week, to pick up a wagonload of sugarcane). And then he began to come in late and drunk. And then many times he did not come in at all. And then she found out that Moisés was running around with other women, right in their neighborhood. That, of course, was when she realized how much she loved him. . . . Moisés would come in. The children would already be asleep. And she would be sitting up in the living room, waiting for him. Moisés would get upset when he saw her still awake. She never talked back to him, but Moisés would grow even angrier when he saw how mute and serious she was. She would begin to cry. Moisés, who hated tears, would grow furious. He would start cursing, and then kick the coffee table. Then immediately he would turn around and storm into the kitchen and start breaking the china. He would come back when all the plates were in shards and begin to slap her in the face. And so they would wind up in bed. The children, by now accustomed to these scenes, would watch the entertainment, or not even bother to get out of bed. The next day Digna would take some of the sugarcane money and buy some new plates . . . For a while things went on like that. Except that the children were growing up—shoes cost more, they needed more cloth for clothes. Digna would feel a strange, secret pride when she heard the neighbors whispering the morning after she had been beaten the night before. "He broke every piece of china in the house again," they would say. And she would hear that, and laugh inside. *The china, the china.* . . . The word, repeated over and over, grew senseless. And it made her laugh . . . Digna felt an overpowering sense of triumph when, on Sunday afternoons, she went to her parents' house with Moisés and the children. And greeted all the neighbors. She, and her husband. It was true the visits always wound up in a free-for-all. Moisés' mere presence set Adolfina's teeth on edge (and he always managed to provoke her), so she inevitably wound up threatening him with her sewing scissors. But were those rows not also part of her triumph? Behind her sister's angry, insulting words, behind all that violence, envy hid. She, and her husband beside her . . . And then one day Moisés came in as usual, late and drunk, but this time he didn't beat her, didn't slap her, didn't curse at all, didn't smash a single plate. He simply said, "Get your things together and wake up the kids." She was so bewildered by that change of attitude that she never even came close to guessing what plans her husband had in mind. *This man,* she thought, *this man, I wonder what in the world he's up to.*

What in the world has he got up his sleeve? Maybe he's found
a better house, I bet that's it. Maybe he's gotten in some
kind of trouble and we've got to run before they catch him,
I bet that's it, she thought, still full of pride. And full of pride
she got all her clothes together, made up two or three bundles,
and woke up the children. They left the house. On the way,
Moisés did not speak a word to her; she still understood
nothing. It was only when she saw that they were standing
before her parents' house that she had the terrifying vision
of what was about to occur. And yet she was not even to be
allowed to rehearse that vision to its end, for at that very
moment, before she could fully comprehend it all, it was
already coming to pass. Moisés called out to Polo from the
street—"Old man!" he cried. "Old man! I'm leaving this piece
of trash of yours out here for you!" And he turned his back.
And it was then that Moisés, for the last time, looked at her.
He turned, and there was such fury, such contempt in his
eyes that even she who knew him was frightened. She was
about to scream, but Moisés shoved her so hard in the chest
that it was a wonder she did not tumble to the ground under
the load of the bundles of clothes and the two children. The
old woman then appeared at the door, crossing herself and
cursing. But by then Moisés had, once and for all, disappeared.
. . . Digna gathered up the bundles of clothes, took one child
on each hip, and went into the house. Those had been, without a doubt, the best years of her life.

We moved into a new house and we set up a sugarcane press
to make *guarapo* with. Life in town is hard. I had never lived in
town but I knew it was hard because I had seen a lot of my
cousins, the girls, turn to whoring to make a living. Or to not
die of hunger, is more like it. Life in town is hard. At least up
there on the mountain you could go around to a neighbor's house
and they'd give you a piece of sweet potato or sometimes even
a piece of pork meat. But here, here you could be dying of hunger
and they wouldn't so much as throw you a bone to gnaw on. It's
hard living in town. I told him. But he had his mind made up
already. So we moved. And every day the sugarcane press would
break down. If it wasn't one thing it was another. But there wasn't

one single day it didn't break down. One day I tried to pull out a piece of cane that had balled up the wringer, and my hand got caught in it. It was chewing up my hand, and it wouldn't stop, and I started yelling. My hand was getting all ground up and squeezed right along with the sugarcane. So then he came in and stopped the machine. But my hand was a mess. Such luck we had . . . But I don't regret a thing. Not a thing. I don't regret leaving home, or crushing my hand to a pulp, or anything. Anyway, it was my left hand. And I don't regret having two children. Or anything that's happened since. Although maybe I do regret it a little. But it's all the same in the end anyway . . . Now I'm going *Hmmm hmmm hmmm*, like that, without opening my mouth. Buzzing and humming like a bee, just buzzing. Singing and thinking, out here on the porch of the house, and squabbling once in a while with those kids. What a relief to be out here all by myself, and now, now when it's almost quiet; now when everybody else is inside and I have the chance to go *Hmmm* and be by myself. Just me, myself, and I, and nobody to bother me. All by myself. And that's the end of it. Because those children are no children of mine. I don't want them to be. Those children, they won't be mine, I won't have it, because I don't want them to be some poor miserable wretched whelps like all the rest of us. That's why—even if Polo doesn't want me to—I'm going to put them down in the register with just their father's last name, and none of mine. They can say anything they want to to me. But he's their father. Maybe he brought me back here and left me and disappeared, maybe he used to beat me, maybe I've never seen his face again, maybe he used to come home half drunk and the only piece of china that would be left safe and sound would be the aluminum platter we stole once at the fair. Maybe every bit of that is true. But I'm telling you, he's still those children's father. And I don't regret that.

Life is not like you'd like it to be. It's just not. And if it were, why you'd want it to be different from *that*. At least I had the consolation of having a husband. Time can ruin things and spoil things and waste things and take things away that a person once had. But the consolation of remembering them, nobody can take that away. At least I haven't gone all rotten or bitter, like my sister that shuts herself up for hours on end in the bathroom, lord knows what for. . . . My sister. Poor thing—even if she practically never speaks to me, it's not because she doesn't like me, it's just that she doesn't have anything to say to me . . . I don't regret a thing.

The first night all we could think about was *that*. And maybe we didn't even think about that. The first night . . . They ought to burn every man alive that leaves a young woman. They ought to catch them and cut off their balls. What future does a young woman who's been abandoned have? What future except to go into the life. That's all the future she has. You think I haven't noticed how men look at me when they come in the shop? Of course none of them are going to propose matrimony, exactly. No. Matrimony is for virgins. For me, bed. Bed, because once upon a time a son of a bitch went to bed with me and then he ran off and left me. Bed—but they can just put it out of their mind. I'll die first.

"You kids—inside, now, it's late. Come on."

Sometimes she was not sure whether the two children were demons or angels. Her sister Celia used to say—although you didn't have to pay any mind to what a crazy person said—that angel and devil was the same thing. Maybe . . . Still, those two children had something strange about them, had something a little gibing, jeering, almost diabolic, surely, about them. *Possessed* . . . "All children are spawn of the devil," Jacinta always said. Although you didn't have to pay any mind to an old woman demented by hunger. The truth was, she didn't *know* her children, even if they were the only thing that lent any meaning to her life, the only thing that made her happy, infuriated her, made her want to curse the world and even life itself. The only thing that drove her out onto the porch and made her sing, with her mouth closed, so she wouldn't burst.

"Look here and see if you see what I see."
"Let me see, let me see."
"Look."
"Oh, my god . . . !"

"What do you see?"
"The same thing you do—nothing."

At first her parents were opposed to her relationship with Moisés. They threatened to kill him; then, to kill her. The old woman vowed to hang herself. . . . But who could resist Moisés? Who could fight it? Jacinta herself finally grumblingly relented. Even Adolfina, in spite of her rage, wound up making him a pair of pants for the wedding. And Polo—Polo was *crazy* about his son-in-law. He would smile at all his jokes, and at all his propositions. Because really, who could resist him?

You got up the courage to come, and you talked to him. And just like always, he told you not to come one step closer because he was going to cut your head open with a machete. But you aren't scared of my father. If you ran out the front door, it was out of the respect you have for the old man. You got up the courage to come, and you even brought that she-donkey of a mother of mine a box of candy. And the stupid old woman didn't even wait for you to leave—she took the box and right in front of you she threw it across the room. And all the candy spilled out on the floor in the corner and cracked and squished. And you stood there so serious, looking at the pile of candy. Lord knows how much you had spent on that box of candy. But it doesn't matter that you had to leave the house—I waited for you out at the fence, and when you went by I threw a little pebble at you, just a little one, so it wouldn't hurt you. And you knew right away. And you ran and hugged me, just like that. And you said to me, just like that, "Let's get out of here." But I said, No, I can't right now. Come back and talk to Papa. "That old man, nobody could talk to him," you said. Come back and talk to him. "I don't want to." Come back in and just talk to him a little. And so you said, "You can either come with me right this minute or we'll never see each other again." So I said, All right, because I couldn't imagine having to live without ever seeing you again. I told you, All right—that night, I told you, when everybody was asleep, I'd sneak out and we'd run away. And we promised to meet under the ceiba tree, out behind the old well.

And so now I'm under the ceiba tree. And you haven't come. With all the work it took me to sneak out of the house. They could be out looking for me by now, for all I know. Virgen santísima, for all I know they've already realized that I ran away and they're out looking for me to cut off my head. Holy Virgin, and you don't come. They'll probably catch me right here, under this ceiba tree, and then I'm ruined and disgraced, because everybody in the neighborhood will think I'm ruined, the same as if I'd already done it . . . Because who's going to believe I haven't done it, or convince my *father* I haven't done it? . . . I feel like laughing— by the time I got back to the house after going outside to catch you, Mama was picking up the candy off the floor and eating it. I almost laughed out loud to see her. After she threw them across the room like that. Nobody will ever understand that old woman. Although when you said we were planning to get married and set up a sugarcane press to make *guarapo* with, I know that made her happy inside. Because that old woman is made out of cast iron, and for her to show she's happy, the rest of the world would have to have already split its sides. But I could see by how her eyes sparkled when you mentioned the part about the *guarapo* . . . I saw how they sparkled. Because there's nothing she likes better than to chew the fibers afterwards. She's the sweetest-toothed old woman . . .

"Digna! Digna!"

"Here I am! Over here!"

"You may not believe this, but the only thing I can see now is an ant with wings, trying to drink water out of the toilet."

"I want to see that for myself."

I would've liked to've been a man. But then again, I'm not sure I would've liked to've been a man. But at least if I had been, Moisés would be the woman, and I wouldn't be here thinking what I'm thinking. I'll tell you, if I had turned out to be a man, I'd have ruined practically the whole world. I wouldn't have left

FOR SALE: Two sugarcane presses. Ball bearings in stainless-steel housing. For information, Peralta Garage, Holguín, Oriente.
—*El Norte*
Holguín, July 31, 1958

75

a single woman sound. I would've liked to've been a man to've been able to do more of what they did to me. But I don't know . . . I think about it, and I tell myself, Stop playing the suffering female, you brazen hussy you—you love everything that's happened to you. You love all this "disgrace," this foul luck of yours. The world caves in on you, and you say you can't stop it. But you don't do anything to stop it, if you could. You're even glad. Because that's just the way you are, you stubborn fool of a woman, you don't regret anything even if you burn in hell for it. You never give in. You love this sadness of yours. I don't know . . . I really don't know. But I think if I had a choice in the matter, I'd say, "I want to be a woman left and abandoned that sits and howls on a suffocating front porch and has two children dying of hunger and sleeping on a lice-infested pallet." That's what my answer would be if somebody asked me what I wanted to be. And then I'd break down and cry, because I wouldn't want to be what I wanted to be and am. I'd start to cry on the spot, but it would be too late. So I'd just get happy again. And then I'd be sad. How happy . . .

"Adolfina! Adolfina! How long are you going to stay in that bathroom! This is unbelievable. You'll be running the reservoir dry any minute now. And I'm about to burst. This is the last straw, my God. What a fate is mine. Not even to be able to go to the toilet when I need to. This is too much. I'm going to call Polo right this minute, and he'll get you out of there if he has to burn you out. You'll see what's what!"

High, triumphant, covered with flowers, she went out into June. Everyone following along, respectful, to accompany her. Someone crying, and those tears were for her. Someone whispering something, and she was the cause of those murmured words . . . It had rained. But now the sun was out. A little way ahead, the earth—open and fresh, cool—was awaiting her. A little way ahead, in among the shrubs and high grass of the hollow, there was a little corner where water stood; now you could begin to smell its particular smell, and hear the whirr of the birds as they flushed up and out of the rough. It was Sunday—what more could have been wished for? It was Sunday, and so everything was different, clean, shining.

Everyone was wearing starched clothes. And the smell and brightness of the country were different too. To die in June, and on a Sunday—what more could be wished for, what more could be asked for, what more could be desired? What occasion, what ceremony could ever compare with the one taking place at this moment, in her honor, all along the red-clay road that gave eloquent, mute testimony to the recent downpour? . . . Baudilio would be among the men, too, serious, in his suit—he who could never stand to wear a suit, even on December 31—suffocating. . . . And she was a little upset to think that the other people might think that this whole cortège, this whole procession, all this harmony and pomp, this whole fiesta—was because of Baudilio, on his account. Because it really wasn't. It would have been so petty, so ordinary, so *common*, if all this had been on account of that. . . . There were other things, principles, callings, other contempts and other terrors much more worthy of concern than *that*. But how could you ever explain such things to these stupid people—all these people . . . How could you make them see that the cause of all this was not so obvious, so simple, so palpable, so vulgar as they thought . . . But now they were almost there. And now they laid down the beflowered symbol of their journey, which was she—the fly, drunken and voluptuous, buzzed incessantly among the flowers. And now they lowered her—the fly, ever cautious, hovered. And now she heard the first shovelfuls of wet, red, heavy, clayey earth thumping on the coffin. And now June, with its many snortings and whinnyings, with its many and varied scurryings and ticklings, with its unbribable, inexorable buzzings, began to tug and pull at her, began to unjoint her, unhinge her, dismember her, take her apart, began to swallow her up. The real nightmare, the real nightmare—had it ended? Or was it just beginning? . . . But by now she was far away. By now there were other things for her to know . . .

The Life of the Dead

How nice it is to float along in the water like this, like I'm floating. Not bumping the bottom or even touching it, so as not to stir it up, and not coming out to float on top, either, so people don't realize I'm floating. How pretty things look from underwater. I open my eyes and everything is changed to a bright white color. I open my eyes and I can see my open hands—so I bring my white hands up to my white eyes in the middle of all this whiteness. How lovely it is, how nice, to float and float and float along in the middle of the river and never touch the bottom and never go ashore—and never stop or be still. Letting the current carry me, carry me along. Carry me, carry me along. In just a little while I'll come to the diving place and then I'll walk on top of the water because there's not a living soul there to see me and get scared. In just a few minutes I'll meet my cousin Fortunato and we'll walk on top of the water, until we realize we're walking on top of the water. And we'll try to submerge. And then we'll get scared, ourselves, just like the people that—do you think?—might have seen us. And finally we'll realize that we're dead and that's why we don't sink. Until we realize that and we submerge, we go down for good . . . But I wonder where Fortunato has gotten off to tonight. You think he's trying to touch things again? Poor thing, he's still not used to this . . . He's still imagining that all this is made up, that it's just "imagined." Poor thing. I feel sorry for him, because I went through the same thing. Poor miserable child.

The radio said, "Holguín, the city of more than two hundred thousand people with just one garbage truck." But he knew it wasn't true. There weren't that many people in Holguín. Of course it was to the radio's advantage, like it was to everybody else's that did publicity and things, to use big, round numbers, and so they included in the number of people in the town (or "city" as the radio kept saying) all the poor devils that according to the census belonged to this municipality (and judicial precinct), even if they had never set foot in the city (and never would, either). Fortunato hated Holguín. Holguín is a city with straight streets all exactly alike. And no matter where you are, you can see the city limits from there. Holguín is a town with sharp sidewalks and exact, square parks laid out in a straight line one behind another. Holguín is a big square-edged rectangular box—a coffin. A city (or town) big, anonymous, and fading to sepia, surrounded by acres and acres that don't quite manage to be mountains, but that won't settle down into flat land either. No tourist has ever stopped to take a snapshot of its bridges, whose architecture is strictly functional—they simply let the water flow (when it rains) under their "arches"; no poet has so far had the gall to hymn a single column or piling of one of those bridges. Nothing "stands out" there; nothing calls one's attention to itself, even if only to be rejected by the eye. It has no ocean, Holguín. To see the ocean one would have to take a bus, travel approximately an hour, and pay at least forty-five centavos. Holguín has no rivers. The prairie around is never very fertile; water flows below ground, hard to get at. There are no trees in Holguín. People in the poor neighborhoods cut them down "just because"; the *nouveaux riches* cut them down so the poor can see their big houses. "Trees block the view," they say . . . The view . . . Holguín is a city that is utterly commercial, which is to say abominable. Everyone there makes a living by selling something. If one is rich, one has one's automobile dealership, or a bicycle shop, a movie house, a small department store, or a garage; if one is middle class, one of the "comfortable," one has a *bodega* with a four-door refrigerator, or a numbers game, or a big butcher shop; if one is poor, one has a little shop in the front of the house turned into a vegetable stand, or a fruit stand, or perhaps one has an ice-cream cart, or a wagon with a horse to go up into the mountains to buy cheap and resell in town. And if one is among the poorest of the poor, then one has one's wheelbarrow to sell charcoal out of, or a wooden box to sell candy from, or a sack full of lemons to walk down the street with, yelling at the top of one's lungs *"Leeeeemons! Leeeeeemons!"* . . . And even the people who have nothing to sell—they sell knowledge to the big sellers. So there are typing and shorthand professors, bookkeeping professors, English professors—the "branches of learning," in other words. Naturally, to keep the inhabitants of Holguín informed about all these varied activities, Holguín has had many newspapers—ugly, vulgar, every one filled with advertisements, even on the front page, and with conventional and convenient patriotism (*jingoism*, which comes down to simple *civic pride*) from front page to last. The newspapers have borne such names as the Holguín *Echo*, or the *Justice*, or *El Norte*, or other odd, dull-sounding names. Holguín has four very poor neighborhoods, a "downtown," and four great preserves of luxury. Downtown one can find the big stores that close at 8:00 p.m., the movie houses that fill and empty twice a day, at five in the afternoon and at eight-thirty at night. In the wealthy neighborhoods one finds, of course, the grand residences, the oleanders, the milky-skinned children, not to mention the voluminous women who remind one of impassive, sleepy hedgehogs or moles with great abdomens, who live here as well. In the poor areas, especially in La Frontera, one finds the bars, the "bungalows" and whorehouses, the wheelbarrowmen, the roads leading nowhere, the Negroes, and Eufrasia's Ball Room, that great center of attraction. Fortunato walks past these places, and they all seem equally detestable to him. He feels he belongs to none of them. Sometimes when he has a peso he goes into a movie house, or has an ice cream, goes to the fair (for in this town there is always a fair going on somewhere), or he may find himself standing in front of Eufrasia's place. Of all the despicable places in the town, Eufrasia's Ball Room is the only one Fortunato has any softness for—it has a certain class, a certain authenticity. At least at Eufrasia's people know how to behave, how to act, they feel "at home," they can be themselves. There is no hypocrisy at Eufrasia's. There is no great pretense. The organ plays. The whores dance. The men, rubbing up against them, try to get their money's worth out of the dance, before the organ stops. Eufrasia—high heels, red dress, big white purse— taps the dancers on the shoulders and collects. Eufrasia is so good at collecting that nobody is known ever to have escaped. And there are occasions, after the collection (for the organ is often generous with the clients), that there's still enough time left for another little squeeze. . . . There is no hypocrisy. The dance is not a symbolic sex act here, it is the very essence of what in those more "circumspect" places it merely represents. Here a whore's cunning consists of knowing that the more she wiggles (but with class, with style, with furious professionalism), the more she allows the client to rub up against her, the closer she dances, the more clients she will have. There can be not the shadow of a doubt about that. Lolín, for example, is one of the most sought-after girls. But at the same time, one must remember that a whore, dancing, must heat the client up but not bring on the climax. If she does, the customer will leave without making full use of the woman; that is, without turning loose the two pesos (the official rate) for a bed—a business from which, it is generally understood, Eufrasia earns not a farthing. Some whores, though, were so very sought after, and so solicitous—Fortunato would eavesdrop on the conversations they carried on with the "clients"—that they might dance three hundred dances in one night. And they would retire toward dawn having cleared more than six pesos. Saturdays, especially, were good nights. Fortunato, after he had worked all day in the factory (making at the time some five hundred crates per day), would go out into the street. He hated the people. Hated the noise of the buses. Hated the sharp-edged sidewalks. Hated his starched, ironed clothes, his fingernails trimmed with Adolfina's scissors . . . And he would come to the Ball Room. Where his hatred, with his gaze, would slide down those figures singlemindedly and hypnotically gyrating, grinding to the unvarying music of the organ . . . But the climax of his abhorrence—or one might give it another name, call it *his desire to love other things*—would come, would be brought about, when he went home again and went to pee, and his eyes would be offended by the greasy walls of the factory. At those times he kicked a chair, smashed the radio with his knee, started stomping cockroaches, vowed to hang himself on the spot. Fortunato would zip his pants and go into his bedroom. "Holguín," he would say, without saying it, and he would groan. At those moments the smell of rotten guavas, like a constant reminder of his destiny, would feed his fury.

I'm going to go get out the seventeen pesos I've got saved up under the mattress, right this minute, and buy a ticket and get out of this place. After all, I've waited longer than anybody had any right to expect. And I can't stand it anymore—I'm leaving. Today.

It's been better than two months since I went to the terminal and asked how much a ticket to Havana cost. They told me nine pesos and forty centavos. I'd already been saving up for a long time. But every time I managed to save up a little something, I always had to spend it. If it wasn't one thing, it was another. But not this time. This time I'm leaving if I have to starve to death on the road.

It's still early. I'd better wait to leave till the whole neighborhood's asleep, because otherwise everybody'll start asking me where I'm going with a suitcase at this hour, and it won't be two minutes till my whole family will find out and raise a ruckus, because my family is the biggest bunch of noisy, set-up-a-ruckus people in the world. Even when they're just talking about things that don't matter one way or another, people walking down the street stop for a minute and listen because they think there's a murder going on in the house. And it's my miserable luck to have to have lived with them since the day I was born.

Since the day I was born I've been listening to my grandmother complain at the top of her lungs all night about her back pains, screaming "I can't take it anymore" till you can't take it anymore.

And for I don't know how long I've been the one that had to step and fetch it for everybody, anything they wanted, from a sack of charcoal to a stalk of plantains in the market for the stand my grandfather has. Or something for Adolfina's headaches that never go away.

My grandfather's vegetable stand is the biggest tragedy of the house, since there are all these rotten fruits and vegetables behind the counter—which my grandfather the stingy packrat won't give away or throw out, so they start attracting rats and cockroaches. The rats and cockroaches prowl all over the dining room and kitchen, and even sometimes get in the living room or go down the hall into the bedrooms.

There's very little ever sold out of that shop. Or rather—it doesn't bring in much. Though if it weren't for the vegetable stand, Grandpa wouldn't have a thing to do and so he'd be spending the livelong day sitting in the house somewhere not talking instead of in *there* not talking. Because he never talks. He'll sit down at the table. He'll eat like he's in a good mood and he likes the food. But he won't say a word. Not a peep. At night, just before seven o'clock when the news comes on, he'll close the shop, lock the lock real tight, and sit in the living room. He'll turn on the radio and listen to the news. One day I could swear I heard him say, Good lord. About something on the news. I could swear I heard him, so I ran out into the backyard and I took advantage of the fact that it was dark and nobody could see me and I made a lot of faces and danced around and jumped with joy. But the next day he didn't say a word again. And since then I've never heard him talk. Except the answers he's absolutely got to give some customer when they ask him about the merchandise or when he tells them how much they're behind in their bill so they can pay up. And even that, I'll tell you, was before, because now he'll hardly open his mouth even for that. Unless it's somebody like Tomasico, of course.

The only customers that come in to the vegetable stand are the people that work in Tomasico's factory, which unfortunately is right next to our house and which starts up so early in the morning if it's working that it won't let a person sleep because of the racket of the motors and the belts and pulleys and the smell of rotten guavas, which is awful, which is what they grind up and make guava paste and guava candy out of.

But we really can't complain that the factory is practically in the backyard of the house, because if it weren't for the factory we'd have all starved to death a long time ago. Tomasico's guava-paste factory is "the lifeblood of this neighborhood." Everybody says so. Everybody that lives around here works there. And of course I do, too. Although now it's held up by the shortage of guavas. Or something. Lord knows.

I got the job thanks to my grandmother, who's the one that went and talked to Tomasico and explained our situation to him. "All we've got to live on is that vegetable stand," she said to him with that face—that face she puts on when she starts telling people how bad things are. "And it brings in so little by the time we take out expenses that if it weren't for the chair seats I've been weaving out of straw we'd have the wolf at the door sure enough." Tomasico blinked a little. He stuck his hands in his pants pockets, because in spite of how fat he is they're always about to fall off him, and he tugged them up to under his arms where he starts them out. My grandmother waited for Tomasico to pull his pants way up there, and she said, "And now with three more mouths to feed, because you know my daughter Digna, her husband ran off and left her, and with two children." And then she tacked on softer and more pleadingly, "Poor things, it's no fault of theirs . . ." Finally Tomasico scratched his head and said, "Tell him to come tomorrow morning and I'll see about putting him to work." And then he added, "But you know, don't you, that it's not steady work, because when the guava season's over, I have to close down the factory." "I'll send him over here first thing tomorrow morning," my grandmother said to Tomasico, firm.

And so the next day bright and early I went over to the factory. I had to wait quite a while for Tomasico to come in. He finally came in, though, and he said to me, "I'm going to have you make boxes. Come with me." We walked along through the sputtering vats of boiling guava and jelly and stuff and came out into a yard behind the boiler. There were two tables set up, with two boys and two girls, or women, at each one, making wooden boxes like crates. "Mariano," Tomasico said, and they all stopped hammering. One of the boys came over to us. "This boy is going to be working with you," Tomasico told him. "So set him up over there. Find him a table and a hammer and nails and show him how to make three or four boxes." The boy hung his head and then he looked hard, straight at me. Before he left, Tomasico said, "Be sure you make those boxes sturdy. And no nails showing outside, or rotten slats. It pains me to see the poor quality you people are turning out lately."

Mariano and I went into the little storeroom they have next to the boiler, and between us, we managed to wrestle a table outside. Then he showed me where the slats were, and the box ends, and he brought me a box of tacks and a hammer. This is not hard work, thought I, while I watched him make the boxes, at better than two a minute. Then he stepped aside and let me do it. I picked up the hammer and started to drive a nail, but my aim was not so good.

At first I wouldn't earn more than fifty or sixty centavos a day, but little by little I got faster at it. There were days I made more than a thousand boxes, which at twenty centavos a hundred, which is what they paid, was better than two pesos. I'd get up early early in the morning. At three, three-thirty, without anybody's calling me—because who wouldn't wake up with that racket of belts and pulleys and wheels starting up. I'd drag myself into the kitchen, drink a little coffee from the night before, and go off to make boxes. In the morning early like that you could go a lot faster and get a lot more done than the whole rest of the day put together, because it wouldn't be so hot. In fact some mornings I'd be shivering from the cold. But as soon as I picked up the hammer and started to drive the nails, the cold would just disappear. When the work would start getting hard would be from about nine o'clock on. By then the sun would be beating down on that tin roof and the boiler would be like an oven and there would be all that steam and smoke coming out of the pipes and valves. That's when I'd go home and have breakfast. Then I'd go back, take off my shirt, and work in my undershirt.

I thought I had such good friends in that factory. Especially the ones that worked with me making boxes. The girls were nice, too, and friendly, and one time I asked one out to the movies with me. But then we couldn't go that day because an order came in for fifteen thousand bars of guava paste, which was the way the factory packed them—in bars—so Tomasico begged us to work overtime because there weren't enough boxes for that many bars. But when the summer was over and the guavas began to run out and be scarce, I began to suspect that I didn't have such good friends as I thought I had. Since the guavas started not to come in so fast and furious, we didn't have to make so many boxes. So there were days when Tomasico would tell us to just make up one sack of endpieces, for example, and another one of slats and bottoms. And so then we'd all work as fast as we could, each one of us trying to make as many boxes as we could before the slats ran out.

One day when I got there, like

ORIENTE THEATER
TODAY ONLY TODAY

DANGEROUS MEN
with
Warner Baxter

Saturday 13 & Sunday 14
EL ALMA DEL BARRIO

!!SENSATIONAL!!
DON'T MISS IT.
—Holguín *Echo* (biweekly)
May 10, 1933

always, about three-thirty in the morning, two of the boys had already made up a big pile of boxes. The sackful of endpieces was almost half empty already.

"Well, you got up early this morning," I said to them, like Hello and Shame on You at the same time. But they didn't say a word, they just kept hammering. The next day I got up earlier than usual, too. But after I'd set up the table and brought out the slats and things, I realized they'd hidden the nails. So I couldn't start till the rest of them got there.

"Where are the nails?" I said.

"They must be where they always are," they said.

But they weren't. So then one of them laughed and said, Oh he remembered, he'd forgotten to put the nails away the day before, so he'd left them behind the boiler, with some empty sacks and stuff.

The work kept falling off and falling off and things went from bad to worse with my so-called friends. One day I realized that when I went home for breakfast somebody had taken at least forty or fifty boxes out of my pile. And to see whether I was right or not I counted them before I left the next day. Sure enough, I had made two hundred and thirty boxes before I left and when I came back there were just a hundred and eighty of them.

"Somebody's stolen fifty boxes from me," I yelled, so they could hear me over the racket of the belts and the hiss of the steam escaping from the boiler.

They all just went right on hammering, although I saw that one of the girls was trying to hide the fact that she was giggling. But they kept on working, not paying any attention to what I had said, so I said it again, and I added, "If I don't get them back, I'm telling Tomasico."

"Stop being a pain in the ass and sit down and go to work if you want to make some money today, because there's just one sackful of ends," one of the boys said.

So I was furious but I sat down and started working, and I even smashed my thumb. But I didn't say anything, or even go *Ouch*, because if I had they'd have all laughed anyway. All right for you, I thought, but when you're not looking, you better watch out. But no matter how hard I watched for my chance to get my boxes back, and maybe some of theirs too, I never could, because they never stirred from the table till the work was all finished. So then I realized that they all stole from each other, and so that was why they never even left the table to go to the bathroom.

I thought about telling Tomasico what was going on. But Tomasico was in such a terrible mood those days that I said to myself that if I told him he'd probably fire every one of us. Me included, naturally. There were less boxes to make every day, then, until we were just working one or two days a week. Finally one Saturday when we were getting paid, Tomasico told us not to come back to work for now, the factory was closing down for a while. He told us, and he looked very serious about it as he was telling us, that it wasn't just the problem of the guava shortage, either, that made him have to shut down the factory, it was that sales were falling off too, since over at the other end of town another factory had opened, with newer and better equipment than his, and cheaper labor, so they could sell their guava paste cheaper too, so all of his customers were going over to them. We all just stood there, in shock. Then we all got together and agreed, and we told him that we could work for less if that would keep the factory going.

But it was no use—the factory closed. Till next year, they say.

When my grandfather found out about the factory closing, his face got more serious than ever, and since then he hasn't opened his mouth once to talk, not even to the customers. They all manage to talk in signs. My grandmother spends the whole day squabbling and scolding him, and she tells him he's crazy as a loon—because nobody just stops talking, just like that, just because they feel like it.

I'm really sorry the factory closed, I'll tell you. Not just because of the money I made—which when all is said and done never amounted to much—but because now I don't have anything to do and I have to stay at home all day listening to my grandmother squabbling with my aunt Digna or my aunt Adolfina or my aunt Celia—who, since her daughter Esther got poisoned and died, is always off in the clouds somewhere.

My aunt Digna is an embittered woman. She denies it. She

says she's not, but I've heard my grandmother say it a lot, and I believe it's the truth. She spends her whole life fighting with her kids. And sometimes she takes a switch and whips those kids till they cry and sob all day long. Those times, there's really no way to stand this house. So I go out into the street, but I don't have anywhere to go. If I at least knew how to play ball. But there's no way—I just can't seem to learn how. And before I'll let other people laugh at me, I'll just not learn, either.

Once—he must have been about five years old at the time—his mother took him to an aunt's house—the Obnoxious One's—and as they were crossing the Lirio River, a man appeared and gave him two pesos. But Onerica grabbed up a handful of rocks and started throwing them at the man. *You asshole,* she was screaming, *you asshole!* And she hit him with so many rocks that it was a wonder she didn't brain him. But the time they got to his aunt's house, Onerica was sobbing and Fortunato had realized that the man was his father.

But what made the strongest impression on him was seeing his mother for the first time so furious that she cried. She never complained about anything, or showed her emotions at all . . . His mother.

I really am clumsy at sports, all of them. And playing games. I've got no aim at marbles, I can never thump it right, or hit the other marbles. And when I try to hit that little piece of wood with the bat and knock it out of the yard, I just swat the air.

So all there is to do is walk. Headed nowhere.

Or stay at home, listening to Digna squabbling and scolding and slapping her kids so hard they're halfway feeble-minded. And screaming, "This is not life! I'm already doomed and sent to hell! Shit!"

I think she's right. But then it's true, too, that it's no fault of her children. There's no doubt in the world that it's her husband that's to blame, since he was the one that left her and that's never sent her so much as a single peso, her or the children either.

When my aunt Digna starts scolding and fighting like that, or after she leaves the kids locked up in the room screaming and kicking, my grandmother starts in scolding *her*; and then Adolfina puts in her two cents' worth from the bathroom, she starts yelling at them to shut up, and my aunt Celia sits in the rocking chair and sings or holds a long conversation with lord knows who that I can never see.

"Why should those poor wretched children have to pay for something that's no fault of their own?" my grandmother says. "When it's you that brought them into the world. I told you not to marry Moisés. But no—you wouldn't pay me any mind, you went off with him, to spite me. You wanted Moisés? Well, try to get him now."

"Leave me alone, Mama," Digna thunders at her. "I'm altogether too worn out and beat down now to have to put up with you too."

"You two she-mules!" Adolfina shrieks from the bathroom. "Don't you ever plan to shut your traps the livelong day? Oh, if only you knew how tired I am of this damnation I'm cast into."

And meanwhile, Celia rocks in the rocking chair and talks, without rhyme or reason.

Sometimes I'd like to do something terrible. I am so tired. The other day I even thought about committing suicide. The idea came to me when I was standing in front of the living-room mirror. My God, I said, this is all just shit. And then I felt this rage coming over me. And I thought about suicide. But then I said to myself, Forget it. It's not me that's to blame, either, that Digna's husband went off and abandoned her and that all day long she beats her kids and screams at them. And it's not me that's to blame that my grandfather's never talked again because he just hasn't felt like it. And it's not my fault either if my aunt Celia's daughter has died or if Adolfina's never found a husband. Forget it. Let *them* commit suicide.

And it was then that the idea of leaving home and all this really hit me the worst.

So today, ever since I got out of bed, I've been turning and turning and turning that idea over in my head.

Asking myself, Where will I go?

And answering myself, Anywhere.

And asking myself again, But *where, where?*

And answering myself again, Anywhere. Anywhere in the world.

And I was thinking about that when the mailman came, with

a letter from my mother. Because my mother, as you know, has been in the United States, working, since five years ago. She got to go thanks to a relative of my grandfather's that felt sorry for her and sent for her. She started making trips back and forth from the consulate in Havana to the consulate in Santiago de Cuba, until finally this relative put down some money and they let her leave. When Mama left, I was still just a kid, and I cried and everything. I remember, she told me, "Don't fret now, as soon as I can, I'll send for you." But she hasn't been able to yet. And by now, I'd say it was pretty sure she won't ever be able to, either. Anyway, I take the letter and I open it.

My dear son

I will never understand why my mother always starts her letters the same, same way, every time. I pray to God that when this reaches you you are well. I am fine. It's cold here now. It's hot here now. Working hard. My mother. . . . Now I am saving a little more money, and I'll see if I can't send you a pair of shoes. I can imagine how things are down there now. Dear son. Dear son. Dear son. Please write. Please write. Why don't you write?

Tweeeeee! The mailman with another letter from my mother.

Your mother, ay, your mother, writing day and night. Tell that poor woman not to worry about this beast. Tell her she has no son, what she has is a goose. Tell her. This boy is going to be the death of me. You are all I have in the world. You are the only son I have. You.

"Another letter from that silly goose that worries about this piece of meat with two eyes in it."

"Good lord! If she only knew he doesn't even read them. I've always said—it's better to raise chickens than children."

Sometimes he would tell himself that he had seen fabulous places, places where, from the very sky, golden galleons, elephants, flowers of unearthly beauty, a rain of crystals, transparent swallows, elaborate carousels would slip down, descend from the sky and fall across the surface of the sea. And one would simply have to see him turned inward upon himself, watch him gaze on the procession of a flock of indescribable birds as they flew by, calling him by name, inviting him to follow. One had to see, yes, how he would spin, leap, how he would cry out from within, and try to reach them. It was a wonder.

I go out into the backyard to sit a while on the dried-up tree trunk. I go out into the backyard, and the first thing I come across is Fortunato, coming toward me with a knife stuck through his throat.

I go out in the backyard, and I start screaming. Screaming. But nobody hears me. And Fortunato walking across the roof of the house, pulling the knife out of his throat and sticking it back in again—once, twice, once and again and again, once, twice, a hundred times.

Then I go into the living room. But in the front room the devils are having a fiesta, and before they can throw me out, I leave. I don't know, I really don't know, where to go. If I lie down on my bed, I discover I've been in bed ten or eleven centuries already, so as soon as I lie down all I can think of is getting up again. If I open a drawer in the wardrobe, to hide in, the beasts start running and flying out like rats, and they scare me out of my wits, so I run out screaming and go lock myself up in the bathroom. But in the bathroom my sister Adolfina is setting herself afire, and she doesn't like anybody to bother her when she's doing that—she's perfectly capable of pulling her arm off and throwing it at me, flames and all, if I fool with her.

So. I don't know what to do. So I go into the shop. Polo's vegetable stand, thinking that in there at least—since the old man never opens his mouth—I can sit for a while in peace. But good heavens, how could I have been so silly! My whole day got off on the wrong foot, so now there's no way out—the old man's in there having a wonderful conversation with Death. And even giving him the best tomatoes, for free. That old coot! The tomatoes he refuses to give Mama so she can make a salad. And there's Death, dying laughing, taking the tomatoes and just swallowing them down as pretty as you please. That son-of-a-bitch Death, there's nobody can refuse him his slightest wish. But I think it'd be best for me to duck out, just in case he wished for *me*. Son of a bitch.

I put up the ladder and climb up on the roof of the house. And that's when I hear thousands and thousands of ghosts fluttering around, and birds of all sizes and colors, all of them—the ghosts, too—flying off like lightning, up into the sky. What a fright I get from all that flapping and squawking. So I ask myself— am I so ugly that even birds and ghosts run away when they see me coming? My God, madre mía, both of you—answer that question for me. It's the only question worth answering so far as I'm concerned. Is Digna so ugly, just tell me, so ugly that she might as well give up? Give up all hope? Am I so ugly there's no use looking out the window anymore? Should I just forget I'm a woman, give up on Moisés altogether? Tell me that—so I can get a running start and smash into the wall of the vegetable stand and crack my skull open and smash my brains out and die, and smash all the hurricane-lantern chimneys to bits while I'm at it. Nobody buys them anyway. Old turkey buzzard, who's going to buy hurricane-lantern chimneys in a town where they practically give away lightbulbs for free? Such ideas that stupid old coot has.

But tell me—am I so ugly?

Sometimes he would also pretend that his mother had died. He would kill his mother just to see himself at the center of a funeral. Just to see himself among the flowers and the wreaths, beside a black coffin, crying. Or perhaps there was more to it than that. Perhaps. Perhaps it was that he imagined her dead because he loved her too much. Or perhaps because he couldn't live without her, or resign himself to losing her, and he knew—he was always a savant, and an idiot to boot— that only death immortalizes what we love. But how could a mother understand such things? Could she—a slow, clumsy woman, living far away, always in the midst of the yelling of strange children, hearing (uncomprehendingly) strange people's voices (for she never managed to learn English)—could she ever have understood that kind of love, perhaps the most overpowering love of all? . . . His mother.

I've read a little bit of the letter. I try to read it all, but I just can't. I'm thinking that someday I'll have to write her, explain to her that last night I went to a dance that ended in a free-for-all with knives and everything. Then she'll write me back and say, "I don't understand why you go to such places. Take care of yourself, you're all I've got." But that's not the worst of it—I'll have to tell her I didn't go into the School of Business because they rejected me, after I took the entrance exam and everything. Although I can't understand how they could; the exam was so easy, plus when I finished I found the answers Irene had given—the daughter of the man that owns the big furniture store by the park—and my answers were a lot better than hers were. And now it turns out that her name is on the list of people they admitted, and mine is not.

I don't understand it. But it must have been because of neatness, or some such thing. And I'm sorry about it—not for me, not for myself, but for her, because she had her heart set on my going to school.

But goodness, that all pales beside this—when Mama finds out I left home, she'll go crazy. . . . So, let her go crazy, but I'm not staying here. I've had enough of this. Anyway, I'll write her a letter and explain everything to her. Or maybe not—maybe it's better to send her a telegram, saying I AM FINE.

It's finally dark.

This afternoon I went to the movies because Digna gave me forty centavos and told me, "Here, kid, go to the movies—I get the creeps looking at you all closed up day and night in the front room. . . ." So I went. I bought a ticket for the balcony for twenty-five centavos and had enough left over for cigarettes and matches.

The movie wasn't bad. But you could hardly hear it for the people hooting and making noises every time it got to an interesting part. Plus the usher was sticking his flashlight in your face every ten minutes to see if you were smoking or to check whether anybody had sneaked in.

I really don't like the balcony, but it's cheaper. In the balcony you get all the people from La Frontera, and they're always being kicked out of the movie or even carried off to jail, because when they're not stealing somebody's billfold or a woman's purse or something, they're smoking marijuana or they've got their blouse off doing all kinds of dirty stuff. Onc time they turned the lights on in the middle of the movie and they caught two women naked in the back row. My grandmother is always telling me they're bad people. *Riffraff*, she says, and you have to treat them like the dirt they are. But my grandmother started hating the people from La Frontera for real after the day the cashbox got stolen right out of the vegetable stand, right out from under my grandfather's nose, who was propped up half asleep against the display cases. That day my grandmother went on a rampage wilder than I ever imagined she could, and I said to myself, Today the old man talks. But no. Not a word. Not a peep. All he did was run his hand over his bald head, and I think he went *Tsk tsk*, like he was upset. *Tsk*, or some sound like that, was all he did.

It's ten o'clock at night now, and my grandmother is listening to the last soap opera before she goes to bed. Digna's out on the porch singing, apparently, but without opening her lips. Although once in a while she opens them to scream at one of those kids.

Celia's out in the backyard, apparently, making faces and doing somersaults. And Adolfina's in bed already.

My grandfather's going all through the house to see if anybody's left a light on, besides the one in the living room, and turning them all off. Every night he does the same thing. He goes into every bedroom, goes into the bathroom, out in the backyard, trying to find a lightbulb still burning so he can shut it off like a flash. "It's like living in a cave!" my grandmother screamed one night when she stubbed her toe on the stove in the kitchen. But my grandfather didn't say a word—he just went on looking for burning lightbulbs.

The soap opera's over. My grandmother turns off the radio. She puts her hands on the small of her back and stretches a little and just like every night she gives a little shriek of pain. She grumbles all the way to the kitchen, into the dining room, out into the backyard, into the bathroom, and then she goes down the hall and into her room. My grandfather is tagging along behind with the bug sprayer, turning off the lights she's turned on as she's gone by.

Other times he would save his mother, but he would kill a cousin of his—though she never existed either. He made her get lost up on the mountain, made her grandfather rape her. He would rape her himself, and then have her hang herself with long shining vines, which did exist, and on which he some-

Now they're in bed.

But Digna is still out on the porch. What will Digna's life be like ten

94

times swung from one creek-bank to the other. But other times one of his cousins would be his hero, his secret lover, his friend. It would be a boy in whom all the purity of the world (all the beauty), all the things that he himself wanted to be (and even perhaps could have been) would be incarnated. And thus he filled the living room, the roofs of all the houses, the rain gutters, his bed, the clouds, with his imaginings. Thus he slowly built up a universe peopled by invisible presences—invisible to others, at any rate, for to him they were the only real, authentic beings in the world, and they gave meaning to his life.

years from now? And twenty. . . ? No, no, I shouldn't think about that. She's probably thinking about that right now, at the same time I am. But I hear her singing like that, with her lips squeezed together, some kind of beehive it sounds like, and I wish time would stop and I could listen to that whimpering humming all the rest of my life. With her mouth closed. Her whole life with her lips squeezed shut.

Like that, so you could barely hear it. . . .

"Let's go to bed," she tells the children.

So then I go to my bedroom and lie down. She's closing the door now. Now she's turning off the light.

Now the house is dark. No doubt my grandfather feels like everything's nice and shipshape. Every few minutes I hear my grandmother in the bedroom next door, which is divided from mine by just a cardboard wall. I can hear her turn over in bed or complain about one pain or another. Then cough . . . Digna's two kids are apparently not sleepy, so I can hear her going on too, scolding them and whacking them every once in a while, which of course makes them yell all the louder. Banshees. Which only makes things worse, too, because then Digna loses her patience and gets out of bed and gives them the licking of their lives. "You damned wretched, wretched children! Let me at least close my eyes! Urchins, the both of you." Out in the backyard Celia is groping her way around and she bumps into the washtub and there's a terrible crashing and banging.

Finally everybody is asleep. This is the moment. I'm going to take that seventeen pesos right this minute and run.

I slowly pack my suitcase. Finished . . . Now, out into the hall. I'll leave a note before I go. Or maybe not, maybe I'll write after I get away.

I'm out in the hall now, and nobody's waked up yet, thank goodness. I almost kiss the floor with my feet, so nobody hears me, and I make it to the living room. But there's a man in the living room. It's my grandfather. My grandfather is standing in the middle of the living room, in the dark, talking. Talking to himself, nonstop. It *is* him. It *is* him. And he's *talking!*

He's seen me. But he keeps talking. He's seen me, I know it. He's bound to yell, call my grandmother. And then I won't be able to leave. But no—he hasn't seen me and he's not paying me the slightest bit of attention. He just keeps talking. What's he saying? I prick up my ears as sharp as I can, but all I can make out is a kind of bubbling, boiling stream of words all run together and confused. Gobbledygook.

I'm going outside.

I'm going to open the door and go outside. Oh, I pray nobody catches me. . . . I'm at the door. If I open it and walk out, I'll never come back as long as I live.

"Good night, Grandpa!"

He looks at me. He looks at me, blinks, and just keeps right on talking.

"Good night."

"Good night."

"Good night." . . . He may have said that to me in that long stream of mixed-up words. Good night . . . Good night.

I'm in the street.

ARE YOU LEAVING CUBA?

WHO ARE YOU LEAVING IN
CHARGE OF YOUR AFFAIRS?

Leaving our bank with your power of
attorney to administer your affairs will
give you the peace of mind to enjoy your
trip free of worry.

Our Trust Department is at your service
to answer any questions you may have
about this plan.

THE NATIONAL CITY BANK
OF NEW YORK—
(with operations in Havana)

We will be happy to send you our booklet
on "Estate Administration" and a model
power of attorney naming
THE NATIONAL CITY BANK
OF NEW YORK
your representative.

—Holguín *Echo*
April 13, 1930

One day I ran into Fortunato throwing
rocks every which way. One of the rocks
hit Tico in the head and almost killed
him. Thank goodness nobody ever found
out who was throwing the rocks.

—Them

THE SECOND
AGONY

His mother was stroking his head, but the stubborn blue impertinent fly was determined to light on his nose. His mother tried to shoo the fly away with her wrinkled hands, hands tired and worn from always washing other people's clothes, sweeping other people's floors, doing other people's dishes, but the fly would take a short hopping flight, buzz around them two or three times, and come back to light again on the apparently irresistible spot. . . . No, now they weren't horses anymore, they were slim graceful colts gliding over a nonexistent gently rolling prairie. There were millions of green leaves, falling. It was a forest. A forest in all its green fullness. And full too of all the noises of a forest, all its rich adornments, and filled with a sound of rushing water which, far off, seemed to reign over all the other magical sounds. If he could only have that place, at least. If only now, at this moment when the quick birds were disappearing into an unbounded sky, and the burning, stinging was growing worse, and everything began to burst in him, to explode, and to dribble away, if only now he could go off running there, machine-gunned still, but into a green forest with lingering, haunting echoes. At least back then, there, before, there were a few trees. There were wide stands of prickly wild pineapple in bloom, and the wellhead, and the ravine. But *here*—where could he hide, where was there to run, where could he take his burning, stinging fury without being seen, without running afoul of those Others who always had to be going somewhere, and always precisely the place where he was, or where he wanted to be? At least back then . . . But how long would he have to bear all this, have to pretend, feign, simulate? . . . Eternally a fugitive from reality, eternally running away, never knowing where to. Being different from the Others, and refusing to be like Them. Feeling, and (worse) showing, that under it all, under the stupid conversations, the grandiloquent gesticulations, the worn, false, wearying repetitions, there was nothing. Nothing more. He wasn't some *kid* anymore; he couldn't afford to burst wide open, scream, shout, yell, shriek that he wanted to die. He couldn't spend hours and hours and hours up on the roof without doing something useful, worthwhile, definite—straightening the tiles, repairing the electric cable, cleaning out the rain gutters. He could no longer allow himself to throw rocks up in the air, high, high up, or roll around on the ground, or sing. He always had to *fake*, and fake that he wasn't faking. Pretend not to pretend, pretend that that orangutan's smile actually belonged to him, that he was as simple, superficial, gratuitously violent, and cocksure, bragging as They were, as everyone was. But somebody was knocking . . . In the afternoon, after the ga-ga-*boom* had stopped, though the nauseating smell of rotten fruit and the hot steam from the still-bubbling jelly still hung in the air, the young men would go and take showers, in the rear of the factory. And they would come out into the evening smooth-skinned, shining, supple, transformed. Inside the vegetable stand, next to the rack of beans and gourds, they would scuffle, wrestle, play, laugh. They would go out in white shirts as the evening was darkening, to meet the girls in the neighborhood, to visit girlfriends, friends, lovers. He would watch them—vibrant, spirited, joking, like young stallions. And sometimes he would make those gestures, too, he would hop, skip, laugh, too. But somebody (there was always somebody) over that way, over there, in a place he could never get to, to destroy him, somebody would always make him look (and feel) ridiculous, utterly out of place, even when the Others accepted him, even when he found himself among that pack of young men kicking up their heels, making a racket, cutting capers, creating a scandal . . . He would go into the bathroom, his only refuge since they had moved to town. There, as he drank one of his most complicated concoctions, he would start making faces, hopping about and stomping on the floor, imitating them all, even himself. He would strip naked and stand in the bathtub under the shower and the stream of water would fall over his naked body and the smell of rotten guava would begin to fade, to be washed off that body impregnated with that putrefaction. His hands, freed for a while from the slavery to that smell, would glide down his body, caress his skin, come to his testicles where they would pause, touching, and then would begin the daily, impassioned masturbation. . . . The hand caressing him—his mother's hand, always tender, calm, always kind, always accepting him for what he was—glided smoothly along his moist, reddened skin and shooed off the fly which, stubborn, kept returning . . . Then would come the cramp. The spasm. A tremor of cold would run over his skin, and he would shiver. The warm whitish liquid would splatter on the floor, be dragged away by the current of water, drained away. And he would feel relaxed, though at the same time frustrated, weary, irritated, and his limbs and joints would stiffen, until he could hardly walk . . . If you could just . . . if you could just. . . . And something began to rain down from that sky. Something, like a net, a suffocating and immovable mockery was upon him, tightening and squeezing his throat, filling his stomach with fear. Sensations, sensations. Once again the awesome sensations. But this time not a sensation of the voyage to dreamed-of places, doubtlessly nonexistent, but rather of a certainty, this time, that he would never visit them. This time not the fantasy of an encounter with that dreamed-of ideal person of blurred and imprecise face, but rather the impression, this time, that that person had already passed by, been lost, been looking the other way when he passed by. It was not events that came to him this time—a grand gala fiesta, an adventure, a great and terrible, tangible fright that he could point to and say, This happened to me, but rather the pallid, distant, and shadowy imagining of those events, and the certainty that nothing, not even something terrible, would ever truly happen to him. The place where all the slugs came out, the dog-rose bush, the magic cousin, the bubbling glasses, the watertree whose roots grew in a little jar and whose foliage, as it grew, covered the house, to shade it from the constant whine of machinery and the never-ending glare—imaginings. Pure invention . . . But life is not to be borne when it is filled with only made-up people and unreal things. Life needs adventure, change, diversity—the pleasures and pains of the traded shocks and collisions of bodies, the running through real, and different, places, the visiting other hells than this. The promise of possibilities—crossing the sea, experiencing other swindles, other agonies, and deaths. Those were some of the things that had to be, that were essential if his inventions and imaginings were ever to have any meaning at all. . . . It was growing dark; the horse had stopped. He was beside a river with a fast, yellow current running through a sandy wasteland. The horse tested the roiled water with its front hooves, and then it backed away. Beyond the sand, in the background, there was a plain like a sea aflame, while in the foreground the river flowed with unstoppable violence. The horse nickered and, blowing a moment, then snuffled the water with its lips. In some open place, on some plain, where there rose no woods or forests, a bird shrieked, high and metallic. And then the light, as always happens in those places where the light is like a fire, was suddenly snuffed out, and the river became a gray-black, heavy-seeming mass that muttered curses at his feet. The horse drew its head back from the water and stood there motionless, its forefeet in the current. One not only had to die—one had to rot as well, and one could not dodge it, and one's suffering never ended, the understanding it all never ended, not even for one instant. And then what? And now . . . what? And even before, back then, what? Except that within that wide, wide region of darkness he began to make out the diverse shades of darkness . . . It was growing dark, and as it grew dark he saw himself eating lizards, raising pigeons, making wine out of rotten fruit of all kinds, beginning to dance, naked. It was growing dark, and all the sounds of the world around deafened him, whispering to him that it was getting dark, and once more there came to him the terrible sensation, once more there came to him the *certainty*—and he was consumed by it, suddenly aflame though dripping wet—that he was always to perish as the butt of some unbearable joke, some awful mockery. Dusk came, the darkness fell about him, and it made him shiver. What to do. What could he do to save himself—and to save himself from what? How could he ever hold back so much stupor, how could he ever hold back that odor of putrefaction which always, always floated through the air, how could he keep back that image of frustration, that sensation of *All is lost* which always, always hounded him? How could he avoid all that—the anguish, the tedium and revulsion, the other terror—and how could he keep down that sense of belonging in some other place (or no place), how could he keep that feeling from suddenly coming over him, all unawares, when he was wet and naked, and, in spite of everything he could do, bathing his hands in sweat? It was futile to masturbate again, futile to dance, futile to turn on the faucet and soap himself again, futile to gesture, cry like Adolfina, or sing with his lips squeezed tight . . . It was growing dark, and he had just set foot on the cold and distant surface of the moon. He began to take the first steps across a dry, dusty, airless sea. He was walking now over a dead land, of narrow and unvarying horizon. So it was as though he were always in the same place. After a while he sat down in that inhospitable place. Apparently it was just impossible to die. Something, like millions of metallic cicadas, was whistling. He listened. They stopped. Everything was suddenly silent. Then he lay down on that ground, and his voice (for he was singing) echoed, ever more faintly, across that empty waste . . . That was when he stole the reams of paper from his grandfather and began to write, interminably so it seemed; that was when his mother went away, to the United States. That was when he decided never again to answer those stupid letters she incessantly sent him. That was when he began to do exercises, in the bathroom, to lift weights out behind the house (though he never confessed any of this to anyone). That was when he promised himself to change his voice, and so began to affect a slightly hoarse, deep, masculine tone. That was when all the girls in the neighborhood began falling in love with him, and at one point he had a girlfriend on every block, he was the Don Juan of that whole part of town, and he began to detest any man who smiled at another man, and he came home several times with his clothes ripped to pieces and his nose bloodied from a fight he had had, over a girl, in the Parque Infantil where all the young people from Vista Alegre (his neighborhood) congregated. And then came the time (for now he was accepted by everyone, he had won them all over by his wiliness, his apparent stupidity, everyone liked and even loved him) when he realized that he couldn't go on anymore, that it was impossible, that he had never been able to stand all this, and that now more than ever before he had to disappear. And that was when he started to look at, and to try to understand, his family, and he began to suffer for their tragedies even more than they themselves did . . . That was when he set himself afire, when he went voluntarily into exile, when he became a grouchy old coot, when he went mad, when, transformed into an old maid, he ran out into the streets to try to find a man . . . And he scraped together seventeen pesos to run away with, but then he didn't; and he vowed to set the house on fire, but then he didn't. And that was when subversive flags began to appear around the neighborhood. That was when he started paying visits to the whores, he and the wildest and fiercest of the young men. And that, or a little afterwards, was when he was listening to the organ one night and he decided to go off and fight with the rebels . . . It was growing dark. They had called out, "Halt! Halt! Stop, you son of a bitch, or we shoot!" And he had stopped. And the nervously trembling "steel pot," as the figures helmeted for combat were called, had yelled for help to other steel pots. And they had stood in a circle around him. So he had sat on the ground, surrounded by a ring of men and rifles—and he still had the big butcher knife in his hand. It was growing darker and darker. And then he was running, and nobody was yelling at him to stop. And as he stumbled, a lizard ran terrified in among some dry weedstalks, and he thought that just at that moment he had been seen, so he ran on, to save himself. So for an instant both of them, the man and the lizard, were running through the dried-out weeds, which made a sound like burning paper, or some far-off holocaust. And as he fled he thought that for the first time in his life it was not a feeling he was feeling, some mere sensation, but rather that something real, *something*, maybe even something worth telling, was actually happening to him. But couldn't you die laughing? Couldn't you just die laughing to think that this, precisely this, an *event*, and an event which to top it off he would never manage to tell, was the single most memorable, most real, and only really truly *true* event in an entire life filled with fantasies built on air and monotonous unyielding pettiness? You could just die laughing, just die. And so, dying laughing, he ran, and there was no way to tell his labored breathing from the laughter.

The Life of the Dead

Walks through vast regions that no man or woman could touch. Voyages through soundless, murmurless waters which could not wet anyone, or drown anyone. Strolls through a timeless stand of trees in which there lived suddenly vanishing birds, on which there grew suddenly dissolving leaves, from which there came suddenly fugitive perfumes. Walks, voyages, strolls, and out there beyond, in the background, there was the day, the same day as always—wide, heavy, white, fixed in the sky, hanging over every possibility. The big day. The only day. That same day.

"Sometimes what keeps me going is the hope that there's another hell, another inferno someplace."

"Me too. But there isn't. And you know it."

"If there *were* another hell, though, that would be some consolation, even if we knew we could never get out of this one."

"I know. If out there beyond this Great Beyond, there were another Great Beyond, we could at least think about the possibility of rejecting this one."

"Or of having contempt for it, even if you could never get to the other one."

"Or desire for it, even if we could never satisfy that desire."

"Another hell, another hell, maybe more monotonous, maybe even more suffocating, maybe even more disgusting and reprehensible than this one, but *another* one, at least."

"Now I see that hell is always what you can't reject. What's just simply *there*."

"You remember that word we still haven't been able to find? That word that's a curse, and a blessing too? That unique word?"

"Now I see that hell is knowing that there is no hell, that there can't be, because that would be a solution to *this*."

"The great solution."

"Now I see that hell is leaving one closed room and going into the same closed room."

"The only room there is."

"Now I see that hell is not circular, not on fire, but just the fleeting, instantaneous present, taking up all the width and breadth of our heartbroken, wounded memory."

"And of our unswerving future."

"Now I see that hell is not annihilating fire—such wondrous good fortune if it were!—but rather an invariable glare which condemns us to see, to eternally *see* that which, by reason of that very glare, we call our hell."

"That which, by reason of that very glare, is unbearable."

"And real."

"Hell is knowing that we have all eternity to wait and watch for our death."

"Hell is the price which must be paid for asking ourselves intelligent, logical questions."

"Hell is knowing that we are here, forever, and now."

"Hell is knowing that now is forever."

"Hell is having experienced all the changes only to discover that everything is the same."

"You run, and when you finally stop you discover that you're in the very same place you were running from."

"*Finally*, you say?"

"I mean at the moment of awakening."

"Hell is the great brightness, the illumination, the *glare* in which I look upon your face, always looking at me."

"Like yours."

"Hell is your face."

"Hell is your face."

"Hell is us, looking at each other."

"Hell is us always looking at the horror, unable to join it, or merge into it, or hide in it, but unable to be devoured by it, either."

"Now we are condemned to jump headfirst, and forever, into vats of boiling guava paste."

"Now we are condemned to live in a house where the breeze-way is filled with a torrent of light that floods and destroys all our dreams."

"Now we are condemned to be present at the collapse of all our dreams, though we are not allowed to collapse ourselves."

"Now we are condemned to live among our own scum and offal."

"And we are not allowed to weep."

"We are not allowed to cry for help."

"We are not allowed to howl."

"We are not allowed to pray."

"We are not allowed to touch, feel, or tap, even with just our fingertips."

"We are not allowed to trust."

"We are not allowed to resign."

"And we are not allowed to join in an embrace of fury. And so to perish."

"Just to look, see, and suffer."

"Just to look, just to look."

"To interpret it, perhaps to speak it."

"But not to perish, ever."

"Leaves pass over my invisible body; I do not feel them."

"Rain like needles tattoos my transparent body; it does not wet it."

"Now it is raining."

"Now the leaves are falling."

"Now we jump headfirst off the roof."

"Now I look at your face."

"Now we look at our faces."

"*Now* is an always that is forever abject, nonexistent, and infinite, like time. Like this weather."

"Now is *this* moment, and that one, and that one too that has not come."

"And we are not allowed to scream."

"We are not allowed to howl."

"We are not allowed to refuse to look at each other."

"Each other."

"Now."

"Always."

"Look at me."

Digna, Jacinta, and God

My mother and God are coming toward me. They're half naked and they've got two big gunnysacks full of something, God knows what, slung over their shoulders.

"Awful! You look awful!" my mother says, and she drops the sack on top of my head.

"What do *you* know," I say to that damned mother of mine, and then I look over at God.

"Don't look at *me*," God says, grunting and puffing, since apparently His sack weighs a lot more than He ought to be carrying.

"So then—I ought to just forget about Moses?"

"What Moses?"

"This old goat doesn't know which way is up," my mother mutters as she throws her sack over her shoulder again.

"So who knows, then?"

"*Who knows, then?* What a question, a person'd think you'd never been born yet. What world are you living in, woman? Listen—the best thing for you to do is get down off this roof before you knock off a roof tile and break somebody's head. We've got to go—we've still got all this stuff to get rid of."

Mama's talking while God sits down on the ridgepole and scratches at His ear furiously.

"What's wrong with Him?" I ask my mother, meaning Him.

"Lice, I suspect."

"Good lord!"

"But that's nothing. One time He got crabs! Nobody knows where from, of course. But He got 'em, anyway."

"Ave María purísima! . . . But where are you going with those gunnysacks? What's in them, anyway?"

"Almond seeds."

"Almond seeds?"

"Uh-huh. This old coot has gotten it into his head that there are not enough almond trees in the world, so we wander all over with these big sacks on our backs, throwing one seed out here and another one over there."

"What nonsense! It's pretty obvious you two don't have much to do with your time!"

"So *you* say. Of course, you're right about one thing—as soon as we've sowed all these seeds all over, we're going to have to get out and chop down almond trees, there'll be so many . . . When it's not one thing it's another . . . But we'd better get going, it's late."

Mama gives God a couple of kicks in the ribs to rouse Him, since He's fallen off to sleep.

"Let's go! Or are You planning to spend all afternoon stretched out up here on the roof of the house?"

And *Thump, thump,* she gives Him two more kicks, this time in the stomach. God gets up. He grunts and heaves the gunnysack up over His shoulder, and then little by little He starts to fly off.

"Well, then . . ." my mother says to me, and she just stands there and looks at me, and I don't know why, but I think she's about to cry, "one of these days I imagine I'll be bumping into you again, and who knows—maybe we can even talk a while, like friends. And don't get all impatient—sooner or later Moisés will come looking for you."

"Oh, I wish, I wish!" I say, with my mouth closed. And then I ask, "But tell me something—am I really so ugly?"

"Tell her," my mother orders God, as they both fly up into the air. She slaps Him and He spills half a sackful of almond seeds.

"Awful! Awful!" the old coot keeps repeating, until my mother finally stops hitting Him and kicking Him.

And so the two of them disappear, off beyond the clouds up there.

An old man. An old man. Now he was an old man. But he still kept scrabbling at that damned scabby ground which, since he wouldn't subjugate it, wound up subjugating him at last. An old man. An old man. And his house was still full of arguing, bickering, bitter women no longer young who had never discovered how to hold a man. A man might have helped him tame his land. But it was not to be. His eldest daughter—tall, skinny, argumentative—seemed irremediably doomed to be an old maid; Onerica had no idea how to keep a man, she never had had, though she knew just enough to let him leave her with a belly, and there was the result of it—the old man's fatherless grandchild, not quite right in the head, always up in the clouds, raised in a houseful of women so *he* was no good for working a farm either, or for anything else for that matter. A stupid child who only knew how to climb trees, and to hate the old man. The old man's daughter Celia, who had always been a little softheaded, had gotten herself in trouble, too, and then she'd been left—and with a daughter, no less, and *her* a halfwit, too, to boot. Only Digna, the youngest, had managed to find a permanent—up to now—husband, Moisés, who though he never touched the land always seemed to have a roll of money in his pocket. How did he manage that? . . . The old man bent and stooped, scrabbling at the gravelly land. And struggling against that gaggle of stubborn furious women, the women as hard and resisting as the land, and as thankless. *Old man, old man.* He was an old man now. Now everyone called him Old Man Polo. Now he was forever to be Old Man Polo. Was he to be doomed forever to bend over that hateful rocky waste? Were fifty, sixty, seventy years (for he had lost count) of hard labor to come to nothing, no merit, no value, no recompense at all? He would rise early in the morning. He would go out into his fields. And the damned land, which seemed to grow more free and independent by the day, less controlled, would already have won another small battle—it would put out weeds overnight, or grow huge rock-hard cracks even a pick could not break up, or it would be covered with thistle. The land would become, virtually before his eyes, a gorge, or a heap of boulders, or a shingly waste, and all the vegetation, the little green there was, would be like tumbleweeds, tumbling off over the brambly, uneven ground (for he did not even have time to terrace his land). So only the rocks were left, the waste of gravelly hard soil, the sharp white limestone rocks they called dogs'-teeth, laughing at him, laughing . . . He had to sell. He *had* to sell. The day before, Moisés had brought a buyer to see the farm, a city man with new money, and an automobile, and everything. And the old man—could be possibly have learned nothing from experience? Could it be that a man's whole life devoted to hoeing up rocks, to wading neck-deep through dust and mud, had still not taught him, made him see the futility of that devotion? He had to sell. He had to. Not to mention that Moisés, who (everybody said) knew so much about these matters, said the buyer was offering much more than the land was actually worth. "Before the guy changes his mind, I'm tellin' ya," for Moisés talked that way, "grab 'im. Selling is the smart thing to do."

This town. This town. If the world were a backside, you'd be the asshole of it. Better than three hours since a soul set foot in this fruit stand to buy so much as a slice of wrapped day-old poundcake. With today's sales I couldn't buy myself breakfast. And the factory worse off every day—they're closed more than they're open now. If things keep on this way, I'm going to have no choice but to close down this shop and give myself over to selling corn-and-honey johnnycakes in the street. "Sell 'em, go on, or we're all going to starve to death." I've never felt so ashamed. At my age, selling corn brooms. Oh lord I mean corn-and-honey johnnycakes, I don't even know what I'm saying any-more . . . But it's better to sell anything, no matter what it is, than to stay here and have to put up with this old woman. Ay, a man makes mistakes in life. That's the truth. You let other people convince you of things and when you look up, you're up to your backside in water and the creek still rising . . . and every-body else on dry land but you. Ay, Moisés, what terrible fate of mine it was that ever brought you to me to convince me to sell that farm! At least up there on the mountain we had our own place to drop dead in. Ay, but a man lets people talk him into things, and when you look around, you're hanging on the end of a rope. No way out. Has anybody ever seen such a family as this one I brought into the world for having bad luck? Of the four daughters I had, two of them were abandoned, one fit for nothing, the other one a widow and crazy to boot, and *really* abandoned, because the man died after he foisted her off on me. Has anybody ever seen such miserable luck? . . . And this poverty, this misery, on top of everything else—I don't feel it so much, I've never known anything else—but everybody in town as bad as we are . . . Nobody's willing to spend a centavo. And it's not just now, either, which is bad enough, but what's to come, because with a black man up there in the President's Palace, there's really no way out. As though we didn't know what brought this on . . . We're starving to death. And people expect you to believe in God! People expect you to pray! Bullshit! It's hard to believe there are people who'd waste their time on that nonsense. Silly old hens!

Geese! Just let some Jehovah's Witness come by here and try to sell me some book, just let 'em try to push some of their literature off on me, I'll bust one of these weights on their head! Trying to bamboozle a man, in this day and age. Shameless creatures, what they ought to do is go to work.

Oh my God, what a trial, what a dreadful trial You have sent me. Now that savage beast of a husband of mine's got his back up against the Jehovah's Witnesses, and he spends the livelong day cursing and blaspheming. What a fate, Lord. And me a Jehovah's Witness. Ay, if he finds out, he's capable of strangling me. Save me, Lord . . . What have those poor Jehovah's Witnesses ever done to him, I'd like to know. Oh, save me!

As so few people came to the vegetable stand, practically all afternoon I was in there half asleep, sitting on the stool propped up against the counter, and so here come these sons of bitches and carry off the cashbox. Me, what was I supposed to do?—by the time I realized what had happened they were long gone. And they're bad people. The best thing is not to chase them, because they're liable to stop on some corner and turn around and bust your head open with a rock or something . . . I saw the kid jump the counter into the back, but I sort of thought it was a fly—I waved my hand at it like this and everything, to shoo it away. The shameless son of a bitch, he jumped back over the counter and was off like a shot, carrying the cashbox on top of his head. And the rest of them ran off so fast it would make your head spin. And once they got away, what could I do? They ran up the hill into La Chomba. And anybody that goes into *that* neighborhood is lucky to live to tell about it. This guy came by here the other day wearing not much more than a burlap sack wrapped around him. And those guys from La Chomba caught him, and after they'd robbed him of whatever little change he had, they stripped him stark naked. And left him that way in the middle of the street. I saw the old woman wasn't around, so I took advantage of her not breathing down my neck every second, and I lent the man an old pair of raggedy pants I had. But I don't know how, but she found out anyway, so I had to put up with her grumbling after all. These damned women know everything. And what they don't know, they guess. These damned . . .

I go out early to get milk for the wild animals in my house. And God forgive me, but they *are* wild animals, the people in my house. It's been years since Polo opened his mouth even so much as to tell me to go to hell. Adolfina hates me so much that every time she looks at me her eyes shoot fire. Poor Celia, don't even mention her. And Digna, every time a child starts crying she blames me. What a fate, Lord. I'm even afraid that one of these days I'll be poisoned or they'll put the evil eye on me. And as though all that weren't enough, now that halfwit Fortunato has taken to making wine. So he's got the whole floor under his bed covered with bottles full of rotten water, and the stink of it would drive you out of the house. And in the middle of the night the bottles explode and go *Psssh* and wake everybody up. If you ask me, the boy's not quite right in the head. Instead of getting out, trying to find himself a woman, he spends the livelong day in there in his room, manufacturing filth or doing some other kind of dopey thing. Good lord. And to top it all, the rats are all the time banging the bottles together and smashing them to smithereens, and then the beasts run out shrieking and squealing, and it's enough to get on *anybody's* nerves. But that's nothing—now there's this elf in the house that steals anything he can get his hands on. He's already carried off the scissors, Adolfina's sewing scissors. And poor thing, she's about ready to scream, because now it turns out she can't even cut out the fabric for the clothes people are having her make for them. Virgen santísima, the sewing scissors. And the worst part of it is, that they say he'll just give the things back when he feels like it, and *then* he throws 'em at your head. Ay, any day I might get up with my head split wide open by a pair of sewing scissors . . . This is not the first elf we've had, either, by a long shot, because we've been carrying this hex along with us for I don't know how long. Since up on the mountain, I imagine. But up there it was different because you'd have a good session over it and it would go away. But in this blasted town you can't even do that, because respectable mediums, what you'd call mediums with any prestige, there just aren't any. So here we are without any sewing scissors and Adolfina looks daggers at me—like I, oh lord, like I was the one to blame. . . . When I think he's carried off two of my nightshirts, of the three I had. But since I hardly use them anyway, it doesn't bother me that much. Let him smother in those nightshirts, for all I care . . . The lack of faith in this house is what's gotten us into this mess. Because even if it's hard to believe, the only person in this house that believes in that elf is me. Me and Digna's children, who say they saw him jump off the ridgepole with the scissors in his hand. But the rest of the people in the house? I don't dare so much as mention him to them; they'd laugh in my face. So here we are. People don't believe in anything. Not even Adolfina, who's the one that's most affected by the elf, not even Adolfina believes in him. She goes around muttering and complaining all day about losing her sewing scissors, but she never mentions the one that stole them. And the old man, don't mention *him*—when I told him there was an elf in the house stealing things, he looked at me like I was crazy. Although he didn't say a word to me . . . What a trial. Things are worse every day. Even the milk—every day the milk is more watered-down, until the other day I even found a minnow in the bottom of the jug. My God, do these milkmen have no shame? And when I told the inspector, he said to me, "But are you saying the poor fish is not entitled to a little milk?" I never heard such sass and impudence. I was furious, I'll tell you. But who could I turn to, God, since this old man won't bother to stand up for his rights to anybody. Such impudence. And if an inspector talks that way, insulting a woman, what can you expect from other people. And us starving to death. And that's nothing—I've walked this whole neighborhood, and I haven't found so much as a quart of even *watered* milk. So I come back fit to bust, with my bottles slung over my shoulder, trying not to let them bang together and break. Suffocating and suffering from all the walking, and now it turns out that damned woman is in the bathroom again and she has been since who knows when. And she won't come out . . . Ay, we're ruined and nobody even pays any attention. I'm telling you.

"The girl's drinking water out of the bathtub."
"Idiot."

I jumped down off the roof in one jump and ran into the kitchen. There was my mother, trying to solder on the handle of the frying pan with a wad of chewing gum and muttering things to herself, making this kind of beehive-sounding gobbledygook that God knows nobody could ever have made out.

"Mama . . ."

"To hell with you. Better than two hours I've been working at this, trying to find the little hole to stick this gum in, and I can't find it."

"Mama . . ."

"Shush."

"Mama, I just saw you up there on the roof, beating God with a stick."

"If anybody else had told me so, I might've believed it, but you're crazier than a loon—forget it."

"Mama . . ."

"There! I finally found the hole! Thank the lord!"

"I saw you up there, and then you took off flying."

"Hail Mary, full of grace, the Lord is with thee . . ."

So then, since I could see that Mama was not going to pay me any mind, I went and found Fortunato. He was scraping a brick to make dust with.

"I just saw God and my mother."

"What crap."

So then I had no choice—I called Adolfina. Though everybody knows she doesn't like to be bothered when she's doing things.

"Adolfina, Adolfina! I just . . ."

"Just let me die in peace for once, if you don't mind. Just do me the favor."

So I went in to the vegetable stand.

"Papa. Papa."

Bananas at three for five centavos. The mangos are going bad on me, but nobody'll buy them even if there's nothing left in the store. People are like that—they see piles of mangos and they won't buy 'em. What times these are, what times. And now this woman—what's she come whining around here for? I hope she doesn't expect me to look at her.

"Papa . . ."

Olives at two for five centavos. Even if nobody buys them at that price, I can't come down. I'm not giving them away. If nobody buys them, I'll eat 'em myself. Or plant 'em—I might get an olive tree to grow out of my ear. Let's see—I'll just take this olive and plant it in my ear and see if it grows . . .

"Papa . . ."

Sweet potatoes at twenty centavos. Twenty centavos, did I say? Well, so be it. Bacon a peso a pound. Whew, expensive, but there's nothing I can do about it. Besides, it's getting hard to find, so I've got to take advantage of that . . .

I leave my father, and on my way back I bump into Celia in the hall.

"Celia, my mother appeared to me, and she was dead, she came up to me and . . ."

"Dead? How can you talk about dead? You don't even know what that word *means*. Ay, the only person in this house that's got any right to talk about the dead is me. Me, who am dead . . . Esther, Esther. Esther? *Esther!* Ay, I can barely remember how your name went anymore. Nor how your face was, either. Ay, what I wish is that I was alive again so I could die again. But listen—you know more about these things than I do—does 'Esther' have an 'h' or not? . . ."

So I left my sister, since when she gets her mind all wound up and running off in that sort of way, with her dead daughter and all, you never know when she'll come out of it. So all that was left was my own kids to tell about what I saw.

Anisia and I were out there playing tag when that witch of a mother of ours comes up to us and says, "Children, I have just seen God and your grandmother up on the roof together." Can you believe Mama, telling us a fib like that? As though we didn't know (because if we don't know then who does, then?) that we had Grandma locked up prisoner in a drawer in the sewing-machine cabinet, and that she wasn't going to get out till she takes God out from under her underarm, because the filthy old woman lifted her arm and stuck Him up in there. And she hasn't lifted it again since. For all we know the poor thing's already dead and rotten. But the blasted old woman wouldn't say Uncle for anything. She won't raise her arm. Though it's a shame, at the same time, that I don't just open the drawer and throw all that trash out, because I've got a whole lot of big giant owl moths tied to a string, and I really ought to keep them in there. It's so nice to go out hunting owl moths at night. You shine the flashlight on them and the silly things just sit there sort of gaga, and they don't even fly away. That's when I creep up on them nice and slow and easy and I grab their wings with just the tips of my fingers. And then I've got 'em . . . My grandmother, before I shut her up in the sewing-machine drawer, she told me the owl moths got drunk on so much light, and they go sort of blind when they see it, and so that's why they can't fly off. So she told me. And she also told me—but by then I had slammed the drawer shut on her—that she knew a way to make owl moths talk, and that if I'd take her out of the drawer she'd teach me. So she told me . . . But ha! She better not even *think* I'm going to turn her loose. Although to tell the truth, I'd sort of like to have somebody to talk to for a while, even if it was just an owl moth. But here comes Anisia, and I'm certainly not telling *her* the things my grandmother told me about.

Ay, if only there had been bells. If only as there had been in other times and other places (for this she had read in one of Fortunato's books), there had been bells ringing out into the air when a young, beautiful person died—in case it was an angel. Oh, if only there had been bells . . . Endless tintinnations, deep throbbing gongs, bursts of brassy ringing, echoing strokes in the June afternoon, announcing her arrival . . . These were her thoughts, behind the closed glass window, as she heard the clapping of the hooves of the horses up ahead, led by her cousins from the country, and heard the rising murmur of the people behind, on foot. And heard also, over her, among the flowers, the stumbling, stubborn buzzing of the fly as it fluttered about, making the most of its unspoiled enjoyment of that bobbing garden. In June.

Wisdom stops at seventeen. Esther was in the fullness of wisdom when she died. She was thirteen . . . I was amazed to see that so many more things fit into her brain than would even begin to crowd in at the door of mine. I was just amazed. But then I realized that she was at the age of wisdom. Afterwards, a person gets stupid. If you're a boy, you get to be a man—and then there's no way out. But while you've still got your being all ahead of you, you possess all the kinds of knowing, all the farms so to speak without having to choose just one to settle on. You can be whatever you want to be—and if you want to, you can not be. Because back then, at that stage I mean, nothing matters. And everything is permitted. So that's why . . . I would look at her and she would look at me. And I *knew* that she knew more than I did. I even came to be a little afraid of her. You have to watch out for the wise ones just the same as for the brute beasts. She sometimes understood things that I hadn't ever even imagined. She'd have you all opened up and figured out before you knew who you were yourself. That's why it was so sad. Knowing so much, she had nothing to be happy about. I've gotten to be that way now, not because *I'm* wise or anything, no, but because she infected me with *her* wisdom. But that doesn't count, because it's something somebody already learned. If I hear somebody say "Shit," for example, and then I repeat it—"Shit"—I haven't learned anything. But not her, she wasn't like that. She invented every word. And when she would say it, it would turn into thousands and thousands of different words. Whatever word it was, any word at all, however repeated it had gotten to be before, she would say it and *Bam!*—it would turn into all kinds of different words. So many, in fact, that I could be dying my whole life long and never say the words she would say with just one word . . . She'd be sitting there, leaning on the windowsill, that blasted factory making all that racket and the smell of rotten guavas driving you crazy, she'd be sitting there, but like she wanted to spread her wings and fly away, like this, or go like this and slip into the cracks between the bricks. She'd be sitting there making signs in the air with her hands, and laughing on the outside so people wouldn't know that she was dying . . . I would come in, hopping from one floor tile to the next so as not to bother her, and I'd find her there, looking like she was dying laughing, but like she was screaming on the inside. And all the time that blasted factory going ga-ga-*boom*, ga-ga-*boom*, ga-ga-*boom*. And the sputtering of the vats, the steam hissing out of the boiler, the stink of those guavas. And that ga-ga-*boom* ga-ga-*boom* ga-ga-*boom*

. . . And what I would want to do would be to shrink myself up, like this, and crawl inside her to see where she was. And the factory going ga-ga-*boom*. And the vats going *sp-sp-sp-ppppt*. And the heat so hot you'd think you were going to melt. And then I could see that she had seen me but was pretending she hadn't, so I'd go over to her and say,

"What are you thinking about, honey? What are you doing?"

"Nothing," she'd say.

Nothing.

The procession came to a halt. Oh, if only the bells had started chiming then. The young men, her cousins, tied up their horses at the entrance. Four men pushed the iron gate open. And she, still raised high, covered with flowers, passed in the gate—floating above the hats, the tilted crosses, the bones, the rocks, the blowing hair. They lowered her. Out at the entrance a horse neighed—somebody was riding up on a mare, you could bet. The grave had been dug the day before, and so the air was filled with the smell of moist earth mingled with the smell of flowers now beginning to wilt. It was the country, the country. Luckily, she thought as she was lowered, her mother had decided to bury her in the cemetery at Aguasclaras, the nearest one to Perronales. The cemetery sat up on a little hill with a view of trees and the river. To get there you walked down a little path bordered with airy-leaved locust trees, lignum vitae, and droopy-flowered stalks of ginger. And so at that moment she felt a terrible urge to thank her mother, to communicate to her, somehow, her happiness. But the earth by then was beginning to cover her. She could feel the perfumed moistness of June over her body. The earth, the earth . . . Suddenly, there was a dry thud, loud, on the wood that arched over her. Somebody had thrown a rock. One of those kids, Tico or Anisia; she wouldn't put it past them. Or Fortunato. He was that way.

So then I went into the toilet—Adolfina luckily was off lord knows where—and I sat down on the edge of the toilet seat, and I started saying, over and over again, "Nothing," "Nothing," "Nothing" . . . Until I saw how terrible that word was. And I still kept on repeating it to myself. "Nothing." "Nothing." "Nothing." Until even with my mouth closed the word was flying around in the air and hitting me over the head. And I covered my mouth with both my hands, but the word came out my belly button, and out from under my legs, and out the ends of my hair. So I choked myself, I stuffed both hands in my mouth at once. But that word flew out of my backside and sneaked out of my toes and it kept swelling and swelling and swelling in my throat, it made a ball this big. Though I still had my hands stuffed in my mouth. But that word popped out of my fingernails. "Nothing," "Nothing," "Nothing" . . . So then I realized that wisdom is over at seventeen.

And I never asked her another question.

Everyone left. First, of course, there were tears, cries, sobs. Jacinta, eternally covetous, stole several wreaths off nearby tombs and put them on hers, the dead girl's. Children leapt about over her, the dead girl. Celia, howling, threw herself on the ground and embraced the earth that covered her, the dead girl. But then, at last, they all left. At last she was alone. Alone with that cursed extension of her flesh, alone with that young body that had hounded her so. Alone with the enslaving, humbling and humiliating, limiting, pushing, pressuring, beckoning body which inevitably forces us to do that which we least desire—that which we most desire—and then we are lost. For still a while she yearned to know how her curse would end, what the end would be of that body that she had borne along, that she had tried to set in the cool breeze over at the window, that she had bathed and powdered, that she had covered (with such sacrifice) with astrakhan, with challis, with crepe, that she had perfumed, that she had solicitously, attentively, austerely, jealously cared for so that it would not become deformed, grotesque, misshapen, that she had put to bed, that she had walked, and that, in spite of all, still clamored, still demanded, still pleaded—and the hounding of it drove her mad . . . Alone with that body, young and cursed, that she had caressed in the dark, given thrilling pleasures to, let have its way. . . . And still it wanted more. When its rest was done, it was hungry; when it was fed, it had still other desires, the itching started, that gnawing. And when she had satisfied its every whim, it grew languid, voluptuous, and it craved, or yearned for, new experience—it even craved new desires, new-imagined cravings, new memories, new pleasures and sadnesses. And that thankless, thankless body would repay all the sacrifices she made for it by growing old, wrinkled, dry, pestilent, stiff—while always demanding *more, more, more* . . . Wasn't it too perverse to live? Was that not the true curse, the worst enemy, perhaps the greatest fraud of all? . . . Wouldn't it have made anybody want to make it burn, explode, once and for all? That too, that too had contributed, had helped her, even commanded her to come to her decision, to have her revenge . . . And now the moment had come—*her* moment. Now there came all the crawling things of the earth, always eager to gnaw, to devour, to eat, to penetrate, to pierce. And in a wave of hoarse muted murmurings they overran her old enemy (her body), captured it, crept around its eyes, crawled through its hair, battered its still-smooth cheeks, scrabbled at the openings of its nose and ears. With waving, waggling, pulsing, eternally moving mechanisms perfected over millions of years, they climbed its breasts, began to mine its legs. And the most fearless of them, the bravest, raised antennae, pincers, dusty legs, and crept in through its parted lips . . . While she watched in triumph. Now forever in June, she contemplated the destruction of her insatiable, selfish, worst enemy. She watched as it was pulled and tugged and pecked at and as, finally, it burst and was pulled apart. But was this too not a triumph for her body? Was this too perhaps not a pleasure for it—being able to disintegrate, to let even its most minuscule particles become tiny bits of joy, of *lust*, for someone, for all the world? Pehaps it achieved at last its ultimate and total ecstasy in finding itself rendered this viscous, slimy, fetid, bloated mass seeping into the earth, dispersing into atoms as it was raped, as all the worms and insects gnawed,

When Fortunato took it into his head not to bathe anymore and to just eat fruitpits, I said, "He ought to be taken to the doctor." But the next day Esther died, and it's just now that it comes back to me what I said the day before that. It's just now that I remember, can you imagine!

---

drilled, tore, *enjoyed* . . . Ah, such bells ringing now. So many bells, announcing this event. So many bells, ringing out to proclaim this rare and unrepeatable moment. Can you hear them?

"Adolfina! By all you love, woman! There's a limit to my patience!"

Now I'll just turn on the water a little harder so I'll drown. I'll turn it up and open my mouth as wide as it can go, and I'll let the water run in my mouth full force, and wash out my insides for me. And let the water run out my backside. I'll turn on the hot water. Boiling hot. So it burns me, so it scalds me, so it burns my skin off. So it boils me and turns me to a roast. Ay, so it cools me off . . . Like this, real real hot, so I can't even stand up in it. So hot it melts me, so hard it knocks me over, and breaks me, and beats on me, like a pitchfork that smashes me in the head and breaks it in a million piees. Oh, let it break me in a million pieces . . . The first thing I'm going to scald is this blasted tongue, my tongue and my eyes. What do I want my eyes for? What do I want my tongue for? What do I want my lips for? Water, water, burning water, steam from all the hot water. Water so hot it's on fire. Fire, fire, fire. What do I want my hands for? Or my face? Or my legs? Or my belly button? Fire, fire. Where's the alcohol? Where's that alcohol? Where're the matches? What do I want my hands for . . . Where's . . .

Whore, and ugly whore, and old whore. Stupid bitch. Old, husbandless bitch. Old, husbandless bitch. Pull out your hair by the roots. Pull out your eyes. Hit yourself a million times. Throw yourself down on the floor. Hop on one foot. Make a hundred shirts and don't charge for even one of them. Make a hundred pairs of pants and don't . . . Wretched, miserable, *miserable* woman. Look at yourself, just look at yourself. I dare you. Look at yourself. Stop jumping around like that. Stop talking all that foolishness about the hot water. Stop hitting yourself in the face. Don't knock out the few teeth you've got left. There they are. There you are. There you've got hold of yourself. There I've got you. There I am—look. And curse the day you were born. And kill yourself for fury. Fury, fury, fury. Old hen. Gristly, stringy old hen that never laid. That never had a rooster. Or a henyard. Or anything. Old hen with mites. Old turkey hen. Barren old cow—I double-dare you. You brag, but when the time comes to do it, you don't have the guts. Come on, come on, let's see. Pick up that bottle like it was the living answer to your problems. Pick it up. Higher. Sprinkle it all over yourself. Light yourself. Let's see if you dare. I dare you . . . It's all words, just words, with you. All you do is hop up and down in the bathtub. Your life has run right through your fingers, do you hear? Sighing, whining, shrieking, that's all . . . That's not life. But you don't dare, you old hen you, do you?, you don't dare finish yourself off once and for all. Because, hold on . . . Just give it a try. Pick up the bottle and sprinkle a little on yourself. Then take a match and light yourself. Run out that locked door like a Roman candle. Set the whole damned house on fire. Light it up, light it up . . . I dare you. Sow. Filthy sow. You just love to bitch and moan. You just love it . . . Old sow!

"Adolfina! Adolfina! I can't stand it anymore! Woman! . . ."

Do it, now. Do it now. Answer her that way. That's the only way you've got left. Strangle yourself with your own bare hands. Jump headfirst into the dry cistern. But first, hammer a million nails into yourself. But before you do that, swallow fifty pounds of soldering paste. But before that . . .

But she never felt so much pleasure as at that moment—fatally unrepeatable—when all the subterranean, crawling creatures fell upon her. A million voracious maggots, great dark cockroaches, supple earthworms, tiny red ants rushed over her body and began to sink in their teeth. And when the devouring of it reached such fury that she was virtually bursting apart, flying into fragments, disintegrating, being carried off in tiny bits and pieces and disappearing as if by a magic wrought by all the pincers, hooks, teeth, stingers, suckers, tongues, and probosces, her joy was so great that she feared that she could not bear it, or perhaps that from one moment to the next she would simply cease to be. And so, to prevent

that happening, she flew away. That was the greatest
triumph—the *only* triumph—to which a suicide might
aspire.

"I see a little girl picking marigolds."
"Dummy. Tell me what you see."
"I see a marigold slapping a little girl."
"Who's the little girl?"
"You. Who do you think?"
"Idiot. I'm going to tell Grandma it was you that hid the
sewing scissors. You dummy."
"I dare you."

Come on, Adolfina, I bet you can't squeeze your throat till your
tongue hangs out.
Frustrated whore. Pathetic burlesque dancer. Streetwalker.
Hooker. Teacher! . . . So the abandoned woman wanted to be a
teacher, huh? Uh-huh, a teacher. Oh, *teeee*-cher! Can you beat
it, a teacher. Who did that crazy old hen think she was? Capable
of unzipping one of my sons' pants! Teacher, huh? Good lord.
You—what you wanted to do was go into the life. What you
wanted to do was bed down every sailor in port. Oh yes, oh yes,
oh yes. Oh no, no, no. That's what *she* wanted, but it's not what
I wanted. And if I did want it, it was against my own wanting
it. Maybe what I want to do is lock myself up in the bathroom.
And start screaming. And start asking myself what I want. Maybe
what I want is just this—to get in the bathtub and turn on the
hot water real real hot. And start hopping up and down, hopping
up and down, hopping up and down . . . I may be living the best
moments of my life right now and not even know it. It's possible
that this is the loveliest stage of my life. I've got happiness seeping
out of my fingertips, and I'm licking them. I'm disgusted from
being so happy. I've had it up to *here*. I want the consolation of
some terrible disgrace, some awful misery, some unbearable bad
luck. Oh yes, I'm happy. Open the guava vats. Poke my body
down in the jelly. Come on, let's see you do it. I dare you, I
double-dare you. You mynah bird. You unroostered old hen. Poke
me. Poke me. Open the bottle. Ay, the bottle. Wheee, the bottle.
Peep, the bottle.

"Tell me what you see. What do you see. What do you see?"

"Nothing. Just a naked woman playing hopscotch."

"Good lord. Who's she playing with?"

"Two lizards."

"I don't believe you. Let me see."

"Look, then."

"Stupid—those are not lizards. They're salamanders."

The Life of the Dead

When, in late afternoon, the glare beings to dissolve, begins as it were to fade into another sort of brightness, and everything becomes golden, fleeting, glorious, so that one would think the world was made to be lost, so extraordinary it all is, then they come out, they suddenly appear in the most golden-glowing and solitary places—as timeless trees burst forth in constantly blooming, delicate blossoms that fall, and fall, and fall, and never fall, of course. They journey, they leap into the sky. They float. They are young, smiling, splashing about though not splashing in the water. They glide down the rain gutters, and the rain gutters do not creak in protest. They investigate flower stalks, explore the flowers, peer at the juncture where the leaves form a whorl of green, walk through vast plains the cold moon silvers without illumination. They are dry in wetness, numb with cold in fire, alone in crowds. They dance, they flow upward to the moon— *there, maybe, there, maybe.* They swing through the sky, they hover over many dimensions, many spaces. They take up pieces of shattered glass, unclassifiable stones, stars. They move with great urns and narrow-necked pitchers through the heavens, gathering, laughing. Utterly, absurdly foolish, infinite, and together.

"Well, now I've told you all about *my* death. Tell me about yours. Tell me what it was like. I'd like to know. I'd like to know whether we all go through the same thing. I'd really like to know. I don't give a hoot. But we've got so much time that I don't know what else we'd do with it. So tell me all about your death. We've got so much time because time doesn't exist anymore so far as we're concerned—since we can't use it, or improve it as the saying goes. So come on—don't be bashful."

"What do you want to hear? You know all about it already."

"So it was just like mine."

"And mine."

"Well, then—tell me what *mine* was like."

"Aw, all right, but it was nothing special. You go over and look down the well, and when your eyes can see down in there, you see we're all of us down there together in the bottom of the well."

"Not one bit different from mine."

"You look over the edge of the wellhead and all of a sudden, *Pssssh*, somebody pushes you in."

"*I* pushed you. But tell me, honestly now, what could you do with those awful people?"

"We could have killed 'em all and kept living ourselves."

"But there's no *style* to that. And anyway, there'd have come other people, almost for sure."

"We'd have killed 'em."

"But you couldn't go on like that forever."

"Till they left us alone."

"If what you wanted was peace and quiet, why here you've got it."

"This is not peace and quiet, this is not being left alone, this is *desperation*, this is *boredom*. Has it ever occurred to you, have you ever stopped to think, what it is to know that we can't even *die* anymore?"

". . . Now we're condemned to live on memories."

"We're condemned to *invent* the memories."

"Now we walk, and we don't move."

"Now we walk, and walk, and walk, and we don't walk."

"I've got a whole bunch of bottles of wine in there under the bed."

"Drink. Drink."

"I've got a rat making alcohol inside a can full of soursop peels."

"Poor beast."

"I've got thousands of sheets of blank paper."

"Write. Write. You won't *say* anything. They'll never *hear* you. But write."

"I've got to tell it."

"So tell it, tell it. You'll get bored soon enough."

"Nobody here cares about anybody else?"

"There's nobody else here."

"But what about me? And you?"

"We're here to be witnesses to that absence. You are my solitude, and I represent to you the certainty that you are alone."

"Take my hands. Take my hands . . ."

"Hush, hush."

". . . Boy, have we been walking tonight! We must be getting almost to the end of the earth by now."

"You still haven't gotten rid of the habit of talking like you talked before."

"*Before* is so foggy that even if I wanted to, I couldn't remember it the way it really was."

"You should be glad of that."

". . . And since I can't see it the way it really was, it doesn't seem as unbearable as it was."

"Although you know only too well that it *was*."

"But at least it *was*. Now I can't even tell myself that I feel anything, or how I feel if I did. I can't even touch myself, or hit myself. Can you imagine? I walk out on the water imagining myself walking on water, and sometimes I practically drown. I'm so happy then—I almost manage to imagine a real river. How happy you get when you feel, or you imagine you feel, that the current is floating you along, dragging you down to the bottom! How happy, how very very happy I am when I imagine the boards and build a house. But what is there to do when we've lost all memory? And yet have to go on."

"If you'd be quiet a minute, we might be able to make it up different."

"If we were quiet a minute, we'd realize so fast it would make your head swim that we don't exist."

"If we hush we can go back and lie down among those marigolds."

"And the wild coffee bushes."

"And the crosses."

"And the red ants."

"And the earthworms."

"And all that."

"Hush."

"Hush."

"*Shhhh. . . .*"

His mother was neither tall nor short. Neither sad nor happy. And not ugly. When it came time to pick corn, his mother would be out in the middle of the field, picking corn, never saying a word. When the dry times came and the seedlings had to be watered, his mother would make trips to and from the well with the cans of water, never saying a word. When the old man decided to sell the farm and they all had to move to town, his mother took the bedframes apart, bundled everything up, and, when everything was loaded, climbed up on the tailgate of the truck (for the old woman and Adolfina were up front, weeping and wailing) to keep the big mirror from banging against the corner of the closet we kept the water crocks in and smashing to pieces. And when things kept getting worse and worse (for things always seemed to get worse), and the old woman would scream, "We're starving to death, this time it's the truth!", and some of them did die, and other ones wanted to die, and all of them (but this was no different from always) were on the verge of madness, his mother began, with the help of a distant relative, to investigate the possibility of leaving the country—to save him (her son). Back and forth, from Holguín to the consulate in Santiago, from the consulate in Santiago to Holguín, his mother would trek incessantly. Somehow able to stand the huffing and puffing and sniffing of Jacinta and Digna, who always seemed to have something to hold against her, to reproach her for, to nag at her about. To hold over her head. His mother. Raffling off a dress, raffling off a stalk of plantains she had bought from Polo—his mother. Patching his pants, dressing her nieces and nephews, being insulted and abandoned the same night she was swept away . . . his mother. Eating almost nothing so the food would go around. With her cardboard suitcase, standing in the doorway now, neither tall nor short, neither blond nor chestnut-haired, not ugly, not pretty, smoothing his hair with her hand, kissing him, waving silently goodbye, his mother . . . Always with an air of resignation, with that calm expression of a person who knows that bad luck, hard times, is not a rare occurrence in human life, but is life itself. Always with that look of sadness and calm, of patience, of a person who knows there is no way out and yet who knows that life cannot be any other way, and that it would be even more absurd if it were. His mother . . . looking at him, sadly, with patience in her eyes . . . This was one of the images of her that he held. Because he did have more. And more . . .

Now I'll swallow some hot water for my sister Onerica. Poor thing, working like a dog and being kicked like one for it. My sister Onerica, worn out from making trips to the consulate in Santiago, starving to death on the road back and forth, just so they'd give her the visa so she could go work like a dog for the Americans. What makes me think about her now is that in this place here, all the sad things in life come together in my head and practically beat me black and blue. What makes me think about her now is that I never think about her. Nobody in this whole house ever thinks about her. We just think of ourselves— which is plenty. I really don't think anybody can blame us for thinking just about ourselves, since that's the same as thinking about the whole world and everybody in it. Because I, at least, carry all the weight of the world on my shoulders. Thousands of worlds, I carry the weight of, *inside* me, and it makes a person's feathers droop, I'll tell you. And sometimes I'd like to vomit those worlds all up, because I just can't hold any more. But I don't— even if I wanted to, I can't vomit up even the tceniest, tiniest world . . . My poor sister, they loaded her boat up and then they left her to row it all by herself. And there sit the consequences—Fortunato. He never reads the letters she sends him, all he does

If she had been like that, was it possible not to hate her? Was it possible not to feel that she was to blame for it all? Was it possible to live, knowing that she was living too? Yet he still loved her . . . his mother.

is sit around all day making up nonsense. Why does my sister write so much? Why all this letter-writing every week? She ought to save up the money she spends on letters to see if she can't come back here someday. But what foolishness I talk—come back for what? Come back to what, if she'd have to turn around and leave again. Because anybody that leaves, once they're gone they just keep going . . . And I don't think she wants to come back, either, even if in the letters she says she does. What would she do here? When you're far away, things look different, but the closer you get the better you see that what's here is just trash and offal . . . I thought it was just at the beginning that so many letters would come. But good lord—there're so many letters there's no room to keep another single one. And the mailman keeps coming. And the letters piling up. Though nobody reads them . . . The mailman goes *Tweeee, tweeee, tweeee* with his whistle, and the letters nobody opens stack up clear to the ceiling. At the beginning I'd sit down in the living room and read the letters out loud for everybody. "My poor daughter, can you imagine going off to Timbuctoo or Zamboanga or wherever it is," my mother would say. "That just goes to show that she never loved us." And I'd say, Mama (with my mouth closed), you miserable she-goat, what do you expect—do you expect her to stay here like us and starve to death? You think your praying fills a stomach. What you need is to be hit by lightning and fried to cracklings, you old bag. That's what I would say with my mouth closed. And then I'd say it one more time with my mouth open. And that would start a row to wake the dead. So then the blasted old hen would get down on her knees and get filled with a spirit and start cackling and carrying on. And the spirit wouldn't leave until the old man took a cudgel, or a big thick stalk of plantains with the plantains all pulled off, as big around as your arm, and started beating her with it. That was how the show would end. But now I don't even bother to read the letters, and the old man never says a word. And the old woman just keeps panting and bugging her eyes out and speaking in tongues, over any little thing, with the spirits. Though nobody pays her any mind. Why just yesterday a spirit caught her standing in front of the cookstove, and it made her blister her hands, but the spirit left before you could say "Shit," because she shrieked and howled like a banshee, and she even cursed God Himself. Who believes in that stuff? Who—with the way things are, I mean—is going to waste his time believing in such nonsense? Me—I'll tell you, what *I'd* give good money to see is God showing His face around here. Let Him be a man and come in here, I'd show Him. I'd bust His face for Him. Listen, you old faggot, I'd say to Him—Why? Why? . . . I'd first say that to Him and then I'd jump all over Him, I'd kill Him and then I'd kill Him again. Why don't You just come down here, You son of the biggest bitch that ever lived. Why don't You put in an appearance down here? Come on. The first thing I'd do is throw a kettle of boiling water all over You. Come see what's good for You. Come on down here, come on.

"Dear sister, I pray God that this letter finds you well . . ." Pray to the devil. Pray to those damned Americans, to see whether they won't raise your salary. Pray to a toad. Pray to those bastards to see whether they won't give you a week off so you can come visit this trash heap down here. Pray to the wild beasts. Pray to shit. "My dear sister . . ." Dear, my ass—"My screwed sister" is more like it. Ay, it makes me furious to see us dying here without being able to stop it or just bust once and for all. Nobody knows how broken down I am, how I've broken down so much I'm practically kept together with old kite string and barbed wire—and I keep saying Wait, wait, wait . . . But no more. I've had enough. No more waiting. *Enough!* My dear sister,
My dear sister.
My dear sister. I don't know why you write. Come over here, God, and I'll box Your ears a little for You. I don't know why you write, since you can surely imagine that there's nobody here that reads your letters anymore. A little closer, You bastard, I'm going to smash You. I don't know why you waste your time, you'd be better off resting a little. I can imagine how worn out you must be . . . Here, I at least have the consolation of getting things off my chest, screaming, yelling, beating those kids of Digna's with a switch. But *you* have to take the tantrums those kids throw that aren't even your own. You have to take care of them. I can imagine you singing lullabies to those impossible kids. I can imagine you . . . and I can almost reach out and touch you with my thoughts. A poor person ought to die before she's

born. A poor person . . . Come on over here, God, and I'll set You on fire. You just try it—come one step closer and we'll see who's got the most power. I don't know why you trouble yourself to write. Nobody in this house even remembers you anymore—not even Fortunato. Not even your own son remembers you. But don't blame him. Come on, You son of a bitch, if You're a man. My God, I'd love to get my hands on You, I'd strangle You with my bare hands. Don't blame him—it's just that the poor thing is crazy, that's all that's wrong with him. We're all crazier than hell in this house. You know what our house is like, my dear sister, so why should I tell you more sob stories. Why should I fill your head up with our trials and tribulations, if your own are even worse—because yours are yours plus ours, while ours are just ours, without yours. Because here, my dear sister, in this house, nobody even remembers that you exist. Nobody. Come on over here and I'll pull out Your eyes for You—though on second thought if You exist You'd have to be blind anyway. And you know it's not our fault if we've forgotten about you. It's this life's fault—this life we're leading. Just to show you how crazy we are—yesterday I caught Mama trying to weld a pan together with a piece of chewing gum. Poor Mama—so many times I've thought of poisoning her with soldering paste. But what for? And now it turns out that ever since I saw her trying to weld that pan together, I sort of feel sorry for her . . . The noise from that factory is so terrible that sometimes at midnight it's still going. And as though that weren't enough, poor Celia spends her life talking about things you can't understand, and the old man doesn't talk at all. Although I'm almost glad of that. We've got enough racket already with the racket from the factory and the Cain those kids of Digna's are always raising. . . . And Digna, the poor thing— that's another one that's always up in the clouds somewhere . . . But as I was saying, with the racket from the wheels and pulleys and all, and the bad words those cursed little cockroaches are always saying . . . Ay, those children. Those children. Wouldn't the best thing be just to cut their heads off before they turn into something worse? Tell me the truth—wouldn't it be better to cut every kid's head off in the world, every single one of them, before it's too late? . . . So whether the old man talks or doesn't talk, it's nothing for anybody to be overly concerned about. Anyway, he always said so little when he *did* talk that sometimes we'd barely notice he was alive. Ay, but that's not true—although maybe on second thought it *is* true. Now that I think about it, maybe he *never* talked and it's just now that we're realizing it. Now that I think about it. Come just a little closer here, goddammit, and I'll bloody Your nose for You. And since now we know for sure that he doesn't talk, we wish he would, thinking that if he talked he'd talk about something interesting— but that's because we know he isn't *about* to talk. Ay, shit . . . And I can't understand where those kids of Digna's have learned to say so many indecent words. Breeding tells. There's no way out. And now they've taken to playing jokes on people—Tico's hidden my sewing scissors on me and I'm playing like I haven't noticed a thing so I can find out where he's cached 'em. Because if I tell him I know he's got them, I could beat him to a pulp with a stick of kindling and he'd *never* give them back, or tell me where they're hidden. So imagine—I've got to be watching the blasted child every minute—and not let him catch me watching him—to try to see where he's hidden them. Aren't I a little old for such carryings-on? And as though that weren't enough, Anisia spends the livelong day with her eye to the cracks in the bathroom wall to see what I do in here. There's no way out, dear little sister. We should never have been born. We should've hanged those two damned old people when they brought us into the world. We should've burned the house down, with them in it, and us gone out into the street and turned whores and then set ourselves afire too. But later on, after we'd lived a little, even if just two or three minutes. Because it's sad just to die without ever having really breathed good air, even for just one second. *That's* sad. Come on over here, God, and I'll claw Your back to ribbons. Come on, You damned old coot, so You can see what it's like from *this* side. So You'll have to bow Your head like the rest of us, and cut Your own throat. Come on, come on, I'll hack You to pieces, I'll slice Your guts open, I'll grind You to a powder. Dog. Donkey. Shit. Animal. My dear sister. My dear sister. You probably ought not to write anymore. Don't write anymore— nobody remembers you. Though we still love you.

"Adolfina! Adolfina! Are you sick? Is that it? Answer me! Am I going to have to break down the door? Ay, my God. We're going to have to break down the door!"

The racket has ceased. The organ has, at least for a while, stopped playing. It may be the organist's break. The children, strangely nestled against each other's bodies, are asleep. The mosquitoes, stuffed full by now, have retired to the darkest corners. The old man's snoring fills the hallway, and produces a strange ringing vibration which at last ends in a long-drawn snort like a death rattle. The moon, soundlessly, silvers the edges of the blinds, makes pale tracery on the photographs. And bathes her hands. She gets out of bed, gracefully and silently, and pulls back the latch. She goes out into the dining room. And now she is standing in the yard.

Don't give yourself airs, woman. Don't delude yourself. Life is shit. Look at me—all by myself with two children so helpless you have to put everything right in their hands. Look at me standing here—alone and nothing to look forward to but more aloneness. Because bad luck, there's no such thing as a little sack to carry it in. You can fill a sack up with potatoes, you can fill your stomach up with food (so they say)—but so far as bad luck goes, so far as misfortune is concerned, it can be all the way to the top and they can still stuff it in and stuff it in and stuff it in, and you're standing there holding the sack for them . . . Till when, o Lord, till when . . . Thank goodness the kids are finally asleep. Now at least I can sit down by myself for a minute on this tree trunk.

What a bunch of slugs all over this tree trunk. This house is full of bugs, and insects, and slugs, and pests. And vermin. Though all the houses in towns are that way—the bugs will turn you out of your own bed. I'm scared to death a rat will bite Tico one day. Poor thing, he's such a pale, skinny little thing—and the rats prowling around this house day and night. And if it were just the rats—but there are those little-bitty fieldmice too, and regular mice, and cockroaches, too. Ay, blasted creatures. Disgusting. If only I could close my eyes right this minute, and say to myself, "I'm dreaming." You're dreaming. Stop worrying, you silly goose, can't you see that this is all just a bad dream? You'll wake up in a minute and be as happy as a lark again, because you'll see that those millions of cockroaches pulling out your eyes were just a bad dream. It was just a bad dream that made you see a rat bite one of Tico's toes. It was just a bad dream that made you feel all alone and abandoned with two babes-in-arms to take care of. It was just in a bad dream that you saw Anisia's shoes falling apart. And saw yourself crying like a silly goose out in the middle of the backyard sitting on a rotten tree trunk. Stop worrying.

And it was just a bad dream that your mother came over to you and said, "Get out of here, get out—we can't have all these mouths to feed in this house."

See? Dreams. Bad dreams. And Moisés telling you to go to hell. Cockroaches in your bed with you. Tico all pale, pale, pale. Anisia screaming because she stepped on a goathead burr barefooted. Life out on the street, like a kick in the belly. Life . . . Life. And it doesn't rain. And it *still* doesn't rain. You watching and watching, to see if the rain won't come. If it won't come. Which it won't. It just won't. Ay, it's not going to rain again tonight. And your mother squabbling and squawking. And the old man looking at you like you smelled bad. You're dreaming. Just dreaming. The pigeons shit on your head, but it's just a dream. The cockroaches scrabble around your mouth, but it's just a dream. Somebody knocked on the door and then ran away, but that was just a dream. Here comes the ice-cream man. It's playing again, the organ's started to play again. What's that song? What song is that? Why, it's "La Cucaracha." *La cuca-ra—cha . . . La cu . . . La cu.* You're just dreaming.

Don't delude yourself, woman.

Out on the porch, sitting on a stool, the old man has nodded off. For some time, the old lady has been watching his head bob as he dozes and then starts awake. Now, though, she tiptoes over to the old man. She slowly slips her fingers into each of his shirt pockets. He is breathing deeply. The old woman cautiously takes out the key to the vegetable stand.

The old man snores on. The old woman goes into the shop. Groping gently, taking care not to bump into the bins and stalls or disturb the rotten fruit or knock over a row of lamp chimneys, she finds a pencil, an envelope, and a ream of paper the old man had hidden under the brown paper bags. The old woman locks up the shop again. She puts the key back where she found it—while the old man serenely bellows. And carrying the pencil, the envelope, and the ream of paper, she heads off for the back of the house.

Well, if I could tell you, I'd tell you that Fortunato has to be one of the most bull-headed people I've ever seen in my life. I believe he's more touched in the head than *I* am. Just imagine— he's taken now to making soap out of ashes and lizard fat. I don't know whether he's doing it to throw us off, so we won't tell him to go get a job, or what. But whatever the case is, so far as *I'm* concerned, at least, *I'm* worried sick. But I won't tell you that, although I wish I could, daughter, because I just barely know how to write at all, and anyway, why upset you with all that nonsense. After all, you've got other things to keep your mind busy; you've got a life up there. I wish you also knew that the vegetable stand has gone from bad to worse and that the only thing that can save us from going under is for me to find a little ewer that according to what a spirit told me is buried under that big mango tree up on the farm we sold on account of that stupid beast of a father of yours. But imagine—how are we going to go digging up a piece of land that doesn't belong to us anymore? Ay, we should never have sold that farm, and God knows I said so. And now God has given us this trial for it. Because if we hadn't sold it, we could go dig up that money right now, and we'd have no problems. But life is like that. Your father got it in his head to sell. And here we are, out of the frying pan into the fire. Things are worse every day. I tell you, if we go on much longer like we're going on now, we'll be having to beg for water by making signs with our hands. I wish if you could you'd have a cleansing session. Although I don't know what the mediums are like up there. Those people up there probably get everything backwards. But try to go see at least a card reader, if nothing else. And try to get her to tell you when you'll be able to come back. And also whether you're going to be rich. The other day a new one moved into this neighborhood that they say is good, and she only charges twenty-five centavos for a consultation. I'm keeping my eye on the old man in the shop to see when he goes off to sleep so I can grab the money out of the cashbox. But lately you'd think he had eyes in the back of his head—nobody could get so much as a centavo out of him. And when he closes up the shop, lord knows where he hides the cashbox. I've been watching him, but no luck so far. He's always been a skinflint. Even just to get this paper I'm scribbling you this note on, I've had to go through hell, and that was with the help of God I prayed for. And even the few little things I take out of that vegetable stand to cook his own meals with, the old rat wants to charge me for them. Can you imagine that? And now with this idea he's got of not opening his mouth—the whole world can go up in smoke for all he cares, he just goes on about his business, not saying one peep to anybody. Even if you don't ever find all this out, I'm going to write it to you so you know, even if you don't know. Besides, what difference does it make whether you know or not?—what's important is my telling it. That way, I've done my duty. And don't think I don't remember you. Although sometimes, I have to admit, I can't remember exactly what you look like. But I think that probably happens to everybody. And anyway, that's not my fault—it's on account of time. Just yesterday I realized that I couldn't quite picture your face to myself—or my mother's face or my father's face, either. May they rest in peace. It made me feel like crying like a baby. But then I thought, Nobody'll remember yours either, in a hundred years. So that made me feel better. Because life's hard, hard. You forget your own child's face, even if you still love her. And maybe it's for the best. Because otherwise what would a person do, carrying around a bag of memories *that* big, filled to running over with faces? With memory after memory after memory. Why a person would hardly be able to get around from the weight of it all. Thank goodness a person little by little loses those memories, as time goes by. How nice it would be to be a person that's just come to a place where you don't know the first thing about the things that have happened there. Or what *will* happen. Just to know—and not any too well, at that—that you've just gotten there, and not even from where, or why. You just *get* there, and you're not even perfectly sure if it's *there* you just got to. You just got there, though, because, well, just because, but you don't have any memory of what's been, back before . . . Now I'll get down on my knees here, in this corner of the house, and I'll pray seven or eight Our Fathers for you. And I swear I won't stop even if my guts start spluttering and popping on me like they do sometimes, so you'll see that I haven't forgotten you, even if I can't quite picture your face. And anyway—what difference does that make . . . .

But the old man stirred from his lethargy. He sat up, for he realized that he almost remembered someone (though perhaps it was a dream, or perhaps a dead person) touching him. Instinctively he patted his pockets. He took out the key and went into the shop. That wretched child, he thought, believing it was Fortunato who had stolen the paper. He hurried out and began looking for him. But at that, he stumbled upon the old woman out behind the house. And he saw that *she* was the thief. The old man tried to grab her by the throat, but the old woman kicked him in the belly. The old man tried to twist her arm, but the old woman bit him on the wrist. The old man then tried to grab her by both ankles and bat her against the side of the house, to bash her brains out, but the old woman kneed him in the face. The old man tried to split her head open with a hoe, but the old woman spun around with a block of cement left over from the bathroom. And at that moment Adolfina ran out of the house waving her sewing scissors.—She'd found them, at last.

In this house there's never any peace. Just listen, just listen to that hullabaloo right under the walls of the castle . . . I come in carrying my dead daughter and I sit down in the dining room, and I say, "Quiet. Quiet." But nothing happens. There is no peace, ever, anymore. I wait for everyone to go to bed, and then I get up very very slowly and quietly and I call my daughter, and then we go into the dining room. But the noise of the day is still here, like it got left behind when the sun went down. And there is just no peace. Quiet! Quiet! And the ga-ga-*boom* of that factory banging at my eardrums.

138

And my daughter just leaves, because she can't stand the racket. Racket, racket, racket. Quiet! Because I want her to come back, come back . . . What did I say? What did you say? Quiet, I said. Nobody can tell me what I said to myself, I said. Sit down, sit down here and let's both rock a while in this rocking chair. Sit on my lap like before. And don't talk, like before. And don't look at me, like before. Be real, real still, I'll rock you to sleep. But that racket! Such a deafening hullabaloo! I think we'd better put some cotton in your ears.

"I think I'd better just die."

Hush, hush, they'll hear you and realize you're still here. Hush. If you'd put some cotton in your ears you wouldn't hear those kids cursing a blue streak out there. If you'd put just a little teeny cottonball in one ear and put your hand over the other one. I can cover up one ear for you if you want me to and then you'll just have the one to cover up. But be still, now. Hush. Don't say bad words. There, there. Don't let yourself get to be like those people we don't know. Hush. The factory'll close in a little while. The old man will lock up the shop. In a little while we'll have a rainstorm and all those bottles of rotten water that Fortunato's got under the bed will get carried away on the river. In just a little while, you'll see. Hush, now. Hush. In just a little while.

"In just a little while I'll take the strychnine and go *Agg-gg-ggh*."

Oh, no, hush. I think I'd better start singing a little so nobody hears you. Close your mouth. Don't make a peep. Just sit here and wait a bit, and you'll see—here, I'll stop up your ears myself. There. Now I'll just rock with the tip of one foot, and you'll sleep. There. Sleep, now. Sleep. Just like . . . I know you can't. I know there's always all this noise to make you jump. I know there's all this glary light that you see even when your eyes are closed. But try, just make a little effort. Sleep. Hush, you people! Shut those traps of yours! Shush! Heathens. Heathens. Hea . . . Now she's starting to be still . . .

*Now Fortunato has taken it in his head
to eat sandwiches made out of lizards.
He goes off out behind the factory. He
hunts down the lizards, smashes them
between two pieces of bread, and bites.
Yuck.*

—Them

THE THIRD
AGONY

There were times he took it in his head to eat lizards, it was true. There were times he took it in his head to make wine, to shut himself up in the bathroom and make horrible faces, to crawl under the bed and masturbate seven times running, to climb up on the roof and burn to a crisp in the sun, to raise slugs, to have a bicycle. It was true. But all those ideas of his, all those obsessions, all those "wild ideas," as other people called them, were but transitory needs, passing fancies, that served only to palliate or put off for a few moments the great need, the real fancy, his one and only desire. There would be one of those wild ideas after another. They would come, have their way, and go. But if one thing in him remained fixed, it was the fatal, inexplicable role of assuming and interpreting others' desperation. The rest of his yearnings, his other whims and caprices would hardly have begun to gnaw at him when he would once again lose interest in them—a week perhaps, they would last, or a month—two at most. But that incomprehensible title of Emissary of Terror, the fact, or state, of his knowing himself to be touched by a fatal gift, by a doom, by some inescapable fate which would at once destroy and shape him, by a thing which would, quite simply, give his life its reason and justification (even when there were times when he himself would attempt to flee it)— *that* was constant. Dusk; the rushing roar of a rainstorm; things dissolving in starlight; as he walked through a place, the smell that would suddenly rush over him, transporting him; looking fixedly at his fingernails; a yellowing sheet of paper blown by the wind; someone saying Good afternoon—those were some of the phenomena which "that thing" would employ to manifest itself. Sometimes all he had to do was stick his head out the door and see the sunlight bursting on the asphalt for that indescribable sensation to make itself felt. And what it would feel like at those instants would be a sort of fever that spread through his body, a sensation like the ticking of a bomb about to explode. And there would be, too, behind all that, the sense of knowing that he was mortal in the midst of an endless, immeasurable fraud, a betrayal, a *trick*—endless and immeasurable in proportion, that is, to *his* existence, to *his* memory, to *his* ability to understand it—and that this fraud, this trick was falling on him from the very sky, and falling on him constantly, and forever. Forever . . . He is out in the backyard. It is night. Everyone else is asleep. The light blanches things—stones, the bottom of tin cans, his hands. And *that thing* comes over him, that thing seizes him, and suddenly it makes him feel superior, strong, alone, and terribly, terribly wretched. . . . He is out in the country. He is a boy. From the arbor he can hear the voices of his relatives talking near the back door of his house as they hoe weeds among the corn. They are the familiar, soothing voices that carry on the ordinary conversations of every day. But there is something behind them, underneath them, underneath those words—something that only he understands; and every word, every sound changes into a sort of challenge, a dare, a terror, a possibility of tenderness, an enigma, *his* enigma, for only he is allowed to understand it. But what must he do? Who must he go to—if, indeed, there is anyone in this town that can guide him . . . He is in the dining room, in the house in town. The radio is playing some popular song, some stupid, ordinary song, one of those songs his cousin Esther likes so much. And there, too, there is some urgent, demanding thing, a thing that commands him, transports him, a thing that lifts him and carries him away, and that leaves him with a myriad doubts and questions, questions different from those that the common days of life bring on . . . And now he is the condemned man, now the chosen one, the man who will not fit in, the man who will not conform, the man who possesses a horror which will not be held to the narrow limits of daily misery. He is the man who cannot listen to a song and say, *I hear a song*—and let that be it. The man who cannot listen to some familiar conversation and tell himself, *I hear people talking*—and let that be it.

The man who cannot simply walk along the street in the evening, savor the moment's coolness like everyone else does, and say, *That's it, that's all there is, this is simply this,* and go no further, not delve into what cannot be seen, not ask questions whose answers in the final analysis only he has any interest in . . . Now he understood at last. Now he understood—the distrust that other people showed for him was justified. For what was he to them if not a traitor, a man who considered himself (*knew* himself) to be above them all, a man just waiting for the moment to laugh at them, a man who would not take seriously the things which in their view justified their existence—the *other*, for them, the thing no one could see, the *useless*? He was a traitor. And if he was to go on living, he had no alternative but always to be the outcast, the rejected, the scorned and despised. For it was not enough for him just to *be*—he wanted to *know*. To see behind things, under them. And that was what was terrible, because underneath things, behind them, was a truth, a scream which rolled all the futile conversations into a ball, a great grotesque gesture which masterfully summed up all the worn-out, clichéd, petty, futile motions which a man in the whole course of his clumsy life is capable of making . . . It was growing dark, it was growing dark, and from one moment to the next he expected the shadows, like a palpable black *thing*, to burst in through the window. It was growing dark, and something far away began to hum, to buzz, and the great unwavering never-ending shriek grew nearer and nearer, and more and more deafening. And he was the emissary of that song—*he* who by virtue of so much grace was doomed, disgraced, and wretched, he who would never again have a moment of plenitude anywhere, for that plenitude, that sense of blessedness, of existing, would always be *out there*, beyond, behind what surrounded him, hemmed him in, and held him like chattel in its constant terror or the formlessness of its forms . . . He is out behind the house, playing with the empty bottles. He is a child. There is hunger—there is always hunger for those who have no strength to rob, to betray, to trick and deceive, to fake it— and who, then, come to this. He has seen his mother crying. He has heard how his grandmother grunts and wheezes as she prays. God. God. But suddenly his grandfather has said "Christmas, Christmas," and that word, bouncing like a ball, has reached his ears, and the word has turned into thousands of words—unsuspected, unique, musical, magical words, words that suddenly open fabulous lands, words that transport him far away, that become cathedrals, boughs that caress his skin, feathery white-capped seas, deep coffered ceilings which never existed, vast landscapes filled with bottles, demijohns, snaking vines and lianas. A great, high, arched portal. Camels wending toward it, and the rain which picks up fragments of colors from a corner of the yard. Go, run across that pebbled sky while into the sinuous channel with its bed of blue stones a man slowly lowers a bucket . . . Was there someone with him, to see that, hear that, be with him at that vision? Yes, someone was there, looking, always, flying away with him, then diving headfirst from the sky with him, or riding off and disappearing into the scrub with him on a spirited stickhorse made out of a broomwood tree—while at the house, lost in a wilderness of smells and endless mazy paths, a cousin, in the rain, rides her stickhorse into the house, carrying a stalk of plantains. . . . Is that not joy? Is that not utter freedom? And is it not a privilege to touch the uncommon, the wonderful, to be a part of those transfigurations? . . . But it is death, too, knowing that Death (always so precise, so punctual, and so aggressive) never fails to strike at last, and so makes our every gesture seem touched with grace and enchantment—those most "dignified," "firmest," most "elevated" voices are threatened, and poetry is made possible. . . . He had to run. He had to jump up, run away, flee, and throw himself into the grass, and then get up and go on. He had to sing. At that very instant, yes, *now*, he felt an irresistible urge to sing, and he brought a hand up to his chest, to make the effort, and he brayed . . . What utter, unbounded joy, what utter happiness. Braying in the grass. My God, what unbelievable happiness. Now he knew what his fate was to be, his end, his destiny. Now, oh now, he said to himself again . . . Had he discovered the secret? Had he finally discovered the word?— Braying, bellowing in the grass. For April was bursting, the day was exploding, it was riddled with the countless burstings-forth of spring. And out there, beyond all that shooting, the libations of the birds, the stand of trees in flames, the bells. . . . And to think that all this was because as a boy he had heard his grandfather say "Christmas." Ah, but you had to be there, you had to have heard him say it, you had to have really listened to the way he said it. *He* had the gift of listening, of seeing, of paying attention. Undistracted attention. *He* was touched by mystery. *He* knew. He was a monster, an artist, a god. Was it possible, then, to die? Was it possible, then, not to trust Death? What, then, was impossible? Where did his power end? Was there anyone stronger, more wretched and ill-favored, purer than he? . . . There was a climbing vine. That much was true, that much was real. Its leaves were green, smooth, tiny, oval-shaped. Its flowers—tiny white flowers—covered the vine like a fine mist of rain. Little wonder it was called the rainshower vine. That climbing vine was just off the breezeway. And it was always in bloom. In the afternoons, its smell and its shade were a blessing, a recompense. That vine could never dry up, he would not allow it. There lay his power.

The Life of the Dead

But her dream, my dream, our dream did not last long (for there is always somebody in charge who won't allow that sort of comfort—or any sort of comfort, in fact), in spite of all I was to sing to her, in spite of the fact that for a while I even managed almost to keep the noise at bay. Then came that situation with Fortunato and all, and from then on that bond between us, that complicity we had, my daughter and I, it's sort of petered away. And so now, I don't know, I don't know really whether I ought to wait for her, or just resign myself to losing both of them—who knows where— and them never knowing that I'm still waiting. Always waiting.

This is how it was:

Fortunato was out behind the bathroom, mashing up tamarind leaves. I came up to him and I said, "I don't know why you're wasting your time making up those bottles of stuff."

And he said, "What time?"

So I said, "Your time, or are you trying to tell me you don't have any time?"

So then he gave a big laugh, and he took off flying. I saw it with my own two eyes, and I didn't doubt them either, because I was already used to seeing Death in every corner. And the person who's used to such things has no call to be scared by little things like Fortunato flying off. I saw him just rise up, as plain as the nose on your face. And from way up high up there he yanked off his head and threw it at me. If I hadn't jumped out of the way it would've smashed me to little pieces . . . And now nobody wants to believe me. But I don't care. If I saw it, what do I care whether people believe me or not. Now, though, the only thing is, I've got a new fear to fear. Bigger than the one before. Because now I know that he knows more than I do, and that he's gotten to a place I've never been able to get to. And that he's died a whole lot sooner than I would ever have expected. And that he's probably talking to Esther at this very minute. Which is probably why she doesn't even come to see me anymore, like she did before. Even if it was just once every hundred years . . . which wasn't so much, or of course so little, either—it was just that for me, waiting, a hundred years would come and go like the blink of an eye. Uh-huh, I'll bet Esther's off with him somewhere right this minute.

I just got here a while ago, and I'm already walking on water. It's not so hard. I just got here, it seems like no time at all, and look at me, as easy as pie, jumping out of trees that touch the clouds down onto the biggest rocks you ever saw. And not a scratch. Look at this—in one jump I can jump all the way up to the moon, give it four whacks, and come back down again and walk along on top of the stand of wild pineapples full of rotten eggs somebody laid. And not even walk if I don't want to. And if I want to, flop down on one of those spiny plants. And say *Whoa* if I want to, and go right off to sleep. I could even turn myself inside out and upside down if I wanted to . . . If I wanted to . . . There he comes. Fortunato's dead, too, though he may not know it himself. It's so hard. It's so hard. Listen to him . . .

I touch the honeyberry tree and I don't touch it. I smash myself in the face with a rock and I don't feel a thing. What in the world—what in the world is this, who ever heard? . . . What in the world is this, that I realize I understand less and less of, the more I see of it? I hug myself real real tight and I feel like there's nobody there. Then I walk along on top of the very tallest plants, and they don't even pay any attention to me. I eat three little baby kingbirds, and the baby birds are still in the nest. And their mother and daddy don't even give me one little peck. I touch my own soul and it's like I was touching air. Because I don't feel a thing. Because I stretch my hands out as far as they'll go, till they fall right off. And I can't touch a thing.

The house has four hot, cramped bedrooms separated from each other by thin walls that keep out any breeze, but not noise. It has, this house, a perfectly four-square living room filled with mismatched chairs with sprung seats, so that they are no longer fit to sit in, but are excellent for bumping into and breaking a leg on. A narrow hallway with one window which opens onto the wall of the factory. A tiny kitchen in which, compelled by some architectural perversity, everyone insists on congregating, and even on bringing guests. A dining room which has no walls, and which is made uninhabitable by flies, the sun, and everyone's odd table manners. The house ends in a small backyard, a place where all the discards, all the trash, all the castoffs of the house come to rest in a loblolly of dirty water from the washbasin and the sink. And at the back there is a pen where Jacinta sometimes will be raising a pig (for she still remembers the roast pigs at Christmastime up on the mountain)—a pig which, bogged in its own muck, shrieks incessantly and gives off unspeakable smells. The roof of the house is of fiber cement. The walls are of concrete blocks and bricks. Off to one side of the small front porch is the vegetable and fruit stand. In the yard there are no trees . . . Jacinta, naturally, hates this house, hates the whole town. She hates the immovable glare which always blinds these dusty streets. One day she watched Fortunato throw rocks out of the backyard and she didn't say a word. So long as he was doing something against the town, she was willing to keep her mouth shut. That afternoon, Jacinta laughed, the first time in a long, long while she had done so. But now that afternoon is a long, long time ago, too. Now she's constantly poking her nose around the house suspiciously, distrustfully, evil-mindedly, staring at the walls, spitting. Jacinta has never been able to sit down on the toilet. Her hatred is still as fierce as the day she came here.

I'm the one that has to keep this house running. Because if it wasn't for me . . . I have to figure out everything all by myself and work things out the best I can. Because as far as the rest of them are concerned, the world can come to an end and they couldn't care less. If there's nothing to eat, I'm the one they blame. If there's not so much as a hunk of pumpkin to throw in the soup for thickening, I'm the one to blame. If we don't have twenty-five centavos to pay the milkman for the one miserable bottle of milk we buy, I'm the one that has to make some story up and go stand there and tell it to him. I'm the man and the woman both in this house—because as far as Polo's concerned we could all be dead and buried, and as far as the rest of them giving a helping hand, o lord spare me. Oh, but I'm going to find that halfwit Fortunato a job. Enough of this lollygagging around here, doing nothing. My blood boils every time I see him off in a cloud somewhere all shut up in that living room reading those novels he reads or making up bottles of filth out of putrid water. I'm going to find that young man a job if it's digging ditches. He'll see if I don't. I'm going to talk to Tomasico this minute, by God, to see if he won't put him to work in the factory, even if it doesn't pay five centavos an hour. Even if it's for nothing. Because, good lord. As long as he gets out of this house. It gives a person the creeps to see him closed up in there the livelong day, like he was a little girl or something. I'm going to go talk to Tomasico this very minute . . . My God, the world's coming down around our ears and we don't even try to get out of the way. They're trying to provoke me, good lord, and they may just push me too far. If things keep on the way they're going, I don't see any way out but by taking in washing. Ay, and what need was there for us to be like we are when we could have been up on the mountain to this day? At least up there you could leave the house with any old rag wrapped around you without anybody paying any mind to how you were dressed or such nonsense. But here all anybody ever does is criticize. As though they were the ones that were going to fill your belly for you when it's empty. We could still be up on the mountain. And I'll bet by now we'd have found that ewer or jug or whatever it is that's buried up there.

"Adolfina! Holy Virgin mother of God, woman! Don't *you* push me too far, too!"

Yes, once she had moved to town she once more began her indefatigable search for a man. She began to dress "fashionably" again, or what she took to be fashionably; she even dyed her hair, though it came out blue. She set the sewing machine in the front door. She stood before the mirror and rehearsed her most seductive smiles. Sometimes—and this, not even in her wild deliriums could she confess—she would stand on her head for an hour or longer, so that the blood would flow to her head and make her skin taut and smooth, as a beauty magazine had promised. But nothing. She just went on pedaling the sewing machine. She just went on growing old. She just went on putting up with Jacinta and her grumbling, the old man, everybody. And putting up with herself, of course. Above all, putting up with herself. One day she threw a fit.

The woman came in with the loudest piece of material you ever saw for me to make her a dress out of. I said to myself, When she gets herself all gussied up in that bright red dress she's going to look like a scorched window curtain. But I took it, and I made her the dress like she told me to make it—tight in the skirt and full on top, so it would look like she had more than she had. I made up that bright red flag for her to wave at the bulls. And when she put it on I could barely keep from bursting out laughing—she looked like a gift-wrapped casket, or an upside-down lightbulb, I don't know . . . But she left as happy as could be . . . But the next day she came in again, with the dress all boxed up. " 'Fina?," the two-faced hypocrite says to me, "can you take it in just a little in the skirt and let it out just a tiny bit on top?" And I'm ready to pop. But she keeps going " 'Fina," " 'Fina," like a cat when it's hungry. And me saying to myself, I hope you get your feet tangled up in that tight skirt and fall face down in the middle of the street. And she says, "Just two little stitches here and four up there." So I did it just like she told me to, I took

it in and I let it out. And she tried it on. And she left as happy as could be. But apparently somebody in her house was whispering in her ear, because the next day she came back with the rag wrapped up in a newspaper and she sort of mews at me again, " 'Fina, listen, I think it would be better with gussets, that way I'd look more, um . . ." So I did it again with gussets. And when she tried it on, she said maybe I ought to let out one of the gussets. So I let out one of the gussets. "Uh-huh, uh-huh, uh-huh" was all I was saying. Meanwhile I was saying to myself, You bitch, I wish you'd go to hell. You want an awful lot of candy for a dime. But I did let out the gusset. And she left with that dress that looked like it was wadded up it was so worked and reworked, and wrapped up in a newspaper. But the next day she came in again with her mother. Her mother, for heaven's sake . . . Since the day mothers were invented, the world's been going to hell in a handbasket. Anyway, the old woman comes in and she says to me,"You, what you do is shoddy work I wouldn't have if you paid me. You've ruined this piece of crepe it took me so much trouble to find for my daughter. Do you think we get our money for nothing, free? Would *you* put on such a dress, I ask you? Don't think we're rich folk. We're starving to death just like you are." And so on and so on, blah blah blah, and the factory going ga-ga-*boom* ga-ga-*boom* ga-ga-*boom*. And people out there at the fruit stand yelling and screaming. And Mama in her bedroom praying at the top of her lungs. And those two children of Digna's screeching and cawing *Stinky-ass, stinky-ass, stinky-ass*, for no reason but to mortify me, because they knew there was somebody there to see me. And that old woman yelling at me. And me thinking I'd worked all week for one peso. And now she wanted me to make the dress all over again.
And me thinking I should have died before I was born.
And the factory going ga-ga-*boom* ga-ga-*boom* ga-ga-*boom*.

"Ohmygod, ohmygod, Avemaríapurísima," I said when I saw Adolfina run at those two women there, and waving the sewing scissors around like a butcher knife. "Ave María purísima!" I said when I heard that screeching and carrying-on in the living room. And I left off praying and ran out to see what was happening. And I saw that miserable daughter of mine stabbing around left and right with those sewing scissors. And those women bellowing and bawling and screeching. Adolfina trying to stab them to death. And me thinking that this made the fifth time this week that I'd had to leave my prayers without finishing them, without even so much as getting to the Our Father. The first time it was to hold Digna back, because she was giving Tico such a whipping it left him half fuddled in the head and I swear if I hadn't held her off him, she'd have killed him. Then next it was to take over for Polo because he was getting swindled in the shop—they were swapping him a bunch of addled eggs for a bag of nice fresh lemons and he never even so much as noticed. Then—then, it was to run get the milk off the cookstove because it was boiling over and nobody else in the house was paying the slightest bit of attention. Then I had to go out and throw a rock at that blasted nanny-goat of Iluminada's who's wiped out practically every sage plant I had planted. And then this—to try to calm Adolfina down, because if I hadn't gotten there in the nick of time, those two women would've been ripped to remnants. Good lord. My God. They never stopped ranting and insulting us, but they ran out the front door like a couple of bolts of lightning. And Adolfina picked up that bright red piece of yard goods and she ripped it to ribbons *with her teeth*, she was so mad, and then she threw it in their faces. Them hopping around and saying bad words. And Adolfina in a fury ripping that cloth to rags and crying. And people would walk down the street and stop right in front of the house to see that show. Me praying to God a policeman wouldn't come along. Adolfina screaming and carrying on. And the factory going ga-ga-*boom* ga-ga-*boom*. Until those two women finally ran off and disappeared somewhere off toward La Chomba, or Yarey, up that way. And then things started calming down a little . . . But I'm shaking now from the fear of it. Because they are not good people. And I lay odds that one of these days they come back and chop us into mincemeat with a machete. Or burn the house down. Or what's worse—put a spell on us. Now I'll have less peace of mind than the little or no peace of mind I had before.

You're standing in front of the mirror and you say to yourself, This is all just a pile of garbage. You're standing in front of the mirror and you're embarrassed to be standing in front of the mirror. Embarrassed that people might think I look at myself like girls do. Like girls do. But I don't care whether I'm "pretty" or "ugly." I don't look at myself in the mirror because of that or anything even close to that. I look in the mirror to have somebody to talk to. Just to talk to. So I say:

"You idiot, what are you doing in this house full of crazy old women?"

"You idiot, what are you doing working in this poorhouse crammed with rotten gauvas full of maggots, and you rotting just like them? Why, even after you bathe you can still smell that smell of rotten guavas, because it's coming out of the inside of you by now."

"You're a rotten guava."

"Idiot."

"Goose, you silly goose."

"You smell like a rotten guava. Here, let me see, let's see if there's some in your pockets. Here."

"What would you have me do about it?"

"Something."

"What?"

"Idiot. Idiot."

"You know as well as I do that I've thought about running away from home. But I don't know whether the money I've got is enough."

"Even if you starve to death, *git*."

"But it's . . ."

"Idiot."

"Maybe. Maybe."

"Idiot. And big silly idiotic goose."

"Maybe I'll make a lot of money and I can make wine out of star-apples. But what you tell myself is true—I don't do a thing here. I'm better off anywhere than here, because here, I'm nowhere. This town is no town, or country either, or anything else. This is something that there's no name for. Here people just sort of pass through, or live a long dying. I don't know, but it's like they're all sort of on the verge of something—on the verge of leaving, or on the verge of death. If we at least lived like we lived before, up on the mountain. I'd go outside and jump in the river and I could swim all day. And I would have my way with the cows. And then lie down in the grass. And forget the world. And so time would pass . . . Until finally, without my knowing it . . ."

"Idiot."

"Idiot."

"Idiot."

"Big stupid goose of an idiot . . . But in town it's different. The sun spends the livelong day making our life miserable. And if I go out in the street I don't have the slightest idea where to go. And if I stay home I think I'll be driven crazy by those blasted kids of Digna's screaming and yelling. And the old woman praying and fighting. And Celia whimpering and sniveling over the death of Esther. And the mailman bringing letter after letter after letter from my mother, every one of which says, You are the only thing I have. You are . . . But wake up, woman—you don't have *anybody*. I don't understand how there can be people that exist with a memory that long. I think they do it to spite you. But I've had enough. I don't want to *be* anything or depend on anybody. Or have anybody depend on me. I want to be what I am—nothing. But for people to know that I'm nothing. So they'll quit fooling themselves. And so they'll . . ."

"Idiot. Idiot . . .Oh, what a blooming idiot."

"I'd like to leave, and the devil take the hindmost."

"Idiot."

"I'd really like . . ."

"Idiot."

★ ★

After dinner she walks out on the porch. She sits down. She scolds at the children playing in the street. She runs her hand over the unpainted wood of the rocking chair. Every single evening.

I wish I was dead. Like I am. But didn't know it. Didn't know I was dead. So I could look out the window at the street and tell myself, Any minute now. And tell myself, He'll be here any minute. He'll be here any minute now. Don't fret now, you silly woman, he'll be here any minute now and he'll slap you first and then he'll sink his teeth in you. And then he'll carry you to bed and slap you three or four more times. And then he'll roll over on top of you and then he'll start loving you. I wish I could think it was going to be like that. Because I still look out the window. Because all I ever do is watch the street. Because all in the world I ever do is try to imagine that in a little while he'll be here. In a little while I'll hear him gabbling and going on and yelling, and I'll start trembling with the happiness of it all . . . In a little while he'll break all the china and take me to bed. And I'll feel something very very cool and nice just barely touching the deepest part of my life. And tickling me. And taking me to paradise. In a little while the smell of alcohol will wake me up out of this eternal distraction I'm in and say "Hello" to me. And push me onto the bed. In a little while. In a little while. In a little while.

"Let's start heading for bed, you kids, it's midnight already."

Once some representatives came—the old man doesn't remember what company they were from—with the idea of turning the farm into a sugarcane plantation. The offer, theoretically, was bona fide. The old man thought it was wonderful. Of course, the land had to be put into shape—it had to be surveyed, fenced, cleared. To afford that, the old man had to sell off practically all the cows. The representatives came in with a load of workmen, cut down all the trees (even the mangos and the guavas), and carried off the wood so there would be free rein for the tractors. "A tractor, a tractor . . ." marveled the old man. Then the representatives disappeared (after collecting for the work their men had done) and they never returned. The farm had been leveled—Not one tree, not one animal left. That time the old man threatened to set fire to the house and jump headfirst down the well. He sent letters, he threatened to sue. He walked to town, came back, went back to town again . . . But when was all this? During Machado's time? Batista's? Prío's? What difference did it make? Bad times all ran together in his memory. In his memory—him surrounded now by lamp chimneys, rotting fruit, and bars of guava paste—bad times, hard luck, disappointments, trials came and went. Came and went. But mostly came . . .

Here comes Tomasico looking for somebody to have a conversation with. I guess there's no help for it—I'll have to talk to him. Here he comes with that two-peso cigar of his and that belly that gets bigger every day. Brazen rascal. You think I'm going to believe that story of yours about how you started out selling guavas and by selling guavas you came to have this factory? Well, go sell somebody else that bill of goods. Nobody makes a small fortune selling guavas, or anything close to it. It's that guava you go to bed with every night, that's what made you, and what keeps you, I don't doubt. Don't tell *me* that in this town such-and-such a rich man got that way because he stole from so-and-so, or is still stealing, or because so-and-so stole from him before that. Manna doesn't fall from heaven just like *that*. As though I didn't know better . . .

"Hello, there, Polo."

I'm not answering . . . Oh, of course I ought to. After all, he's the best customer I've got, and the *only* one that never owes me so much as five centavos.

"How are you, Tomasico?"

"So-so, just so-so. No better than I look, anyways. A little perturbed. Waiting for a truckful of crate slats to come, and it doesn't seem to want to get here."

"I know how it is."

Always griping. Like he wanted to keep me from asking him for something. Me. The idea. As though I'd ask him for the time of day.

"So . . . And if it doesn't hurry up and get here I'm going to have to close the doors for at least a week. Maybe two."

"Whew. Quite a problem. And there's no other way to get them?"

"Oh, I'm sure there is. Cost you an arm and a leg, though. And I'm not one to be taken advantage of that way. I've worked too hard and I'm still working too hard for my money for somebody to think he can get rich off me."

"It's the truth."

I don't know what he was trying to tell me with that last mouthful he said. But I do know one thing—the only thing he knows how to do is act the bumbler and tell people his troubles. And me, here I sit, dying of starvation, but at least I feel better than he does, because I can at least say, "Well, bub, I'm screwed, and that's all there is to it. I'm starving to death and there's no way out of it." . . . I can say that, and that gets the whole load off my chest. I've griped myself clean.

"I won't pay more than ten pesos a thousand. That's plenty. You'll probably disagree, but you sit down and figure the costs any business has got, and you'll see—there's always more headaches than profits. It's always the same story. And then you're always the one that's got to solve everybody else's problems. And if the factory goes under someday, *you're* the one that gets made the scapegoat—everybody else, why man, they just go get a job somewhere else, what do they care. And it's over, so far as they're concerned."

"That's the truth. It certainly is."

I better think about something else before I take that belly and pop it. "That's the truth. The very gospel."

"And on top of that—I'm telling you this in confidence, now, d'you hear?—sales have really gone down. If things go on like they have been, which I'm pretty sure they're going to, I'm broke, bankrupt, swamped. I'm sunk."

"No!"

I wish, you jackass. Although I can't even be glad you're screwed, because then Fortunato will be left high and dry, and he'll be sitting in the house again getting underfoot all day or hanging on one of the vegetable-stand doorposts like he was before. You'd be ready to throw a bucket of boiling water at him to shoo him off.

"And how's my grandson doing in the factory?"

"Your grandson?"

"Fortunato."

"Oh, Fortunato. Well. . . . Well, I'm going to be frank with you, the boy's a worker, you say to him, 'Put this sack of slats over there,' and he'll do it. And you say to him, 'Peel me a thousand guavas,' and he'll peel them for you. But he's got no initiative. He's got no pep. If he doesn't smash his finger, his head hurts. Or he loses his hammer. But there's always something. Anyway—it's the young people, they've got no interest in working. I remember when I was eleven years old . . ."

Now he'll start in telling me the story of his childhood, and I'll have to sit here and listen to it all again and go "Uh-huh, uh-huh, uh-huh." Or "Uh-uh, uh-uh, uh-uh." Till he's good and ready to get up and stretch and go. But I know what I'll do—I'll think about something else while he's talking. I'll sit here and think about something else, and that way I can laugh at him on the inside. I'll be laughing at him, the great goose . . .

"By the time I was eleven . . ."

I'm laughing at you, you big sluggard. And you don't suspect a thing. I can say anything I want to without opening my mouth. I can wish you were dead without saying a word.

". . . I was already working like a dog."

Which is what you are, exactly what you are. But I'm not even going to pay any attention to what you're saying, you swindler. I'm laughing at you this very minute. I'm wishing you'd burst wide open right now, you toad.

"Like dogs, we all worked, me and my whole family."

What peace of mind to know nobody can ever guess what you're thinking. What peace of mind . . . You bullfrog!

"What do you see now?"

"Just a candle flame fluttering and hopping around."

"If you keep telling those stories I'm going to crack your skull wide open and call Grandma."

"But it's the truth. Look . . ."

Today there's such a sadness on my shoulders that I'm practically coming apart inside with it. It's like I wanted to cry. But I feel like it wouldn't go away even if I did. It's a feeling that I don't know where it came from, or how it landed on me, or when it plans to go away again. The saddest sadness, and it says, "Idiot. Any day now you'll be a thousand years old and you'll still be nailing boxes together in that rotten guava factory. You're a dummy. You're about to be an old man, and your life will have slipped right through your fingers. And you'll have no idea how or doing what. Your life will just have slipped away, as clean as *that*, and you won't even know what the word was supposed to've meant. Your life will have slipped away, and you just sitting there hammering and hammering and hammering.

"And life just easing away from you. While you hammer your thumb. Life zinging away out the window, or through the first chink it can find. And you smashing your thumb black and blue. You sticking nails in your fingers. While life oozes out the first crack it comes to. And you . . . Idiot. Idiot. Idiot."

And dinnertime comes and I still haven't come out of this blue funk I'm in. Grandma serves up the food but I hardly eat, because this sadness just won't allow it. I look at the spoon and I feel like screaming. I look at these people, and I feel even more like screaming. I look over at the washstand, and I feel like crying. I don't know what it is, but even the *Brrrr, brrrr, brrrr* of the pigeons up on the roof sounds sad to me, telling me there's no way out anymore, and for me there never ever will be, ever. So I leave my dinner sitting there and I stand up nice and slow so nobody notices that I'm practically falling apart inside. And I walk out to the breeze-way like that, which here people call the porch. But I can't fall apart out on the porch, either, because Tico and Anisia are out there playing "Don't touch the ground," and if they see me crying the first thing they'll do is run off and tell everybody. So I play the idiot and stick my head in the cypress tree. And pretend I'm looking for something I hid there. And that's where I start sobbing real real softly. And I start forgetting about Tico and Anisia, so my sobbing starts getting louder and louder. And louder and louder. And then the animals come. And so I start dancing with the animals. And the animals practically shake themselves silly laughing. They take me by the arms and throw me up on the roof. And they pull me down again. And they carry me out to the backyard. And they hang me from the tree that had been cut down once already but that they had set up again. While meanwhile I kick and kick and kick.

But the wild animals are rolling around on the ground, watching how my tongue starts sticking out. Watching me turn all different colors. Watching how so as not to give up altogether I start laughing too, and I laugh and laugh and laugh. Practically howling. And everybody dancing. Everybody dancing. While I practically split my sides laughing . . .

But where's my mother? What's become of my mother? Where's my mother got off to? How can I have lost sight of my mother, my goal? . . . Somebody told me her story, and it's as sad as all the rest. My mother following a hen out into the stand of spiny locust trees. And my mother always dying out there in the brambles, losing that hen in the locust thicket. My mother always back there, or up ahead somewhere. In some other hell.

My Mother

After the rain you'd think the world had come to an end. Everything looks so pathetic that you'd wish you could walk around with your eyes closed so you wouldn't have to see anything. Or just see things you made up yourself. Or things you wish you could make up. But I can't close my eyes— Mama told me to follow that old hen, because you can bet anything you want to that she's laying eggs out in the locust thicket somewhere. So here I am getting all scratched up and tattered, like a wild mountain she-mule in among these brambles. And that shameless hen—you'd think she knew I was following her, she runs so fast. And sometimes she cackles and flaps around in the air two or three times. But I'm hot on her trail, even if it means my legs get scratched to pieces, because if I go back home empty-handed and tell my mother I lost the hen and couldn't find her nest, she'll pick up a stake and cudgel me. Even if I scratch myself to pieces and tear my dress, I've got to follow that blasted old hen . . . But she's not as blasted as I am—because at my age I've no call to be doing what I'm doing, or for things to be going like they're going. You take Nicanor Parra's daughters there, for example—they're no poorer than we are, or any richer either, for that matter, and do you think they'd be out in the middle of the bramble patch following some crazy hen? Hah! . . . Oh, but in *my* house I'm the pack mule. Onerica, do this, Onerica, do that, Onerica, come here, Onerica, go there. And I do it, though I don't know exactly why. And without a peep. Not a peep on the outside. I mean, since I'm saddled and bridled, I may as well let them ride. And besides—if I didn't it'd just be all the worse, because then I'd have to spend the livelong day listening to Mama picking at me and scolding and grumbling and Polo calling me a lazy slut. My blood boils (though nobody can see it) every time my father calls me a lazy slut. I don't know why. But my blood boils. Mama calls me one name after another, and it's like water off a duck's back. But my father can look at me and say, "Lazy slut," and I feel like my life is so miserable that I might as well jump down the well—though nobody would ever guess it. What misery! And on top of that, to have to be taking care of my sister Digna, because Adolfina does nothing but water the plants and mop the parlor floor. Waiting, and waiting, and waiting . . . You'd think life was no more than one long wait. That's why I refuse to live—I'm not waiting for *anybody*, not me. Up here, cooped up here on this mountain, who's going to come for me? Who's going to come take me out of this locust-tree thicket? Who, I ask you? But Adolfina is such an optimist she spends her whole life planting a chinaberry tree over here and sticking a picket fence over there around the flowers so the cows don't come in and eat them. Or trample them. Carrying water and white-clay dirt to dust the floor with, with her bare hands, putting ashes around the morning glories so the ants don't eat the bark off the stalks, or watering the shower-of-gold . . . It breaks my heart how people can fool themselves so. It breaks my heart to see her, in the dry times, which is most of the time around here, how she carries water up from the ravine to slosh on the floor to mop with. And then to watch her sit out there in that breezeway full of wasps, waiting for somebody to come by. Poor thing . . . And sometimes the wasps eat her alive. Her face swells up so, it scares you. And even like that, with her face swelled up like a watermelon, she'll go and change clothes, get all powdered up so she looks like a cockroach that's been in the flour, and go sit out in the breezeway again, to wait. And Mama, the thick-headed old biddy, out there muttering in the kitchen—"If women to-day've got no better idea than *that* how to keep their places, little wonder nobody'll show them any respect or even look at them a second time—the more painted up the less men around—and I'd rather have my daughter dead than have her . . ." Going on and on and on like that, muttering and grumbling. And Adolfina turning old, sitting out there in the breezeway. The wasps dropping down on top of her hair burned red from all the sun it gets when she carries up the water to pour on the floor. Adolfina turning older and older, just sitting in the breezeway. And Mama out there grumbling in the kitchen . . . What a fate is mine!— I've lost the hen. I'd be better off dying than going home and telling Mama.

Dear son
I pray God
when you get this letter
you are
fine.

I was sitting on a rock crying, out in the middle of the locust thicket. I was wishing I'd hurry up and make up my mind to die, so I could get up and go down to the river and jump in . . . I was crying, and I had already forgotten that it was getting on to be night. I had even forgotten why it was I was in the middle of the locust thicket crying.

All of a sudden I heard twigs cracking nearby.

WHO WAS IT

I was just sitting there. When Misael comes up to me, sweating all over.

"Woman, what are you doing out here all by yourself?"

"I was following a hen."

And before I knew what to think, Misael had my arms

pinned to my sides behind a locust tree, and he was squeezing and rubbing up against me. How could I ever have imagined that he of all people—because, why, everybody felt like he was practically part of the family, because he had worked ten years or more for Polo—that he of all people would be capable of doing such a thing to me? He had practically been raised with me . . . And such a thing had never entered my mind.

You just dissolve inside from happiness. You tremble when you see that. You see yourself for the first time, and so it's like seeing everything for the first time. And you forget everything, for the first time in your life . . .

Now all I can hear is your panting, and your hard breathing . . . Now those locust trees come back to me, and I can feel how they scraped my backside, and I can hear the way those blasted crickets were shrieking. And I feel like myself again. But it's like now there was no salvation. I don't think there's any salvation for me anymore.

Now all there is is your heavy breathing.

"Adolfina! Adolfina! I tell you I can't hold it anymore!"

The first time, as soon as I could get up and I saw him with his pants still down around his ankles, I ran off like a wild woman for home. But the next day I didn't run. I didn't move a step. And we stayed there a long time—both of us naked as could be in the middle of that locust thicket. Not even thinking that anybody could come through that way and see us. Not even thinking.

"Believe it or not. Now the only thing I see is a little girl littler than you are, drowning in a dry bathtub."
"How stupid."

And we both wander off naked through that locust thicket, and now it's almost night. Dark night.

"What now?"
"Now the smoke has blotted everything out."
"Fibber. Why don't I hear anybody coughing, then?"

The moon looks like it's gotten snagged on something behind the clouds. And can't get loose. We take advantage of
its getting snagged like that to stroll around for a little while
through the locust thicket. Naked, the both of us. The moon
finally gets unhooked. And we take advantage of its getting
unhooked and floating out of the clouds, and we lie down on
the dry bed of leaves the locust trees have dropped.

Tell me
whether you get
plenty to eat
every day.

What would people say if they saw us walking around
naked in the middle of the pasture? My lord! and with that
big fat moon hanging up there in the sky . . . What on earth
would people say if they saw us like this, naked and walking
around with our clothes in our hands? Virgen santísima, if
you don't feel like forgiving me, then don't. I couldn't care
less anymore.

The water little by little slides through my legs till it gets
up to my shoulders. The water is cold and it's full of all
different colors from the light. Misael walks over to me, with
the water up to his knees. Misael naked . . . And I look at
him a second, but then I feel terribly embarrassed. So I dive
in. And under the water I start laughing. Misael naked.

"Just imagine, now that halfwit has taken it in his head to
make toilet water out of rue leaves. And he's got the poor
rue plant looking so pathetic that it breaks my heart. You've
seen what a demon that boy is. Instead of running after the
women . . ."

He waited until no one was in the
kitchen. He ran to the table and pried
the lid off the can. And he started eating
crackers as the tears welled in his eyes.

I start eating crackers while these tears roll down my face, right out of my eyes. I'm crying out of rage, goddammit, and I can't stop eating crackers, because any minute now they'll come in and hide the can from me. I'm crying from sheer rage at seeing that there's nothing I can do to make things better, even for myself. You'd think the world would just come to an end. It ought to, if it knew what was right. Somebody ought to drop an atomic bomb, and put an end to it. Any day now I'll be seventeen years old, and then what's there to live for anymore. Seventeen years old and mashing my fingers to a pulp for two stinking coins to rub together. And having to listen to the griping and grumbling and backbiting of these damned bitter women . . . Shit! I'm going to sit down this minute and write my mother and tell her to send for me right now. I'll wash dishes, I'll sell newspapers on the corner, I'll sweep the street. Anything. But I can't stand another month in this house. Oh no . . .

"Eating crackers again! You ought to be ashamed of yourself, you glutton! You inconsiderate pig! So big and such a halfwit. You never think about anybody else."

I'm leaving, I'm leaving, I'm leaving I'm leaving I'm leaving I'mleavingI'mleavingI'mleavingI'm . . .

This time I'm leaving. You want to bet? You'll see!

"How inconsiderate! The crackers we all have to eat. That was for us all. Get out of here, get to work. *Do* something."

Cock-a-doodle-doo. Cock-a-doodle-doooooo.

Grapáck. Grapáck. Grapáck. Grapáck.

I'm leaving. Oh, not really?! Uh-huh, I'm leaving. Aaah— what a yawn, excuse me. Yay! He's leaving. At last! You don't say—you suppose he's taken into account the suffering that'll give his grandmother? She'll probably die of it. Yes, oh yes, he's thought of it, that's why he's doing it. Oooh—what an inconsiderate, ungrateful, thankless child. Oooh—such patches on those pants. Ave María santísima—the patches have taken over the whole pair of pants. But he looks dimwitted.

I'm leaving.

I'm leaving.

Look at him.

"But you come home at this hour? And without finding that

nest? You ought to be whipped with a fencepost. You ought to
be turned into kindling. You goose."

You silly turkey.
You simpleton.
You idiot.
You halfwit.
You piece of meat with an eye stuck in it.
You heifer.
So old and such a goose!
Crazy as a loon!
You ought to just die.
You're no daughter of mine.
Get out of here this minute and find that hen.
Always up in the clouds somewhere.
Always out woolgathering somewhere.
Always a little touched in the head.
She-mule.
Where the devil have you been all this time?
Ay, shit!
Tra-la-la-la-la. Tra-la-la-la-la-la-*laaaaa*.

At first she herself didn't really know what was happening.
She would grow tired more quickly as she hauled water up
from the well. She would feel a little dizzy. She would suddenly feel terribly, terribly sad, and then other times she
would be so happy she would be tempted to jump up and
hang from a tree branch and swing. Even into the second
month she couldn't quite put her finger on what was happening to her. Something was changing. But those little pains
that came over her periodically, that stream of blood that she
had never understood—that no one had ever bothered to explain to her—had gone away . . . So it was only later, at around
six months, that she realized, though she still could hardly
believe it, that she was pregnant. And at that point she began
to do what she believed ought to be done in a case such as
this, to abort the child. Instead of two, she would carry four
cans of water. She would hop on one foot. She would climb
the cherry tree and swing down on one of its limbs. She would

drink all the concoctions she heard mentioned (in the conversations she herself brought around to the subject) that might serve her ends. But no luck. She achieved no results whatever. Her belly went on growing. Her legs began to swell. And she started getting pimples all over her face. At night, while the others slept, she would frantically pummel that bulge she carried. And she went on doing that, all through the night, to the rhythm of the others' breathing and the croaking of the frogs out in the yard. Sometimes the dawn would break and she would still be pummeling herself . . . And still she swelled, and went on swelling . . . And all her efforts were futile. It was then that, desperate, she saw at last that she could not avoid her fate, though what she could do was cover it up. And to that end she made herself a burlap garment like a corset, and she bound it so tight around her midsection that as she made her trips down to the well she felt—with joy, almost—that from one moment to the next she might be asphyxiated. For a while her desperation was so fierce that she actually convinced herself—sometimes for a few moments, but sometimes for days on end—that she was dreaming, that none of this was true, and that if it was, it certainly wasn't happening to *her*. And she would cry, out behind the chinaberry tree. And several times—out behind the chinaberry tree—she swore to hang herself, and then she would try to smother herself by holding her nose and refusing to open her mouth. Several times, she tried that. And several times she was on the verge of victory. But then somebody would always kick, somebody would call, somebody (there inside) would weakly protest. And so then, red-faced, sweating, she would open her mouth and gasp for air. And her belly would regain its rhythm, its orderly throb. It was around that time—perhaps she had only a few days to go—that she became suddenly beautiful. The blotches and pimples vanished from her face. Her blood began flowing as it had before, her skin grew smooth and taut, shining, white, and her eyes took on an extraordinary hue—sweet-violet. Her hair, which till then had rebelled in wiriness, grew straighter, softer, obedient to her fingers as they played with it in surprise and delight. Everything about her took on a calm, a kind of fullness of being, a plenitude derived from a mysterious saturation, a sort of triumph . . . At home she was watched resentfully— her family understood none of this, nor asked (nor gave themselves) any explanation, though they felt, in some sense that they could not understand either, betrayed. Celia would say that she was pale, Digna that she had gained weight, Jacinta that she was more dimwitted than ever, Polo that she was more slovenly. Only Adolfina, who had a little suspicion of the truth, a little fear, a little envy, would look at her and groan. And so Onerica managed to hide her pregnancy until the very day of the laying in . . . That day, just as the sun was rising, the labor pains began. At first she stood them, but then she began to softly moan. At last she threw herself to the floor in the parlor, screaming. The old woman ran back and forth almost hysterically, carrying a pot of wormwood tea (to settle her bowels), or a towel. But Onerica, now in her own bed, went on writhing, and her wails grew louder and louder. That afternoon, when Polo came in from the fields, Onerica was kicking the walls, yelling, frothing at the mouth; her face was paper-white from her bleeding. "What now?" Polo said. "Lord knows," Jacinta responded as she stirred up a batch of rue tea and poured hot water over ironweed for a bath for her. "It's got to be some hex." "You and your hexes can go to the devil," the old man spat, splashing his feet in the washtub. "Some of that garbage of yours you call food is what's got her insides all torn up." "You savage," the old woman muttered, poking up the cookstove. The old man, who had had to wrestle a calf practically to the death that afternoon, removed his feet from the water and picked up the washtub to dump it on the old woman's head. And the old woman by this time had a burning piece of firewood firmly in her grasp. But at that moment a noise—a noise they had never in their wildest dreams expected to hear—began to fill the house. It was the loud, terrified crying of a newborn baby. The old man's hand went to his waist for his machete. The old woman stood there, holding the brand aloft. Digna and Celia, who were shelling corn out in the cornpress, ran in with their mouths agape. Adolfina, in the dining room, threw down her sewing scissors and groaned, and then she let a burst of laughter escape her. And everyone ran for the bedroom.

And so Fortunato was born.

And Misael ran off that very day and not a hair of his head was seen thereabouts for a long, long time.

And so Fortunato was born.

And Mama held the baby up as high as she could and showed it to Papa.

And Papa said, Kill it, kill it.

And Mama said, I can't—kill it yourself.

And so he said, Hand it here.

And so I jumped out of bed and screamed, Wild beasts! Wild beasts! And then I got back into bed.

And I could hear how the frogs outside were going *Nrrrr, nrrrr, nrrrr.*

Louder and louder. And softer and softer.

And I closed off my ears to everything else and just listened to the frogs.

And Fortunato was crying and crying and crying.

And so Adolfina then came to the baby's defense.

And Adolfina said, If you kill it I'm burning this house down with every one of you in it. You wait till you're asleep. You'll see. I'll burn you all up.

And the old man, it looked like he wanted to hit Adolfina.

And so Adolfina picked up the kitchen knife.

And Mama started praying and screaming and carrying on.

And by now I was practically asleep again.

And Mama still praying.

And Adolfina swooped down on Papa with the kitchen knife.

And so Papa put the baby down on the floor and ran for the mountain.

And the baby crying and crying and crying.

And the old woman was cursing now and she got down on her knees right in the middle of the parlor.

And he was up on that mountain for close to a year.

And she started praying the Credo.

And those frogs going *Grnrrr, grnrrr, grnrrr,* as hard as they could go.

And I couldn't go to sleep or stay awake either.

And Adolfina leaned up against the closet for the water crocks and started sobbing and crying and carrying on.

And I felt like crying too.

And so Mama then came into the bedroom and said, Who is the father?

And I said, I don't know.

And the wild beasts had laid that baby down on the table and he was crying and crying and crying.

And the wild beasts would play with the baby—they would tickle and goo and try to make him laugh.

And that baby on the table screaming and kicking.

I said to myself, It breaks your heart, he's so little and he's already having such a hard time of it . . .

And Mama said to me, You have to know who the father is.

And I said, No.

And so she said, Whore Whore Whore—you, what you ought to be is dead.

And that baby bawling and crying.

And my pain started again.

And so finally I could let it out and cry, but real real softly, so you could just barely hear it.

And the frogs were still gabbling and croaking.

And I thought, Those frogs know how to make themselves heard, all right.

And I thought, Those frogs, they're probably happy.

And so I thought, A person ought to be a frog.

And I thought . . .

And Mama got down on her knees.

And the old man disappeared up on the mountain.

And so Fortunato grew.

And me trying to get the papers fixed so I could leave.

And the wild beasts and the demons slapping me in the face.

And so here I am, not speaking any English.

And the pain crept higher and higher and higher, like a little brown spider.

And the hen just will not show her face.

And night caught me up there in the middle of the mountain.

And the beasts tickling me.

And me writing and writing and writing, and nobody answering me.

And me taking care of spoiled brats.

And me saying goodbye to Fortunato.

And there always just being barely enough food to go around.

And everybody else but me with the right to make demands on people, ask favors, take advantage of people.

And so I had to leave Fortunato. Abandon him.

And me trying to sleep.

And me trying to find the way out of that house.

And me . . .

And that baby crying.

And me so happy I'm almost crazy.

And me, Oh lord, how happy I am.

And that baby crying.

And that baby crying.

Crying.

Every day Fortunato wakes up dead, up on the roof of the house, with pigeons roosting on top of him. Every day, it's always the same story—that white cloud of pigeons that flies off the minute I go Cheep cheep, *and then Dead-Fortunato gets up on his feet.*

—Them

THE FOURTH
AGONY

But yes it could, it could dry out. That vine was dried out and withered by the unending smell of rotten guava mash that hung about the house, in the air. It was withered by shrill voices, hunger, the never-ending squabbles and racket. It was withered by nights of Fortunato's futile wandering. It was withered by this new inferno so terrible and so violent that it left room for no further dreams or evocations. The vine was dried out by the constant letters from his mother, the uninterrupted grumbling and muttering of his grandmother. It was dried out by all the things he did not know, the unknown things which therefore pushed him on, and yet which paradoxically pressed down on him so hard that they asphyxiated him—the uncertain future, and the certainty on the other hand that if there were someone watching over him, a guardian angel perhaps who could make or change his fate, it was someone watching over him precisely so as *not* to let him escape. The vine's shining green leaves were perishing, withering, they were growing blackened and shriveled by the burning, shimmering-hot street one had always obligatorily to cross, by the fiber-cement roof one had always obligatorily to live under. Its sweet-smelling tiny white flowers were falling, falling, a shower like snow that melted straightaway into steam, so quickly they disappeared under his constant bursts of anger and resentment at his own powerlessness, his own impotence, under his constant bursts of fury at the impossibility of escape. And the vine's perfume and the murmuring of its leaves now mingled horribly with the deafening racket of wheels and pulleys and the acrid piercing smell of the guava jelly that seemed to have flooded the world . . . Get out of bed. Pull on stinking shoes, *quick*, at some ungodly hour before dawn, and then pull on a pair of stinking pants. Splash a little water on your face. And run to where the crate ends, crate slats, and little nails are kept, so you can start hammering them together. Make a thousand crates that day. So as not to starve to death. To get that peso. Hammer, hammer, hammer. And every *tck* of the hammer—sometimes a person missed and hit a finger, or even a hand—was a blow to the trunk of that lovely, sweet-smelling, shining green vine that grew and grew and covered the whole house. At every *tck* of the hammer that plant shuddered, shook, and a shower of leaves and white flowers disappeared into the vat the guava jelly bubbled in. And at last, when the boiler freed itself of its heat and steam and blew out its hissing whirlwind-cloud, it utterly blotted out the plant's silhouette; and when it passed, when the valves were closed and the steamcloud had melted away, all that was left was the skeleton of that great vine, still smoking—and reeking of rotten guavas . . . But listen, if it hadn't been the factory, or the work, or the sun, then the times when the rains dragged on forever or refused to come at all, or the chain of hurricanes one after another battering down everything in their path, or the (apparently) natural human tendency to wipe out every trace of green would have killed the great green sweet-flowering vine anyway. And if not those things, then some other hell would have come along. He knew that. He knew it. In spite of his desperate efforts to hold on to even one branch or tendril of it, one leaf, that scar on its trunk out of which the sap sometimes dripped and ran, one tight-furled bud (which probably, which *surely*, now would not be given the time to bloom), he knew that that place, that landscape, that *consolation* (which of course was probably in the final analysis just another sort of prison, magnified and made beautiful now by recollection), all of that was irrecoverable. As irrecoverable as that now-remote past and as unreachable as the life he had before him. Now that he knew they were lost, even the most disgusting, hated places became sweet, loved, venerated. Now, as he got to his feet and ran again, though he could barely keep himself upright, he understood (he *saw*) that *any* place is to be preferred to having no place at all, to being always in someone else's power, to being able to count on not even a tiny, burning place of one's own where one could be alone with one's own, personal ill luck. Now, at this instant—the fly buzzing once more on his nose (that fly so like him, wanting to possess a place all its own)—everything conspired to show him how much meanness, pettiness, and futility this present time held, if the mere act of remembering a past (almost equally crippling and detestable) was enough to keep us alive, sustain us. And so he ran. Now everything was clear. He ran. Now everything was unbearable. He ran. Now everything became a symbol, an allegory—even this stupid race he was running—a crabbed and miserly augury which was so obvious that there was no need even to interpret it. And as though all this weren't enough, he'd once had a dream: He and two women were walking through a stand of trees toward the house, up in the country. At first he didn't recognize the two women, talking as they walked along beside him. But then he saw that one of them was his mother and the other, one of his aunts—though he had so many that in the dream he couldn't remember her name . . . They were coming back home through the trees, back home to the house in the country after living for many years in the city. They were only coming back for a visit, though, across land which no longer belonged to them. To a house with a new owner. His aunt's hair was long and yellow (*bright* yellow—fake, no doubt) and she was talking to his mother. They were talking about the way he was dressed. The whole conversation turned on a pair of pants he was wearing and which, according to his aunt, were too tight—they had to burn them. His aunt put great stress on that— they had to burn the pants—she came back to the point again and again, she insisted. His mother nodded, though he couldn't quite make out her words. They were walking through the trees near the house in the country, the place of his childhood, and yet time and time again, quite often, under a custard-apple tree, or up in the branches of a mountain plum or in the top of a palm, or hidden among the leaves of a manzanillo, he would come upon a group of people he knew, people who had never before been in this place he was walking through now. People he had met in the street, or in his grandfather's fruit and vegetable stand, in the factory, workers, guava-paste peddlers, hideous shrieking public school "misses"—people that life had forced him into contact with, people he had had to deal with every day, say hello to, even make friends with. His mother and his aunt went on about his pants—he couldn't recall now which pair it had been—that had to be burned, and his aunt (perhaps for spite, most probably out of sheer unmitigated spite) would shriek even louder and more shrilly each time they passed close by one of those awful groups of people, who would stand or sit there rigid, self-assured, and look at him, as though they had been born to be sitting up in or standing under those trees—taking his measure with their censuring eyes, grotesquely inquisitive, prying, smug and mocking. At last he and the two women came to the yard. The new owners of the house had abandoned it, boarded up its doors. But from the outside everything looked just as it always had before. And he stood there motionless, looking at it, that enormous pile of palm branches and palm thatch and boards cut from palm trees, all of which the sun, the wind, the rain had faded into gray. His mother and his aunt discussed whether they should go in. If I go in there, he said to himself, I'll die. Apparently his mother and his aunt did not hear; they opened themselves a little hole in the thatched walls and disappeared inside like two great curious rats. He stood there looking. Now there were no weeds or grass around the house, just perhaps the shade of some tree he could not quite find. For a while he stood there outside, remembering. From time to time he heard distant explosions, hollow, rumbling, monotonous. What sense did this return make? What was there in that house where he had spent his childhood? Was it possible that he had been happy there, and that only now that it was all gone—and utterly irrecoverable—he was to be allowed to see that, to recognize it? But happiness lies in the moment it is lived, not in the moment at which it's later recollected. For if not, he thought, then everything is a great joke, a fraud, a hoax, a trick, and no happiness exists at all. And suddenly, looking at that great sprawling ramshackle house with its smoke-blackened roof and its frondless palm-leaf thatch (for the animals ate the thatch away) where a gust of wind blowing down the breezeway banged a sheet of tin that was almost falling off the roof, he saw himself now—big, ridiculous, a man—and he could not contain his laughter at thinking that just moments earlier he had had the nerve to use—even with reservations—the word "happiness." Big and stupid and ridiculous—again a faraway report—in a house which no longer belonged to him, which never had belonged to him . . . There, *there* was the place that childhood had mythicized. The hollow where the dishwater made a loblolly (he had launched a boat there once), the enormous cookstove patted by hand together out of white clay and ashes (he had roasted a sweet potato there once), the great cornpress made with palm boards (he had started a business there once, a stable, and once it had even been a corral for guinea pigs). And he saw, or once again confirmed, an axiom: The worth of the place we once lived in is not implicit in the place itself, but in the kind of life we lived there . . . What if he went in? What if he suddenly pushed aside those palm fronds, as his mother and his aunt had done (who, by the way, had not yet reappeared), and went into the house? What if he walked once again through the kitchen, saw the great dining room, and even climbed up on the long dining table? Maybe then, maybe then . . . because if there was one thing he was sure of, it was that even if in all the places that had come afterwards, or that were imposed on him afterwards, he had left, as everyone did, a part of his life, this place was the only one worth remembering, calling up in his mind, *invoking*, the only place which in spite of all, or because of it, was worth reconstructing, reinhabiting. And what if he should climb up and dance on the roof of the house, peek into the corner room—hens roosted up there on the roof, rats ran along the ridgepole and over the thatch, spiderwebs and wasps' nests lurked—where his cousin Eulogia, the cousin no one remembers, had taught him to blow smoke out his eyes! And what if he ran over to the well, and looked up again at the sooty kitchen ceiling! Wouldn't he be saved? Saved forever? And so he looked again at the great bristling, crackling, ramshackle house of palm boards and stripped-bare palm thatch—*it still exists, it still exists!*—and he pushed some thatch aside to squeeze through, and he ducked in. Quickly he came into the kitchen. But something had happened there. They had cut the kitchen in half. The new owners, no doubt with a view to expending less energy, to moving about less (a practical family), had raised a wall which cut the room to half its previous size, so that the cookstove was no longer its center but now was rather up against that wall; it was impossible now to walk around it as before, to chase someone around it, to jump over it. And to make things worse, the stove itself was no longer the same cookstove. It was now a common piece of kitchen equipment—made of bricks, tin sheets, and cement. He immediately left the kitchen and went into the dining room, a small room now, almost totally taken up by half of the old long table (for they had cut it in two) around which there barely fitted (and then only because they were pushed close up to its edge) six short stools of the sort whose seat fitted under the table, leaving only the backs shoved up to the table. And when he saw this, he felt like running into the parlor. But one no longer got to the parlor through a linked chain of breezeways with their rain gutters; now there was a wooden hallway with doors opening onto small useless bedrooms. Before he stepped into the hall he stopped. He felt he was being smothered, asphyxiated, that this was not the house, that obviously he had somehow been tricked. He made an effort to go on, even to run, but now there began to break out all down his arms, all across his chest, a rash, an armoring of prickles, a carapace of unutterably harsh gooseflesh which spread so quickly that in seconds he could barely move a muscle. He looked over at the table—there were thousands of tiny frogs, but not frogs exactly, either, tiny gray animals, rather, likewise mailed and armored with bumps and ridges, and they were hopping heavily, sometimes to fall and land upside down, there to lie immobile, contracted and contorted in a sort of *rigor mortis* into pitiful positions. He was forgetting something. Something, at that moment, was slipping from his memory, and yet it was, he knew, the only thing that could save him. He remembered to look up to the ceiling. Surely up there everything would still be the same. Look up at the ceiling, see the smoke-blackness clinging to the ridgepole, the great spiderwebs, the wicker hamper suspended there that kept rats and mice out of the vegetables (and would there still be bats way up there in the dark?)—but again, he was forgetting something. What should he do? What was it? And his carapace went on swallowing his body, it was reaching his face, it was petrifying him completely, and his eyes now could only look straight ahead, down the long narrow hall with useless doors like sentinels frozen forever at attention. He remembered—look up at the ceiling, go into Eulogia's room, run into the parlor, climb the trees in the yard. They'd all leave, they'd all have to go if he took full possession again. But the walls of the house were closing in now, his suit of mail was constricting his throat, and so weighted down was he by his coat of metal nails, his armor and helmet, and so rigidly was he fixed there, that he could only look at those walls rushing in upon him, like some nightmarish vise. And as he was being asphyxiated, he thought he heard someone talking somewhere, in one of the narrow rooms nearby. Somebody—no, two people were talking a mile a minute, loudly and mindlessly, extolling the advantages of a cookstove with two burners (and here he thought he could stand no more of this), and praising small kitchens where "you didn't have to wear yourself out running back and forth all the time," their very words, to go to the table in the dining room, back to the kitchen, and back again. They went on chattering, gabbling, rattling away. And the walls inexorably moved inward on him, and the metal slag of his very body squeezed him tighter and tighter, pulled him downward, now buried him completely. But when the ga-ga-*boom* of the factory shocked him awake and he shook himself and looked about and saw himself under a roof of fiber cement, the two women were still gabbling shrilly and stupidly about lord knew what passing triviality. It was his mother and Adolfina remembering, as they poked through the charcoal ashes in the kitchen, and what a racket they were making of it all, dying laughing, remembering the horrors—now, thank God, past—perhaps to forget the horrors of the present . . . With his eyes now open, Fortunato followed the laughter and the clatter of the unburned pieces of charcoal as the two women poked among the ashes. With his eyes now open, he heard, farther off, that other deafening din of wheels and pulleys and steam valves opening to a hiss and a rushing whirlwind of steam. And with his eyes now open he stayed in bed a while as the hands he raised in the air under the mosquito net began to resemble claws and his face began to writhe into horrible grimaces. And one leg rose up, straight up, drew back, and kicked out at the mosquito net, which then tumbled down upon him, upon his open eyes, like a cloud given no time to wring itself out into water. He got up. The sun was still not up. But the

And to think it was all on account of a hen that got away . . .   —*Onerica*

clattering din next door grew in rhythmic speed and intensity by the second. He had to get dressed. He had to pull his shoes on, *quick*, and run grab his hammer, *quick*, a fistful of nails (all he could handle at once), the best sackful of crate ends, *quick*, before the others got there. Now he was out on the street . . . Oh, but who could resist, at that moment when day had not yet dawned and yet the night had passed, who could resist at that moment stretching a hand out into the void, raising it gracefully, lightly, then gently arching it just at the fingertips, and then, there, in the privacy of the dark, the mosquito net, perhaps wrapped only in the mosquito net, invoking a strange, foreign dance, a ballet, or emitting some shriek, some neigh, some baa, some brief death rattle perhaps, just as the sun came above the horizon . . . But he controlled himself, he left that plan in the air, suspended, postponed, and in silence he drew back the mosquito net, and in silence he began to dress, frustrated somewhat, still sleepy, drowsy, and, as always at that hour of the day, unconsciously aroused . . . Because there was that, too—Control yourself, reject, deny, avoid (moments before the sunrise) *that* feeling—which grew more insistent day by day and which furiously and undeniably, unavoidably, inevitably demanded its satisfaction. . . . There was that, too. Even now, at this moment when the *real* itching should have transported him to a stable reality free of foolishness and imaginings, even now, at this moment when the holes he'd been shot full of should have given him no chance to go off on tangents, no chance to think of dancing airy dances or making werewolf faces in the dark, even now at this moment there was *that*, tapping him on the shoulder, interrupting this great event that at last was happening to him, *the only real thing in all my life*, when he was trying so hard to sing, hop along on one toe, claw his own eyes out. Oh, to sing that song he'd heard his grandmother sing—*what* song?, how absurd—as at the same time, with the most delicate yet firm insistence, little pebbles were popping against his chest. Now, now, now, Lord, *that* itching would come back. Even now, when he was practically brushing the ground with his cheek. Wasn't this, then, the perfect moment to begin to sing in that voice of a Valkyrian contralto —the stones and pebbles, like snare drums, popping against his

chest—that lovely, lovely song? Now. At this very moment.
Right now.

The Life of the Dead

I've been wandering around out here looking for my dead cousin
Esther a long time. And little by little I start recognizing that
I'm underwater. And touching things that don't exist. I go back
to the house I lived in when I was a child. Who'd I ever have
believed if they'd told me how things can change? . . . Who'd I
ever have believed if they'd answered my question whether a
person always stays the same or whether a person is always
changing?

The dead man is looking for his dead cousin. Touching things
that don't exist because *he* doesn't. There ought to be a law
against people looking at the things they looked at when they
were boys and girls. There ought to be a law against people dying
and going on living. There ought to be a law against people sitting
on the stool they sat on when they were boys and girls. . . . Now
everything is so different. Now it's like things are all deformed.
Now I see that time is truly lost forever. I'm looking at myself
and I feel like it can't be. I look at you strolling along under the
soursop trees and on top of the branches of the tamarind tree. I
see you stay up on a branch a while and then drop off, and land
in one of the corners of the kitchen. I see you. I see you . . . I see
you stand for a while over by the cookstove, and then grope your
way into the dining room and then grope your way into the parlor.
I see you. Listen to how they're talking about you in the parlor.
Listen to them talking . . . "It was a long time ago," they're
saying. "He left, and we said, Well, if he left, it's because he's
dead. But that was a long time ago. Now, probably, we'd figure
it was something else . . ." Those are just "those ideas" of yours.
Those are just "those ideas" of mine. Those are just "those ideas"
of myours. If you open your eyes now, you won't see anybody in
the parlor. And nobody'll take your arm. And nobody'll say, Sit
down, child. And nobody'll tell you a story. And nobody'll say,
Sit down, child, here, sit down. And nobody'll fuss at you, or
scold you, or make you mind. The only person here with you is

Nobody, and that's why you feel so safe, and so protected. These are just your imaginings, these are just my imaginings. There's nobody. It's the Nobodies. Go ahead, if you want to. You can go into the breezeway, and past the breezeway there's the yard, you can go out into the yard, and there are the chicken coops, and the corral for the cows that died of the whatever-it-was. Out there you know is the edge of the world. Out there is your cousin, sitting on the fence. I make a sign to her and she opens the gate for me, at a twitch of her unreal finger. I make a little sign at her that's just barely a sign, and the fence goes *Psssssh* and like magic it opens of its own accord. Now we can walk out to the cornfield.

Hand in hand we'll go, my dear cousin, to see whether it's true that the mint plants are still alive. To kill a grub or two if we find some. And to play hide-and-seek, like we were still kids. Like we were still.

The fair—like almost every fair—is held once a year, in the main open field near the hamlet. For the grown-ups, the fair offers the Ferris wheel, the Octopus, the Meteor, the Rotor, the Hammer, the Airplanes of Love, and a shooting gallery; the roller coaster is too unwieldy to bring to these out-of-the-way places. For the children, there is the carousel, or "merry-go-round," as the children are taught to call it, with the organ in the middle whose music can be heard through the whole fair, and the little boats, the pony ride, and the bumper cars. For young and old alike, the fair offers the spectacle of a woman with long blond hair who climbs up to the top of a tower and dances on a tiny platform high above on one foot, does acrobatic tricks, holds on to a rope with nothing but her teeth, and finally, after dangling by her hair, leaps into space— landing, in a brilliant bathing suit of sequins and spangles, safe and sound on the ground . . . The fair, of course, is the most marvelous event celebrated in all that region. Everyone goes. Everyone dances, flirts, pinches, drinks—or at least mills endlessly about the grounds. Everyone has to move, and to look, to gape in wonder. Starting six or seven months ahead, the preparations for going to the fair begin: men save some of their harvest money to buy something new to wear—

a pair of pants or spurs—and to have the rest to spend; girls fatten a hog, sell their turkeys, or, if they are even poorer, they weave straw chair seats or pick guavas to sell to buy themselves a dress or a pair of shoes. Every young person must, for the fair, have something brand new to wear. The men, self-assured, scrubbed to a shine, greet each other with strange, grand gestures, showing off their gold watches, their new hats. The girls, with great shoulder pads, new dresses and shoes, deep white purses, suddenly take on an exotic air— perhaps because all week they have been rubbing their skin (their arms, legs, and faces, at least) with white-clay earth and lemon juice. Even the old folks are capable of selling a heifer so they can buy themselves a new pair of false teeth to wear to the fair. A great public, pagan festival. A fiesta. The fair is the granting of a wish, the culmination of a wait, the only real opportunity these people have to show themselves off, to satisfy that eminently human need. . . . Everyone is there. They wheel and turn, they dance, they ride their rearing horses, they argue, they drink, they smile—some of them have fist fights and some of them slap their children. But everyone is there. Showing off, strutting, strolling, waiting, hoping, searching. And the organ music swells. The music.

There I was being bored silly at the fair.
There I was with my feet killing me.
There I was so tired I could have dropped.
There I was, dying, I was so bored.
There I was, wishing I could die.
Thinking.
Thinking that nobody had asked me so much as to have a bite of something sweet with him.
Thinking I must look like the yolk of an egg in this yellow dress.
Thinking it would soon be sun-up.
Thinking that no man had asked me to dance yet.
Thinking that now nobody would, either.
Thinking that I'd wind up a dried-up old maid.
Thinking that nobody in our family would ever get married.

Thinking about Adolfina.

Thinking about Onerica.

Thinking about Celia.

Thinking about myself.

Thinking that now there was no way out.

Thinking that I left the starch sitting out to cool in the stand of wild pineapple.

Thinking that the dew would fall on the little starch we've got for all the clothes in the house.

Thinking that tomorrow would be Monday.

Thinking that Monday we had to wash all the clothes.

Thinking that then it would be Tuesday and then Wednesday and then, and then, and then, and then.

And.

The organ music playing and playing and playing.

And people dancing and dancing and dancing.

And me like a soul in limbo over in a corner somewhere.

And me watching the other girls having a good time.

And me thinking that it was all Mama's fault for not letting me give myself a home permanent.

And me wishing Mama was dead.

And me laughing on the outside in case anybody was looking at me.

And me with my mouth dry.

And nobody asking me to have so much as a snow-cone with him.

And me with my feet all swollen.

And nobody asks me to dance even if they step on my toes.

And now nobody even looks at me.

And nobody asks me to dance.

And nobody flirts with me.

And nobody even yells, "I wish you'd get hit by a lightning bolt!"

And nobody so much as notices that I'm alive.

And nobody gives me so much as a slap in the face.

So then

I went out beyond where the fair was, into the field.

So then the organ music sounded so, so sad to me.

So then I realized, as I watched those people going around

and around and smiling, that I didn't have any claws to grab on to life with, like other people did.

So then I realized that without claws, it's impossible to survive.

So then I realized that I was dying.

So then it sounded like the organ was crying.

So then I started to cry, too.

So then the organ and I are crying our eyes out.

So then I felt like the world was coming to an end and I realized that a woman alone is nothing, that a person without another person simply does not exist.

And then, without realizing it, I stepped in a mud puddle.

And then I muddied up my hands real good, too.

And then I ran my hands over my face.

And then I walked on my hands and knees in it.

And then I gave a scream louder than the organ.

And then I mewed like a cat in heat.

And then I broke out laughing.

And then I lay down in that mud puddle.

And then I rolled in that mud puddle.

And then I started crying, a whole lot softer than the organ.

And then I saw how sad everything was.

And then I saw an owl fly over way way high up and curse me.

And then I got up and started walking around again.

And then I started dancing, all by myself, in the middle of the road.

And

then along came Moisés.

And he said, What's wrong with you?

And I said, Nothing.

And he said, *Some*thing's wrong with you.

And I said, No, nothing.

And he said, You look like a sow in a pigsty.

And I said, Your mother's a sow.

And he said, Don't you say anything about my mother, who's dead, may she rest in peace.

And I said, I don't care if she's dead—I am too.

And he said, Well *I* care—you sow!

And so I slapped him with my muddy hand.
And then he slapped me.
And so I slapped him again.
And he slapped me.
And I slapped him.
And he slapped me.
And he slapped me.
And he slapped me.
And he slapped me.
And he slapped me.
And I started crying, I was so happy.
And we walked all through that field of grass.
And then we went out into a canefield.
And we didn't do anything in the canefield.
And the music of the organ had stopped crying by then.
And the music of the organ was just music.
And the music of the organ, you couldn't even hear it anymore.
And I said to myself, You are Digna.
And I said to myself, You are being born, Digna.
And I said to myself, You're being born, being born.
And then we got up on the road again.
And we went back to the dance.

"Polo! This is the limit! This is the straw that broke the camel's back! Adolfina's been locked up in that bathroom for better than two and a half hours already, and there's no way to budge her. So you go see what *you* can do, because I've done all I can do. And stop playing deaf with me, you old coot, because I know you can hear—and hear plenty! What it is, is, you want to play like you're off in the clouds somewhere so you don't have to solve any problems. But if you think *you're* blasted and be-damned, you take a look at *me*. And if you don't want me to talk to you, why then I'll SCREAM! And if you don't want me to scream at you, then I'll take a broomstick and I'll crack it over your back for you. You useless old fart! You shameless old goat. I don't know why I ever married you. Ay, my God, forgive me for rebelling against my fate, but no matter what You say, I believe I've got the right to fight with this old pervert. Go on, git, you old cuss, get that daughter of yours out of that goddamned bath-room, because if you don't I'm going to throw a fit. I'm bursting, I tell you! I can't hold it anymore. Get her out of there this minute or I'll set this house afire. I can't take it anymore. Ay, I can't hold it anymore. Show that you're a man, even if it's just once in your miserable life! Go on, *git!* Why don't you move? Move, you old fart, move! I've had it up to here! Up to here, I tell you. Noooo moooooore! Ay God, ay, God, ay God. Get that woman out of the bathroom! Ay, I can't hold it in anymore, I can't do it, I can't. Ay. Get this old man out of my sight. Take him some-place far away from here. The devil's behind this, I tell you. He's to blame for these miseries and disgraces. You old blockhead. You numbskull old coot, you, it's your fault for selling the farm. Ay, the farm. Ay, the farm. *Ayyyyy*, the farm. Ay . . ."

Has anyone ever seen such things as get in that girl's head—whoever heard of locking yourself up in the bathroom and not coming out for two hours? I'll tell you the truth, I can't figure it out . . . Ah, old woman, but if you think I'm going to say so much as one word to you, you've got another think coming. So far as I'm concerned, she can lock herself up in that bathroom till kingdom come, I'm not going to give you the satisfaction of fussing at her and making her come out. She can rot in there first, for all I care.

"Ay, get her out, get her out of there!"

I'm going to sack up these mandarin oranges, to see if I can't sell 'em, because they're starting to get soft and if the people see 'em, they'll never buy 'em in a million years. Good lord, everything in the store is rotting in the stalls, and nobody so much as walks in the door. If this keeps going like it's going. If this keeps going . . .

"It's *you* she takes after, with these crazy ideas of hers. It's all on your side of the family. Why, everybody in your family died crazy—if they didn't hang themselves they busted their own heads open on the rocks. *I* know. *I* know. Miserable goddamned luck I had the day I met you. Miserable goddamned . . . Ay, my God!"

But it turns out I don't have anything to put the oranges into, because I never had any sacks to speak of, and now all the wrapping paper I had, that blasted Fortunato has ruined writing filth all over it.

"Every day I regret that much more that I ever married you!"

Old woman! Old woman! You better get out of my sight if you know what's good for you, because as tired and worn out as I am, one of these days I'm going to shy one of these weights at your head, and *then* you'll wish you'd listened to me.

"Go get that woman out of the bathroom! Lord only knows what's happened to her in there."

Can't be any more than what's already happened to her. You just mind your own business. Stop poking and pushing at me or you'll live to regret it. I'm telling you . . . Here, let's see . . . let's see what there is around here that I might wrap these stinking mandarin oranges up in . . . She can spend the rest of her life locked up in there so far as I'm concerned. And anyway, the little I ever go to the bathroom, why . . .

"Go on! Git! I'm going to throw a fit!"

Here comes Tomasico again. And this blasted old woman and her carryings-on. The shame of it. I wish the ground would open and swallow me up. If I could just grab her by the neck . . . But here he is already . . .

"Hello, don Polo, how are you doing?"

The tightwad, and always calling me "don" Polo. If you ask me, he's making fun of me. That's what it sounds like to me. The smug goddamned skinflint, he got the picture in two seconds—he heard this old hen cackling and squawking and he's come over here to poke his nose in . . .

"Just fair to middling, Tomasico. Sitting here waiting for somebody to come in and haul this stock away."

"Oh, the sales are awfully slow."

"Slow! Today all day, all I've sold is two bunches of soursops."

"Lord help us!"

Oh yes, he'll talk to Tomasico. The evil old goat. But to me— to his own wife—do you think he'll utter a single word! Why is he that way with me? With *me!* I slave from dawn to dark. I've never done anything but sacrifice myself for the rest of them. I'm telling you, there's something fearful going on here. The evil in this house must be something fearful, and I mean it! People would rather talk to dogs than to us. And then we won't even talk to each other! My God, take this trial from us. Take this terrible trial from us, because I am just simply tired.

When it rains, which is rare in these parts, sounds seem to become different somehow. The rain washes the air and even the cracks between the wooden boards clean. The rain unclogs time itself, and the music of the organ comes high and clear through that crystalline air. The music and the laughter of the people drift across the fields and flood the house in which the family is sleeping. Everywhere, everywhere—like it or not—the music of the organ, high and clear, fills the air, the whole night long. This afternoon it rained.

Lolín was called "the Chinee," no doubt because of her eyes. Big wide eyes—sad? Lolín didn't mind being called "the Chinee"— on the contrary. "Chinee" is one of those nicknames that gives class to a whore. Like all the whores of La Frontera, Lolín loved red-colored cloth, Mexican ballads, and long fingernails. Like all the whores, Lolín began her work in the evening, at the bar, continuing it into the night, and, if some client requested it, ending up in bed at dawn. Like all the whores of La Frontera, Lolín is from the country, from another town, adores her family, and is poor. Like all the whores, Lolín is extremely sentimental. She sings.

She saves a little money which she later lends to someone and therefore loses forever. Like all whores, she lives alone, she is lonely, and she cries, generally, Sunday night through to Monday morning. And, like all whores, she would be capable of letting herself be killed, of letting herself be ruined (which is always what seems to happen in these cases) for the first man who treated her decently. Fortunato is secretly in love with Lolín. He goes to Eufrasia's place almost every night to see her; he has idealized her big eyes—which perhaps are not so much sad as, simply, big. Fortunato would like to kidnap Lolín, elope with her, flee. But there are the other men. And they all know that Lolín is a whore. So therefore, in the presence of those others, he has to treat her like one. And when he goes out with Aby or the other young men from the neighborhood, he has to talk like they do, treat her like they treat her. Turn into them, turn supple, fierce, like them. Although he has never confessed it, Fortunato has written novels in which the main character, the star, is Lolín. In one novel Fortunato and Lolín, after a daring daylight robbery, make their escape in an enormous automobile and flee the length of the Island; they make love wherever the notion strikes them, as their enemies tighten the net around them. In another, she is the remote, famous singer who comes briefly to Fortunato's small town. She looks at him once, calls him over, and makes him hers forever and ever . . . And meanwhile the organ plays on and on, and he, Aby, and the other young men wait for the Chinee to get rid of that fat drunk so they can proposition her. Aby, the smoothest, will speak for them all.

Anisia thinks she's going to beat me at smashing plates. But she's off her rocker if she thinks so for very long. Nobody smashes plates like I do. She'd better not even *think* she can beat me! Right now, while she's snoring in bed, I'm going to get up and go smash all the china in the china closet and all the crockery in the kitchen. Right now, I'm going to take every one of the plates and I'm going to throw them at my grandmother's head while she's asleep. And tomorrow they can talk as much as they want to, what do I care. What's important is to beat Anisia at breaking things. Boy, am I going to laugh tomorrow when she gets up and sees there's nothing left to break.

But what on earth—Anisia's already at the crockery! . . .

"You goose, you thought you were going to sneak in ahead of me. Well, you're a halfwitted moron. I got here first, so I'm going to be the one that smashes all these plates and crocks to smithereens."

"At least give me one plate. To smash on the old woman's skull."

"If that's what it's for, take two."

"Oh, good, I'm going to crack 'em on her thick head."

"Walk real slow."

"Real slow . . ."

"Slower."

"Like this . . ."

"No. Slower. Look—fly, like this, like me."

"Like me, you mean."

"Uh-huh. Like this."

"I hope nobody sees us. I hope nobody finds out we can do this stuff."

"Ssssst. Talk with your mouth closed."

"I *am* talking with my mouth closed, stupid."

"I didn't realize it, since I could hear you whinny."

"We're almost there."

"It's so dark."

"I don't know if my aim's good enough to hit her in the head."

"It's so dark, I can't see my hands in front of my face."

"Duck!"

"Do you see something?"

"Of course not. I can't see a blessed thing."

"Me neither."

"There's nobody in the bed."

"Nobody? Good lord, where are those two old coots at this hour?"

"Maybe they're in the closet."

"Or in the chamberpot."

"Look under the bed."

"There's somebody under here."

"Fortunato! It's Fortunato!"

"What are you doing here?"

"Nothing."

"Fortunato's under Grandma and Grandpa's bed snooping, to see what they do when they go to bed."

"Blasted kids!"

"We're gonna tell!"

"You're crazy, I wasn't snooping, I came to steal the cashbox the old man keeps under the bed. But tonight apparently he put it somewhere else."

"Did you ever hear of such a thing—a dead man stealing money."

"I want it so I can dance with Lolín."

"Did you ever hear of such a thing—and for what else?"

"And to make wine with."

"Did you ever! . . . A dead man dancing and drinking wine!"

"Let's get out of here before we wake somebody up."

"Yeah. Let's get out of here."

"Let's run on our big toes."

"Let's bite an ear."

"An ear."

" 'Bye, Fortunato."

". . . nato."

"Goodbye. Goodbye."

". . . 'bye. . . . 'bye."

"We'll leave you while you're still asleep."

"We'll leave you while you're still awake."

"We hope you rest in peace."

"We hope you find the cashbox."

"We hope you get to dance."

"We hope you get stinking drunk."

"Rowf. Rowf. Rowf."

"We hope you wake up and are still asleep."

"We hope you live and die again."

"We hope you die and still think you're alive."

"We hope you live and think you're dead."

"We hope you're dead and know that you're dead because you're alive."

"We hope you live dead."

"Rowf. Rowf. Rowf."

No. Since long before night. Since early that evening. As soon as it cleared off. After dinner—and they ate early, as they had in the country—the music of the organ was there—very very loud, full-bodied, sonorous, booming—echoing off the walls of the front porch, and even off the puddles of water left by the rain that Tico and Anisia now stir up with sticks and rocks, and then with their hands. The music.

I would tell myself, Your time has come and gone. You've already had everything you were ever going to have. You've tasted everything you were ever going to taste. Nobody else is going to come, even to say, "I hope you get struck by a bolt of lightning." Nobody else is going to come and ask you what's wrong, even if you roll around in a mud puddle. Now the organ can cry its liver out, and nobody is going to come along to try to console you so the organ will stop crying and just play music like it always did.

Your time has come and gone and you never even noticed.

That's what I would say to myself. But then right away I'd turn around and say, Don't say such things, woman. Don't say such things. And I would console myself—for no good reason, it goes without saying. And when I thought *that*, I'd turn unconsoled again. And so then I'd run all around the backyard or through the vegetable stand, but I couldn't find any consolation anywhere. And so it would go. Until I realized that it was true, what I'd started out saying was true. And so now that I practically know that what I was telling myself is true, the only thing that relieves me at all is giving myself over to Fortunato's pigeons.

Letting them peck my face and then lift me up and fly way way up high with me. And from way up there let me go so I drop.

If you people knew how peaceful a person gets when you know that there's no way out. When the pigeons, who take a little bit of my clothes, each one of them, in their beaks, when they fly up with a person and then let you fall through the air. Then. *Then.* It's those seconds when a person is really and truly free. *Free.* . . . So free that all a person can think about is crashing on the ground, so a person can get free of so much freedom.

The Old Woman and the Sun

I go out for a walk down the street to try to breathe, and the goddamned sun, the first thing it does is slap me in the face. I go outside—but that ga-ga-*boom*, ga-ga-*boom*, ga-ga-*boom* is still following me, and it slaps me in the face. I tell you, there's no way out. Wherever I go, it's all the same. I'm a poor worn-out old woman, and I still can't get a minute's peace. And if I stay in the house I go crazy from the number of devils there are in every single corner. In the cookstove. Inside the pots and pans. And even in the empty cracker tins. Everywhere! And if I go outside for a little walk, the god-damned sun won't let me raise my head. "Son of a bitch!" I say to it. But the moron doesn't even bother itself to answer me. It just shoots such a blast of fire at me that if I didn't jump out of the way I'd be fried to a crisp by it. And then it just goes on about its business, like nothing happened. I go in under the few trees that are still left in the parks, and the son of a bitch, I don't know how it does it, but it sneaks down through the leaves and branches and all and shoots a jet of fire right at me . . . There's no way out, I tell you! I could die two times over and I'd never find a minute's peace! . . . So I try to run away from the sun by hunkering down in an alley. But so what—the bastard is smarter than you'd give it credit for, and it sli-i-i-i-ides across the asphalt right over to where I am, and it slaps me in the face. In the forehead. On the hands. Until I'm singed and brown all over. Until I can't even breathe. Until I'm in such a state that I don't even care one way or another. But that's still not enough for the sun—it keeps poking me, and prodding me. And it turns my hair to charcoal dust. And pulls off one of my fingers. And it keeps on, and keeps on, and keeps on, until finally I take off running down the street. And the people that see me say, Good lord, look at that old woman run. You'd think the devil was on her tail. But those people must be halfwits—can't they see that the sun's after me, lickety-split, and if it catches me it'll fry me to twenty kinds of a crisp?

Staggering and half burned to cinders, I finally make it home. But the door's locked. But the door's locked. But the door's locked. Ay, the door. Ay, the door. My god. My God. How can You allow such things to happen to me? How can You allow it?

The sun's still hot on my trail. And the goddamned door locked. And I knock and knock and knock and knock and knock and knock and knock. And the people inside say, She's knockered! But the door's still locked.

"Open up."

And I say, Knockered my ass, the door's locked, you idiots. But the people inside won't open it. Those sons of bitches won't open the door. Open up, you sons of bitches!

But instead of opening the door, what they do is bar it. I can hear them throw the bolt. I can hear them piling things up against the door so I can't knock it down and get in. "Now it's *your* turn, now it's your turn," the voices say. "Your turn on the outside of a locked door, outside . . ." And the sun is practically on top of me. The ball of fire is so close it can practically reach out and grab me. So I bang and bang and bang on the door. But they refuse to open it. They refuse. *It's got me!* The sun has got hold of one leg. And I go *bang bang bang bang bang*, but nothing happens. The animals won't open the door for me. Help. Help. *Gotcha. Gotcha. Gotcha* . . . Ah . . . Ay . . . Help . . .

Help. *Gotcha*, you old biddy. I've practically burned you to a crisp already. *Ayyyy*. Somebody help me. You wait, you just wait, I'll burn you to cinders. I've got a leg already. Ay, the sun's roasting me alive. *Gotcha*.

"Open up."

Ay. It's frying me to a crisp. Open the door. Open the door—I'm melting. Open up.

And she went mad—but this time the old man wasn't at the vegetable stand anymore to see them come take her away.

I'll tell you, there are days I don't seem to have the energy to lift a finger. Days you just want to sleep and not wake up for a thousand years. But I haven't always been that way—I remember once, when we were living up on the mountain, a storm

Fortunato and the Moon

It was truly the biggest moon one could ever have hoped to see. A strange, far-off moon, lighting up the sky, at precisely the moment he left the house with his suitcase and the seventeen pesos in his pocket. A cold, timeless moon, scudding across a papier-mâché backdrop—uncouth, inhospitable, and unreachable. There was music, too, utterly clear—the sound of the organ, over in Eufrasia's

caught me under the almond trees and I had to stay there all afternoon. I remember that when it cleared off, little streams of water were still running over my feet, and the sun was shining on the water, and the birds were making such a fuss that I could have stayed there forever listening to them. And then, I don't know where from, there came over me such a wave of happiness that it was as if at that very instant all roads were open to me and I was part of that shining water flowing down through the almond leaves scattered on the ground. I just stood there, I don't know how long it was, because at that moment time had simply disappeared. I was floating. It was like I guess being in a state of grace would be. And that seemed to want to tell me that something wonderful happens sometimes, and it can even come in through your feet.

—*Digna*

Ball Room, going around and around endlessly, timelessly, and as terrible and invariable, as disapproving as the moon ... What to do? The moon, high and cruel, implacably glared down on him, watching him with its fixed frown. ... If you stop and think about it, then there can truly be no salvation; if you hesitate, if you think, if you waver for even one second, you are doomed. Listen to that organ, listen to that nagging drone, listen to that perpetual humiliation. Listen, and flee. Run ... But the moon is cold and angry, as well. The moon is a presage of the new shocks and collisions, the new frustrations that await you if you flee. Its inevitable humiliating glare will strip you naked, it will follow you to the ends of the earth; it will throw your silhouette across the endless landscapes of loneliness and solitude, poverty, all the new torments to come. What to do? The moon—horrible, timeless—illuminates him, throws his shadow across a motionless expanse of deserted streets. Its expression—its age-old face like a battered whore's—was saying, "What can *you* do in the glare of my light?" And then, he stopped walking (he had not yet passed the first corner), put his suitcase down, and looked upward. And he saw the unvarying face of the Great Whore who, high above the piercing babbling of the organ to which all the other people whirled and whirled, coldly and haughtily flowed on, forever, through her cold and desolating sky.

What are you doing out there? Come on, come inside. Come in and lie down. Walk inside, slowly, quietly, so they don't find out that you've been trying to run away from home. Don't let them get wind of that, because they'll write your mother and your mother will die from the worry. Come on, put that money back in the mattress. Put it away. Put that money away. You! You better mind me, now. Put that money back in the mattress and leave it there for a present for your grandmother on Mother's Day. That's the best you can do now. Come on, come inside. Such ideas you get!—imagine trying to run away and wander the face of the earth. Ay, Fortunato, it takes a man to do that. Come on, sneak back in here. Nice and slow. That's it, that's it. Tiptoe down the hall and get into bed without turning on the light, and make as little noise as you can. The old man and the old woman are snoring, but they sleep as light as a cat. Hurry, now, don't let them catch you out here in the middle of the living room . . . But why did I turn back? I have to get out of here. I don't want to live in this miserable bad-luck house anymore . . . Come on, go in your room. That's it, on tiptoes. Over to the bed. Now I'll hypnotize myself. If I make up my mind to, I can go to sleep. You can dream if you feel like it, child . . . Dream. Just dream.

"For the love of God, Adolfina, I can't wait any longer!"

You are in bed, and you pull the covers up over your head. In bed, and you snuggle down as hard as you can in the sheets. If only you could be an ant forever. But even if you were—then what? If only you could be a water rat and swim underneath all the trash and garbage that floats on the top, and come out floating yourself, far, far away, and then dive underneath again. But even if you were—then what? If only you were a big owl moth and could hide in the fields around the house you used to live in. Fly in among the dark cool grass and bushes where nobody would come and bother you. But even if you could. But even if you *are* one—then what?

Hiding in there among the grass and bushes, you'd want to be something besides an owl moth. Because the life of an owl moth is hard. Very often other animals jump on them, or other owl moths pick fights with them over the best leaves and things. The other owl moths.

Snuggled up there in the sheets, thinking about a million

things. Now you're going to get the urge to leave home again. It's going to come over you. Here come the fury and the stink of rotting guavas, and the fit the old woman is throwing at the bathroom door. And the cockroaches walking right on top of the table. And . . . And now you'll tell yourself, Tomorrow, tomorrow I'm leaving, tomorrow I'm getting out of here. Tomorrow. . . . But you are doomed, Fortunato. You are doomed because Onerica was your mother and your father, and therefore you have to live for Onerica. Because life is not for giving you what you dream about being, it's for making you be what necessity demands you to be.

No!

But there's no reason to get mad about it. Cry, if you feel like crying. Fall completely apart, if that's what you feel like. Poor kid. If you feel like pitying yourself, you can pity yourself and everything. But there's no cause to get angry.

Yes there is!

You may as well get used to seeing those cockroaches as just another part of your life. Because they're a part of life, period. My poor boy. So hard-headed. What's to become . . . Ah, good, you're practically asleep already. It'll be daylight soon. Soon you'll get out of bed and get dressed and go off to the factory. But isn't the factory closed? Never mind that, it's the only thing that's in view for you . . . Soon I'll pick up the hammer and nails and start enjoying my hard luck and miseries. And start planning new hard luck and miseries.

I can already hear the steam from the boilers. I can already hear them cleaning the vats. Somebody's tightening and greasing the belts.

Ga-ga-*boom*.

Ga-ga-*boom*.

Ga-ga-*boom*. Get up, you slugabed, the factory's reopened. The crate ends came in. Everybody's already out there hammering the crates together. Get up, you sleepyhead. In a minute, in a minute.

No! It won't be like that, goddammit!

At first there were only rumors, scattered pockets of protest, and—as always occurs in these cases—a great many words.

And besides, they (at first) who had always been harassed and oppressed, always been hungry, humiliated, always the butt of swindles and unkept promises, always been frustrated—why would their senses have been attuned to the shifting nuances, the shifting tides, the shifting winds of the political situation? That sort of thing was for people with something to gain—or lose. Up until then there had been one invariable law for the poor man; like all inexorable laws, it appeared in no written code. All it said was that a poor man had to work forever, and starve to death. But then things got worse. It wasn't just words anymore, it wasn't just the single, almost random gunshot from time to time in the middle of the night. It was bombs going off everywhere, it was red and black flags unfurled on every corner, appearing just before dawn as the city (supposedly) was sleeping. And leaflets. Leaflets full of threats and impassioned essays, leaflets full of insulting truths about the government, leaflets scattered in parks, in streets, in doorways, on front porches. Many men, especially the young men, became recruits of the government—and for their helmets were nicknamed "steel pots." They were given a uniform, a rifle, and twenty-five pesos a month. Then they were sent up into the mountains, where the rebels were. But there were many more young men who went up into those mountains on their own, to become rebels themselves. By 1957, Oriente Province was virtually divided into two separate governments. In the country, the rebels held sway, preventing the campesinos from taking their produce to market, setting ambushes for the army (when there were weapons enough), and even raiding the small towns. In the cities, government troops used their entire brutal arsenal of persecution, blackmail, pressure, torture. By the middle of that year the lights were out in Holguín, water began to be scarce or to fail altogether, there were food shortages. A plane machine-gunned a building. And young men began to appear on the highways without fingernails, without eyes, sometimes without testicles.

The pigeons lift me up and carry me away. Pigeons. And they whisper in my ear not to be afraid—whenever I want them to, they'll set me down again. Pigeons. I've bought my daughter Esther a pair of earrings and a pin. The pigeons lift me up, and then way up there they turn me loose, and I come tumbling down. What really hurts is that they told me they wouldn't drop me. But they did. What really hurts . . . By taking in washing and ironing I've bought my daughter Esther, who'll be a woman any day, a purple-colored pin and a pair of purple-colored earrings too, about the color of that greenish-purple kind of sugarcane. The brooch—the truth is, it didn't cost me anything. I dithered around and acted like I was a little halfwitted and then when nobody was looking I tucked it in my bosom. But the earrings cost three pesos seventy-five centavos. Three pesos and seventy-five centavos of my hard-earned money. The way things are these days, you have to be crazy to spend three pesos seventy-five centavos on such trifles. Nobody but you would ever do such a stupid thing. But I don't care what people say—that money was mine, and it took a lot of work to scrape it all together, too, so I can damn well do what I please with it. The pin looks so nice on her, like that, on her bosom, and I can even tell that it stands out a little, because she's beginning to get breasts already. So any day I'll have to be buying her brassieres and everything too. Good lord, life is just spend spend spend. Where am I ever going to get the money to keep her in clothes and shoes? What got into you— buying that plain little thing a pin like that? Nobody but you . . . You ought to have bought her a pair of shoes. It's pitiful to see her slapping around in those cheap house slippers she wears. . . . She hasn't put on the earrings yet, because first she's got to have her ears pierced. They haven't been pierced yet. I could never get up the courage to have my own ears pierced. And by the time I turned around I was an old woman and my ears were so tough there wasn't a needle that could be pushed through them. And if there had been, my ears would have rotted and turned black. Ay the pigeons. Ay the pigeons. The . . . By the end of the year I may be making things out of air, but she'll have a new dress to wear. She will. You'll see.

The city without electricity. No lights. Totally blockaded. There is no movie house anymore. There are very few places anymore where a person can travel at night without being stopped or even machine-gunned. Outside the official centers, there are almost no places where rum is sold, where there might be laughter and talk, where a person can still shout or rub up against another person. Only the Ball Room in La Frontera is still open. Eufrasia, who is wise in the ways of survival, somehow managed to get her hands on a dozen carbide lamps and a permit from the Regiment signed by the colonel himself. Some people said Eufrasia was an informer for the government, which was why she had been allowed— so far—to open her Ball Room. Others said that Eufrasia was a secret agent for the rebels, and that the big fry among the rebels met there, which was why the government allowed her to open, since sooner or later—when the time was right— there would be a raid. But be all that as it may, at this moment the organ is playing, monotonous and clear, apparently louder than before because of the absence of the other noises that once competed with it. Every night.

Sometimes I stop being Adolfina and turn into Fortunato. And I *am* Fortunato. I sit up on the ridgepole of the house and I have long conversations with the pigeons and I pick up two or three scorpions and pop them in my mouth and swallow them just like *that*, or maybe I let them sting me in the eyes. Sometimes I am Fortunato. But other times I turn into a table leg. And I stand there for hours and hours and hours just being a table leg. And when I get tired of being a table leg, I turn into Digna. One time I turned into a chameleon and it was three months before I turned back into Adolfina. I'm Adolfina now. Adolfina thinks there's no better way to not-live than to always have Death on your back like this. Adolfina knows that the only way to bear life is by not-living it. You throw away all the trivial things and just think about the big problem . . . I would go for walks in the park with Death, who would constantly be tugging at my skirt, so I wouldn't stray too far. And he would say, Sit down over here. And Death and I would sit down on a bench and wait for the time to come, and I would watch how he'd push me here and pull me there and poke at me to be still, and I would almost burst. But at the same time it comforted me inside. And I would say to myself, There's one thing you'll never lose. There's one thing that time, goddammit, and this never-ending hurry-scurry and this terrible hot wind have never been able to take away from you. And that's your memories. The made-up memories. Because I . . . *Claaaaang!* Death, as calm as could be, was waiting for me to show up on the wings of a kingbird. Me, and Death. Can you hear that racket? I would go flying, and I'd be hanging between heaven and earth for hours and hours and hours. Like that, just hanging there—thumbing my nose at time and laughing at everything as loud as I could. Just flying—looking down at all the people. And laughing. Laughing. And looking at myself, too, down there on that bench. And sometimes I would take a tear from my eye and gargle it. And sometimes I'd go visit Adolfina someplace I knew she wasn't. And since she wasn't there, I'd wait.

The people in the house are asleep. Or at least they are lying in bed in the dark. The light of the moon reflects off the fiber-cement roof which the sun and rain have polished to a soft patina, and off the zinc sheets of the factory, now closed. Out in the yard, an empty can, a broken pail, the remains of what was once a bicycle twinkle. The organ is playing, and its music—loud, clear, and forever unchanging—also floods the town, now illuminated by nothing but moonlight . . . Later, as always, there came searches of the houses, mass executions, horribly meticulous tortures, the closing down of virtually every store and business—even Eufrasia's this time. Humiliation and hunger were absolute . . . Later yet, the general terror reached such heights, the total oppression was so widespread, the hatred aimed at every man, woman, and child was so fierce, that there was no choice but to think about this new and terrible state of affairs. They had no choice but to forget their personal hatreds, their merely personal grudges, and look at this new hatred, this new feud that had descended upon them all, and which required all their strength and even their most deep-seated powers of loathing to bear up under . . .

And then.

Madre María, mother of God, there's not a drop of milk left to give the children. Things are getting harder every day. What is to become of us? Those goddamned rebels have got everything cut off. My God, and the militia said they were going to burn down our house. The house burning down, and me fried to cracklings. Madre María—and Digna's poor children crying for their milk. And us not having even enough money to buy a little bit of sugar on the black market with, so we could at least fix them a sugar-tit to make them feel like they were eating something. Ay, if only I could finally sleep tonight. Oh, Virgin Mary, if only I could close my eyes and *Bam!* doze off just like that. And if only my kidneys didn't ache like they ache. And the mosquitoes didn't eat me alive like they do. I have to thank you because at least the factory finally closed, this time it looks like for good, so even if we starve to death we don't have to be hearing that ga-ga-*boom* night and day and day and night *till it drives you* CRAZY! But ay, Holy Virgin Mother, if only there would be milk again. If only things could be straightened out. And this house go back to being *some*thing, even if only just what it was before. And Holy Virgin, show that old donkey Polo the way—because even if he won't pray, I'll pray for him. Help Adolfina, too, because the poor thing, every day she gets more worked up and furious over any little thing. And help her not have those fits of locking herself up in the bathroom, God. And take this rheumatism off me, Lord. And if You can help Digna get rid of that evil spirit that's in her that makes her hum and talk to herself all day long with her mouth closed, I promise I'll climb the Hill of the Cross on my knees tomorrow morning. And make the old man talk, God. O Lord, enlighten this house. Please let everything be straightened out and make the vegetable stand prosper. And end this plague of mosquitoes. O my God, and make Adolfina's sewing scissors appear again so she can cut out that dress for me. And also the butcher knife so I can peel the plantains—if we ever get any again. I'm going to keep in touch with You, God. I'm going to raise my hands and sprinkle medicinal water in every corner of this house. Medicinal *and* spiritual water. Forgive us, God. And give us faith. And charity. Give us charity. Dios te salve, María, the Lord is with thee, blessed be the fruit of thy . . . Santa María. Santa María. Santa María. Pray for us now, pray for us sinners. O God, these mosquitoes. Amen.

But what was God for them? God was above all the possibility of crying their lamentations, their only real possibility. God offered them the occasion, which all men and women need if they are not to become absolute monsters, of being children from time to time, with their whining and their complaints, their anger, their fits of tears, seeking protection from On High, the Father Who watches over us from Heaven. But God, cruel and remote, was also the Great Flim-Flam Man, the Bad Guy, the Jerk whose fault all of this was, the Boss you could blame everything on, take to task, and even renounce, revile, reject—impassionedly. Since He was superior and to all appearances pitilessly unyielding, God made it possible for them to satisfy, in one Being, the sacred and essential necessities of both leaning on someone, indulging their need for dependence, and insulting someone or something, rebelling . . . God, cruel and ungraspable (with a somewhat sweet, vacuous face, however, which they believed had been precisely copied in the sweet, peaceful, and somewhat vacuous image hanging on the wall in the living room), was the possibility of refuge too, the possibility of comfort, of poetry, of that love (the highest mystery of all) which all men and women instinctively seek. God was He Who at the most unbearable moments of their lives would take up the burden of their terrors. God was He Who when there was at last no way out (which is what always, sooner or later, occurs) would take up the burden of their infinite pain and misery, and Who would console them for their unending humiliations. God was He Who listened unprotestingly, never growing bored or impatient—perhaps because He wasn't listening. God was the Venerable, the Great, the Highest, the Being Who always watched over them and Who therefore had to be respected, or at least taken into account. And as He was a worthy and respectable Lord, our Lord, it was He as well Who offered them the opportunity to manifest, to make clear, to *mate-*

rialize, the last straws of their fury—by cursing Him. God was their good fortune, someone superior to themselves Whom they could publicly malign, and even damn to Hell. God was the Great Fraud, the Father most loved, the Omniscient One (ah, paranoia), the Faithful Spouse, the Eternal Watchman. God, with His concept of sin, was covered with glory, filled with enchantments, and also the One Who had defined all the successive incarnations of pettiness and meanspiritedness to which Man is prey—that is to say, He'd defined all simple human experience. And besides all that, or beyond it rather, God was the possibility of the infinite, the *Beyond* itself. The fact that someone—loving, sweet, soft-bearded, white-robed, and smiling (for so they picture Him)—might at last (and from the Beginning) be waiting, to reward them for all the undeserved brutality they had suffered . . . Ah . . . The resurrection of the body. The forgiveness of sins. The life everlasting. God.

"And now. What do you see?"

"I see boiling water coming all the way up to the neck of a blind hen."

"Good lord! And she can't fly away?"

"What for?"

"But what if she gets boiled alive! If she does, what'll we do then?"

"Then it'll be *your* turn to dance in the bathtub."

"And what then?"

"Then me."

"But can't it be some other way?"

"What for?"

"And what about after that, and after that, and after that—who'll be the next one, and the next one, who'll always be in line for after that? And what does that *after that* mean—if it's just as unbearable, if it's just like *this?* And what about after that, and after that, and after that—what then?"

"Ha ha ha—after that . . ."

The news comes while I'm cleaning off the front porch—it makes you sick to see it so muddy. The news comes and I refuse to hear

After that, things became so completely unbearable that we had to forget our own hell, like it or not, and adopt the hell that was for everybody alike.   —*Fortunato*

what they have to say. I refuse to hear a word of it, because everything has already happened. Because everything that's going to start happening now, I've already seen it. Where? I don't know. But everything I do, I know I've already done it, and everything I hear, the words are all sort of out of kilter from my already hearing them so much. And it's terrible hearing again what I've always been having this feeling about, this intuition I've had, and what I've always been suffering.

The news comes while I'm sloshing water across the floor of the front porch. And trying to get rid of a couple of those awful ants that are trying to strip the rue plant naked of every leaf it's got.

After that, a woman's uterus was pierced with a red-hot iron rod because she had gone out in a red skirt and a black blouse—the colors of the insurrection.

The voices say. The voices told me. They say the voices told me.

Listen to the voices.

Me pouring bucket after bucket after bucket of water on the porch. Why do I have to wash off the front porch? Tell me, Adolfina, you dead woman that walked all over town last night looking for a man to go to bed with you. Tell me, you dead woman—what kind of work is this, trying to make the floor of the front porch sparkle?

"Did you people hear about it!" the voices said. "There's a man hanged out there, out there by the manjack grove. And they say it looks a lot like Fortunato." Woman killed last night when she couldn't find a man to do her the favor. Woman killed . . .

After that a campesino's entire family was burned alive. After that a boy, just a kid, was hanged from a tree at the entrance to town. One of many boys.

After that . . .

"And they say he was beaten something awful."

And they say it broke your heart to see his face.

And they say he didn't have so much as a single centavo in his pocket.

And they say he was young.

208

And they say apparently he didn't work for a living, because his hands were as soft as a woman's. Soft and white.

And they say it's Fortunato.

And.

I would slosh out the water and even let it get my feet wet. Two of those ants were drowning, so I put the broomstick down on the floor for them, so they could climb up it, and save themselves.

"You better get out there before the militia take the body away. Why don't you go tell don Polo? Go on, Adolfina, you're the sanest one in the family." You, because for you there's not even the cold comfort of madness. "Tell him that there's a boy hanged out there in the manjack grove that looks like Fortunato. According to the milkmen," who thank goodness risk smuggling milk into town once in a while, "he was apparently a student or somebody that had never worked the land, because it doesn't look like he ever worked very hard with his hands. I thought of Fortunato—he's the only person around here that hasn't had to break his back in the fields."

The ants, my dear woman. Oh my dear woman all alone and creeping up fast on fifty. Woman killed last night when she didn't find. Those ants, my dear old bag, are practically up to your hands. I put the bucket on the floor and start sweeping the water with the broom. The rue plant is practically stripped clean. The ants scurry off the broomstick onto my hands, and it's then that I kill 'em. Now that I'm dead I'll give one quiet scream and then I'll die again. They say his hands were nice and soft, like a woman's. The way things are . . . Crazy, that boy.

It has to be him, Adolfina. Go on, tell the others, but tell them so they don't find out. Although sooner or later they'll have to know. Sooner or later. Sooner or later. What if I start singing out here, in the middle of the front porch? If I start singing and dancing with the broomstick out here, the people walking down the street will say I'm crazy. Or that I'm really really happy. If I cut off one of my ears and swallow it down in one gulp, people will say, She's crazy as a loon. If I hop on one hand and then mew like a cat seven times and then take off all my clothes and start jumping up and down on just the tip of my little toe, people will say, Take her away, she's gone berserk.

Get the straitjacket. Throw her in a padded cell, and lock the door.

But I've never been as sane as I am now, thinking all these things.

And if I sat down right here in broad daylight and started sticking my tongue out at people, what would happen? What would they say?

I put down the broom and turn my back on the empty bucket and I go into the living room.

"We know," a herd of animals tells me, dying laughing and rocking back and forth on the sofa.

We already know, we already know.

I'll walk down the hall and start screaming in the kitchen.

I'll scream as loud as I can, and I'll tell Mama that Fortunato's been hanged. I'll go out to the fruit stand and I'll scream at the old man that Fortunato's been hanged. With his soft hands . . . They say he didn't die from the hanging. They say he was dead before they hanged him.

They say.

They say he was beaten, and his eyes were gouged out, and his testicles were squeezed to a pulp. They say he was raped, because they've got experts at raping men.

They say.

Now somebody'll have to write Onerica. Who? I'll do it. Dear sister, I drop you this note . . . If only they'd let me get down the hall. If the demons would only stop slapping me and let me get to the kitchen.

If I can get to the kitchen, I'm free.

If I can get to the kitchen and let out a scream. If I can get to the kitchen and spit it out. If they'll let me go in the bathroom. If they'll allow me to pick up the bottle of alcohol. If only the demons would let me by, all these princes, all these animals, all these wild beasts . . . If only they wouldn't laugh so loud, if only they wouldn't climb up on the roof and jump headfirst into my hands. . . If only they'd just be still. Let me tell my news. Dead in a manjack tree.

Mama, Mama, Fortunato's dead and hanging from a manjack tree.

"Holy Mother Virgin. Oh my God . . ."

_____

Digna, Digna, Fortunato's dead in the manjack tree.

"Ay, if Moisés were still in this house, this would never have happened. Quick, run find Moisés."

Celia, Fortunato's hanging in the manjack grove.

"Ay, my daughter Esther. Ay, my daughter Esther told me about this last night. Ay, my daughter Esther . . ."

Papa . . .

"Bananas two for five centavos. Mandarin oranges at half a peso. The soursops are going rotten on me . . ."

Just let me make it to the kitchen, and I'll never ask for another thing as long as I live. Just let me be the one to tell the news. Just to the kitchen. The kitchen. That will be your goal. Dead woman—tell those wild animals and those angels to let you into the kitchen. And then into the bathroom. The bathroom. That is your true goal. That is your final goal. Tell those pigeons not to flutter and flap around so much up there on the roof. My life as a pigeon was not easy—I got I don't know how many mites and lice and things. You demons—don't scream now, just as I'm about to talk. If you can get to the kitchen, you're practically home free. If you can make it to the bathroom, you're totally liberated. There's Fortunato knocking at the door with a rope around his neck. They say his hands were as small and soft as a girl's.

Just let me make it to the kitchen.

What an unconscionable lot of ants I've got climbing up almost to my hands.

Just two or three more steps. Two or three steps, and *bingo!*

There's your sister, out there crying behind the house.

Listen, listen, people.

Tell these ants to make way, I'm carrying in Fortunato, who's dead.

Tico and Anisia are setting the house afire.

Ah, I can't stand all these compliments and all this gallantry from so many princes. You see? Ever since last night, they just won't leave me alone. What a chorus of princes, my lord, what a gang of princes. What a number of princes . . .

My dear sister . . .

Mama's at the cookstove. If I tell her the news she'll cross herself and drop to her knees and burn her hands in the lard that she's got in the skillet. I better tell her later. Digna's yelling at the children and singing, like always, with her mouth closed. What do I gain by mortifying her? . . . The old man won't speak if I tell him. Though on second thought, he might. But I don't want to make his life any harder . . . The old man . . . he's the only one that ought not to be told about these things.

I'll go down the hall and start singing.

I'll get to the front porch and pick up the bucket and the broom. I'll fill up the bucket with water and scrub down the floor real good. One by one, I'll scrub till the tiles shine, till I can practically see myself crying in them. Fortunato's out there hanging from a manjack tree, and I'm scrubbing the floor, and Onerica is taking care of children in Timbuctoo.

Onerica's babysitting in Timbuctoo.

And the old man is crying, locked up in his fruit stand. Watching us leave, one by one. Watching us leave . . . Before an old man cried, the whole world ought to come to an end. If I ever said "My God," I deserve to be set on fire, this very minute. Mama makes her food without tomato, or garlic, or any salt at all. And Digna sings as she sits on that rotten tree trunk out there in the middle of the backyard. I bet I get ingrown toenails from all the water my feet have sloshed around in. Here comes the ice-cream man. After all this time! . . . The ice-cream man is not a bad person—as though there might be a person that existed in this day and age that wasn't a bad person. Sometimes he'll stop and talk to me, and his ice cream sits there and melts in the sun. But he just talks and talks and talks. I'll tell you, I don't even know what he talks about. Have you ever thought how strange the word "talk" sounds? There are words like that. We say them all the time, and then all of a sudden we realize that they're different, strange, maybe they even come from another planet, or they came from somebody that lived here before us and then couldn't or maybe forgot to pick them up and take them with them. So then they, the words I mean, they have to let themselves be adopted and misused by us even while they try to act like they're just one of the family. Anyway, he talks about stupid things, all kinds of nonsense, but at least he talks to me—and it's wonderful that a person just comes up to you and starts up a conversation. Wonderful not only in this day and age, but any time. Always. Here he comes. Good morning. Good morning.

The kids'll run up any minute and start driving him crazy, one asking for strawberry and another one for vanilla and another one this and another one that, and the ice-cream man talking and talking and talking, and he's not a bad person, but I'd like to know where he gets the milk to make the ice cream with, and I'd like to have some ice cream, but I don't have a centavo to my name, and I'd be embarrassed to accept such a gesture.
Gesture . . . What a word—
What language is that? If you had twenty-five centavos, you'd have some ice cream, you spinster, you unloved thing, you old woman.

I better finish scrubbing and sweeping down the porch. Or else I'll have to go back and start all over again.

And so I'm scrubbing the porch and the ice-cream man comes, and without my asking for it or anything he gives me an ice-cream cone. Free—
a pistachio one, no less, my favorite, oh thank you.
I bet any day now the ice-cream man asks me to marry him.
"Thank you very much!"

The kids in the neighborhood tried to kill us again. They stoned us. Now neither Anisia nor I dare go outside, because as quick as lightning all the kids start yelling at us and calling us names and throwing rocks at us, and we have to run and hide because otherwise they'd crack our skulls wide open. And the one that's to blame for it all is my grandmother, that blasted old woman that squats down and prays in every corner of the house at the drop of a hat. The other day they caught her making crosses in the air at the butcher shop, because according to her it was a miracle it was open. Everybody dying laughing, while she's making all these crosses in the air. Until this one informer for the government said Grandma was

EXTRA!!
On Nov. 13, rebel forces of the "Antonio Guiteras" Company, No. 9, under the command of Cdr. Gómez, took the town of San Luis, Oriente Province, an important rail center lying some 30 km. north of Santiago. From this front, as well, there are reports that reinforcements sent by the dictatorship from Palma Soriano to San Luis

were pushed back and heavily hit, suffering more than fifty casualties and the destruction of short-wave equipment and armored cars.

—*Bulletin* of the Revolutionary Army, No. 1, Nov. 15, 1958. 1 ctvo.

really praying for the rebels and then another one said she was really praying that Batista would die, and things went on that way until the women from that Yarey barrio pushed and shoved her out of the store and refused to let her buy any meat. Crazy old woman. So now we're the ones that have to pay for it, because all the kids in the neighborhood are out to get Anisia and me. And we're not going to have any choice but to tell the elves to poison Grandma, or stab her in the neck with a pair of scissors, or spirit her away—anything, so long as she's gone for good. We're not going to have any choice but to tell them to do that.

"These children have got an evil spirit in their bodies. Look at how they look at me. I think you ought to give them a good cleansing with peppercress, and flog them with an arbor vitae switch, and lock 'em up in their room."

At noon the glare seems to glow from the very walls, the stones in the yard, the sparse plants, and the fiber-cement roof. The glare sifts in through windows and cracks and under doors, and it floods the porch. And its desolating, corrosive, blinding power is such—its sheer *glare*—that it allows one to see nothing but itself. Things become transparent. And people become mere shapes, shimmering auras gliding about between the walls devoured by the light. Blinded, they seem to swim, float through that thick, luminous medium (though drowning in its brightness). The old man props a stool against the doorway, and soon he dozes. The old woman, back in the kitchen, wields the instruments of her destiny with skill and fury. Adolfina is still in the bathroom. And Tico and Anisia tie Celia to the rocking chair in the living room while she talks to herself and waves at phantoms in the deserted street . . . It is at that moment that Digna, in the midst of that pulverizing glare, walks down the hall, right under everybody's eyes (though they yawn unseeing, for they are plunged into desolations of their own), and goes out into the backyard. There she sets a ladder against the wall outside the bathroom and climbs up onto the roof. When she reaches the roof, she goes over to a pile of rubble left there and begins slowly and carefully to remove the heaped roof tiles, to lift away pieces of fiber cement and scraps of lumber, until she has uncovered a rickety old steamer trunk. Digna now glances all around, to be sure that no one is watching. And she opens the trunk. Gingerly, almost respectfully, she rummages through the papers, the boxes, the empty jars and bottles, the dead cockroaches, and all the other useless relics which time, the habit of squirreling things away, and poverty and unhappiness have left. At last she digs down to the bottom of the trunk, and there her hand discovers the object of her desire. It is a wad of white fabric, moldy now and mildewed, yellowing, which she caresses with her fingers, crumples again, and then, again looking about to check that no one is watching her, lifts to her lips.

I knew that happiness was a thing that didn't last. I could feel happiness tickling at my nose, my hair, my lips, sometimes even at my earlobes, and it was like I had God by one leg and could touch the sky with my free hand. And I knew, or felt, that that was the coming and going of happiness, all at once. Because that's the way it is. Because I've never kidded myself about what was actually possible. Because even when I was lying in bed with him and I could smell the smell of rum all over everything, I still saw myself as alone. And I would get so sad. I knew so much happiness wasn't possible. I knew it was almost like a dream. Or something that's not supposed to be enjoyed completely and fully right at the moment, but rather later on, when it's gone. Now, for instance. Like a dream, and by the time it's starting it's already coming to an end. I know it's got to be that way, though I'll tell you the truth—I don't like it one bit.

Then, she puts Moisés' pair of underwear back in its place. She covers it with the papers, boxes, empty jars and bottles, and other leavings of the past. She closes the trunk. She hides it again under the wood, the fiber cement, and the roof tiles.

Once more she looks around to be sure that no one has seen her. And then, laughing great gusts of laughter, she begins to descend the ladder. . . Her secret. Her great secret. She has a secret. . . . And then she took to climbing up onto the roof above the bathroom every day. And taking out the pair of Moisés' old underwear, smelling it, and laughing out loud. And then, she took to laughing out loud all day long. And then she would sing, while she was up on the roof. And then she took to hunting spiders, lizards, rats—invisible to the rest of the family. And then, following what had become a classic tradition, she tried to kill Tico and Anisia, her own children, who brought such a thing about by doing nothing but laughing at her day and night. But they jumped out of the way just in time, so that only the old man and Jacinta, running in when they heard the shouting, received the bath of boiling water. And then.

The pigeons have gotten furious—they've thrown us out of the house. Now we all have to live up on the roof of the factory. At noon, when the zinc roof heats up, we start pacing from one corner to the other; and then as it gets hotter and hotter, we run, our feet burn so—we can't put them down on the zinc and we certainly can't keep them up in the air. So we run, like a bunch of madmen, while really it's just our feet burning to a crackling. Or we jump up and down and jump up and down. You cannot imagine what it's like to live up here, on a white-hot zinc roof that burns you like fire in the daytime and freezes you at night. It's awful. And as though that weren't enough, now it turns out that the whole neighborhood has taken a terrible dislike to us all, so people stand out in the middle of the street and yell things at us—they call us witches and voodoo doctors and I don't know what else, and they say we ought to be hanged from a lamppost. All of that, they scream at us. Poor Mama, I don't know how we got her up here. Up here so high. And now she spends the whole day walking along balancing herself real carefully from one sheet of zinc to the next, and sometimes she slips and falls and is just hanging there by her slip off the factory eaves while a whole crowd of people gather out in the street to watch her fall. But so far she's always just hung there . . . Esther and Fortunato spend their whole life lying on the ridgepole, looking up at the sky like it was the most natural thing in the world to do, and when there's a hailstorm they just open their mouths to try to catch the hailstones. And I'm the one that's screwed, because I'm still waiting for Moisés and I know he'll never think to look for me up here. I bet he's already gone to the house, but since he probably knocked on the door and nobody answered, he's left. Ay, and now he won't come back again. Damned pigeons. I told them those birds were evil. Every animal that flies is evil, because they know about how inferior we are. But nobody paid any attention, so here we are. This is the upshot of it. And the worst thing about all this is that we're all turning into pigeons, but without wings. Just yesterday I heard Fortunato—when he said something he sounded just like a homing pigeon, and Adolfina answered him and she sounded like a pigeon too. I tried to make them be quiet. I ran crying all the way across this white-hot roof to tell them to hush. And as I was getting over to where they were, I realized that I had started sounding like a pigeon myself. I tell you, there's no way out. We've caught the devil's own mange, and little by little we'll turn into lord knows what. At least when I was a pigeon I could get to see Moisés. But I could swing on the devil's balls or turn into a bluebottle fly for all I'd ever see him again. I know that. So what do I care—I'd as soon be one thing as another, because no matter what, I'm always going to be Digna-the-piece-of-trash-that-got-left-in-the-road. Digna. A piece of trash. Abandoned. Abandoned and with two children to bring up. And a whole life to die in.

Goddamned lice. I've got them all over me. When my wings sprout (assuming they do) I'm going to burn them off. I don't want to be anything more than I've ever been—a bird burning her own wings off. Wings, my ass. Where are these famous wings, I'd like to know? . . . A bird that knows that no matter where she lights, she's going to get a fist in the chest, two raggedy children, and a bundle of clothes tied up in a sheet. Her hope chest.

And then two men and a woman came. The men were tall and thin, old; the woman was burly and strong. The three of them tried to convince her to get dressed and come with them. Jacinta, who was still limping from her burns, stayed right behind them, hopping along holding her skirt away from her legs with her hands. But Digna refused to get dressed; she would just laugh and from time to time she would give a kick which invariably landed on the husky woman's shinbone. The old woman was crossing herself and loudly praying to heaven. Adolfina, locked up in the bathroom, was sobbing hysterically. And so the procession made its way down the hallway—Digna (giving kicks that always landed in the same place), the fat woman, the two tall stringy old men, and the old woman hopping with her skirt between forefinger and thumb. At last, when they came to the kitchen, Digna whirled about, ripped Jacinta's skirt off her, and before anyone could stop her she threw it into the cookstove. Then she leapt in one clean leap up onto the table and began to dance. Every time one of them tried to get close to her, she gave a kick at the person's chest and laughed. Finally, one of the men vaulted (with considerable grace and agility, actually) up onto the table and very genteelly offered her his arm—which she, moved, took at once, at which point the two of them intertwined in a frenzied dance. Digna shrieked with joy. At one of the wildest moments of the dance, the man clasped her in his arms, lifted her into the air, and tossed her down to the burly woman, who caught her as though she weighed nothing. Then, with care and gentleness, she lay her down on the floor, took her by both arms, and immobilized her. The three of them then picked her up and carried her down the hall and out onto the porch. The whole neighborhood was outside in front of the house, waiting. They did not have to put a straitjacket on her, or catch her in some sort of psychiatric armlock. As soon as she was inside the car, she began to wave at all the people, and to smile ever so brightly. Beaming, she waved goodbye.

"Ay, Adolfina! For all you hold dear. I swear I'm going to get the colic if this keeps up, woman. Ay! I've been waiting to use the bathroom for three hours! Adolfina!"

The old man saw it all from his fruit stand, and although she could not see him, he waved goodbye through the crack in the door. Then, in a loud, deliberate voice, he began to inventory the lantern chimneys, the boxes of matches, the plantains, and the rotten tomatoes—the only merchandise that was left. But all was not well. Suddenly, his voice broke at one number and it would not go on. His voice was hoarse, harsh at the best of times, but now it fractured into a fine, airy, desperate moan, a wail, like a rat at the exact instant a man steps on its tail. The old man. The old man then—still like that rat—stuck his head under the counter. He stayed in that position all afternoon. At nightfall, when he pulled his head out, Death was sitting up on the counter, taking off and putting back on a sandal which was apparently hurting his foot, and which changed in little blinks into an iron boot, a hammock, a blind snake, and then at last a leaf from an almond tree. " 'Evening," Death said pleasantly to Polo, buckling his sandal. Apparently it had stopped hurting his foot now.

Ay, and things going from bad to worse every day. Now we're done for, for sure. Yesterday I finally just grabbed the washstand and chopped it to kindling and threw it in the cookstove so I could cook. Although today I'm not going to worry about the fire, since we don't have any food.

And besides, almost nobody in this house eats.

If only I could cry for Polo, but what for? That dratted old man, God forgive me, but he never worried about anything. What a husband I get, my God. If he took me to bed, which he did, it was because there was no other way out for him. Ay, but now I really ought to bury the hatchet.

Or if I could cry for Fortunato. But what for? What good would it be for him to be alive? What was he ever good for? And anyway, the others have already cried plenty. Ay, Lord, I bet nobody's going to cry that many tears for *me*, when *I* kick the bucket. I'd be better off to cry for Dead-Esther. But what for? She never gave *me* any thought. So far as she was concerned, I never even existed.

Or if I could cry for crazy Digna, who's locked up in that

place where they won't even let me put my nose in. Place full of women wearing uniforms, and where all you can hear is yelling and screaming and banging, and then . . . But what for? Can a crazy woman answer your prayers? Or for dead Adolfina—Adolfina-always-burning-to-a-crisp. But no. Cry for that hussy who's always doing things to spite me and vex me and put me out?—that hussy I'm certainly *not* going to cry for . . . Or for Tico and Anisia, who've turned out to be a couple of mischief-making heathens, and who I've got to be always watching to make sure they're not trying to poison me. But who do You want me to cry for today, Lord? For my dead mother? For Celia, who I don't know how she could ever die, because the poor thing never lived? But I'm not crying. I don't feel like crying for them. So, since I don't quite know what to do, I finally go into my bedroom. There sits dead Adolfina, like always, rummaging through the box of snapshots.

I went to the chifforobe and took out the box they keep all the old snapshots in. I've looked at those pictures a hundred times already. But every once in a while I do it again—I keep a lookout, and I wait till nobody's in the old man and old woman's bedroom, and then I slip in and get the pictures. The first one I pick up happens to be one of me—I've got a neckerchief tied around my neck so tight it looks like I was trying to strangle myself. I must have been about eighteen in that picture . . . These have people I don't know in them, or maybe I've forgotten who they were, distant relatives or something. . . . Esther on her thirteenth birthday. Esther with a bunch of her girlfriends . . . Esther in the park. Looks like the one that lasted the shortest time has the most pictures.

I was sitting there, looking through the photos, when Mama came in and stood there with her mouth half open, staring at me, amazed.

"What are you doing?"

"Nothing. I'm not doing a thing."

"You're looking at those pictures."

"Well yes. Look at yourself here with Polo, the day the farm was sold. You're standing there dying laughing . . ."

"Ay, that's because that's what that photographer wanted. My God, don't show me those pictures, it's bad luck."

"Look at Polo here, in front of his vegetable stand when it was closed."

"Woman, put those things away. . . . Let me see the face the old man had on . . . Let me see."

"Here's one of the whole family taken together standing under that big old tamarind tree. You remember that big old tamarind tree, Mama? We'd all sit under it to shuck corn. And you'd make up the lemonade and bring it out to us. And we'd sit out there shucking corn and telling stories and laughing as hard as we could. We were all young back then, in that house. Back then practically everybody in the world was young. It would practically be a party to shuck a whole wagonful of corn sitting under that tamarind tree."

"Here's Digna and her two children with Moisés in the middle. That Moisés always came out looking so good in pictures . . ."

"There was nothing so much fun as shucking corn. And sometimes you'd get inspired and make coconut candy. If you only knew . . . sometimes I'd want to die at one of those times, right then and there. It would have been worth it to die. A person didn't have any aches or pains, there were no worries worth worrying about, everything looked happy, and anything at all was an excuse for a good time. I'd roll around in the dry corn shucks and I would feel so happy that I could have died right there. I'd listen to the girls telling stories while you passed around the coconut kisses, or the coffee, or whatever it might be, and I'd say to myself, I couldn't be happier—if I could die right this minute, I'd die happy. And Polo off somewhere, in a corner, with shucks practically up to his neck, and actually talking—to everybody! And you passing around coffee and coconut kisses. And me shucking corn and listening to the girls laughing and talking. And the men, too. Because men would come to the shucking. All the men and boys in the whole coun-try . . ."

"A picture of Fortunato when he was six. He was always so ugly. And screaming at the top of his lungs."

"As soon as they heard there was going to be a corn shucking, they'd come like bees to the hive. You could hear them laughing and talking for miles before they got to the house. And the pile of corn getting higher and higher. And people laughing louder and louder. And I tell you I felt like getting me a handful of that laughter and eating it, or stuffing it in a box and keeping it, and opening it once in a while to listen."

"Here's you gathering mussels in Santa Lucía. Look at your hair standing straight up—there must have been a lot of wind that day . . ."

"I'd be opening that box this very minute and listening to that laughter. What does laughing taste like, I wonder? What does it look like? Laugh, laugh, go on—like you did that time you put salt in the coffee instead of sugar. Let's play like we're sitting under the tamarind tree. Let's play like time doesn't exist anymore, and we're all dying laughing in the middle of that lake of corn shucks and the waves of talk. I've got corn weevils all over my skirt, and they're tickling me, and I feel happy. We've brought out a million lanterns and lamps and lights of all kinds, to light up the place under the tree. 'You have to be careful with all those lamps,' Papa says. Now here come Primitivo Leyva's daughters and the Pupo girls. This is a party. Corn shucking at my house is a party. The girls have all come up and said hello to me, and asked me all kinds of questions about everybody. If anybody were listening, what would they think, do you think? What would they think we were?"

"I didn't come out too bad here. But with that halfwit Polo beside me, holding up a broadside about Chiba's that covers my face completely!"

"If somebody were to hear all that racket, they might even go crazy themselves, from not understanding how there could be so much happiness in the world. Because that *was* happiness, but since it was, we didn't recognize it. Those nights we felt like we were something besides people working their fingers to the bone at a corn shucking and having a shivaree—and the way those oil lamps winked and sputtered. Those nights we knew it all but we pretended we didn't know a thing, we'd make ourselves sick on coconut kisses and laugh without even knowing what we were laughing at, or maybe just laughing at some silliness. Those nights were, and they still are, the only thing worth saving in my memory my whole life long. The only thing that ever put a sparkle in our eyes or made us sing with our mouths closed when we looked around, the only thing that still sometimes makes me feel so sorry for you, Mama, and for me, and for everybody. Because I'm still sitting under that big tamarind tree. Because I can still feel those corn weevils crawling around on my legs and climbing on my skirt. And still hear Primitivo's daughters laughing. And see that parade of boys from La Perrera. And I can still play like I'm innocent and naive. And not tell a soul that I already know it all."

Death went on fluttering around the old man. But the old man played dumb—he simply went on counting nonexistent grapefruits and bananas. Death was in no hurry, so he flew around and around the fruit stand. But finally he sat down on the tomato baskets, and the old man winced as he heard the sickening squashing sound of the tomatoes bursting and spitting out seeds. Someone outside was calling. "Here's your abandoned daughter out here." "Here's your burned-to-a-crisp daughter out here." "Here's your hanged grandson out here." There was always someone outside yelling something unfair, horrible, insulting, and calamitous—things by which he, the old man, was always hurt the most. "Here's your daughter dancing with a Negro," someone was shouting now. Inside, the old man and Death were playing hide-and-seek. The old man turned into a chigger, and Death was hard put to find him, since the chigger crawled inside an empty spool of thread. Outside, the old woman was calling Polo, but Death caught her shouts and threw them back out into the yard. So the old man didn't hear her calls. "Open up! Open up," the voice of the old woman was shouting out there, and then she would kick at the termite-riddled walls of the fruit stand, so that had it not been for Death's deciding that her voice would not penetrate that sanctum, the vegetable stand surely would have come tumbling down like the walls of Jericho. "Open up, you son of a bitch, open up!" But Death went on catching her words and furiously hurling them back through the cracks in the walls. *Whatever became of all your fury, whatever became of all your violence, where is your rebelliousness now?"* If the old man had looked out through those cracks he might have seen himself, in a landscape that might have been this Island's but which actually lay far beyond the grayish hills and over the demon-infested ocean. He was climbing up into the top of a dry, dusty tree to blow the conch shell, for his mother had died and he was alone in the house. . . . Death picked up a lantern chimney and out of pure devilishness he smashed it on the floor. The old man bent over to pick up the pieces, and at that, Death started tickling him from behind. The old man dodged away laughing, and then suddenly he heard the brief explosion of a voice—a quick, sharp sound which Death, his hands full tickling the old man, had not been able to catch and toss back outside through the cracks. The old man heard that sound, a sound like the wail of a person who has never before complained in all his life, or like the rending of someone who after suffering centuries of infamy at last simply bursts. The old man listened again— the sound was disappearing, giving up the struggle, apparently. He raised his bald head and looked Death in the face with his bright, dry eyes. Death set the lantern chimney he had just picked up back in its place and passed his long fingers across the old man's smooth skull, with the same tenderness with which a mother touches a child unfairly punished. Then the old man put his arms around Death's waist, and Death gave a quiet chuckle. The old woman, outside, utterly rabid with fury, began to try to bite her way through the wall. And the young demons practically split their sides laughing when they saw pieces of teeth spew from the old woman's bloody mouth. The youth blew the conch shell again. But still no one came.

"Open up! Open up, Adolfina! There's a limit to my patience!"

Dance, dance. The water spills over her thin, disheveled hair as she dances. The water bathes her body, which is always boiling hot. The water floods her always-open eyes. The water, which sizzles and almost evaporates when it hits her skin, wets her body yet cannot put out its flames, and cannot surfeit it . . . The water, spilling from the pipes with all the force a brand-new, unfiltered aqueduct delivers, and especially since it hadn't worked in months . . . The water, rushing turbid and violent and cold from the pipes . . . The water, and her dancing and dancing and dancing in its spray . . . The water, and her leaping about in the bathtub which is not a bathtub. The water, covering her body as she—frenzied and utterly alone—tries to throw every bone out of joint, to the tune of that rushing stream . . . of water.

No matter who comes, I'm not opening this door. Not to anybody. I'm going to leave it like this, with the bolt on. So nobody can come in. So they'll leave me be. Especially today, when there's all this water. Especially today. . . . So they'll leave me alone and let me dance with everybody in the world. I'm not opening the door for *any*body. They can just think again. Nobody. Because my life has flown by, without my even knowing how it's gotten past me. Just flown by—while I've been taking care of layings-in and throwing out bedpans full of piss. But I'm not taking it anymore. This very day I'm going to leave this house and go out and go to bed with the first man I find. Or a horse, for all I care, or a lizard. Or a dog. Anything. In just one minute I'm leaving this house. I've had enough of this denying myself things in exchange for nothing. You've had enough of this, Adolfina. Go on, get out in the street and find yourself a man. Go out there and strip naked in the middle of the park. Do anything you feel like doing. Go to bed with any man that comes along. But do *some*thing. Do something. Do something. Ay, I want to do something.
    If you stay here in this house you'll hear that wall clock going *Tick-tock, tick-tock, tick-tock,* and there'll be no way out. If you keep living in this house the very walls will start eating your face away. If you stay here you'll turn into a piece of wet brick,

and your face will turn that greenish color of vegetable soup. If you stay here you'll never be able to expect anything but the coming of Death. The others made up their minds to leave—and they did, too, they went anywhere, as long as it wasn't here. Onerica, Esther . . . All the men left while they were still young, before the curse of this house destroyed them—even Fortunato finally got his nerve up . . . If you stay here—the coming of Death, that's all, when you're old and alone. With my arms shriveled up from never holding anybody in them. Get out in the street, woman. Get out and start howling under some tree. Get out in the middle of that gunfight and beg somebody to kill you. But do *some*thing, Adolfina. Do something, because things are beginning to come clear. And you now have all the earmarks of a faded chest of drawers, or a wall with the paint flaking off, or a rusty flatiron. Do *some*thing, you piece of rotten lumber.

Do something, you knife with the handle broken off.

Do something, you sofa with fleas.

Get out of this house and start hunting.

Get out into the street and smile. Wiggle your bottom. Run. Get out into the street and do something to justify being alive. Do something—you scissors with no cloth to cut!

And then she died.   Yes, she died. There was a bombard-
                                    ment. A rebel band made a daring,
                                    desperate raid on the town in broad
daylight, in the middle of the afternoon. Their plan was to steal some weapons. There was a fight, the rattle of machine guns, even a hand grenade. Once they had gotten what they had come for, the rebels scattered through the part of town the family lived in, shooting wildly into the air, into walls and windows to cover their retreat. At that, the army in turn ordered the entire neighborhood bombarded, to kill them at any cost. It didn't matter that houses and their inhabitants were destroyed as well. In fact, that was part of the army's plan—official reports stated that the entire area was enemy territory, for if not, how could the rebels have been allowed to hide, to get away? The little red military planes took off, and they flew across the town. As though inspired by the music of their own engines, they carried out their mission

rhythmically and with precise discipline. It appeared, in fact, that one of the objectives of those machines was the asylum Digna was in. Not one wall of that building was left standing. But some of those who lived there did flee the building and were saved—including Digna—though later they died. Ear-splitting explosions.

So then I went outside, and all of a sudden I realized that the world was coming to an end—and about time, I say. So I didn't even flinch, I just looked up at the sky which was crumbling and falling down. You should have seen that for yourself, the sky cracking and falling all over the place, and me walking through the pieces all over the ground! Me walking with no idea where I was going. And not worried about not knowing. Walking along like a person who knows that the end has come but that you have to go on because there's no alternative. Like a person who knows that nothing but silence will ever come to us, silence and a bigger loneliness than has ever been known before. Like a person that's run out of hope. Like that, just walking along with my hand shading my eyes. Skipping. Flying through the air once in a while. Giving a little scream, and then singing like I always do—with my mouth shut tight. Looking for my children and wanting to not find them. Asking people and then running off before I got an answer. Walking along and feeling like a fine white mist was freezing my stomach. And it was like I knew everything and had seen everything. And it was like even after I'd gotten past the end, I still knew as little as I'd known before I'd known a thing. And it was like I was being born right out in the middle of a field of bitter chicory plants and was screaming for them not to let me be born. And it was like I was hearing the whole world shrieking just seconds before it vanished, with me the only thing left. Me, surrounded by some kind of terrible fire that was reaching out and reaching out its fingers to grab me. Reaching out and reaching out, down through a sort of hall, down through a sort of a hall with no end.

ONLY LEFT FOR SALE ONE SUGARCANE
PRESS—SIX STAINLESS-STEEL PARTS ON
BALL-BEARING MOUNTS. May be seen at
Calle Arias, No. 36, for a demonstration.
                                        —*El Norte*
                        Holguín, Sept. 29, 1958

When night is almost fallen, millions of naked women emerge like lizards rushing out from among the trunks of custard-apple trees. When it is almost pouring rain, and the sky is ripping, and the demons split their sides laughing and scream at us, Come, come. When the day is done and the day begins, and everything is one great frozen fire. We go outside, Fortunato and I. With our wings shooting sparks and our beaks wide open so we can swallow lots of air and swell ourselves up, we float up until we blend into the flock of turkey buzzards that're always watching from way up there—sometimes we entertain ourselves by pretending that we're kingbirds. And we keep going up and up until we disappear into that bluish-colored glare. And into the whiteness that all the birds make flying back and forth, who knows why or where or where from. We go higher and higher, until we realize how high we are, and then we fall—like always, right into the Palace of the White Skunks, where all of them, lined up in the Great Hall holding long spears, are waiting for us. We fall into the arms of the beasts, that is to say, and since they had thought we were lost forever, they almost start to have a little affection for us.   —*Dead-Esther*

One night I saw Fortunato having a conversation with the rotten tree trunk that's out there in the backyard. He was telling it something terrible and crying his eyes out. He was crying and roaring with laughter. I said to myself, He's crazy as a loon, and I ran for my bed. That was a long time ago. Now I wouldn't know what to think.—Them

THE FIFTH
AGONY

Because there was always that problem, too. Not to go mad. Have strength enough to bear without (truly) bearing, to (seem to) accept, without accepting. Have courage enough to (seem to) play the game, so that he did not betray himself, so that he did not lose his reason, his judgment, or his mind, did not lose that almost ungraspable thread which is the thread of every man's own particular and inarguable truth, the *authentic* truth, the truth that no one else knew and that would never be any good for putting food in his belly, or for making his family happy, or for muting the racket of the belts and pulleys, or for reducing the blinding glare. Because above all else, above the screams and insults, above the inexorability of time's devastations, the menace held by daily living, above all that pointless, stupid racket (which for all its pointlessness was nonetheless unbearable, which added so heavily to the weight of his frustrations, which so tainted the outcome of every real, memorable, important undertaking that it might well be the thing that finally did drive him mad)—above all that, at all costs he had to keep lucidity enough, strength enough, courage enough to see (dimly, through the night), over there, that faint thread, that filament which for all he knew existed only in his imagination, which in fact for all he knew might well be nothing but one of the forms by which infamy manifests itself to us. Out there beyond, there was the night. Not blue. Not white. Not soft. The night. Period. The night with its ugly street corners and dirty clotted water. The night taking form in clouds of mosquitoes, in the bottom of a huge cauldron scoured furiously. The night with its fires, with its shrieks of red children and abominable dogs as starving and hysterical as their masters. The *real* night, with its unending sewers, its high thick walls, its undodgeable tracers—flashes of fatal powder . . . As you stretch out your hand, as you grope ahead in the void, as you try to catch yourself—is there anyone who will come to catch you, and help you stand? Is there anyone who will even see that you are crying out for help? And that someone, if he comes, might not he be precisely one of your enemies? . . . He had had to listen to so much nonsense lately. *Always.* But what was sure, what was certain was . . . what *was* certain? . . . Out there, the almost metallic rustling of small beasts—like him, sweaty, stinking, and, like him, howling. Shrilly squeaking, bitter, betrayed, like him. What if he just stayed still, what if he didn't move, what if at last he turned himself over to those claws and pincers and teeth? "In the fall . . . the leaves . . . in the fall . . . the trees." Was there anything he might recite now, any witty (memorized) piece declaimed in a loud distress-filled voice that might immunize him against that incessant rattle of machine guns? He knew a song. His grandfather had taught it to him when he was a boy. And he would sing it in the breezeway, under the rain gutters, or sitting at one of the corners of the long dinner table. The song (in a great wealth of tears and self-pity) told the story of a child born fatherless, since his father had "fooled" his mother and run away. The boy "becomes a man," goes off to war, and "in revenge kills his father." The last verse of the song went like this: "And that's the way boys act who really know how to love." He could never forget that song. The national anthem, maybe, of course, he might forget the national anthem—but that song? Never. Its lyrics, its catchy tune reverberated endlessly across that plain, that field, that pasture—his life walled about with insults, with hungers of all kinds, with humiliations of all ages past and present, with dreams and idiocies of infinite and useless variety. Smells that were never enjoyed, words that distance had stripped of their honest note of resentment, places and times that no longer existed except in this moment when, though utterly irrecoverable, they were evoked. And out there, beyond, what *was* there out there? The absolute certainty that the terror would hang—fixed, unwavering, and indifferent—over every little daily calamity, over every small triumph, for it was a terror which needed no din of wheels and pulleys, no stink of rotten fruit, no brutal and brutalizing government to frighten or eradicate its victims, because it was the true, great terror, the great solitude, it was the certainty of Death—already knocking at the door, already knocking . . . And if he still somehow managed to break through this circle of his pursuers (which was difficult enough) and at least for the moment escape (which was probably impossible), it would still be there—stalking him, waiting its chance to eliminate him, constantly grinning at him. Now he had no God, though he still had the sense of an eternal fraud, a con game, a terrible practical joker, perhaps, hanging over even his slightest torment—bringing his hands up to his shirt, feeling how wet it was, turning his eyes up to the sky. What were those stars doing—twinkling as fierce as noon, and just as hellish? He no longer had God, though he still had the certainty that someone, or fate itself perhaps, was forever watching—over the stars, over fiber-cement roofs, over the twigs of a thistle plant, over toilet bowls. He no longer had God, but he had the utter certainty that that adversity (or adversary) was there, right there, standing even in the way of his mad flight, that its ears were pricked up for the least rustle of the grass, sensitive to every vibration, that it was always ready to denounce him, to sway and stir like the maggots when (long ago, in the country) they felt the light as he would raise the cover of the privy. He no longer had God, and he did not have a face square-jawed or oval and seductive, or utterly impassive and unmoved, a face unassailable, a face without anger, without flashing eyes, without sparkling teeth—things which, perhaps, would have exempted him from these philosophical quandaries. He had no God, and he did not have those fierce, egotistical, self-assured gestures that other people had, either, he had no possibility of school, trips, fabulous parties. He had no God, and he had no slave plantation, no vast eternally green gardens, no 1958 Oldsmobile—the latest model—no important position in an important firm, no kingdom—things which surely would have diverted his mind toward new religious doctrines, or left him time to think one up. He had no God, and he was unable to be like the others—fully stupid, or fully happy, or fully wretched. For the truth was that at times he felt that someone or something was calling him, and he wanted to see who or what it was, he wanted, without knowing why, to whistle as he got dressed. The truth was that sometimes he, too, had almost possessed some bit of the silence, the dusk, the darkness, the almost-felt . . . He had no God, and he had no trust in His new representatives, either, who assumed (in all seriousness—passionately, even) the divine role of fraud on a grand scale. What was he doing there then, full of lead, sweating horribly, bursting inside, lurching through the grass, through screams, through the rocks? For somehow it did all matter to him; he actually had *faith*—that was the word, that was always the word. Many times he had been Adolfina—he had suffered as she had (or perhaps more) the urgent need to be embraced, penetrated, to have his throat cut, to be strangled and asphyxiated, to be annihilated in the name of love. Many times he had been Celia, and he had discovered the splendor of traditional sufferings, and of madness. Many times he was Digna, and he learned of the other faces of betrayal and of solitude, faces which he would have thought impossible, unbearable. Many times he had been Polo and Jacinta, and he had learned at those times the terrible extent of fury and of frustration, the necessity for rancor and for blasphemy. Many times he had been Tico and Anisia, and he realized that in order for a man to survive, he had to possess two essential qualities—innocence and cruelty. Many times he had been Esther, and like her he reasoned (not without terror) that voluntary death is the only pure, disinterested, free act a man may aspire to, the only act which saves him, invests him with a halo of fascination, and, perhaps, bestows upon him some tiny bit of eternity and even heroism. Many times—all the time, really—he had been all of them, and he had suffered for them, and perhaps when he had been them (for he had more imagination than they did, he could go beyond the mere here-and-now) he had even suffered more than they, deep within himself, deep within his own, invariable terror. And he had given them a voice, a way of expressing the stupor, the dull horror, the fear, the blind terror which they, surely, would never be fully able to know or to suffer. Because there was that, too, the bearing all the wretchedness of the others on his shoulders, the suffering for them, the trying to understand it all, the trying to understand *them*. There was that, too—the infinite transfigurations of terror. His vocation as interpreter, spokesman, unblinking observer, scrutinizer . . . God, God—still without being able to invoke Him fully—and what about himself, when had there been time for himself? He had always yearned for time for himself, his own time, to howl in, and in which to howl his own particular howl. He wanted to speak his own story—*himself* banging the walls, dancing, vomiting in the bathroom, slapping his own forehead (for he had sinusitis), and now shot, wildly fleeing his pursuers, the skin of his face scraped raw where he had fallen, fleeing through kicks, "Halts," clattering rifle fire, and fever-chattering teeth. *Himself*—outside time, groping through the darkness, suffering for them all and, all alone, taking the risks—himself unable to bear it, destroying himself for the others; himself loving, hating, and even trying, at someone's orders, under the threat of the doom set by someone else, to transform himself into another person. Was that other person him? His real self which had been put on earth to be transfigured, to suffer, to rebel, and, always, to do so alone? Why? What for? Knowing there was no possible protest, knowing there was no reward or recompense. Apostasy for the pure (justified) sake of apostasy. Rebellion for the pure sake of rebellion. It was then—or perhaps before, perhaps forever, perhaps even a little while later—that he realized that that was his reason to live, his goal, his end—*Now, now*, he thought— that only through violence and by means of those transfigurations would he be able to find his own true self, his rent and raveled fulfillment—find plenitude. How would he be able to bear it— with that face (his eyes were brown), with that din, with that heat, and, to boot, with that terrible knowledge? He had no God— he had only, sometimes, that unreachable itch, that tickle, which he could not give name to even at the moment of its coming and which sometimes came and went and left him nothing but the renewed sense of being stalked and hounded, and of being frustrated . . . How nice, then, if he could hop from one tile to the next, move about the house, give up, give in, and, hopping on one foot in a crazy game of hopscotch he invented for himself on the front porch, come at last to the place on the porch where he could watch all the people pass by (quickly sometimes, indifferent and casual sometimes, happy sometimes), watch them as he cried or sat in the shade and cut all those warm, invisible, unclassifiable animals' little throats (the tiny beasts that were he himself) or lay down on the sofa languidly (they had put a new seat in it) and caw, caw. Was that not a wonderful verb—*caw?* . . . To hell with that smell of rotting fruit, forever floating in the air. To hell with the night. What were those stars doing? There they were, though. What the devil could be said at this late date about a star—what purpose did it serve, what was its usefulness? Were stars not made to be tamed, to be mastered, to be controlled, to be devoured, to be gulped down in one gulp, to be used now, *now*, at once, to be vexed and mortified, insulted, and then kicked, battered, and discarded, and then, just for fun (and there lay the key to the changing frauds and betrayals), to be locked away in cells of iron where, doubtless, they might be smothered, their screams muffled forever, after a few hours' imprisonment? . . . Still, there they were, pale and distant, bathing his convulsion-racked body in steely light. There they were, cold, unattainable, sparkling their remote unwarming sparkles. The stars . . . And the night with its mysterious beckonings and its pointless endings. To hell with that body, that young, damned body which was always in the way, always a hindrance and a burden—too big, too simple, too slow, too much, too much, too much—always in the wrong place, always yearning after something, burning. To hell with that face, those eyes especially—he didn't know what to do with them, where to rest them, they were so big and sad, like cows' eyes, that they were always unsettling people, inspiring mistrust in anyone who looked into them. To hell with that hair, which seized the least excuse (some light breeze, a tree branch) to grow wild and uncombed. To hell with his sweat-dripping hands, his rumbling, growling belly, and that tickling itch as well, that strange melody, that rhythm, that gooseflesh, hair standing on end, which commanded him to tell the story—now, at this very instant—to speak, to say something which would endure, something new and terrible, perhaps the inner pain of that very urge to speak, perhaps the real pain at the moment of the burst of gunfire. To hell even with the doubts and self-contradictions that made him leap from one terror into another, make decisions for everyone, suffer for them all, and still go on. To hell with the variations of fear and wonder, the infinite scenarios, the speculations, the projected encounters—which now had come to pass. To hell with it all. Oh, just to be able to let himself go, to be able not to have to look for that probably nonexistent thread of truth and meaning anymore. Grimaces and ugly faces, oh, just to be able to make faces and to kick against the pricks, to dance on four wooden legs, howl on his hands and knees, crawl on all fours, on his hands and knees gobble down all the blue-black nights he never got to see. To walk freely, lightly, decidedly, triumphantly (on all fours) now that he was rid of all that—all the things that annihilated (and justified) his existence—the infinite sounds, rackets, dins, and the single, unique melody. Oh what a swaying dance . . . Yes, because there was that too. As his face was now touching that dirty, resistant matter, the earth. Even at that moment when the end was rushing upon him—and that fly once more as well, that fly which was determined to rest on the site it had chosen for its own—even then, he had to do everything he could so as not to go mad.

The Life of the Dead

Early early in the morning we go out, Fortunato and I, to pick stars. We take a real real long pole with a hook on it and we cut them down, or sometimes we throw rocks at them and knock them down. But there are always a few that don't want to fall, so when that happens I jump up way up high and pick them off with my fingers. The stars are like live spiders. One of these days I'll show you one so you can see. And if you ask me to, I might even give you one to keep. Uh-huh, they're exactly like live spiders, and sometimes they get pretty mad, too, and then they shoot sparks out of their eyes and everything. That's why I'm real real careful when I pick up a star, so it doesn't set my arm afire and burn me up. Just yesterday one fell and hit Fortunato on the head and left him as bald as a billiard ball. It was this great big huge star, one of those that just won't give in, and that get furious when you pick them out of the sky. This star, after it had burned all of Fortunato's hair off, it came running after me and shot fire at my eyes, and if I hadn't shut them, I'd be blind today. But I'm no fool, I closed thcm as tight as a clam, and I put my foot on the blasted thing, to stop it. You ought to have seen that sight—as soon as it felt me stepping on it, it stopped shooting out sparks and started little by little getting dark, and making little soft snorts and bellows, until finally it was just a piece of charcoal, and I threw it in a mud puddle . . . There are getting to be fewer and fewer stars. All morning I bet we haven't picked more than seven or eight—and even so, some of them weren't worth keeping. Fortunato says we ought to start looking for something else to do. And I know he's right. I know that sooner or later we're going to have to stop playing this game. But we ought to go slow. Slow. Nice and slow. Don't worry, Fortunato—in a little while, when we've picked the sky clean of these sparkly spiders, we'll find something else. But what about after that? . . . Don't you worry.

Out behind the old well—which is where we live now, Fortunato and I—is where we meet every afternoon. And I take out the big clay pitcher with the narrow neck (so it's real dark inside) where we keep the stars prisoners. Sometimes Fortunato cries, like he was still alive. And so then I, just to keep him company, I play like I'm crying too. The stars wiggle and jump around in the pitcher, and sometimes one or two of them even get away from me. But all I have to do is look at them real hard and they come back, all bedraggled-looking, and crawl back inside. Fortunato doesn't stop crying, but I tell him they've gotten used to the bottom of the pitcher and they really don't feel comfortable outside it anymore. That could be true, too. They've been prisoners so many years now that it may be that they think the black bottom of that pitcher is the sky. A great big huge sun goes past us real slow and sort of grudgingly says Good evening. Fortunato watches it go away and he cries even louder. The stars start stirring and rattling around in the plugged-up pitcher. I cry too, but it's probably just because I've gotten in the habit. And so on, until it's night. Or maybe day. And I think that maybe this is all a big lie I'm telling. But I know it's the truth. I think that maybe I'm just a girl and that what I want is to move somewhere else where there's not so much racket and carrying-on, where the guavas don't stink so, and where somebody'll come along and ask a person if she wants to get married. I think, though, that by tomorrow I'll be wanting something else, something that's not this nonsense of poking at stars with a long pole with a hook on the end of it and keeping them prisoners until they shrivel up and practically die inside a moldy old clay pitcher like this one, which my grandfather used to carry watered milk in, to sell to the townsfolk. Back then. I. Fortunato. The pitcher. There's the big one. They're ringing the bell. I mean the horn—. *Gracáck. Fracáck. Grapáck.*

Oh, I forgot—sometimes stars fall without my having to pick them. They fall all by themselves and they beg me to throw them in the pitcher. When we stop playing this game, what'll become of them? There's all kinds of stuff in the sky.

Night. Gunfire and the organ at Eufrasia's Ball Room lend monotonous rhythm to the neighborhood. The moon moistens its cold embittered face in the clouds. Someone is snoring, someone is moaning, someone tosses and turns in the sheets, howls softly in the silence (which is not silence but the merging of all the shrieks, rustles, howls, and moans into one anonymous, vague, ungraspable yet rhythmic sound). This is the hour at which Celia gets slowly out of bed, walks out to the backyard (sometimes stumbling into the washstand or the radio or a wall), leans the rickety old wooden ladder up against the roof of the bathroom, and climbs up. When she is on the roof, balancing laboriously, she slips over to the pile of rubble (pieces of roof tiles, old lumber, empty cans, and sheets of zinc) that buries the steamer trunk. Celia looks about cautiously, then opens the trunk. Now intent on what she seeks, she paws through the objects in that rusty antique—old spoons, pieces of glass, empty jars and bottles, a pair of underwear she pushes aside indifferently—until at last, there at the bottom of the trunk her fingers find the treasured objects she has sought. Her hands tremblingly bring into the silver light the intimate things that were Esther's—her first brassiere, her first slip, her first pair of high-heeled shoes, a pair of pink plush bedroom slippers, a lock of her hair from the last time it was cut, a piece of fingernail, the butts of the candles that were set about her when she died, one of the flowers from a wreath, one handle from the bronze casket. Funerary objects, pieces of clothing, bits of her body, all are set out on the roof with patient ceremony. Then, the ritual begins. Celia kisses the slip, holds the brassiere up to herself to try it on, slips her feet into the shoes. One candle in her hand, another in her mouth (she chews it), she begins to dance, making fantastic gyrations as she balances precariously on the slippery roof. She whirls and dances among the funerary relics, the rags, the glinting gewgaws, the residue of a body, and the lights. And the indifferent, perhaps even non-existent lights of the night shine on her as she dances.

The ones that are not alive are the ones that are really alive. They're the realest ones. We came to earth not to be ourselves, but rather to give life to *them*, the ones that are gone. The ones that had enough self-respect to leave, to turn up their noses at us, they're the real ones. And so we live—we that have never lived—we live for the dead people that got condemned to eternity for turning up their noses at life. They live in our unending admiration for them, in our timeless adoration of them. They are forever made even larger by our limitless frustration. They are, in a word, in our hands, in the hands of us cowards who only manage to bear our own existence by leaning on *them*.

I let myself be dragged along into the house by that racket—*so young, so young, and she actually managed to* . . . I was numb, dazed, and terrified.

And I started to dance.

I came in and I picked her up, dead, with one finger. Because she weighed less than a feather. Because she *was* a feather. With my dead daughter balanced on one finger, like a juggler with a plate of meatballs, I started dancing all over the house. I jumped, I ran, I took off flying, and then, like always, I had to put her in the box. In the box, me and my daughter. Me, dead, in the box.

Me and my daughter dead in the box. If you could have seen how light she was. If you had seen what a tiny thing I was carrying in my arms. If you had just seen—she weighed less than a dried-out corncob. I was walking around holding her in my fingers like she was a sugar ant, one of those tiny ones that don't bite or do anything. Me dead. Me dead. Me dead. Carrying my dead daughter. I balanced her just like that, as easy as pie. What a pity you didn't see me. What a pity you couldn't see that—me holding my daughter up in the air, walking all over the house, until I went out in the backyard. With my daughter dangling from one finger, and me carrying her as light as a washerwoman carries a bundle of clothes on her head. My stiff stark daughter on my finger.

Out in the backyard, the beasts and the witches were practically having a ball. I walk out there through that bunch of beasts, holding my daughter up over my head. I walk right on top of those beasts, and nobody so much as dares open their mouth. Out in the backyard me, my daughter, the witches, and the wild beasts.

And the dried-up tree trunk in the backyard.

Somebody ought to know that at that moment I was almost enjoying my sadness.

Somebody ought to know that I was making my sadness richer and richer. I want you to know that I myself was that backyard. And I walked right on top of myself, and I consoled myself. And I cried for myself. Trying to find peace in myself and asking myself, Why? Why? Why? like I myself was God. And I got no answer from myself.

I want you to know that I tried to calm myself. But I couldn't control myself. And I couldn't even tell what myself had become. And so things went, as the afternoon turned into night. And the next day they came in and they said to myself, "Come, woman, it's time to say goodbye to her." Out in the backyard, they said that to me. And out in the backyard I asked myself what sort of creature myself was, to go on being I myself. And why myself ought to go on dying and dying and dying, when I myself knew very well that I myself was dead.

And when we thought to finally look around, the two of us were hugging each other tight, and the photos were scattered all over the bed, and we were crying our eyes out.

Tell me the truth—how many times in a life does a person have to die?

Tell me the truth—how many deaths can happen to one person in one day?

Because I've lost count. I swear, I've lost count, so I'd appreciate it if you, my dear wild beasts, would answer me that question. Come on. Why don't you answer me? Answer me that question. How many deaths? . . . But listen to that music. Did you hear it? You didn't hear it. You don't know what you're missing not hearing that music. You don't know what you missed. A person ought to always be listening to that music, or otherwise just die one time.

I'd rather have been—if I could have had my choice in the matter before that first death, I mean—I'd rather have been a big fat pitcher, or a little tiny spider. I'm empty and I'm constantly getting filled up—and people wash me, and set me up in a place where I won't fall or get knocked off and broken, and then thirsty lips will be constantly drinking from me. Ay, what a wonderful life, and me shining and sparkling, and not caring about anything, never getting a wrinkle, and desired by everyone . . . I'm a spider. I weave my web. And I sit down to wait for the flies to come.

I've spun out my web, and I'm all tangled up in it. And I die in a tangle. Now come the flies.

I get up early. And before the sun is up I jump way across, from one place to another, spinning threads out of my belly. My belly is full of fine, fine threads. Maybe one day I'll jump from one branch to another, thinking I still have lots of thread inside, and . . . That might happen. But for now my belly is stuffed absolutely full, so I don't have to worry about that. The only thing I have to concern myself about now is weaving my web. And then hunkering down right in the very center of it, and waiting.

And I go on like that, until the sun comes out behind a leaf. I've seen it do that. And then the fly comes along, not paying much attention to what it's doing, and the spiderweb stretches, and springs back. My dead daughter in the spiderweb, right next to the spider. I have waited for this moment. I have waited and watched for this moment. I have spun this moment. Now I can eat her. *Clcc, clcc, clcc.* The spider and the daughter. The spider walking along on the spiderweb toward the daughter. And the sun through the leaves.

Be. Just. A. Spider. And not think about what this thing called loneliness is, or about not having anybody, or about loving but wishing you didn't.

And then going out into the street with your hands on your head.

And looking at the light. And not looking at the light.

And coming apart inside, and almost coming apart outside.

While it rains, or doesn't.

While the thunder and lightning flash, or don't.

While you die, or you don't. While you die. While you're buried.

While you think.

Think, while the family looks at you from the kitchen and says, She's crazy as hell. Sit down and think, while the family says, She's crazy, crazy, crazy. As a loon.

She's crazy. To think . . .

Out there, sitting in the middle of your soul. The tree trunk. Your soul is a dead and dried-up tree trunk. Sitting on my soul, I meant to say. Sitting there, as though there were still things to hope for, to sit and wait for, or things to say, or to not say . . . You people that can see, tell me whether there's anything else out behind the privy. You people that can see, tell me whether there's anything out there beyond my hands when they stretch out and grope in the void.

Christmas . . . The table groaning with roast pig and my daughter Esther walking on all the plates.

The plates.

The table set.

Death on the plates. The table.

Now I feel how wonderful those weekend afternoons were when we would go up to my father's meadow. I would fill my skirts with great fat plums, and I'd come back home like that, with my skirt like a basket, full of plums, and I'd skip through the stand of prickly wild pineapples. And I'd dump the plums out in the grass, listening to you. And then I'd sprawl out in the grass myself, and watch the sun cross the sky like a big fat owl moth, while I ate plum after plum after plum, listening to you . . . Lying on my back on the ground, looking at the sun and at the plums before I ate them. I wish I could sing. I feel like singing. I'm going to sing. I'm going to start singing any second now. Now I'm singing—my dead daughter and me, being buried. Once more that song. And up in the sky, the beasts splitting their sides laughing. Cover my head and feet.

Throw dirt in my eyes.

Put a spell on me for the first man that comes along. Some halfwit threw a rock on me. Ay—this coffin is made out of rotten mastic-tree wood. Ay—saying Shit is like saying Good morning. What can I say to convince myself that I'm saying something? If I give a howl, I'll be a she-cat in heat that sharpens her claws on the roof tiles and goes off to find a husband. If I give a bellow, I'll be a broken-necked cow rolling around in the rocky stretch up in the pasture. If I cry, they'll say, She's a woman betrayed. If I sing, they'll say, She's a woman singing. If you sleep. If you eat. If you walk. If you get out of bed. If you go out. If you skip. If you cry, or if you don't. If you scream. There's always the perfect definition, even for your howl. To brand it once and for all.

Saddled and bridled. I'm being saddled and bridled and branded once and for all. Try to understand.

The grippe to end all grippes, settled in the croup . . . Try to understand.

How sad—to look at your hands like this, lying on your back under the ground. And bring them straight up to your face. After this slap the world comes to an end after this movement the world comes to an end comes to an end and still goes on.

Things now take on the same terrible shapes they always had the house sprouts a harpoon like the claws of a crab from the ridgepole there grows a claw spurting blood and a huge spider is singing out behind the coconut palms

the coconut palms against the sky things take the same terrible shapes they always had they take them again the house sparkles and glints and gives great strange howls of laughter

and a woman with a tiny candle between her fingers covered with burns—can an angel have died

a woman sitting on top of a bottle of anisette crying—can it be that a boy has died or a girl or an angel

a witch rocking in a hammock and chewing up live lizards—can it be that a little girl has died

a chorus of wild beasts crying their eyes out and making soap bubbles in the washtub—that is the death of an angel a demon playing a marimba in the air—that is Death playing with the rusty wheel of an old bicycle

an old woman putting out the fire in a cookstove—that is virtually Death in the flesh

an old man counting bananas and crying—that is something worse than death

two children peeking through a crack in the wall and asking why that candle is lit in broad daylight—that is death in life

a woman with her mouth shut tight—that is what follows death

another woman sprinkling alcohol on herself—that is the beginning of life

another woman with her hands on top of her head kicking the empty bottles in the backyard—that is the death of my daughter

something worse than death

almost as bad as death

shit—thats Death I tell you

look look its Death all right

I swear on your mother its Death

ave maría purísima what Im looking at is Death

I may be dreaming but that thing standing over there isnt that Death

dont tell me that dont tell me

over there over here I meant to say look look

there he is

Celia didn't dance on the table when they came to get her. She danced, as she often did, up on the roof. She was up there all one night, walking back and forth along the roof tiles like a nervous hen too scared to jump. The two men and the woman apparently were in no hurry this time. Jacinta made them coffee from the supply she'd bought on the black market, crossed herself, and, obviously terrified, looked at the visitors every time the clicking of Celia's heels was heard on the roof. Celia was softly moaning. She cast into space strange, aristocratic gestures utterly unlike herself. And sometimes she seemed to be pushing someone away (though not at all violently), someone who had lighted on the end of her nose. By the slowness of the motion of her hands and arms, that person apparently weighed a good deal. When they went up for her, unlike Digna she offered no resistance. She put out her hand, smiled, and greeted them with discreet formality. And she allowed herself to be led away, almost glad of it, it seemed. Still, she tightly clutched the brassiere that had belonged to Esther—and the visitors, quite intelligently, did not attempt to take it from her. But when she was in the car she cast the garment away, apparently of her own accord. And smilingly she waved goodbye. Tico and Anisia waved back.

And things worse every day. The vegetable stand a failure. The factory closed. The whole town without lights, since there are rebels behind every fence, as the saying goes. Trees full of hanged men. And hunger up to the oarlocks.

REBEL FORCES ENTER SANTIAGO DE CUBA

Forces from Company 3 gained entry to the city of Santiago de Cuba, penetrating as far as the warehouse of the Miller Company, where they seized a delivery truck. They also entered the bay at Santiago, passing from La Socaja to the Spanish colonial fortress of El Morro. At the pier in La Socaja they confiscated a large boat, which they then used to get to Key Smith, passing directly in front of the Naval Officers' Club some 200 yards away. When they reached the key they took over the harbor pilot's house, where the only functioning telephone in the area was located. A man named Martín was captured

And there's no way out.

Because there's no way to win this or lose it, either, anymore.

There are too many militia.

For twenty pesos, anybody'll go with the steel pots.

Ay, Moisés, who'd ever have thought I should never have listened to you. And the worst part is that it won't do for me to complain.

And the worst part is that I have to play deaf and dumb for them to leave me in peace. Has anybody ever . . .

Ay, Moisés, my lord.

And what's more, he leaves the woman with me with two children.

And things worse every day.

And me shaking in my boots because the whole neighborhood knows that in this house we're not on the government side.

there and accused of collaborating with the dictatorship, and his Oriente Province government employee's identification card was confiscated.

Shaking in my boots.

And meanwhile Iluminada, the policeman's wife, she decides to buy all of the little stock I had left—on credit, since she knows I'm not going to screw up my courage enough to go over there and collect what she owes me. Fifteen boxes of matches she bought just this morning. Has anyone ever heard of such a thing? I think what she wants to do is move the vegetable stand over to her house, lock, stock, and barrel.

Ay, Moisés. If I were up on the farm right now, I'd go out and kill me a sow and eat it. And the devil take the hindmost.

But here—things are different here. If you keep your mouth shut, you're with the rebels and you don't want to be found out. And if you talk . . . well, see for yourself what happens to people that talk.

I tell you, things are getting worse every day and I don't see any way out.

That's the only thing in the world that Jacinta and I agree on—there's no way out.

If I sell a sack of charcoal, they come investigating to see where I got hold of a sack of charcoal. And if I don't sell it, they come investigating to find out what I do with all that charcoal.

So I tell you—
there's no way out.
And things are getting worse every day.

Eufrasia's Ball Room is closed. Although people say she's trying to get a permit to open just for the army. She'll get it, too. And then things'll be all the worse, because it'll be open and I won't be able to get in. Seems like things get worse every day. Honestly it was pretty much the same to me whether I went to Eufrasia's or not, but since all the guys in the neighborhood were going, I went too. Now that it's closed, though, I spend all night doing nothing, not going any-

And thee, oh dreamer, who art visited to excess by the moon, so that thou exhaust'st thyself in vain activi-

ty, learn thou the possibilities of sleep.
    —*The Magic Mirror*,
    "Dreams" (a poem)

where. Because I haven't got a peso to my name, so I can't do anything. What's so bad about that is that practically every night the electricity is cut off, so there's no alternative but to go home. And sit on the front-porch wall. And grit my teeth at my grandmother's grumbling and complaining. And everybody else's, too.

People say the rebels are close. I sit on the wall, and I think. Sometimes you can hear shooting, and you'd swear it was right beside you. The lights all off. My grandmother grumbling and arguing with everybody and bumping into things because there aren't even any candles. So they say they're close. . . . Now there's not even anything for breakfast . . . I think the best thing I can do now is go off and join the rebels. They're real close now, and sometimes they come into town and everything. Last night there was a skirmish right over there, on the Hill of the Cross . . . The factory closed . . . If I had a peso, I'd go to the movies. But I couldn't go tonight anyway, because there's no electricity. You can't flush the toilet, either, because there's no water, and the stink is terrible, even out here on the porch. If I could just go to the Ball Room. I wonder what's happened to Lolín. If the bathroom didn't smell so awful, I'd jack off thinking about her. Although to tell the truth, I thought it would be different.

"Adolfina! Adolfina! If you stay in there much longer we'll have to break down the door and put a stop to this!"

I'm going out this very night. This very night. I can't stand living cooped up in this house looking at all these damned dead people that think that *they're* alive and *you're* dead. I'm sick and tired of it. I'm sick and tired and I feel like screaming. This very night I'm going out. This very night. I don't care where, either, I'm going out. Somebody else can stay home and turn into an old maid. Somebody else can take care of other people's children and sew clothes for the family for free, like a slave. I'm sick and tired of it. Ay, I'm so tired of it I even feel like banging my head against the wall again every time I remember that my youth got away

248

from me before I ever knew it was gone. But tonight I'm going to get all that back. I want to get it over with and either die or be saved, once and for all. But not just keep on dying by inches. Not keep on rotting here in this cockroach hive. Here in this ocean of whiners. That's for old people. I'm not an old woman yet. *You* tell me—look at me—isn't it so, that I'm not so old? Isn't it so? You tell me. Tell me right now. Tell me.

I'm going out!

The old man again heard the noise of a car in front of the house, and he never for an instant doubted what was happening. Now it's Celia, he thought. He tried to look out through a crack in the wall, but Death had stopped up all the cracks so the voices from outside couldn't get in. So then he climbed up on the tallest display case and tried to look out through the spaces the fiber-cement roof left where it met the wall. But those cracks were closed up, too. So then the old man (for now the automobile was pulling away) slowly waved goodbye, responding the only way he could. As he was waving, he lost his balance and he barely kept himself from tumbling down off the top of the display case. Death, rocking on the dry stalk of what had been a bunch of plantains, cackled. And the old man slowly climbed down. He reached the floor and sat down on his stool. Death then beckoned him with a provocative gesture to rock the stalk he was sitting on—Death liked to rock. The old man did not rise from his stool, he simply raised an arm and began to push the stalk, rhythmically, carefully, like a father pushing the swing his favorite child is swinging on . . . "*What has become of that divine rage of yours, what has become of your violence, where has your rebelliousness gone?*" Once more as he heard those questions—he did not know where they were coming from—the old man felt they were climbing up his rickety, wasted body and slapping him in the face. How could it be that a man who'd dared cross the sea, renounce his mother, kill, steal, blaspheme, hate, how could it be that a man who had done all those real, courageous, manly things, things moreover necessary in order simply to live, to get by, and to reach that exalted status *Man*—how could such a man have fallen so low? How could you have brought what should have been your glory to such a muttering, petered-out end? . . . And the old man felt the blows to his face growing ever fiercer, until it was impossible not to react—for an instant he stopped rocking Death on his plantain stalk, raised both hands to the spot from which the voices seemed to come, and showed his callused palms, his dry, stiffened fingers, his misshapen, horny fingernails. He raised his hands. Those masses of flesh, those claws, those clumsy armor-plated stubs, their joints now almost frozen in stiffness and pain—*those wrecks*—those were his hands. And suddenly the voices ceased, abashed, it seemed, before the evidence, the product of eighty years of feverish and impassioned work . . . For it is not the grand defeats that ruin a man, it is the daily frustrations, the everyday injuries, the meanness and pettiness of day after day—into which meanness, unconsciously perhaps, yet necessarily, you fall. And so it grows meaner every day . . . And then the old man, satisfied with the result of his gesture (for at last they had listened to him, at last they had understood, if only this once, at the very end of his life, that it was he who'd been right, all along, that it was he who was the victim), reached out once more to grab the end of a stalk of what once had been a grand bunch of plantains, and he began to rock it. To rock Death, who had witnessed that scene with great apparent satisfaction. And then Death, as though inspired by the rocking, began to sing to the old man.

I will go out!

I thought it was different from that. But it's nothing at all. Big deal. There were three of us—Aby, Cipriano, and me. And every one of us had to give her two pesos. The first one to go with her was Aby. I wanted to go last. It was really no big thing. And two pesos. Good lord. A thousand crates.

In about five minutes Aby came out and he didn't say a word. Not a peep. He ordered a beer. He drank it, but then he still didn't say anything. So then Cipriano went in, and by then I was shaking, but I didn't say any-

REVOLUTIONARY ARMY FORCES ATTACK EL COBRE Troops under the command of Capt. Roberto Arenas penetrated into El Cobre this week, capturing one Jeep from the army and causing five casualties. Two Springfield rifles and three revolvers were also captured.

—*Bulletin* No. 2,
Nov. 21, 1958, 1 ctvo.

thing. And I ordered another beer. But Aby, the asshole, apparently he noticed I was a bag of nerves, because he said to me, "If you drink it's all the worse, because your bladder gets full and you can't get it up." That might have happened to *you*, I told him, but I can be about to burst and I can still do the job, don't worry. And I had another one. And my goddamned hands started sweating.

Luckily, at that hour the Ball Room was practically deserted, so I sneaked my hands in my pockets and dried them off on the inside of my pants. But you'd have thought the goddamned things had a hot spring inside them, because it was a whole stream of sweat they were sweating. Then my forehead started sweating. And I was trying to dry the sweat off my forehead with the sweat off my hands. I'll tell you the truth, it looked at that instant like I was raining from the inside out. And I was saying to myself, Any minute now Cipriano will come out and it'll be my turn— and I sneaked my hand in my pocket to try to wake myself up a little down there. But it was as dead as a doornail. So I ordered another beer. Aby broke out laughing like a madman. And the organ was playing "La Barranquilla":

The cayman's up and gone,
He's gone off to the riverbed.

And there I was poking at myself with both hands stuck in my pockets. But nothing was happening. And Aby dying laughing. And the organ going "The cayman's up and gone, the cayman's gone." And then Cipriano came out. "Not exactly out of this world," he said, and he borrowed my matches. Aby was leaning on the organ by now, singing, and then he grabbed two whores that were dancing around in front of us. The matches had gotten wet, so they wouldn't light. These songs the organ plays never seem to end—the cayman could have got to the riverbed and back fifteen times already. So to make a long story short, I sucked up a little foam off the head of the beer, and I headed for Lolín's little room back there.

From back here you can barely hear the music—maybe because it's all closed up in here with no windows or anything. The Chinee is lying there naked and I'm taking my clothes off. My hands are hardly sweating at all anymore. There's no electric light in the room, there's just a kerosene lantern with the chimney all smoked up, just like at home . . . "Ow, your hands are cold," she says when I snuggle up beside her. When the lantern chimney gets completely black, it explodes. At least that's what my grandfather used to say, every night, the minute he saw Adolfina light the wick. But my grandmother said that was horsefeathers, the old man was saying that just to keep us in the dark, because he was too stingy to burn five centavos' worth of kerosene. The more I think about it, the worse it is, and my hands are sweating like crazy. Good lord, I thought it was something else.

"Did you finish yet?"

"Not yet."

"Let's go, man, hurry up."

"You better do it with your hand."

"Just like the others. Poor little thing. I bet it's been months since it saw food. Let's see. Like that?"

Around the lantern, the moths fly around and around and around. You can watch them fly around and around the chimney, which is practically red hot. You watch the moths and you see the first one fall. And burn to a crisp. Dear son—Tell me whether you're well. You still haven't told me whether you received the can of Chinese lunch meat I sent you a while ago . . . Oh, or the pair of shoes, either, which were the best quality, even if they were used, and I think they were your size . . . Now, now. Now, kid. No, not yet. Not yet. Like that? I knew that was what you wanted. You baby—I'll bet it's your first time. The moths fly around and around and around and the smoke makes the chimney completely black. Now Adolfina will take a piece of newspaper and clean it. But it'll be back the same way in no time. And the moths go around and around and around. It's that they can't stop. Anybody would think they just can't . . . That old man, what he wants is for the chimney to explode so he won't have to burn his five centavos' worth of kerosene. Good lord—in all my life I've never seen a more miserly man—that's the stingiest man I've ever seen. I think he doesn't talk so he can squirrel the words away someplace. Oho, but I'm not giving him the satisfaction of seeing the lantern chimney burst. Even if I have to be a slave and spend all night long cleaning that chimney. Even if I have to do that and be a slave, I'm not going to give that damned old coot the satisfaction of seeing that lantern chimney explode. Old miser. Now, kid. Now, come—now, it's getting late. I'm coming, I'm coming in one second—just a little more, a little more. There's the mailman with the letter from your mother. Go out and get it. Poor woman—every day she writes a letter to that halfwit, and he never writes back. He doesn't even read her letters, that's the latest thing. Do you know what it means for a mother to spend her whole life working for him and him not even to read her letters? He's a heathen beast! Aren't you ever going to come! Let's go, kid, let's go, it's late and I've got other things to do. Hurry up. Let's see. Maybe a little saliva on it. Let's go. Let's go. Oh that's it oh ah ooooh . . . Now he's taken to raising pigeons. And sometimes. Ooooh, that's it that's it keep doing that. I'm telling you, the boy is a halfwit . . . Ooooh, that's it. I say he's crazy as a loon—do you know he's got the whole floor under his bed covered with bottles of water all mixed with molasses and hot peppers! He says he's making wine! Is that crazy or not? Crazy as a loon. It must be an evil spirit. Ay, what trials this family must suffer. Come, come, come now. But he refuses to go to the temple. Come on, kid, get it over with. He refuses to get a cleansing. Come on. Come on. Oh, but the one to blame is that blasted old fart of a grandfather of his, because he's the one who taught him not to believe in anything. That old man puts about as much faith in God as in a horse. But I'm going to make him have a cleansing. You'll see. Tomorrow morning I'm bringing in the mediums and we'll give him a good purification. And Esther, too. Here, now—relax, relax, now. Don't stiffen up. Relax, I'm telling you. Ay, but your hands are so cold. A real live wire, huh? So the mediums came in and started walking in circles around the parlor going *Heh heh heh* and they sloshed a little water on my head. With the cold I've got and those crazy women throwing water on me. Finally one of them went into convulsions and fell down and started kicking and saying she had Maceo's spirit in her and she was dragging his chains. I couldn't stifle a hoot. Come on, now, or do you plan to spend the night on top of me? Do you know what it is to say she had Maceo's spirit in her? That was the last straw—I couldn't keep from bursting out laughing. And at that, the medium—spirit and all—she came up and slapped me in the face. That was something! Whoever heard of a spirit hitting anybody? "Well, but since it was Maceo's spirit. Maceo was a soldier . . ." said my grandmother when I tried to explain why I'd slapped the medium back. The moths fly around and the lantern chimney is black as pitch. Come, damn it, or I'll leave you with it just like that! Old man, old man, old man, I'm not going to give you the satisfaction of seeing that lantern chimney burst. Old man, old man . . . Here I sit, with a piece of newspaper. But good lord, look at all these dead moths inside here. This house is the biggest plague in the world. During the day there's rats and cockroaches, and at night there's moths, mosquitoes, and more rats and cockroaches to boot. And the one to blame for all this is that blasted old man who not only won't clean the cornpress or put tin sheets around that sugarcane crib, he wouldn't even pick up a corncob in the middle of the floor if he tripped over it. Won't lift a finger. Come on, kid, come on. I can't even wiggle it anymore. Here, what do you want me to do? Come on, *come*, or are you going to keep me in here all night? Oh, don't touch me with those cold hands. And now here, in this house, do you think he ever cleans out that store of his? That fruit stand of his full of rotten fruit that nobody'll ever buy. That goddamned fruit stand. And the rats in there prowling around all night . . . Because I certainly didn't let her get away with it—I reared back and slapped her so hard it knocked that spirit right out of her. So then she attacked me like a wild beast—she tried to scratch my eyes out. But then my grandmother jumped in and started beating on me too, and saying, Satan! Satan! This boy's got Satan himself inside him! And then she threw herself down on her knees and I kicked her so hard in the back of the neck that I almost killed her. Then the old man came in through the back door with a stalk of bananas in his hands and he starts smacking left and right, hitting everybody he could reach with that big stalk of bananas. And the mediums started screaming and howling. So I managed to escape—although wet to the skin and covered with bruises. But wait a minute— was that how it was exactly? Never mind—I'll tell it another way the next time. Relax, relax. Don't stiffen up. Let your body go . . . Hit him with the broomstick the next time he locks himself up in the privy. Spoiled brat. Lazy good-for-nothing sluggard. Piece of meat with a pair of eyes in it. Wild beast. Idiot. Horse. Ave María purísima, I tell you, what there is in this house is the devil himself in the flesh. Our Father, forgive us our sins . . . Dear son. Dear son. Dear son . . . I'm flying. I'm flying. The mosquito net ripped open. Goddamned old goat, I'm not going to give you the satisfaction of seeing the lantern chimney explode. Now. Oh, that's it. That's it. That's *iiiiiit* . . . Raising pigeons up on the roof. I don't write you because I don't have anything to say. I wish you were dead! Dear son. How many moths die every night, burned to death in the lantern? A lot. A whole whole lot.

Let's see. Who's next? Two pesos, in advance. Great. You can't make enough money for breakfast, even. Try to come, now. Come on. I believe in. Son of a fucking bitch. Don't talk about my mother . . .

There comes Fortunato with his face beat to a pulp.
There comes Fortunato with his pants all ripped. How disgusting—you can see the crack in his behind.
There comes Fortunato with his eye all bloody.
That riffraff in La Frontera practically stoned him to death.
He ought to defend himself—he's a man.
Don't you *ever* plan to come? Enough of this. I'll give you your two pesos back if you want me to.
Now he's taken to getting out of bed at midnight and standing there like a zombie looking out at the backyard.
He stopped smoking.
He got drunk in the bathroom with that scummy water he keeps under the bed.
Ayyy, that's it—suck it.
Now he's yelling and vomiting all over the bathroom.
I found him out behind the house with a temperature of 104.

Dear son. I'm sending you a razor, the best money can buy. Because I know you must be shaving now . . .

Go see what's wrong with that slugabed. He doesn't seem to want to get out of bed this morning.

Jerk-off, jerk-off! Big jerk-off!

"And what do you see now? Tell me what you see."
"Smoke. Just smoke."

1. Versions

He'd left his pillow lengthwise in the center of the bed and pulled the sheet up over it so it would look like he was sleeping. I was the first one to realize that he wasn't there. And the first one to read the note he'd left on the foot of the bed: "I'm leaving. I'm joining the rebels, because I'm not doing anything here. Don't tell anybody."

"I'm leaving to join the rebels . . ."

I really don't know the first thing about life. I'm a woman abandoned with two children that do nothing but mortify and spite me. But that part about "I'm not doing anything" almost gave me goosebumps, because it made me ask myself whether *I* was doing anything either. Whether anywhere in the world *he* would ever do anything. Whether any of us anywhere ever do anything.

"I'm leaving" . . . I can't even say, "I'm leaving."

"I'm leaving" . . . I can't even afford myself the luxury of saying to hell with it all and running away.

REBEL OFFENSIVE
CONTINUES
After the surrender of the militia stations at Cueto and Güaro, troops from the "Frank País" Second Front have surrounded the headquarters at Mayarí, putting it under severe attack. Enemy communications have been cut throughout Oriente Province. The retreat of the main body of enemy troops has been cut off by outnumbering rebel forces. Territory has been taken between Camagüey and Oriente provinces. The resistance offered by the dictatorship is weakening everywhere.
—*Bulletin* No. 1,
Nov. 15, 1958, 1 ctvo.

I took the note and went and read it to Mama, who was in the kitchen at the time poking around in the charcoal can to see if there wasn't a little piece of charcoal to throw in the fire. And

I went out in the hall. And as I squeezed that piece of paper tight in my hand, something kept telling me that I was never going to see Fortunato again. Something kept telling me, You're never going to see him again. Something kept telling me. But I didn't want to listen. Mama still hadn't gotten the cookstove lit.

Good lord. To think I paid two pesos to get a handjob. I *deserve* to be laughed at . . . Although I'm pretty sure the same thing happened to Aby and Cipriano. I thought it was something else.

—*Fortunato*

2. Versions

I still hadn't gotten the cookstove lit, because in this accursed house there's not so much as a tiny chip of charcoal for a person to get a fire out of, when Digna comes in and says Fortunato's gone off with the rebels. Just like that, just like slapping me in the face with it.

Can you imagine how inconsiderate? Dear god. I'm a sick old woman. And to tell a person such news that way. I think she did it on purpose so I'd faint. Or have a stroke, more like it. Because you can see as plain as the nose on your face that what these savages want is for me to get it over with and die. My God, I tell you, these people are going to be the death of me, before my time. As sick as I am. Ay, virgen santísima, I'm alive by a miracle. By your miracle, sweet Virgin Mary.

I was talking to Cipriano, and he says he'd rather go and be a steel pot than join the rebels. I don't know what to do. But I think I ought to go with the rebels. And besides, what good would twenty pesos a month do me, which is what they pay a steel pot. Informers get thirty-three pesos and thirty-three centavos, but I'll never do that, never. I believe I'll go with the rebels.

—*Fortunato*

I threw myself down in front of the cookstove and right there on my knees I prayed to God to take this dark cloud from over us.

3. Versions

I snatched the note out of Digna's hand and ran out in the street screaming. Screaming. Yelling and screaming. Fortunato's run off with the rebels! Fortunato's run off with the rebels! I stood there on the front porch and started screaming like a madwoman. Ay, him too. Him too. I was screaming for him. Screaming because we'd lost him. And for the first time I forgot all about me—Adolfina—a woman alone, a husbandless woman, a woman . . . For the first time I forgot all about myself and cried for somebody else. I cried for that poor boy that's lost, probably forever. I cried for him and for his poor heart-sick mother working her fingers to the bone far far away from here. I cried for life itself—because it couldn't be any dirtier or uglier if it tried. Or any more two-faced. And after I realized all that, I finally realized that I was crying just like I always did, too, crying for myself.

"Peek in there to see what you see now."

"Just you and me trying to drown."

"Will we make it?"

4. Versions

Now we're fixed. Any minute now the militia will be here to burn the house down, and the vegetable stand with it. Can you imagine a woman so idiotic! Of course, though, now the one that's screwed is me, because I'm the head of the family. Now they'll come and search the house and maybe even carry off the sacks of charcoal I've hidden out behind the bathroom. What do I need to be mixed up in these messes for, and in my old age? Just tell me that— what do I need such troubles for? And especially since nothing's going to be solved by any of this anyway. Let them go tell somebody else that when all this is over things'll get better. Me, though, now that I'm old and have learned not to trust anybody, especially the man that promises you something for nothing—me, they can save their breath on. What difference does it make whether Juan or Pedro's

Another rebel detachment penetrated the city of Santiago de Cuba at another location. The highly mobile patrols fired on the army and, one block from the cemetery of Santa Efigenia, on the Dos Caminos–El Cobre highway, they burned a short-wave transmitter. Within a few minutes they came across another short-wave transmitter. The rebel contingent inflicted three casualties on the troops in

charge of the first transmitter and two on the second.
—*Bulletin* No. 2,
Nov. 21, 1958, 1 ctvo.

running things?—the little fish always gets swallowed by the big fish sooner or later, and I'm the littlest fish there is. And I'll tell you, things are worse now than they ever were before. That's just the truth of the matter. And they think they can straighten things out with popguns . . . Cut the crap! The government's the one with the guns. And leaflets and popguns are never going to bring it down, you can mark my words. And now that dimwit goes and gets himself mixed up in this mess. They'll search the house—they will! And it'll be me that'll have to answer for it. They'll probably ask me where I got the charcoal from, and I don't know what I'll tell them. The way I made sure nobody found out I had those sacks of charcoal hid back there— not a soul in the house knew about them. When Jacinta finds out, my goose is cooked. But I didn't tell her about it for her own good, because I know all too well what a racket these women make and how worked up they get over any little trifle. Why, look at that great goose Adolfina—just to make people notice she was alive, she grabbed that note that *other* peabrain left and ran outside with it and started reading it out loud at the top of her lungs in the middle of the street. So now of course the whole neighborhood knows. Then the army will find out, too, and the police and the militia and the whole world. And me in my old age having to go through this. Do they think that now that half-wit's up in the mountains with the rebels the government is going to just roll over and die? You could die laughing, you could just die laughing—if it weren't that the one that'll have to pay for it is me. Otherwise it would make you laugh. Just die laughing. Idiot!

5. Versions

He went to bed early, as he had had to do for many weeks, since Eufrasia's Ball Room had been closed to everyone except the army and the town had lain in darkness and there was an order to shoot any young person walking through the streets after nightfall. In

> Let us sleep, and draw the curtains so the moon cannot slip into our alcove.
> —*The Magic Mirror*, "When the Moon Shines" (a poem)

some of the neighborhoods a good distance away—Blanquizal, Pueblo Nuevo, San Andrés—he had had girlfriends. Now he began to recall how many shoe soles he had worn out, visiting those girlfriends, and for nothing . . . One of them, the one who lived in San Andrés, lived practically out in the country, in the middle of a big pasture. There was a long narrow ravine running through the grass, and to get across it you had to go over a high-arching bridge with no handrails. The great pleasure of the trip had lain not so much in visiting his girlfriend as in crossing that bridge, especially when (at the official hour for visits) it began to grow dark . . . But where was all this coming from? He had to go to sleep so he could get up early, before everybody else, and go join the rebels . . . But like always, he could not sleep. There was a sound which only he could hear. There was a creak in the wood, a rustling of cicada wings, a buzzing of mosquitoes, someone snoring long and jerkily. It was a devastating sound, and the moonlight sifted through the blinds and glowed against the mosquito net like a candle behind a pane of frosted glass. A smell of cockroaches, heat, noise . . . And he smelled it. He could actually smell it. And he knew he had to leave. But he also felt that he had to stay. He felt there was always some decision to be made, some choice. You always had to choose between two impossible alternatives. He had talked with the other young men, his friends; he had told them his plan. They thought he was joking, though they pretended to take him quite seriously. Then, when they saw that he indeed was serious, they began to joke about it. Finally there was only Aby left. Aby knew how to think, he had to understand. Go off with Aby to join the rebels. Go off to the Sierra to fight together. He would defend him. Shots—and he, machine gun in hand, would keep him from being killed. He'd kill every steel pot there was, and then he would carry his wounded friend's body into the depths of the forest and there he would make him well again. He would fight, shoot, defend his friend. Except sometimes that bridge would butt in and beg to be crossed. That arch in the middle of a wide green plain—there is where he should go in the evenings, to sit and be calm . . . When Aby saw that Fortunato was speaking in a hoarse, confidential tone, he began to talk about other things. A whole new truckful of whores, country girls all of them, had just come in from Jobabo, he said, and they were working in San Isidro Park in the afternoons. They charged less, since the times had gotten so much worse. And so the two young men parted. But not before he had sworn to Aby that he was going with the rebels. He had confessed it to him in a strangely serious voice, looking straight into his eyes. If he didn't do it now, Aby would never respect him again, and he would tell all the others, and he wouldn't be able to show his face again. But it would have been so nice if the two of them had gone together, and never have had to see the others again. Weren't they different from the rest? Aby talked about going places, going to Havana, or to one of the Keys . . . A burst of gunfire; then, silence. The moon shining on the mosquito net, suffocating him, and sleep would not come. He started softly rubbing his toes, his feet, his legs, his knees (Didn't he used to have a scab there? It was gone . . .), and then he lay his hands on his groin. Again, but now farther off, he heard gunfire. If he masturbated he would fall asleep, surely. His body was now so used to that ceremony that just getting into bed was all it took to excite him. But tonight was different. His fingers brushed his member, caressed it, rubbed it, but no erection came. He thought about "the Chinee"—tall, well built, standing in her underwear with a lantern in her hand. This image had never before failed him. Then he thought of Lourdes, the girl with the big firm tits. Here there was a slight twitch, though his penis did not fully stir from its lethargy. He thought then of Irma, the girl who lived on the other side of the bridge—a little heavy, and pale. But they all lost their faces, they dissolved and blurred, he could not hold their images. So there he lay a long while, futilely exerting himself, sweating under the mosquito net, trying all the faces he knew. Only when Aby appeared—tall, thin, in his tight pants—to usurp the others' places, laughing, walking through strange vegetation, did the rhythm of his stroking increase—and in a whirl of fragmented, desperate faces and strange falling leaves, Fortunato at last achieved his tranquilizing goal . . . He rose before dawn. He put on his shirt (for he had gone to bed wearing his pants, so he only had to close his fly), set the note he had written days before on the foot of the bed, set his pillow lengthwise, and covered it with the sheet. He went down the hall, his shoes in his hand. And at the front door he slipped on his shoes before he went outside. The neighborhood was sleeping. When he came to the Gibara highway, he began to feel the early-morning coolness. And he became once more a boy, walking along the highway. Confidently, he set his shoulders and kept walking.

6. Versions

I heard those beasts cackling and squawking, and I said to myself, Somebody has died. But what was there to worry about? When you're dead, can anybody still be alive? So what was I going to worry about?

I heard the cackling and squawking and laughing of all those wild beasts, and the jumping up and down of the demons. And one came over to me and slapped me twice in the face. And then he hopped away cawing and dying laughing . . . "What's happening?" I said. And the beasts died laughing.

What's happening, what's happening? But I wasn't afraid. And I wasn't sad. Or anything. I didn't feel a thing. Because I had already felt all that already, so much that I couldn't even tell anymore whether that was what I was always feeling or whether I just couldn't feel any of it anymore even if I tried.

I heard those beasts laughing. And an angel all teary-eyed jumped into the cookstove, but he didn't even singe a feather, because in this house Mama never lights a fire anymore. Sometimes because there's no charcoal, and sometimes because there's no food to cook. But either way, the cookstove's always stone cold.

"What's happening?" I said, and I called my daughter. But my daughter didn't answer me. So that's when I realized that it was Fortunato.

Because I'd had my suspicions for a long time. And that's when they were confirmed. I figured out it was Fortunato. You had to be the one that had died if my daughter didn't come running to hug me the second I called her like I did. It had to be you. So I cried for myself like I never thought I ever could. I cried for this new aloneness that comes now and that leaves me dead two times over.

Ay, it had to be you if she didn't come running to put her arms around me.

Ay, it had to be you that was dead if she didn't come announce the death to me.

Because they didn't have to say another word to me anymore—I knew you were dead. I didn't have to hear another word, because I knew that even if you weren't dead yet, you were dead.

Stupid beasts, if they think they're going to make me sad by telling me the news, they're mistaken. Because I knew it even before it happened.

If you're happier with him than with me, don't you fret. Don't you worry about me, my daughter. Stay with him.

If he can make death different for you, don't fret yourself over me. I want you to go with him. Don't answer my calls even if I call you. Rest in peace. I'll just sit down here to cry over myself and to cry over these poor beasts that give this news to me—and so late. To *me*, a woman who knows what has happened, and what's happening, and what's yet to happen. Do you hear—what's yet to happen. In fact, let's *all* cry.

7. *Versions*

It's a lie! It's a lie! It's all a lie! What *really* happened is that when they finally saw that they were between a rock and a hard place, when things got so bad that there wasn't so much as a sweet potato to put on the table, Fortunato left to go live a while in his aunt Emerita's house—the Obnoxious One's. She's a fearsome woman, and the whole rest of the family hated and despised her, to the point of never even mentioning her name—and for no reason but that when her husband died and she was left a widow, she had managed to make a decent life for herself all by herself and didn't completely die of starvation like the rest of them were doing—which of course was practically an insult to them. What really happened is that Fortunato stayed there all that time without visiting the rest of the family or picking up the letters from his mother. And he lived there hounded and bothered by his girl-cousin (the aunt's daughter)—who for a long time (at dances, in the living room, in the backyard of the house) and even before he lived at her house as well, had never let an opportunity slip by to make her intentions known to him, so to speak—so of course now that they were living in the same house she made herself truly unbearable. So unbearable, in fact, that Fortunato even got a little worried that he might fall in love with her and wind up living for the rest of his life with that horrible shrieking aunt that was always sloshing water on the floor and mopping, shaking dust out of things, cleaning, doing practical and therefore of course useless things. What really happened is that one night, when he realized that he couldn't stand another minute of his cousin's "advances," or of his aunt's glaring at him with her eyes full of hate, or of the boredom, the food without any salt in it, the doing nothing all day, he made up his mind to carry out this plan he had been hatching for (it's only fair to admit) months and months and months. What really happened is that that night—his aunt had gone all through the house, in the dark, with the insect spray, just like his grandfather always did—he went to bed early. And with mosquitoes buzzing all around his head (because it's only fair to admit that the mosquito net had a hole in it), he scribbled a note, saying he was going off with the rebels, and then (it's only fair to admit) he masturbated three times, and then at first light he got up. And he left, setting his pillow long-ways in the bed and covering it with a sheet, to make it look like it was him, still asleep. . . . What really happened is that the next day it was his *cousin* (logically enough) who ran terrified over to tell the rest of the family. And what really happened is that Adolfina, with Tico and Anisia tagging along behind, showed up at the house of the Obnoxious One. "If he had been with us, this never would have happened!" she was screaming. And curs-ing and crying and hitting out at everybody (even at the cousin, it's only fair to admit, who got a cuff in the head for her help in the matter). And then Adolfina snatched away the note. And she screamed (it is only fair to point out) all the way back to her own neighborhood. What really happened (as it's only fair to admit) is that that was what really happened. Oh, really! *Grrrr*, really.

Grapáck!—really.
Ga-ga-*boom!—really.*

The unhappiness of what really happened, which did happen like it happened, and so happens to be beyond haphazard telling, has left a telling bruise on all. Is that not true? Oh, the truth . . .

So then, when the old man and old woman's snores grew deafening, and Tico and Anisia stopped bawling from the whacks Digna had given them, and the organ could be heard, and the moon filtered through the window and silvered the litter in the backyard, and the house was one low, long-sustained, and rasping breath, a breath that rose and fell, swelled and ebbed, its rhythm never faltering, Adolfina sat up, got out of bed, opened the wardrobe, took out the shining dress—that one—the high-heeled shoes—those, there—fixed her hair, made up her face, put lipstick on her lips, pulled on a pair of long sheer stockings, and, on tiptoe, went into the bathroom. She lit a candle there and stood before the mirror and looked at herself as she walked, turned, smiled, waved. She still needed something. More color, a more attractive hairstyle, a little perfume, some talcum on her bare shoulders, redder nails, her lips more glistening, her earlobes whiter, covered by her hair, and her hair down a bit more on her forehead as well. She went to her room and made all these changes and then, still on tiptoes, but quicker, she ran back into the bathroom, lit two candles this time (the last there were in the house), and examined herself. She needed to throw a long stole over her shoulders, a long knit covering for those protruding collarbones. And do something with her eyelashes, make them longer, thicker, darker, and hide the bags under her eyes—maybe even a little padding for her hips, not much, but quickly, quickly, weren't they out there waiting for her? Weren't they dying for her to come? Weren't there dozens of men lying in wait for her? Was this not her big night? Tip-toeing, almost flying, she flew to her room. She did all the things she'd thought of, then holding her breath she brushed her hair once more, bit her lips to give them more color, patted her cheeks several times to bring up the blood in them, tightened first the garters that held up her hose and then her belt, and wrapped in the great shawl, trying not to slip in the dark hall on her teetering heels, she ran, *flew* to the bathroom mirror. She examined herself once more. Still there was something missing. She still needed something to complete her trousseau. A big white purse, a silk fan, a feather-bedecked hat, a hairnet of crystal beads, gloves—but my god, were glass-bead hairnets still in fashion? Why not—and anyway they always flattered her so. She ran to the wardrobe again—she heard the organ clearly, the unvarying tune echoing loudly against the walls of the closed factory. She had to control herself, she had to get ahold of herself. She couldn't load herself down with too many garments, it might be a hindrance to her plan. And might it all not make her look a little . . . ridiculous? These days people had learned to appreciate such a little fixing up. . . . She opened the wardrobe, took out the purse, the hairnet of crocheted crystal beads, the fan, the gloves, but she didn't dare put on the hat. No need to go overboard, she thought. But one feather, maybe . . . that might not be too bad, and a necklace, and maybe a set of tinkling brass bracelets, that was always attention-getting, and a good way to be noticed in the dark, especially, a good way to stand out. She slipped on the bracelets, snapped the clasp of the necklace closed behind her neck, patted herself three or four more times on the cheeks, and slipped the feather in her hair. . . . But wouldn't a ring be nice? A pair of pretty earrings? She put on the ring, the pair of dangling earrings. And thus, nervously metallic, she returned to the mirror. But didn't she still need a little something to cover up that greenish color under her eyes? And shouldn't she raise the hem a little on the dress? And wouldn't a little chain look cute on her ankle, even if it was an aluminum one? Oh God, and that music, that music . . . She could wait no longer. She heard the music, heard the far-off clamor, heard the rustling of her clothes—her dress made of crinkled crepe rustled softly as it brushed her legs, her flesh, her skin, and something began to rise in her, something began to push her out toward the street, something made her color so that she no longer had need (as she looked one more time in the mirror) to pat her cheeks again.

But oh, if only she had long thick lashes—false ones, maybe. She had heard they were the latest rage, eyelashes that gave butterfly kisses to inflamed cheeks. But she could hold back no longer. Someone was calling, someone was awaiting her. All those men—leaning against walls on every street corner— were waiting for her. At last, she blew out the candles in the bathroom, closed the door, and looked out for a moment at the backyard filled with moonlight and the music of the organ. She stretched out her hands toward that light, and she danced for a moment, all by herself, to the sound of that music. She tried on several expressions that she thought would be seductive. She smiled. My big night, she thought. And then, clinking and utterly bewitching, she stepped out onto the porch.

This is my night. What I don't find tonight, I'm never going to find. My night. If I don't come across something tonight, I may as well give up. I know this is the end. I know that once the sun comes up and I go back home all by myself, it'll be worse than being dead and knowing it. This is the end—and it's your night, Adolfina. Your night at last.

Somebody's waiting for me on every corner. Somebody's calling me. Somebody's making a sign to me to come a little closer. Somebody's walking up to me . . . Ay, Adolfina, it makes me want to laugh to see you like this. You look like a scarecrow dressed in sequins. You look like a palm tree after it's been hit by lightning. Listen to them calling me. Listen to those men going crazy over me. Who's that girl over there that's so pretty? they're saying. Where did that exotic creature come from? Who is that princess? I want to meet her, introduce me. I want to talk to that woman, I want to ask her to marry me this instant. Can't you hear that multitude of men going mad for me? Which one will I choose? . . . Which one will I accept as my own? . . . Your night. This is your night . . . Maybe a little more makeup will do the trick. Let's see now, a little more lipstick. And a touch-up on those eyebrows. Ay, God, my nose is shiny again. Ay, you can even see my blackheads. More rouge! More powder! Just a dab more . . . There!

8. Versions

I got up at midnight, just like always, to try to get a breath of air without having to listen to those children whimpering and the old man and old woman snoring. When all of a sudden I see a woman with a neckline practically down to her navel walking down the hall right out onto the porch where I was standing.

"Adolfina!" I said, and I touched her, because I couldn't believe it was her. "Where on earth are you going at this hour, and dressed like that?"

"Sssh. I'm going out looking for a husband, any way I can. I can't stand this anymore."

"Adolfina!"

"Sssh. Hush, *please,* and if you don't please, then go ahead and scream. Do anything you want to. I don't care."

"But woman . . ."

"It's getting to be too late for me."

And so I said to myself, Am I seeing visions? Can this be my sister? But then I said, But what a selfish pig you are. You've lived *your* life, but not her. How can you judge her? You selfish pig! You ought to get out and help her. You ought to get out there and try to find her something yourself. Selfish pig!

So before she left I fixed her hair a little and wiped off the lipstick she'd smeared all outside the outline of her lips, I made her kiss a piece of paper so it would stick, and then I stood there for a long time with that piece of paper in my hand. Adolfina just looked at me; she didn't say a word. And I looked at her. Because what was there to say.

9. Versions

The police came and said, Does Polo Ramos live here? Speaking, I said. They came in the house. And they searched it high and low. They even looked under the mattress. "You better watch yourself, old man," they said, "we know you've got a rebel here." And I was about to say, But why blame me for what that good-for-nothing muttonhead does? But they didn't give me time. What they did give me was a shove, and then they left like a bolt of lightning. Jacinta hadn't even finished making them coffee. I went in to the fruit stand and started throwing out the rotten bananas. These days, nobody eats bananas . . . Luckily, they didn't look out behind the bathroom. That's where I've got the sacks of charcoal hid.

As I was going past the dam, the men who were there guarding it called me and asked me where I was headed. I'm going to see my father, I said. Who's your father? Julio Pupo. Where's he live? In Velazco. You're not a student? No. Take care, then, all right? All right, thanks. And they let me go. Trembling inside, I crossed the bridge there at the dam. And when I calmed down a little I realized I was practically running.

I get to Velazco at noon, with the sun so hot it splits rocks. I've got exactly forty-eight five-centavo pieces in my pocket. If I don't find the rebels fast, I'm going to starve to death. The town is no great shakes. People don't even notice that I'm not from here, they treat me just like anybody. As hungry as I am, the best thing I can do is go into some greasy-spoon and eat up these forty-eight five-centavo pieces.

I bought seven slices of pound-cake at twenty-five centavos apiece, so I still had thirteen five-centavo pieces, which I finally threw in a big mud puddle so they wouldn't be clanking and rattling in my pocket. I went to the park and sat down. I'll tell you, I still haven't seen a sign of the rebels anywhere. Although no police either, much less the militia. Strange. I wish I felt like I could ask somebody what's going on in this town—whether the rebels have got it or whether it's the steel pots. But I better not. Better just wait and try to figure out for myself what's going on . . . Here comes a Jeep. Finally. It's the rebels . . . But good lord—if those are the rebels this war is never going to end. Rifles held together with rusty wire. And some of them didn't even have rifles. If that's the way things are around here, I might as well go back home. But I'm not going back home again even if you tie me up and drag me. Good lord—I think those are the rifles the Spaniards used in the nineteenth century, which if I remember right, while they were loading them the Cubans slaughtered them with machetes.

—Shawls and scarves are a great aid to glamour. The elegant scarves so fashionable now are very important to the beauty and general "look" of a woman, and they work their magic whether they are used simply to protect a hair-do or to shield a woman's sensitive skin from the cold and rain.
—*El Norte*
Holguín, June 6, 1958

"Where's that old bag come from at this hour of the night?"

"Don't ask me. Probably some whorehouse around here that we haven't found out about. That's the way things are—nobody ever tells you what's going on."

"She looks like a turkey buzzard with the mange. And look at how she wiggles."

"I wouldn't jump to conclusions—if it itches she could still probably scratch it for you."

"For *you*, maybe—I think I'd rather hump the bedpost."

You're in the street at last! At last! Now to use all your weapons. Now to play all your trump cards. Now to fight like a lioness. Pick up that soldier coming along there . . . He looks like he's in a hurry. Move . . . Too late. What a shame. My God, I'm no good at this. What a pity. Oh, look—there's some men standing on that corner. Go on over that way, whore, and try to snare one. But walk a

"So you've come to join the rebels? I about figured that, son. The minute I saw you come into town, I said to myself, That one's not from around here, and I kept my eye on you. I bet you're from Holguín, or Aura, or Gibara. I'll tell you, a person these days is used to seeing strangers come in every single day. Just day before yesterday seven boys came in from Holguín. Business majors, at the college,

little more gracefully, my God. Look, sway your hips a little. Use that fan. That's it. And flirt as you cruise by.

all of them. I took 'em out to the camp myself and I believe they're still out there. Waiting to be transferred up into the Sierra. So you came to join up too. And by the looks of you, you didn't bring a gun or anything. Much less money . . . Well, boy, I'm going to be honest with you. Of the eight brothers and sisters in our family, the only one that hasn't gone off with the rebels is me. And not because I wouldn't have liked to, either. It's just that I've had to stay in town to solve all the problems that come up and to take care of the family. Let's go over to my mother's house and you can eat—you look like you're half starving. Tomorrow morning's time enough to talk about joining the rebels."

"Hey! Old woman! Where're you going at this hour of the night dressed up like a prize heifer at the fair like that? I'm telling you, the dew falls on you, you're liable to melt, old woman . . ."

Did you hear that! They called you an old woman. Did they! No, they weren't yelling at me. They couldn't have been. Oh yes, oh yes, listen—they did it again. Ay, old woman. Ay, old woman. Listen to them laugh. They're dying laughing, and it's at your expense. Jesus! Imagine them calling me an old woman. Why, I'm just a baby.

They called you an old woman.

No. *No.*

Hey, old bag, what are you doing so late outside your house, the way things are? . . .

Me, an old lady? Ayyyy. . . !

10. Versions

The ocean is inside this seashell, going *Whhhhh, whhhhh, whhhhh*. I put the seashell to my ear and I hear the ocean— *Whhhhhhh*. And sometimes my ear even gets wet. Anisia wants me to give her the seashell. But she can just forget it. This ocean I've got locked up in here I wouldn't give to the devil in person. Forget it! I'm not handing over this seashell to anybody.

Before, it was just lying there on the floor, holding the door so it wouldn't slam. Just a doorstop, so nobody ever even noticed it. Just sitting there, but my aunt Adolfina decided to throw it in the trash, because somebody told her that when there was a big seashell in the house, the women in the house never got married. And so since she's as crazy as a loon to find a husband, she gave it to me and said, Throw this in the trash. But it was as I was carrying the seashell out to the trash to throw it away that I discovered that it's got the ocean in there inside it. And then that was when Anisia started just *dying* to get her hands on it. So then when my aunt Adolfina saw that I hadn't thrown out the seashell, she almost killed me, and now she's practically foaming at the mouth she's so mad at me, and following me around all day to see where I've got it hid. But they're going to be awfully disappointed, the both of them, because nobody takes this seashell away from me. Over my dead body. So they can just get used to the idea. I even sleep with it under my pillow. But since it's so big and lumpy I practically have to sleep sitting up in the bed. But I love to sleep that way. I love it even if I don't like it very much. I say I love it so they can't get any hold on me and try to change my mind.

I love it.

Virgen santísima, it must be practically sun-up already and I still haven't found a thing worth having. Oh my lord. It's true some of them have flirted a little bit with me, but when they come closer and say two or three words they just walk off. Besides, they all smell so strong of sweat and rum that it practically knocks you over. Ay, but now there aren't even any of *those* around. . . . Here comes a Negro . . . Oh, if my family saw me talking to a Negro like this. But so what—in the dark you can't see anything anyway. I better hurry. But good lord, in this fog you can't even see where you're walking. Ay, I think I turned my ankle. I know—I'll scream and see if that Negro will come to my aid . . .

"Ay-y-y-y-y-y. . . !"

ANY SPRAIN GETS QUICK RELIEF
WITH SLOAN'S OINTMENT
KILLS PAIN FAST!
—*La Justicia*
Holguín, Mar. 11, 1933

Velazco is flatland. The ground is red and clayey, and one drop of water turns it to mud. The town consists of two thousand wooden houses and one central street which at the same time is a long park, flanked by four stores of various kinds, all now closed. Velazco does not touch the sea. The mountain range called the Sierra de Gibara—which rises behind it white, blue, and perpendicular—prevents that. Velazco is a sort of Holguín in miniature, though more attractive, more "typical," more "picturesque" to the eye of the traveler who arrives and plans to leave soon. It is even more suffocating and mean-spirited than Holguín for those who live there. At nightfall, after dinner, the young people sit in the long, narrow park. "We, the youth of Velazco . . ." they say. The young person with family in Holguín, or who goes there often, can afford to look down on this sort of statement and the conversations it leads to, and even scoff at it openly. Velazco is lowland, flat, and fertile, an excellent region especially for growing grains of all kinds. Almost everyone lives on grains—the planting, cultivating, harvesting, and selling of them. Velazco is also, like Holguín, an eminently commercial town. Velazco's main street, the street that runs through the park, is of cobblestones, but since all its other streets are dirt, when the rainy season comes (and it lasts practically the year around), red mud covers the stones, the benches, the walls of the businesses, and the wooden columns that support the roofs over the sidewalks. Sundays, even in the midst of this reddish quagmire, the people are miraculously white and starched, and they seem to float above the muck, when in reality they skillfully hop from stone to stone. They visit one another, stop on street corners to chat, stroll through the park. Velazco has two funeral parlors, two gasoline stations, one movie house, and one hotel. Now that there is no electricity, the movie house shows no movies, the hotel is closed, the gasoline stations have been confiscated by the government. The funeral parlors are open seven days a week. Since the rebels have taken over all means of transportation, men and women have gone back to using horses, wagons, and carts, and even the occasional buggy that happened to be out in one of the outbuildings of the old families' farms. Early in the evening the young men come trotting into town. The puddles of reddish water reflect the bright white lights of the carbide lamps. Velazco, with its tile-roofed wooden houses, its narrow muddy streets, its men on horse-back (now, too, generally carrying pistols), its red-clay-stained face is of all towns on the Island the one that most resembles those picturesque, violent, and unreal towns we have come to know from American westerns.

"And what about your mother—does she know you've joined the rebels?"

"No. She doesn't know."

"Ay, poor thing! When she finds out . . . We mothers are always heartbroken inside. Sooner or later . . . Imagine—I had eight sons and daughters, and seven of them are up in the Sierra. And the other one's risking his life every day right in this town. Because at least the ones in the Sierra are safer; those of us who stay behind down here are apt to find the militia coming in the door any time of day or night and wiping us out. Look what happened the last time they came. Look how they left my store! They came right into the middle of town shooting, and they kept shooting till they left again. Windows, walls, everything, they shot anything they felt like. They didn't care where they were shooting. Thank God my son Lencho wasn't at home, because if they'd caught him, I'd have had to put a black crepe ribbon on the door that instant. Ay, and as hot as it is, to be dressed in black! But I'll tell you, sometimes I ask myself if I oughtn't to be dressed in black from head to foot every day anyway, so many people turning up shot and dumped out there in the streets, and I keep thinking one of my sons will turn up dead out there too. Look at that window broken to bits. They barreled through town, just wrecking things. And shooting like wild men. Why, it's so bad that I'm almost used to it by now, and every night we pull the mattresses down onto the floor and sleep that way, just in case . . . And the worst part of it is, nobody knows when it'll all be over. The last time they came through I had to give them two gallons of lard. Two gallons! And if I hadn't, they might have killed me. They're capable of it. And if you knew how many informers there are—*dozens!* Sometimes you don't know whether you're talking to a rat or a revolutionary. I mean even the informers inform on each other, and once or twice one's been hanged before the government realized it was one of their own—so then there's no choice but to hang the *other* guy, too, the one that ratted on the one that got hanged. Who's *also* one of their own. Ay. I hope you're not an informer. My son is such a good, noble man . . . Though I don't know—he's the only one that hasn't gone off to join the rebels. My God, is that possible? Is it possible that he's an informer and that when the militia come, he'll turn me in? Why did they take it all out on *my* store? Look at that other plate-glass window over there. It's not touched. But then, who can you trust? It's the truth—in bad times you can't trust *any*body. *Any*body. Not even your own sons. I've heard so many stories about other places . . . Take me—couldn't *I* be an informer, and talking to you this way just to get your confidence? . . . Are you an informer? Am I an informer? Who can you trust? . . . When everything's turned upside down and backwards, and the whole world is falling apart—then everybody turns informer just for the sake of informing. To save their own skin . . . But what nonsense. Look at that set of scales—they got it so whomperjawed it'll never give the right weight again! Do you think if I was an informer they'd do that to me? Poor boy, your family's probably out looking high and low for you. Come in here and have something to eat."

11. *Versions*

I am the *real* owner of that seashell that's got the ocean inside it. I'm the one that picked it up and heard the ocean the first time. Tico thinks he's going to get to keep it, but he's going to have a terrible disappointment there, because this very night I'm stealing it. You wait and see. You'll see . . . As soon as he's good and asleep, I'll sneak in and slip it out from under him and replace it with the mortar and pestle for mashing up the garlic. Boy, is he going to be surprised when he wakes up.

Holy Virgin, the Negro's walking away. He looked at me like I was a piece of lumber, he helped me get up, asked me if I was all right—all the while me thanking him and trying to make a little conversation—and then he just turned around and walked off. What do I have to do, what can I do that I didn't do? My God, do I have bad breath, is my makeup smeared? Ay, if I only had some of that really good vanishing cream I'd have had a man long ago. And these hands, and these legs, and this blasted hair that no matter how much I comb it always looks like a cypress tree run through a washing-machine wringer . . . Good lord! No luck. No luck so far. What it is is that this town is hopeless. You can count the men in this town on the fingers of one hand. And there's not even any electricity. How can I expect them to appreciate me! Goddamned town. Probably another town's got thousands of men, crazy to meet a woman like me. And me standing here on the corner, all by myself and without a ray of hope that anybody'll turn up at this hour. I'll go to that other place. I'll go there. I'll go there so fast it'll make your head swim.

"What do you see now? What do you see?"

"Nothing. A piece of tapeworm jumping around like a whole long tapeworm."

"Oh, tell the truth. What do you see now? . . ."

I've been in Lencho's mother's house for better than a week now, and I still haven't been able to go off with the rebels. When it's not one reason, it's another, but whatever it is, they still haven't been able to take me to the camp. I feel funny being here, with so many people that come in to eat. Lencho's poor mother. I don't know how she manages to find all the food and get it cooked for this battalion of people. I really don't know what to do. Whenever a Jeep comes into town full of rebels, I feel like running out in the street and telling them I want to go with them. But it would all be the same in the end—to join up I'd still have to wait for the order from the camp. But I feel bad about staying here. Yesterday all there was to eat was a plate of peas and one piece of sweet potato per person. I don't care whether there's that or not a thing at all, but Lencho's poor mother, when she put the food on the table she said, "Today all I could get ahold of was this little bit of peas . . ." But I'm not going home again. I'm staying here no matter what. Tonight when Lencho comes in I'm going to tell him to take me to the camp. . . . A gun. If I had a gun, or any kind of weapon, things would be different. By now I'm sure I'd already have been with the rebels.

SETTLEMENT TAKEN BY
REVOLUTIONARY FORCES
A platoon of rebel soldiers under the command of Capt. Oscar Rico has taken the small settlement of Yateras. The troops later marched on the military encampment there, where they seized six Springfields and three M-1 carbines along with other materiel.

—*El Norte*
Nov. 5, 1958

A man! A man! Even if he's the ugliest man in the world. All in the world I want is to be able to stretch out my hands in bed and touch something other than me myself and I. Me lying there beside myself. Me touching myself in the air. But what's wrong with me? What should I do now? . . . I know—I'll go to San Isidro Park. I've heard people talk about that. But first let me put on some powder, even if it's by Braille.

"Name."
    "Fortunato Estopiñán."
    "Age."
    "Seventeen."
    "Student?"
    "Yes."
    "What kind of weapon did you bring?"
    "None."

Washington, D.C., Jan 3.
—UPI—The United Press reported that in an interview in the Cuban capital with Pres. Batista, the president answered questions relating to international affairs. The chief of state is reported to have said, among other things, that in spite of modern nuclear arms and the advent of the Space Age, the countries of Latin America would continue to determine for themselves their own way of life. He also said that he supported closer ties between NATO and the OAS, adding that those ties should not weaken the status of the United Nations.

—El Norte
Dec. 3, 1958

If you have deep lines at the corners of your mouth, puff out your cheeks as you apply powder so the powder won't outline the wrinkles so much. And besides, it's a good exercise to keep them from getting any deeper.

—Isabel de Amado Blanco, "A More Beautiful You," Cuadernos populares, Havana, 1958

"None? . . . Well, kiddo, believe me, I'm really sorry, but without some kind of a weapon you're useless. We can't do anything with you if you don't have a gun or *something*. You tell *me*. You want to go out there and be cannon fodder? We have a serious problem here, and it's not men, it's weapons. Every day an average of a hundred men or more show up here to join up, and I have to tell them to go home and take it easy till we've got weapons for everybody, unless they want to find themselves a gun, in which case they can come back. It's just the reality of things. Now, then . . . If you want to, you can wait around a few days until we get another contingent organized that's scheduled to go up to the Sierra Maestra. But stay here as a full-fledged rebel—that you can't do. You tell *me*—what'll you do if the whole goddamn army shows up and you don't even have a BB gun, let alone a pistol to stand up to them with? You tell *me* . . .

Nothing! No luck at all! Here I am in San Isidro Park, and still nothing. You can hear a lot of laughing and smutty talk out there in the dark, and you can even see couples going off into the underbrush over there—but me, nothing. This is the last straw. Not even a goddamned raggedy bum will wink at me. Oh, there are men sitting on the benches, bunches of them, but the only thing they do is watch me when I walk by on my high heels. They don't even whistle . . . But I'm not giving up. This is my night. I'm going to go into a bar. I'm going to order a drink and I'm going to pick up the first man I see. And what's more—I'm going to hitch up my dress. That's what you ought to do, you goose. But get going. Hurry up! It'll be tomorrow any minute now, and you'll still be standing there with your finger in your mouth. Honestly, what a night you picked, you whore. Everything's pitch dark, and you can count the bars that are open on one hand. You can even hear shooting over there somewhere. Maybe the men doing the shooting are handsome. Young and handsome. Such a lot of wasted energy, my lord, such a lot of youth. But let's get going. Let's go into the first bar we find open. That's it, that's it . . . Go in and laugh like you were an experienced whore. Ay, I'm so embarrassed, what if my family sees me? . . . I'm so embarrassed. What if somebody I know sees me? . . . To hell with being embarrassed, that's never helped you go to bed with anybody. And don't be such a goose, nobody'll see you anyway. Nobody from your neighborhood'll be around here at this hour of the night, much less the way things are. But wait a minute—where were those shots? Where are those men? Maybe I can find *them* . . . Or maybe they can find *me* . . . Maybe that was a signal for me to follow . . . Because it's way past midnight and you're still walking these dark deserted streets. This is no joke, do you hear? So make up your mind—you either wake up or you're screwed. I mean you either get screwed or you're screwed, because you know very well that this is your last chance. Once the sun comes up, all your hopes and dreams can just forget it. Because you'll go back home again then, and you'll sit down and stare at Death, and you'll be taking care of Death and saying Good morning to Death every morning of your life. Giving him first one hand to hold and then two and then taking him in your arms and then finally—you crazy old husbandless madwoman— squeezing him like this, as tight as you can. Until you finally feel like for the first time in your life you possess something all your own. All your own. And nobody else's. For all eternity. . . . Crazy. Miserable crazy woman what a shame old woman old woman ay look at that old woman *my* shes an old old woman— Adolfina! Adolfina! why are you dressed like that woman whatll the people say if you go out in the street that way my *god* my daughter has turned to whoring sweet virgin mary whatll people say so thats Adolfina huh but wasnt she don Polos daughter uh-huh she certainly was the daughter of the man that had that big farm up on the mountain up in Perronales he was a millionaire I swear yes sir that woman you see going along there painted up like a barber pole thats her you see things get turned upsidedown and then somehow they never get turned rightsideup again there she is there she is flirting with every man in the street but I wouldnt do it with her if all it cost was twentyfive centavos how could you you skinflint if youve never got a five-centavo piece to your name and how long is it shes been streetwalking like that I dont believe the day she finally went to pieces the day she finally went around the bend for good I dont believe that anybody knows what day it was for sure but they say one night she ran out of the house like a madwoman and stripped off every stitch of her clothes in the park and that ever since then shes been the way you see her now ave maría purísima if my daughter did such things Id run a stake through her heart I swear but thank god all my daughters are as pure as gelded ponies why Ive never had the least problem with a single one of mine at least in that way because they all came out boys and Ill tell you the truth its a shame and a pity when a poor man has girl daughters because if they dont marry some goodfornothing twotimer they marry a man thats so poor they all starve to death and if they dont get married at all thats even worse because theres nothing worse than an old maid daughter because they wind up wanting to boss you around and its even possible that even without getting married one day they come in with a belly out to here and *that* thats terrible Im telling you Im telling you the truth . . .

"But look at that—if somebody had told me that that woman was don Polo's daughter, I'd have called him a liar. I was looking at her and looking at her, and I honestly couldn't believe my eyes' own witness. My heavens, if that's really her . . . And skinnier than a fingerling caneshoot. And look how she wiggles her backside, she does it so we'll follow her—and plow her. But I'm afraid I'm not the man for such acrobatics."

"Well, if I had a peso I'd climb aboard."

"For shame, man, with one of your best friend's daughters!"

"Why, that's exactly why I'd do it . . ."

"Good lord!"

"Shh, here she comes . . . Maybe I'll just give her a little pinch on the fanny."

"Leave her alone—poor thing's gone off in the head, is what it is."

"Here she comes . . ."

"Can you believe how that woman's walking!"

"Shh!"

"So you're Polo Ramos's grandson?"

"Uh-huh."

WALKING

Walking is an art, an art that can be learned and learned easily if you pay attention to these guidelines: Stand with your feet together and your toes pointing forward. Place your heel on the ground first, immediately touching the floor with the outside of the foot and then with the toes. In other words—heel, arch, toes. Keep your knees loose, and you'll soon see that your weight shifts effortlessly from rear to front. Don't drag your feet. Swing your arms in the opposite direction to your feet—that is, swing your left arm back as you put your left foot forward. And you'll see how smoothly you seem to glide.

—Isabel de Amado Blanco, "A More Beautiful You," *Cuadernos populares*, Havana, 1958

"Well, I advise you to go home and stay there. Because I want you to listen to what I'm going to tell you— and this is just between you and me, do you hear?—this is never going to end, not in a hundred years. I know that as well as I know I'm sitting here talking to you. You can go to the bank on it. Out here we're all starving to death, but there's no way this government is going to go belly up. Of course the rebels aren't going to give in so easy, either—they'll still be fighting when Gabriel blows his horn. But for you to think that this is going to be finished with four little pellet guns held together with fence wire— forget it. So do what I tell you, kid— go home. Crawl under the bed till this blows over."

Again she watched until the old man dropped off to sleep out on the front porch—because now, since there was nothing to sell, the old man spent the livelong day nodding on the porch. Then she crept over to him, as silently as a cat after a canary (though with her legs cocked to run), slipped her fingers into the old man's shirt pocket, felt around, and with just the tips of her fingers gently lifted out the key to the fruit stand. She quickly opened the door, grabbed some wadded paper used as stuffing for the lantern chimneys to keep them from breaking, picked up the pencil, closed the door again, replaced the key in the old man's pocket, and in practically one hop jumped into hiding out behind the house.

Dear daughter—I'm writing you these few lines to tell you that something terrible has happened. Ay, but I don't know how to tell you. It's so awful . . . Ay, my daughter, I believe the devil has gotten into this house, and I don't see any way to run him out again. Ay, the devil. And I'm writing you I don't know how, because no matter where I go the devil's right behind me grabbing the paper out of my hand and burning it up in the cookstove and scolding at me, saying things like "You crazy old biddy, how can you do such things, keep still, you old woman." And slapping me two or three times right in the face. So hard that if I had any teeth I'd be toothless because he'd have knocked them all out of my mouth by now anyhow. Ay, daughter, things here would make a person fume. Just fume. Ay, and there's no way out. Ay, and we're all starving to death. I swear to you, even if you don't believe me—starving absolutely to death.

I believe the jig's about up, daughter. I believe the game's about over. And the devil after me with a flaming oil lamp to poke it in my eyes. Ay, because he wants to see me blind. He won't let me have a moment's peace all day. I don't know how I'm managing to write you this letter. Trembling all over with fear is how, because I know if he catches me, he'll kill me. Ay daughter, has anyone ever had such hard luck and miseries as we have! Ay, and as though that weren't enough, I've got a chigger on my foot. Ay, and it itches something terrible. Itches and itches and itches. Like the devil. Ay, but the devil won't have me scratch my foot because he says he can't sleep with all the racket the scratching makes.

Ay, but I can't stand the itching. That chigger, you ought to see it. It's *that* big.

But that's the way things are around here. So I'm writing you this letter on a piece of stiff paper no better than cardboard. The cardboard the old man had wadded up in one of the lantern chimneys.

Ay, and the minute he sees me using this last piece of cardboard he'll knock my brains out, so as not to miss a chance to knock my brains out.

Ay, and there's no way out for me.

Ay, and that goddamned chigger biting me.

Ay, daughter, and I hope you never come back.

Stay up there and wash dishes.

Stay up there and sweep floors.

Stay up there and take care of shitty-britches kids and wipe old people's asses.

Do what you have to do,

my daughter—but don't come back to this terrible fate, not even in your dreams.

This is the ends of the earth.

This is the end of the world.

This is the last straw.

Here we are, between the devil and the deep blue sea. Between a rock and a hard place. Between shitting and going blind. Imagine—there's not even a bite of rotten sweet potato to swallow.

And the town in the dark. Because those goddamned rebels have managed to screw up everything. So the town's in the dark. Ay, but I already told you that. And the mediums don't even dare hold séances anymore, because they're scared they'll be taken for revolutionaries and carried off and shot or thrown in jail. Because there are even women mixed up in this mess. The whores—they just do it to find themselves a man.

Ay, so that's the way things are. Ay, and things'll get worse before they get better, too. I say so because I know. Ay, how awful. Just as an example—I can't even go outside and walk down the street after seven o'clock at night.

Ay and Adolfina spends the livelong day locked up in the bathroom and she won't come out for the Lord Himself. Ay and every day it's the same thing all over again.

Ay and me about to burst. And the whore locked up in there. Doing what, I'd like to know.

And meanwhile Digna has taken to singing with her mouth

closed, and I say any day now she's going to explode from being as bull-headed as she is. And meanwhile Celia gets out of bed in the middle of the night and starts carrying on conversations with herself—and sometimes *she* sings too. Ay, but she does it with her mouth altogether *too* open. You'd think it was a frog with the cramps. Ay, if you heard that racket . . . Anything's better than having to listen to that crazy woman Celia, because ever since Esther died, all she does is do nothing and stay up in the clouds all day. Ay, and sometimes I'll tell you I almost think it's a trick on her part to keep from having to wash the dirty clothes, because before, she was the one that had to do the washing. I don't know. And may God forgive me for thinking so. But sometimes I almost think it's nothing but a show. A show she puts on so she won't have to lift a finger. You'd have to see it . . . What you'd really have to do to find out is cut open her heart with a machete, to see what she's got inside there.

Ay but who's going to be the one to cut her heart open with a machete?

Ay but meanwhile she lies around like Miss La-de-da herself.

Ay, that poor Celia doesn't lift a finger, and maybe it's true that she's crazier than a loon.

Ay, daughter, what a trial, what a trial this family is to me.

Ay, daughter, and may God keep what I'm about to say a secret forever, but the other night I saw—I was about half awake and half asleep—I saw a rat as big as the chifforobe crawl across my bed and stand behind the headboard with its paws on its hips. Ay, it was awful! The devil right here in this house. Ay, if you'd seen that rat's eyes—they were blue. They were red. They were yellow. They were green. It didn't have eyes at all, it had burning coals, and they were sputtering and sparking and shooting out fire—while it stood there dying laughing. The goddamned creature—standing there with its paws on its hips behind my bed. Dying laughing. Laughing, this big rat, like some god. Ay—and now that I say that, I wonder if it wasn't God Himself . . . Jesus! What am I saying? . . . But maybe . . . Ay, daughter, anyway—to make a long story short, what I wanted to tell you was that your son Fortunato has run off with the rebels. Ay, daughter, your son Fortunato has run off with those goddamned no-goods!

Ay, and there's no way out for us.

———

Ay, and what a terrible fate is mine.

Ay, Fortunato with the rebels.

Ay, and surely by now he's dead.

Ay, what a fate.

Ay.

Yes, daughter, the dimwit went off with the rebels. Because I also want you to know he's turned into a dimwit. Ay dimwit, dimwit. A halfwit.

A certified case. The dimwit's gone halfwitted. And lately he's been making perfume out of cats' whiskers and grapefruit-tree leaves. Ay, poor Fortunato—by now he's probably stiff stark dead. And I don't know whether to throw out those bottles he's got under his bed, or to wait . . . Because who's to say he's not dead. Who's to say he's not alive, though, and then he'd have my hide for throwing out his bottles full of old bar-room piss or whatever it is. Ay, who's to say one way or the other . . . But at any rate, I'm writing you this letter so you won't say I've forgotten all about you. That's why, even if I'm shaking in my boots—because I know that any minute now the devil'll come out here and gouge my eyes out. Ay gouge my eyes out and cut off my hands ay cut off my hands if he catches me writing you ay daughter because thats what

> We went to see the captain up in the Sierra de Gibara. And he told me to wait a few more days, because another contingent was leaving for the Sierra Maestra in just a few more days. So here I am. Waiting. And eating the little there is to eat in Lencho's mother's house. I tell you, I feel terrible about it. But what can I do . . . Not even dead am I going home again.
> —*Fortunato*

weve come to in this house because the devil has cast a spell on us and he has his will with us and Polo locked up in that fruit stand without saying half a word even if theres nothing to sell he locks himself up and Tico and Anisia have broken every plate in the house ay if you saw that and Fortunato he left a note saying he was going off with the rebels because we were a bunch of simpleminded women and we didnt let him do anything about anything ay the plates ay my plates . . . thats what he said in the note ay but the worst thing about it is not what it said its what it *wanted* to say ay the worst thing the worst ay the worst ay as though that werent enough the lantern chimney smashed to pieces last night when a big huge moth got down inside it the biggest owl moth you ever saw and it didnt want to get burned up inside the chimney so it jumped around and knocked it over and the chimney landed on the floor and smashed to bits and the moth was jumping and flopping around with its big huge black wings on fire until finally it burned up ay and who knows what omen that burning up on fire was and so now we *are* in the dark because Polo refuses to give us another lantern chimney because he says itll just bust to pieces again in no time too ay and if you could see how he babies those lantern chimneys hes got in the fruit stand its like they were his own flesh and blood the apple of his eye so then now those children of Dignas put chairs and things in the middle of the hall so Ill bump into them and fall and break my legbones ay because they want me to die the goddamned ungrateful children ay those children of Digna and Moisés they are terrible ay and that Moisés that got my daughter Digna pregnant two times and sent her back to me a mess ay that Moisés that dragged us into this hell we are in ay and as though that werent enough now Fortunato has gone off with the rebels and theyve killed him so open your eyes daughter dont fool yourself because thats the way life is ay life ay life

ay, life.

Ay, and I do mean life . . . Yessir, just set yourself right about this, because what happens here is you try not to die all at once so you can see what it is to die a little bit at a time. Ay and me that's seen so much, every day I tell you it looks more like we ain't seen nothing yet. Ay-y-y—here comes that wild beast. There the devil is now. One of the worst of them. Ay, I hope I don't get caught with this letter, I hope I don't because if I do I'll have to eat it. Ay, that goddamned devil, ay, there the devil comes. Look at that devil. Ay . . .

Ay-y-y-y . . .

"What are you doing with that piece of cardboard, Mama?"

"Nothing. I was trying to make a lantern chimney out of it."

"Let me see."

"No, it's for a chimney . . ."

"I said give me that paper, you damned old crone!"

"Oh my God, take this life from me. Take my life from me this minute."

"The paper! The paper! You old biddy!"

"Why aren't I dead! Dead!"

"You miserable old she-ass—let me see that paper!"

"What I've mothered is a wild beast! A wild animal! A beast!"

"Let me see it! . . ."

"Ay! God! Save me!"

"So you're writing poor Onerica."

"I wasn't going to mail it. It was to show God I still remember her."

". . . 'Adolfina never comes out of the bathroom . . .' You're right, Mama, I've never come out of the bathroom."

"Ay, I'm going to scream. I'm going to burst your eardrums screaming!"

"If I hadn't come out I wouldn't be standing here before you this minute."

"*Ay-y-y-y-y-y!* She's killing me! I'll be a martyr in heaven to my own thankless daughter! *Ay-y-y! Ay!*"

They sent forty-seven men and seven women back after they'd gotten practically all the way to the Sierra Maestra. They say they're not letting another soul in without a gun.

Now I *really* don't know what to do.

They tell me the news when I'm with Lencho in the machine shop that used to belong to one of his brothers. I'm making bullets with a file. They tell me the news. The file looks like it hears the news too. The file has lots of tiny little teeth on it. If you saw that file . . . I run all those little teeth over the rough casting to give it the shape of the nose of a bullet so it goes in the body easier. The file, with all those little round teeth, in my hand. They won't take anybody unless they at least have a rifle. So these are your hands, Fortunato. And if you take one of these hands and cut it off, everything will still be the same. Because these are just hands. These are your hands, and they're

THE WEATHER

The National Observatory forecast for tomorrow includes some rain for the western portions of the Island and mild temperatures throughout.

—*El Norte*,
Dec. 14, 1958

holding a file that's dying laughing and grinning with all its little tiny nickel-plated teeth. Or whatever they're made out of. And there's Lencho, feeling sorry for you. So you can't join the rebels anymore. If you don't have a gun you can't join the rebels. What can you do without a gun? There's the file. There's the half-finished slug. Somebody'll take that slug and make a bullet out of it and shoot it. Somebody besides you. For you, that's not a possibility. Put the file down. What are you doing in this place that's not for you?

What place *is* for you? What do you do when you're around men that know what they're doing—or if they don't know, don't know that they don't know? Fortunato. But *you* know. You know you don't belong here. Or there either.

Now leave this place, forget this world. Back there, the chorus of those accursed women laments your going. They're crying their eyes out back there. And your mother . . . Ay! don't give this blow to your poor mother, young man.

Ay, you little rascal. Here, let me brush my hand over your hair. Here, let me pat you a little on the back. Come on, man. You're still just a little boy. A little boy! Look how your grandmother is crying over you. I want you to know that Polo—yes, Polo—rented a bicycle and went out looking for you. Poor old man, three pesos they charged him to rent that bicycle, and within two blocks of the house he had a blowout. Try to imagine Polo riding a bicycle when the tire blew out. He went head over heels. Isn't that hilarious? Oh, but you're crying. Here, here. Let's see how you're crying. *Baaa baaa. Baa-aa-aa-aa.* Remember? The billy-goat goes *Baa-baa-baa.* Laugh, laugh. Let's see . . . Put the file down and go back home. *Baaa.* You tried to get away. Crazy. But you can make it up. Home. Home to the weepy women the little sissy goes. Home again, home again. Jiggety-jig. Jiggety. *Baa baa baa.* Home again. The little sissy goes home again to cry in his granny's lap. That's the way little billy-goats go. *Baa-aaa.* Here now, here now, listen—How do billy-goats go? They go *Baa-aa-aa.* Good! Good! How smart he is. All right, now one more time.

"No. I'm not leaving, goddammit."

288

12. Versions

The situation in the northern part of Oriente Province, under the rebels, was this: The rebels had occupied the smaller towns and maintained almost absolute control over the roads and the campesinos. They were organized into "fronts" and "columns" encamped of course in the most mountainous and isolated regions, into which the tyrant's army had great difficulty penetrating. The northern rebels possessed few weapons, and those were, by and large, antique rifles used in the War of Independence, plus some Springfields, and pistols. When there was a machine gun, it was kept, logically enough, in the main camp. In truth, in the northern part of the province it was more fear of the rebels than the rebels themselves that speeded their victory. The campesinos, "oriented," took care to spread that fear. They reported that the rebels were armed to the teeth with all sorts of modern weaponry— *efficient* weaponry. The people of the towns also broadcast these reports. And when the soldiers, the "steel pots," went on scouting missions into the countryside, they were so deeply under the power of suggestion that the least noise sent them scattering. The rebels ran, too, of course—and with reason—when the army made one of its ravaging sweeps through all the towns and villages of the northern countryside. In the southern part of Oriente Province, from Bayamo southward, the rebels were more numerous, had better weapons, and held more strategic locations; they could stand up to the government troops. But in spite of all that, a detachment of ten thousand well-armed men (and in that the government needed not to have spared any expense), with the tanks they already commanded, and protected by air cover, could have wiped out the rebels in a very short time—had they had the will and the courage to do so. But they lacked the passion, they lacked the anger, the rage fed by years of injustice; they were not surrounded, they did not have the certain knowledge that they could never go back. Those advantages, the rebels had. . . . In the north, the army's raids came oftener. The rebels, when the army struck, simply retreated into the hills, and the towns they had taken returned to the hands of the soldiers of tyranny. The army then leveled everything in its path—the soldiers set up camp for several days, sacking, burning alive the campesinos whom informers reported to be revolutionaries or their sympathizers. During those marches through the north it was only very rarely that a rebel was killed, or for that matter a member of the army. The civilian casualties, however, were great.

The rebels also had their Bulletins, their organs of propaganda which though clandestine reached a large percentage of the population. The rebels received real military training, at least in the major encampments. And their discipline was better than the army's.

Most of the rebels wore beards, and they were not in the habit of bathing any too frequently. Some wore red armbands which said "Libertad o Muerte"—Liberty or Death. So as not to starve, they ate beef which they "requisitioned" from the large landholders—who, intimidated, "donated" it. Often the rebels shared their beef with the poor campesinos—which meant with almost everyone. Sometimes to get needed weapons they would storm a military camp or barracks. If one of them was killed, his body generally had to be abandoned to the enemy. If the body was rescued, the wake would be held at one of the campesinos' houses in the area and, without flowers or other funerary accoutrement of any kind (sometimes not even a coffin), the body was buried in a field somewhere. The rebels feared the little yellow buzzing airplanes that constantly flew over the fields and pastures, dropping bombs. But the shrapnel generally hit an oven for making charcoal or a cow or a house or a campesino. The rebels had quickly learned how to dodge air raids.

For transportation they of course took over civilian vehicles. They "attached" them—that was the word then in use. If the owner was a person who held little brief for the regime-to-come, he could write his vehicle off for lost. If he was a sympathizer, the assumption was that he had freely loaned it—probably forever. There were of course also underground organizations that collected funds for the rebels by going house to house, or by selling bonds or by soliciting and reselling used clothing, and so on.

The revolutionary press was eternally optimistic; from its news reports one would have inferred that the tyrannical government in Havana was about to fall at any moment. But the truth was that even that would not have been sufficient for victory had the rebels not had two infallible allies—indignation and right.

Just at the period during which Fortunato was hanging around Velazco, the army was making preparations for a great sweep through the area of that town and all the nearby countryside, over to Gibara. Into Velazco came then one day troops led by a captain of the dictatorship's forces, a man famed for the brutal murders he had been responsible for throughout his career. He took the town over, shot it up mercilessly; he hanged many people and burned many others alive. He seized all the food in town and then continued on northward, shooting, sacking, burning. His motto was "There's no turtleshell tough enough for a fire that's hot enough . . ." The rebels, dug in up in the hills, could hear the noise of the gunfire. That was in December 1958, or possibly late November; that is, one month before the government fell and the rebels took power. The man who carried out these operations was named Sosa Blanco, and his victims had to await the coming of the Revolution to be avenged: He was shot.

Most of the men fighting with the rebels had no very clear idea about the future, no fixed philosophy or principles by which they lived their lives. They were simple men, fighting against a dictator, and so when the Revolution triumphed (as the phrase unavoidably had it), many of them—who knew no more than anybody else in the country what the real story was—were more surprised than anyone at the way things turned out.

"It's a matter of balls, and that's why we're going to win this thing," said Lencho, and he took the first swig.

We were all sitting in one corner of his mother's store. We'd found a stock of rum. So we're there drinking and I'm already as red as a tomato. "Pass it over here." "Drink, drink—drink all you want to, there's more where that came from." And when they give me the bottle I drink more than I ought to so I can show them I'm used to drinking.

"Open that other bottle there—it's good stuff."

"Good stuff or horsepiss, it's all the same to me, long as it warms me up inside."

"They say the steel pots put gunpowder in their rum to give 'em a kick—and so they don't turn pussy."

"That sounds like them—bunch of girls. *We* drink it any way we get it."

"Open that other one."

"We can win this revolution with one hand tied behind our backs!"

"Pass it over this way, will you."

"Take it easy—that's the last one."

"Well, sonny, I believe your old lady's got her bottle or two stashed away back there somewhere. A businesswoman to the last . . ."

"She *did* have . . . I haven't left a drop for her."

"You have to get up awful early in the morning to beat old Lencho here."

"But what's wrong with this Holguín city boy? He doesn't drink much, does he? Has he had enough already?"

"He's a good boy. Came to join up with the rebels."

"You don't say!"

"He walked all the way."

"Well, that takes balls all right. He *walked?*"

"Walked. And now they won't take 'im because he didn't bring a rifle with 'im."

"What shit."

"I can't believe it. What're you going to do?"

While everybody else is drinking, I go to the bathroom and start throwing up. From the bathroom I can hear the loud talk of all the drunk men out there. I'm vomiting. I'm puking my guts out and crying like a woman. Everybody else is getting drunk and having a good time and I'm in here puking . . . Now I really truly don't know what to do, because I don't want to stay here with Lencho and these people but I don't want to go home either. Throwing up and bawling, like a sick calf. If those men see you they'll laugh in your face. Lencho comes in and sees me throwing up. He asks me what's wrong. And I throw a little vomit on my face so he won't see that on top of everything I'm crying too.

"Well, I'll tell you what *I'd* do if I were you—I'd go back home and just wait real quiet."

"Don't be stupid, kid. Stay a little while longer. They're

bound to send more people up to the Sierra sooner or later. And then you're in."

"What you've gotta do is join the army—be a steel pot. I'm serious, be a steel pot. They give you a rifle, and you bring it back here."

"Why don't you just kill a militiaman and take his rifle? If you do *that*, they'll take you before you can turn around. With as few guns as there are around here, they'll take you with open arms!"

"Let's have another drink, and then we'll think about how to do this."

"Don't be stupid—tell your mother to send for you. Go to the United States. And when this is all over, come back. That's the best way, the one with the least risk involved anyway. A lot of people have done it, too, I'll tell you. They'll be heroes when it's all over. Don't be a fool . . ."

"Drink—and you do whatever you feel like."

"Kill a militiaman."

"Good idea."

"Go home."

"Drink, drink."

"Whacha gotta do is . . ."

"Lissen, lissen to what I tell you . . ."

"*Lissen* to me. . . ."

"So you chickened out, huh?"

"Pay attention . . ."

"No. Do this . . ."

"There's nothing like meatballs . . ."

"Do this, and this, and th . . ."

"What a hullabaloo!"

"*Grapáck, grapáck, grapáck, grapáck. Grapáck. Grapáck.*"

Well, kiddo, what you've got to do is kill a militiaman, and take his rifle. I'll let you use my own knife.
Look:
You sneak up on him and

Kill a Rifle. I mean a militiaman. Hey, soldier! Here I am and I'm gonna kill you. Hey soldier. Hey. Just turn your back to me—that's it—so I can stick this knife in. Hi, there. Hey? Hey. Hey? Hey. Hey? Hey . . . Good lord, is he *tall!* Put a ladder up or you'll

you stab him
like this.
You take his gun away.
And you get back here
on the double.
And that's it.
Okay?

—*Them*

never reach his shoulder blades. And he's still growing. Still growing. So climb him. Hey, soldier. Hi there. But what a tough hide he's got. I stab him and stab him and stab him, and instead of going in, the knife just bends. Oh Christ. The knife's turned into a file. And good lord, the file's dying laughing. Good lord, the file's flying off. I knew that file had something against me. Now they'll say I'm a thief and I've run off with their file. I've got to try to find it, I've got to try to find it and get it back no matter where it's gone . . . But look where it is—way up above those clouds.

"So it's a question of you not being able to join the rebels without a gun. It's a question of . . ." Of what? They say it's a question of. Oh, but they're talking about the question. But do you mean to tell me you don't know what the question is? Well, listen, listen: That is the question. There's the rub. Therein resides the difficulty. That raises the question. And there the problem originates. How do you like that question? Not to put too fine a point on it—a soldier and a rifle must be killed. What is the real question? Or can't you face it? Ay, the kweschun. *Kawkawkawkawkawkawkaaaw kaw kaw* . . . Get a rifle. That is the question.

I've left San Isidro Park, and I curse the day I ever went there. Now I'm on the corner where The Hot Spot is. They say this place is famous for the number of men and women that come here. But now they don't sell so much as a cup of coffee—and I don't see a soul. I'm going to stand on this corner for half an hour, and if nothing comes along, I'll go down the street a block.

"Adolfina! Adolfina! Virgen santísima! What can that woman be thinking about, staying in there all day today—is she *never* coming out of that bathroom? Holy Virgin, make her come out of there before I lose my mind!"

And if nothing comes along down the street a block, I'll go down the street another block.

And if nothing comes along two streets down, I'll go out on the highway.

And if I don't get at least winked at out on the highway, I'll go to Mayra the Mare's whorehouse—I've heard people talk about that place too.

And if nothing comes along there—I'll go to Eufrasia's Ball Room.

And if nothing comes along there—I'll go to the Oasis.

And if I get to the last whorehouse on the line and nobody's paid me any attention, I'll stand in the middle of Calixto García Park and start screaming.

And what if nobody listens?

Then I'll stop and start laughing out loud.

And what if nobody listens?

I'll start howling.

And what if nobody *still* listens?

I'll climb up a cottonsilk tree and start calling people to look at me.

Be careful. You might fall and hurt yourself.

Hurt myself?

Hurt yourself a lot. And imagine if a policeman catches you up in that tree—what'll he think? He'll think you're putting up a flag for the revolutionaries. The way things are, you'll be hanged on the spot. You better just go on back home.

Not a chance. This is my night. And if nothing comes along in Eufrasia's Ball Room, *or* in the whorehouse, *or* in the bar, then I'll start knocking on doors. I'll go house to house. I'll strip stark naked and start going house to house, knocking on doors.

And what if a dog chases you!

Ay, I don't know—tell me what to do, tell me what's wrong with me, tell me what I don't have that keeps men from even getting near me.

YOUR VOICE

What is your voice like? Is it high, low, piercing, sweet, shrill, well modulated? Have you ever wondered? Possibly you haven't, and yet your voice is what makes the

I've made up my mind what I'm going to do—I'm going back to Holguín.

I'll walk into my house and I'll take the butcher knife.

And I'll watch a militiaman till I see my chance and I'll stab him with the butcher knife.

And I'll grab his rifle.

And I'll run.

And come back here.

And say, Here's the rifle, so can I stay here with you?

And they'll say, Sure, okay.

And everybody will look at the rifle.

And they'll say, Wow, it's brand new. And they'll say, How'd you get it? And they'll say, We were just kidding, Fortunato. And they'll say, See, we were right, we *told* you to do it this way. And they'll say, Can you beat it, you'd think he was such a nincompoop, and he's got balls as big as Maceo's.

And I'll be able to join the rebels.

And they'll say.

I left the corner where The Hot Spot is without anything coming along. I went down the street a block, and ditto. I went down the street another block, and ditto again. Now I'm out on the highway out of town. The only things on the road are army trucks and tanks, and you'd think they were bolts of lightning. I think I'm going to have to move on again. Now all that's left are the whorehouses. And the ironic thing about that is that I don't know for certain where they are. It'll be a laugh if I have to stop somebody in the street to ask where Eufrasia's Ball Room is. Here comes a militia-man. I'll follow him. Here I go . . . But my goodness. My God, I've walked so much my legs can barely carry me. And to top everything off, my shoes are completely falling apart on me. Ay, my only shoes to go out in!

I say my goodbyes to Lencho and his family and sit on the counter in the store to wait for the truck.

I'm going back to Holguín to kill a soldier. Now one of Lencho's daughters is crying—I can hear her from here. What crybabies Lencho's kids are. Lencho's wife looked at me with her big brown cow-eyes, but tired-looking. Poor thing, I can imagine what she's going through. When the food was put on the table, her eyes opened real wide, and it looked like she was going to cry. And like she really was having to force herself, like it was against her own will—that was how she ate the peas, and it looked like from one minute to the next she was going to burst out crying. I watched her, and I could tell she was saying to herself, If Fortunato wasn't here, we'd all have that much more. I knew that was what she was thinking, and I knew she was right in thinking it, too . . . I don't believe there's anything any sadder than sitting down at the table and having food left over because there's so little of it that nobody feels like taking the last bite—leftovers, and nobody gets enough. There may be lots of sad things in the world, but that bowl full of peas sitting there in the middle of the table, and everybody looking at it and nobody taking what their stomach craves—that bowl there, I don't think there's anything any sadder than that. I don't believe there is. In fact, I know there's not.

And now I'm waiting for the truck that'll take me to Holguín. I'll come back here on foot, with the rifle real well hidden on me. I'll come running all the way back, in fact, and it'll feel like two blocks, not like all those miles. I won't even get winded. The truck driver is a friend of Lencho's and that's why I can get a ride with him. He's got authorization to go to Aguasclaras, and up to now he hasn't had any trouble with the guards at the dam, although they say that now they're searching everybody, and that anybody that looks the least bit suspicious to them gets pulled out right there and thrown in the river. They've done that to a lot of people, I hear . . . Lencho comes over to the counter to say goodbye. Everybody's heard that I'm going to kill a militiaman, so they're all hanging around me like I was this strange creature.

"You're crazier than hell."

"Good lord!"

"But he's just a boy!"

"He looks about half simpleminded."

"Oh, but he's an old man by now."

The truck finally comes. I shake hands with Lencho, and I don't know why but the most terrible sadness comes over me. Somebody hands me a knife and says, To the hilt. Leave that here, the driver says. If they catch us with that pig-sticker we'll be in for it. So I hand the knife back thinking, When I get home I'm going to grab that butcher knife and scram. Now that I'm leaving, I really don't want to very much. My rebel days are over, it looks like.

Go back home, sissy. It's the truth—I almost feel like throwing myself on the ground and being an I don't know what—anything but a kid that runs away from home and then has to go back. Anything but what I am. But what nonsense—all I'm going to do is walk in the door, grab the butcher knife, and walk out again. I tell Lencho I'll be back in two days. Maybe less. Maybe . . . Take care, they say. Maybe . . . And so you go back home.

What a laugh! You lazy good-for-nothing! Who got you into this mess? So now you're going back home. Oh, I could laugh till I split.

"Take care."

"I'll be back with the rifle in two days."

"Bring cigarettes. We never see any around here anymore."

The truck pulls away, and now you can't bear to be going back. You honestly thought this business of joining the rebels was going to be different. But it's not what you thought it was, because what a person *thinks* can never be what *is*, for exactly the reason that it's thought. The truck driver is shaking inside. If they catch him, they'll skin him alive. If the militia guards at the dam flag him down, they'll have his balls. And all because of you, you dimwit. All you're any good for is complicating other people's lives. Let this be a lesson to you—next time you just stay at home and don't stick so much

EL CRISTO BASE TAKEN

Late on the night of Nov. 26 forces of the "Antonio Guiteras" Company No. 9 took the military base called El Cristo, which had been un-

der siege for several weeks and whose last hope lay in reinforcements which the dictatorship unsuccessfully tried to send to its aid. The reinforcements were pushed back five separate times on the San Vicente highway, near Santiago de Cuba. The enemy suffered 13 deaths, lost 80 men taken prisoners, and had several wounded, two of whom were turned over to the Cuban Red Cross.
—*Bulletin* No. 4,
Dec. 2, 1958, 1 ctvo.

as a finger outside to feel the wind with. Do you hear!

"I'm coming back, by God."

I asked the soldier what time it was. And he said it was exactly two forty-five. Then I asked him for a cigarette. And he gave me one, without a word. I said, Do you have a light please? And he lit my cigarette without a word. I noticed he was walking a little faster. I said, You think it'll stay hot? And he said the National Observatory was predicting rain. And now he *was* walking faster. I said, Weather like that, best thing is to go in a bar and have a drink with somebody. He told me he never drank when he was on duty. And now he was practically running. So then I said, Weather like that, best thing is to get into bed with somebody. But I couldn't catch what he said back. Because now he was really *running* . . . The smoke gets in my nose and I start coughing. To think— a cigarette had never touched my lips before in my life. So I threw it down. Now I'm going to Eufrasia's place.

We're about to cross the dam. If we get across the dam, I'm saved. If I can manage to get across the dam without the guards stopping me, I'm home free. Now you're crossing the dam. You're shaking. And suddenly you realize it's raining. They're almost sure to stop the truck. It's almost sure the guards'll catch you and say, Ah, you silly goose, so you planned to run off and join the rebels, we heard about you . . . And they'll arrest you and carry you off to jail. And then there'll be no way out for you. The truck is on the dam now. The truck is going across the bridge. On the other side the guards are waiting for you with their machine guns. "I feel like I've got my balls in my throat," the driver says. And you— what about you? The water running over the dam sounds like the end, like something you can't even explain to yourself. It's a sound so continuous, so loud, so deafening and full and invariable that it's like it was from another world, from some planet

ruled by different laws from ours . . .
The water's almost red because it's
rained so much lately that all the rivers in the whole countryside are
stirred up, and they all dump into this
dam. Look at all that water running
under the truck, which is rolling over
it like an ant crawling over a floormat
woven out of vines. Look at all that
water, and look at me, and look at
those guards over on the other end of
the dam. They're getting closer. Now
they'll stop you. Now. But now you're
not in the truck—somebody's thrown
you out the window, and you're
floating.

You're floating along under that
reddish water. You're almost down to
the turbines. You know if the suction from the turbines gets
you, there'll be no escape. You know the turbines are calling
to you. Listen . . . Now I'm floating under this red-colored
water and I'm almost down to where the turbines are. I'm
about to be under all this water forever. I open my eyes, and I
can't see a thing. I stretch out my hands, and all they touch is
this thick water. The current is howling. And it looks like
everything's about to be over any second . . . It's raining. The
truck is just about to pass the guardpost. "If they stop us,
we're done for." The guards raise their arms. Then they wave,
and with that one motion your life keeps floating—on top of
the water this time. The driver sticks his hand out and
waves back. That means we can go through, we're already
through.

You can go on. You can go on. That means for the mean-
time you've escaped. Boy. *Boy.* Anyway, it's true that it was
raining.

Raining, and still no luck. I went into Eufrasia's Ball Room—I
knew it was the Ball Room by the organ and by Eufrasia herself,
because even if I didn't know her, she was painted up just like

I'd heard about her. And the men there! And all of them in uniform . . . Playing the pro, my stole slung as carelessly over my shoulders as a queen's, my fan half open, holding my purse so it brushed my thighs, and walking in elegant little steps, I made my entrance. I paraded right into the middle of the dance floor, wiggling my whole body and clicking my high heels—I even winked at Eufrasia so she would see she could trust me. But the whore, what she did was laugh out loud. But I acted like I didn't know what she was laughing about, I laughed too—but I didn't stretch my lips too wide, so my face wouldn't crack, like all the beauty tips say. Then I stood as tall as I could and gracefully walked on, my crystal-bead hairnet in place, over to one corner. The organ started playing again, and I started fanning myself. I was sweating . . . Finally a policeman asked me to dance. As we were dancing, I could see he was exchanging signals and laughing with a lot of his friends that were watching us from the other end of the dance floor. I tried to dance him farther away, but he wouldn't budge. We danced almost the whole duration of one of those songs the organ plays—which is a long time, I'm here to tell you—and we never exchanged a word. . . . I didn't have the slightest idea that the man gave you a fifty-centavo piece to dance with you, until Eufrasia came up and said to me, Okay, cough it up, you just get two ten-centavo pieces of it. And she looked me up and down like I was a criminal. What are you talking about? I said. The half a peso, she said with her teeth gritted. What half a peso? The half a peso the gentleman gave you. Don't try to tell me you didn't collect—all the whores here collect in advance so they're ready when I come by. Ain't that right? And the goddamned policeman said, Uh-huh, he'd already paid me. And I said, But that's not so. But Eufrasia just kept saying, Cough it up. And the policeman's friends—they're all standing around us in a big circle dying laughing. So finally just to get it over with, I opened my purse and I threw a half a peso at Eufrasia and I ran out of there as fast as I could go, with the whole place howling—it was just *gales* of laughter. I've never been so mortified. Can you imagine her thinking I cared about keeping thirty centavos that didn't belong to me? . . . But look how it's been raining. And my clothes are drenched. I bet I get a cold and don't live to tell the tale. Although this tale I'm not going to want to tell anybody, I'm afraid. Oh well. Better try the next place.

COLDS
GIVE IN FAST
to Bromo-Quinine.
Take it early and
stave off dangerous complications.
Bromo-Quinine
Laxative
Look for the name.
—*El Eco*
Holguín, Oct. 17, 1932

The truck has dropped me off four miles from home. I better step over here in the grass and dry out a little while I wait for the sun to come up so I can go home and get the knife. I'll just be there a second. Five minutes.

—*Fortunato*

I sat down in a park. I threw down the fan, which by now was falling apart, pulled off my sopping-wet stockings, wrung out the stole, and opened my legs a little bit so my skirt would dry out. I waited for two hours. An old man came by and struck up a conversation. We talked about his children. About how hard everything was get-

I've been walking all the way from Aguasclaras, but I'm coming to Holguín now. But maybe I should wait till it gets a little later. I'm exhausted.

I walk and walk and walk. I go into Mayra the Mare's whorehouse. I leave Mayra the Mare's whorehouse.

Now I'm in the Oasis. This is the last of the whorehouses. Over in one corner there's a table with four men all by themselves. Looks like they've had quite a bit to drink. They're singing. I think one of them was winking at me. I straighten my stole, kick off my shoes, and start dancing, holding my glass-bead hairnet in my teeth and unbuttoning the front of my dress with both hands. I'm right under the carbide lamps. In the spotlight. So

ting to be. We talked about all kinds of things. Until he said good night and walked away. And I headed for the next place. At least my skirt was dry by then.

—*Adolfina*

BIRTHDAY OF THE POPE
The birthday of His Holiness Pope Pius XII, born Eugenio Pachelli, was celebrated with various activities. All Vatican offices were closed, and newspapers published greetings for His Holiness, wishing him long life in the service of the Church.   —*El Norte*
June 3, 1958

LATEST NEWS!
The triumphant advance of the Revolutionary forces continues with the occupation of the town of San Luis. Forty-five rifles and a great amount of materiel was captured.
—*Bulletin* No. 2,
Nov. 21, 1958,
1 ctvo.

TODAY
MARTI THEATER

ONE HOUR WITH YOU
—with Maurice Chevalier
—*La Justicia*
Dec. 20, 1934

then one of the drunks puts his arm around me and asks me to have a drink with him. He seems seriously interested. We drink and dance. At last, Adolfina! At last you're dancing, the way you always wanted to. Another drunk comes over and wants to dance with me, too. But the first one doesn't want to turn me loose. So I throw down my stole and dance with both of them at once. With two men. With three. With four. Dancing.

"There's a whore in there carrying on something awful, taking off her clothes and dancing with a whole tableful of drunks. I think the broad's from some other town, because I don't remember ever seeing her around here and I never forget a face. You ought to see her—she looks like a hundred-year-old bedraggled hen about half plucked. And all gristle. I don't know what women like that think life is all about—why don't they save up a little money and retire before it's too late?"

"Like you should have done?"

"Oh—and what about you, bitch!"

"You wrinkled bag!"

"*You're* the one that's wrinkled. And rotten—you stink!"

"Oh, you want to fight, huh! Well here then! Take that!"

"Ay! You she-ass! I'm going to scratch your eyes out!"

"The one that's gonna yank out your gizzard is *me!* I'm sick of your insults, you whore! Take this!"

"*Ay-y-y-y-y!*"

Look how I turn. Look how I spin. Look. I look like a spinning top. I *am* a spinning top. Oh I love to dance like this, with everybody. I love to go around and round and round and never stop. Around and around. Around and around. Just like a top.

Around and around.

Look. Look. Look. What spins. What whirls. What turns.

I am the queen of tops.

I am Adolfina. Touch me. See for yourself that I am Adolfina. Look at me, all of you.

I, Adolfina, go walking through this goddamned shitty town . . . Can't you see me? I've left the last whorehouse on the arms of a bunch of drunks.

ORIENTE
THEATER
TODAY
GRAND PREMIERE
SEVENTH HEAVEN
with
Janet Gaynor &
Charles Farrell
plus
AMOR A MEDIANOCHE
*
SATURDAY AND SUNDAY
THE LOST BATTALION
—*El Norte*
Sept. 6, 1958

I honestly did everything I could. That's the saddest part of the whole thing—everything's *done.*

I tried to excite one of the drunks but no chance—there was no way that poor soul was going to be able to cut the mustard. So I helped him over to the part of Calixto García Park where there's all that undergrowth and I tried to sleep with him even if we didn't do anything. I tried. I said, Sleep, now, sleep, go to sleep, you're all right. Nothing's going to happen to you. And I sang to him like one of those grandmothers you don't find much anymore. Me singing to a drunk in the weeds in Calixto García Park, Holy Virgin Mary Mother of God. Adolfina sprawled in the grass with a stinking old drunk.

Me and the drunk.

But not even so much as that did I manage. The son of a bitch got up don't ask me how and started yelling and saying I'd stolen his wallet. And he was cursing a blue streak. And yelling and

cursing like that and calling me terrible, terrible names, he stag-
gered off to where all the whores were—because they'd changed
parks and now they were sleeping around in Calixto García. And
they all came running over to where I was still just standing there
paralyzed, and they started screaming *Thief! Thief!* at me, till the
drunk worked them up to slicing me into lunch meat with their
knives . . . I honestly don't know quite what happened next. I
know that I started screaming to high heaven—so loud I even
surprised myself. And that I started swinging my purse around
like a battle-ax. I was kicking and hitting people with my purse
and using my elbows and teeth and everything else against that
pack of maddened whores—*dozens* of them. I remember that.
But I honestly don't know exactly what happened next, except I
was screaming so loud and kicking and biting and swinging my
purse so hard, and I was so mad and so furious and so enraged—
that all of a sudden all the whores were running off like streaks
of lightning, and even the drunk disappeared . . . So then I made
one last try. I pulled up a whole lot of more or less dry grass and
piled it all together like it was a body. And I lay down on top of
that heaped-up grass and I started whispering all these things to
it. I said all kinds of sweet things. But it wasn't the same. It's
not the same to lie down next to a pile of grass as it is to lie
down next to a person, even if that person is about as close to
an animal as you can get and still be more than half human. Even
if he's the ugliest animal in the world.
So there I was
until I said to myself, Get up.

Till I said to myself, Can it be that you've fallen so low just
so you can see the truth?

Till I said to myself, Enough. Uncle. That's it. And I opened
my eyes. And all of a sudden, I saw things—the few raggedy trees,
the street, and you, you ruin of a woman. How is it possible to
live for nothing but to look down that straight street with just
a few trees here and there, also straight and stripped bare? How
is it possible to go on living after you've realized that all those
square houses on a straight street that peters out into a flat field
is all there is? How is so much tenderness, so much desire, possible if all there is is that straight street to display it on? . . . I'm
going to get up, and I'm going to brush this wet grass off my face

and clothes. I'm going to put one empty hand in the other empty hand and I'm going to try to make it home. I'll walk down this straight street. I'll turn at that square corner. If I make it home, I'm saved. Saved from what? If I make it home, I'll be restored. Restored to what? If I make it home, I'll be protected. Protected against what? If I make it home, I won't be dishonored. Dishonored by who? If I make it home, I'll have had my day—really had it . . . No! I'm not going home till I've made one last try. There's always one last try after the last try. But where's my hairnet? And my stole? And my fan? And my stockings? And my purse? And my feather? My God. I've lost my whole outfit. I'm even missing one shoe. And the sun's coming up. It's almost daybreak! And gunshots again. What a lot of gunshots, such gunshots! Listen to that, listen. Things are really in earnest now. What a racket, madre mía! Have you ever heard such a racket! . . . I'll make my last try to the tune of those gunshots. To the tune of that big gunfight I'll start dancing right here. Dancing, and calling, and cawing, and singing, and howling. Like this, like this. What a gunfight. My lord, such shooting! And me dancing. Me dancing my joints out of joint in the middle of Calixto García Park, to the music of that shooting. Me like a whirling dervish. Me dancing my insides out. Me stripping myself stark naked to the music of that gunfight . . . And here they come! Here come the splendid men! They're almost here. At last! They're coming closer, they're looking at me, they're touching me, they're pinching me to see if I'm real, they're dancing with me, all around me, everywhere. What men, what men! And they're still coming—lord! They're desperate. They're going mad for me! . . . So young, so strong, so hungry. Lord. Look at their muscles ripple under their clothes. And see how gentle they all are with me, how sweet and rough at the same time. How tender and how hungry for me. Don't fight, don't argue over me. Ay, such uniforms, such shoulders, and the way they move their legs . . . And now they're picking me up, lifting me higher, carrying me away. Holy Virgin Mary! And every one a prince.

My knights in shining armor.

"Let's go!"

*   *

ORIENTE THEATER
TODAY—PREMIERE—
TODAY
THIRST FOR AFFECTION
with
Leonora Ulric
BOMBSHELL
with
Jean Harlow
—*El Eco*
Dec. 23, 1935

Knock on the door. Wait. Who is it? It's me, Fortunato. Ay, my God! Knock.

"Don't open it, don't open it, the son of a bitch will ruin us! Don't open it!"

Who is it? It's me, Fortunato. Ay, Fortunato, I'm so happy you've come back home again. You don't know how we've suffered. Come in.

"Don't open it!"

It's me, open the door, they're following me. Open up, open up.

Where have you been all these days? Nobody knew anything about you . . . Knock, knock, knock. This is the door.

"Don't open it!"

The house. This is the house. Jesus! This is the house. There comes the neighborhood pansy back home again.

Oh, but that's the son of Onerica the husbandless.

The organ music sounds like crying, the organ music sounds like . . . They say when they first saw her she was alone, and then she was with a Negro under the San Andrés Bridge. They say they saw her. But I don't know whether that's the truth or a lie . . . I know so little, really. I think about it and I tell myself, It's not true. But who knows—maybe, on second thought, it *is* true. I know so little, really. What do you think? Ay, and they say the Negro was a common criminal.

Oh, that's that great goose that doesn't know how to do a thing.

A halfwit. And he's knocking and knocking and knocking. They say now he refuses to cut his hair. If you ask me, he's a queer . . . Like father, like son. His father—because I know who he was—he used to put on a uniform like he was in the militia and go around holding up lottery-ticket vendors in the middle of the highway. You never heard of such things happening back in my time.

Knock!

Back then things were different. You said it—they were different as all hell! . . . There's an old woman out there begging. Give her something. Here—take this, one day it may be me in your shoes.

"The old woman's out there crying."

Your mother's an old lady crying and making a bedpan sing.

Your mother. And she laughs. And shows her gums. Your mother . . .

The bedpan's not singing. The bedpan's crying.

Don't you hear how that bedpan's crying—your mother is playing it, blowing across the hole in it like it was a flute.

"Give her that money, you!"

You're standing at the door. You're knocking on the door. Now they're coming to answer the door. They'll open it. They won't open it. I tell you they'll open it. No? Yes? The Revolution's over. Inside, the old lady will play the bedpan someday. And you'll have to listen. And in fact you're already listening. And you're almost accompanying her with your knocking. Knock. Knock, young man . . . They finally open the door.

Followed by a choir of princes and knights in shining armor I go back home. I, Adolfina, the loveliest of them all. Surrounded by a great choir of princes, I return to my palace. Tell them, they don't have to believe *me*. White knights and red knights and blue knights and yellow knights and black knights and green knights and purple knights. And princes as tender as young boys that have just begun to flower. Princes as young and spirited as unbroken horses. Violent, well-turned, blond-haired princes. Princes and knights of all colors, as radiant and young as I myself. As life itself.

I and the princes.

Adolfina, the lady of the knights. I return from my grand gala night. I return from my procession through the streets of the great city. I return in the midst of conversations, propositions, and gallant compliments. Be still, my princes, I have given orders to the servants to open all the doors. Come, do not hold back, there is no need for timidity. Be not so gentle, gentlemen. Come, enter, and tell me stories I have never heard. I am so sated with banqueting . . . Tell me something that has never been heard. I will give orders that we be served in the Great Hall. But come—the portals are flung open. Let us go inside.

THE FLY—II

But the fly can soar to notable heights. It may be seen flying about cow manure, it is true; it may be seen hovering about the intestines of a dog just run over by a truck, it is true; but it also investigates the hanged man's tongue, and lights on the horse's mane, the highest leaf on a bay tree, and (though perhaps by mistake) the rose. Millions of persecution-years have sharpened its wits—it almost always can foresee our intentions. Before we ever make the fatal move, it flies away. Scientists, specialists in the field of entomology, and many devoted amateurs have given themselves with all the passion of the poet to the study of this legendary insect. More than fifteen hundred varieties have been classified. We know that it is harmful, persistent, and immortal. It arose, of course, long before man. Indisputable documentation exists to prove that the fly was present at the crucifixion of Christ, at Clytemnestra's and Marie Antoinette's bloody executions, and that it triumphantly buzzed about over the mummified bones of the first pharaoh. The fly also inhabited the funeral shroud in which was laid the first emperor Lao-Tse, the Great One, the sacred ruler of the First Dynasty. Perhaps from that fact derives the hypothesis that the fly's favorite color is yellow. But its great weakness, as we all know, is for window-glass.

PART THREE

THE PLAY

(ADOLFINA *opens the door and walks into the living room. The* CHORUS OF PRINCES, *after they have closed the door, follow her closely, solemnly reciting the most exalted passages from the Song of Songs. From time to time they lift Adolfina's skirt, revealing her burned, blackened, twisted calves and thighs. In one corner,* CELIA *kisses her dead daughter and then throws her over her shoulder and runs off with her like a bundle of dry kindling.* DIGNA *sings with her mouth closed. Through the door to the hallway the* CHORUS OF WILD BEASTS *enters, with* DEAD-FORTUNATO *in their arms, and never releasing him. From the ceiling the first* DEMONS *begin to descend, sliding down a rope tied to the roofbeam.* POLO *picks up the spraygun and starts spraying fog all over the living room. The* PRINCES' *declamation grows softer until it fades away completely. Listening to the ocean which crashes inside a seashell,* TICO *and* ANISIA *enter; they are wearing masks made to illustrate some of the faces of Death.)*

TICO *(to* ANISIA*)*: You give me that seashell or I won't tell you what's in the bathroom.

ANISIA: I'm not giving it to you, because I know better than you do what's there and what's not there.

TICO *(his voice eager, taking off the mask)*: What? *(Replaces the mask.)*

ANISIA *(holding her mask firmly in place)*: A little girl trying to drown herself in a dry bathtub.

TICO *(raising his mask, so that only the lower half of his face shows)*: Cold. Cold. You're ice-cold.

ANISIA *(masked)*: An old lady walking on her hands.

TICO *(faster)*: Cold, cold, cold.

ANISIA *(still faster)*: A seashell without an ocean inside it.

TICO *(at full speed)*: Cold! Cold!

ANISIA *(without mask)*: That! *(Points toward* ADOLFINA *surrounded by* PRINCES.*)*

CHORUS OF PRINCES *(reanimated, circling around* ADOLFINA*)*: You are lovely, lovely. *(Some* PRINCES *stick their hands up under* ADOLFINA*'s skirt, only to pull them back quickly, startled, pained, and somewhat frightened.)*

(The first loud knocking is heard at the front door. No one seems to have heard it. ANISIA *hides the seashell.)*

DIGNA *(going out to the backyard)*: I'll just sit down here and wait for Moisés to come. And when he comes I'm going to ask him just one question, and I'm going to stay sitting down. I'm not going to get up . . . *(*DIGNA*'s voice is drowned out by the din of millions of birds which sing, fly away, shriek in a deafening cacophony. Breaking into that uproar,* CELIA *enters with her dead daughter sitting on her shoulders, giving the impression of one tall, unreal, deformed being. As* CELIA *speaks,* ESTHER, *furious and in silence, pulls out tufts of* CELIA*'s hair.)*

CELIA: Haven't you seen a hen with her feet tied together go by here? Poor thing, I've been hunting for her so I could untie them for her. Poor thing, she must be half dead. But listen, you mean nobody has seen a hen with her feet tied together go by here? You might have. She had to've come this way. Tell me whether you have or haven't seen her. But wait— was it a hen? . . . My lord, now that I think about it, it wasn't a hen. It's more like a guinea pig that's just been smashed to a pulp. Tell me whether you haven't seen a rabbit that's just been smashed to a pulp, or a hen with her feet tied together. A white hen, or a rabbit, or an ant with green feet. What was it . . . two woodticks jumping rope? A hen that can't walk? And Esther—what about Esther? Where's Esther? . . . Ave María purísima, this house is *filthy!* *(The racket grows loud again, then softer, then dies away.)*

ADOLFINA *(squatting, walking with her hands on her knees, a bottle of alcohol balanced on her forehead and a box of matches between her breasts):* I am the incarnation of loveliness. Inside me live all the forms of tenderness in the world. My purse is the most beautiful purse that ever was. You people can *have* your tragedies. I contain all wisdom, and I am the queen of that choir of princes and white knights that is always with me, following me, pursuing me madly, filling me with delight. Look. Listen. Touch, feel, hear them.

TICO and ANISIA *(marching militarily, their masks under their arms):* Oh stinky-ass, oh stinky-ass, oh stinky-ass. *(Thunderous applause, followed by the notes of the national anthem.)*

ADOLFINA *(hopping to the tune of the national anthem and slinging the bottle of alcohol into the air, then catching it):* Because I invent my own refuge, and I crown myself queen.

CH. OF PRINCES: You are lovely, lovely. *(ADOLFINA bends down as the PRINCES place a crown on her head.)*

TICO and ANISIA *(marching):* Oh stinky-ass, oh stinky-ass, oh stinky-ass. *(Repetition of crowd effects.)*

DIGNA *(going to the door):* But is it possible that any other man than Moisés exists?

ADOLFINA *(swinging her arms and hips, answering DIGNA):* "I am black, but comely, O ye daughters of Jerusalem, as the tents of Kedar, as the curtains of Solomon."* *(She returns to the CHORUS OF PRINCES, who, from center stage, beckon her with provocative gestures.)*

TICO *(laughing):* Cold, cold.

ANISIA: But I'm not giving up.

DIGNA'S VOICE *(from the hallway):* All right, you kids, come in here and stop playing with those bugs around the light.

TICO *(removing his mask):* Your mother's calling you.

ANISIA *(straightening her mask):* Us. Your mother's calling us.

2 DEMONS *(picking up the masks which TICO and ANISIA have thrown on the floor as they exit to the dining room):* Oh, the mother. The mother . . . *(They squat down and shit in the powerful beam of a spotlight. They clean themselves and go off hand in hand singing a children's marching song.)*

---

* All quoted material is taken from the Song of Solomon, unless otherwise indicated.—Trans.

ANISIA'S VOICE *(from the dining room)*: Behave yourself—act your age. Try to behave like a child.

TICO'S VOICE: We *are* children.

ANISIA'S VOICE: I alone know everything.

TICO'S VOICE: I alone know that you don't know everything.

ANISIA'S VOICE: And that other people won't know everything until we know everything.

TICO'S VOICE: And that we won't stop knowing everything, because nothing interests us.

ANISIA'S VOICE: I'm a young child so old that there's not an old person left anymore who can remember when I was young.

TICO'S VOICE: Or old either.

(They enter the living room.)

ANISIA: What do you want to play now?

TICO: Let's play Crack the whip.

ANISIA: No. Let's play House.

TICO: Let's play King with the bottles.

ANISIA: Let's play Dead.

TICO *(softly)*: Tag.

ANISIA *(more softly still)*: Hopscotch.

BOTH *(almost inaudibly)*: Sssh, there's your mother. And mine.

DIGNA'S VOICE *(from the bedroom)*: Aren't you kids ever going to be still all night! You two are going to be the death of me! I'm damned! I'm cursed and gone to hell already!

TICO *(picking up his mask)*: I'm to the point where I can't take it anymore!

ANISIA *(picking up her mask)*: Goddamned wretched kids—are you trying to kill me with these sufferings you put me through?

DIGNA *(sticking her head out)*: Inconsiderate brats! Spoiled little whelps! Go to bed!

TICO: To bed!

ANISIA: To bed. Let's go to bed. *(They remain standing, rigid. For a moment everything becomes unreal. TICO and ANISIA resemble two statues in some strange setting.)*

* *

(Silence. The PRINCES *are arm-in-arm around* ADOLFINA, *who is lying on the sofa. The* DEMONS *one by one slowly climb up the rope to the ceiling.* POLO *reappears in one corner of the living room. He drops the spraygun. He blows out the only candle still burning and walks toward center stage as he moves his lips and opens and closes his mouth, as though he were talking to himself. Now is heard the second loud knocking at the front door.* POLO, *staring up at the ceiling, goes on talking to himself.)*

CH. OF WILD BEASTS *(in a corner)*: The Pleiades are in the center of the sky—a sign of rain. And the Southern Cross stands more erect in the sky than it ever has before. Though it is difficult to predict the sea-wind. The entire crop may be lost, just as it was last year, and next year . . .

A DEMON *(sliding down the rope)*: And the year after that!

CH. OF WILD BEASTS *(in a circle, dancing around* POLO*)*: They've offered to buy the farm, and I can barely see my own hands before my eyes.

1 WILD BEAST: And the grass starts growing, and it grows and grows. *(He becomes the grass.)*

2 WILD BEASTS: And the grass grows higher and higher, and it grows as high as the house. *(They become the grass growing tall.)*

3 WILD BEASTS: And me an old man, sitting in the breezeway, watching the grass grow.

CH. OF WILD BEASTS: Grow. Grow.

1 WILD BEAST: Ay, I'm choking! This grass is choking me to death!

CH. OF WILD BEASTS *(still circling around* POLO*)*: They've made me an offer on the farm. There's the Southern Cross and the Pleiades, and the Plow—but who's to say that they'll be there tomorrow? And that a big wind won't come and level the corn? And that we won't have to all turn beggars on the road? Life in the country is hard. So hard. There's no bad luck as bad as having to live at the mercy of the clouds. There's no bad luck as bad as having to always look up at the sky, to see what the weather'll be like today and what it'll be to-morrow, and what the weather might be like the day after that. And a person down here on the ground not able to do a thing about it. And the sky throwing down lightning and thunder and bolts from the blue and wind and flaming boulders and hailstones and floods.

(The DEMONS, *blowing wind out of their mouths and backsides, bring on a storm.)*

CH. OF WILD BEASTS *(terrified, covering their ears)*: In March the wind is terrible.

2 WILD BEASTS *(clinging to each other in terror)*: In March the wind will practically pick you up off the ground, and blow you off your own land, into the next hell down the road.

1 WILD BEAST *(with both hands high)*: You, in *this* world, only hear that terrible March wind. That wind blowing over my bones. That accursed wind that blows and blows and blows, blowing across things that fade away. The wind, laughing at my fading away.

CH. OF WILD BEASTS: Useless old man—what are you waiting for to get you off this rocky hillside? You're going to starve to death. You'll be sitting in the breezeway and the house'll be coming down around your ears. And you won't be able to hold it up.

1ST WILD BEAST: And you won't even be able to pick up the fallen pieces and throw them in a pile.

2ND WILD BEAST: And you'll try to cover yourself with leaves, and palm branches, and old pieces of cardboard.

1ST WILD BEAST: And the wind will stir up that trash and leave you naked, and you won't even be able to cover your own filth, old man.

A DEMON *(slapping him)*: Sell the farm, sell. *(All the* DEMONS *blow harder; some blow out shit.)*

CH. OF WILD BEASTS *(closing the window)*: Here's the wind. And us with the cows out on the other side of the river. They're bound to drown. And me here just sitting, listening to the sound of that conch shell heralding my own death. Listen to that conch shell—it's the same conch shell I blew the day my father died, may he rest in peace.

2 DEMONS *(loudly)*: Listen to that conch shell—it's the same one my father blew the day his father died.

CH. OF WILD BEASTS *(loudly)*: Listen to that conch shell—it's also the same one my father's father blew the day *his* father died.
A BEAST *(shrieking)*: The conch shell, the conch shell, the conch! *(Blows the conch.)*

(The old man paces the living room as the DEMONS *beat him and try to trip him. The* CHORUS OF WILD BEASTS *closely follows his steps, never turning loose of* FORTUNATO, *however.)*

CH. OF WILD BEASTS: As in a dream I see my life—tumbling away through the little piles of cowflop in the pasture.
2 DEMONS: As in a dream I see myself, climbing the custard-apple tree to announce my death with the blowing of the conch.
A BEAST: Because I am alone.
JACINTA: Goddamned old coot, you'd have been better off going under once and for all than selling our land. It's your fault if we don't have enough food to fill the cavity in the one rotten back tooth I've got left. And on top if it all, you get stingier every day. I've had it. One of these days I'm going to trip and cut my own head off, you keep this house so dark. Believe me, it'd do you good to turn on the lights and stop talking to yourself. A *world* of good. You selfish old man! But even if you bust, you old miser, this candle stays lit. Old coot, you're even stingy with the dead. You won't pray, you won't even let me light a candle to their soul. Plus you spend the whole night long out there in the living room standing in the dark talking to yourself. That miserliness of yours has driven you crazy. From now on, I'm going to be the one that runs this house!

(When JACINTA *screams the word "house,"* ADOLFINA *gives a start and then sits up slowly on the sofa, while the* PRINCES, *somewhat fearfully, step back, watching her from a distance.)*

ADOLFINA: In this house the wild beasts hop and flutter like moths, and Mama puts out the little food there is on the flyblown table. *(The* PRINCES *step back farther.)*
CH. OF WILD BEASTS *(coming toward* ADOLFINA*)*: In this house. In this house. In this house!

2 DEMONS *(hopping closer)*: In this house there is an old woman tied to the cookstove that's never lit.

3 WILD BEASTS: In this house rats scurry around night and day, and you can never even close your eyes anymore.

1 DEMON: In this house there's a demon who won't let me be.

2ND DEMON: Who stalks me.

3RD DEMON: And who asks me who I am and what I'm waiting for, and what I've done, and why I'm alive.

CH. OF WILD BEASTS: And who asks me what I will do.

1 WILD BEAST *(running terrified out of the* CHORUS*)*: In this house there's a terrible wild beast that makes faces at me when I look in the mirror. Me, who am so young and innocent.

CH. OF WILD BEASTS: Spiders fly like gnats and I, poor boy, I watch the sky fall down on me.

ALL THE DEMONS: And I, poor boy, sometimes I wish I could hold it up so it wouldn't.

CH. OF WILD BEASTS: In this house, in this house, in this house.

CELIA *(entering, with* ESTHER *atop her)*: In this house the pigeons have rebelled and thrown us out. They beat us and scream "Git. Git." In this house my dead daughter. In this house.

POLO *(entering)*: In this house there's an old man who doesn't know a thing about the world, who knows it all, who doesn't know a thing. Who wishes for death, who wishes for life. Who says, I can't stand it, and who consoles himself by counting bananas, counting rotten bananas.

1 WILD BEAST: And the seven stars in the Pleiades.

1 DEMON: And the years gone by.

1 WILD BEAST: And the days he has left.

1 DEMON: And the days he has left over.

JACINTA *(entering with the mortar and pestle on her head)*: I am the angel of this house, and yet they treat me like a dog. *(She remains standing, precariously balancing the mortar and pestle on her head.)*

DIGNA: In this house there's a madwoman that sings with her mouth closed and that hops on the roof on one foot, and with her eyes closed too, and that sits at midnight on the rotten tree trunk out in the middle of the backyard. And sometimes she looks like a woman that's been sent here from another world.

CH. OF WILD BEASTS: In this house there's a chorus of wild beasts that I talk to once in a while, into whose hands I deliver myself once in a while, and that I quiz once in a while.

TICO and ANISIA *(entering hand in hand wearing their masks)*: In this house there are two terrible brats that think they know it all.

ALL THE DEMONS: In this house there's a mailman who never stops blowing his whistle.

CH. OF WILD BEASTS: In this house you can always hear the far-off sound of a conch shell.

2 WILD BEASTS *(one to the other)*: They say a boy blows that conch, and that he's telling the world that his mother has died.

POLO: Listen to the sound of that conch. Listen, people.

ALL: Listen.

(The long-drawn sound of a conch shell being blown. DEAD-ESTHER *and* DEAD-FORTUNATO *enter. Everyone else freezes. The* WILD BEASTS *and the* DEMONS *become a forest.* TICO *and* ANISIA *are the river. The rest of the family are stepping stones the two dead youngsters cross the river on.)*

ESTHER *(hopping from one stone to another)*: It's been a long time since I've lived with that family.

FORTUNATO *(helping her)*: They were all crazy.

ESTHER: It's hunger that brings on those things.

TICO *(still as the river)*: In this house there's a girl who little by little has filled up a whole bottle with strychnine.

ANISIA *(river)*: The girl's got the bottle full to the top now.

TICO *(river)*: In this house there's a boy that's saved up more than seventeen pesos, and with that money he's going to run off.

ANISIA *(river)*: And never come back.

FORTUNATO: Listen to them calling us.

ESTHER: They look for me everywhere, high and low, but they never find me. They look for me, but I'm floating, floating—without touching the bottom or ever coming to the top either.

FORTUNATO: They look for me everywhere, high and low, and here I am on top of the house, listening to the mailman's tweet and the honks when my grandmother snores.

CH. OF WILD BEASTS: Because I'll never even have the satisfaction of knowing that someone has blown that last sad sound for me.

1 DEMON: For I have tried to plant in the sea.

2 DEMONS: But now I cannot even plow.

CH. OF WILD BEASTS: Because I am dead. And the wind carries away the earth that should have covered me. And I am dead and lying among the rocks. Exposed to the air, and to the sun, and to the disgust and rage of everyone that passes—they look at me and spit.

1 DEMON *(crying)*: Sell, oh sell.

(JACINTA enters, stumbling into the furniture, knocking over a vase which smashes to bits on the floor. She also falls.)

JACINTA *(getting up)*: You old wolf, I've fallen down three times today already on account of your turning out all the lights. As though one candle cost so much to burn. A person could kill herself in this house from your miserliness. Ay, my knee-cap's broken into sixteen pieces. You skinflint. What a miserable goddamned fate my fate has been. Ay, you miserable stingy old coot.

1 DEMON *(slapping the old man in the face)*: Old wolf, old wolf!

JACINTA: Damned old fart, you ought to have died before you sold that farm. It's your fault we're starving this minute worse than a hog on a short tether. And you get stingier every day. But this is the last straw. Any day now I'm going to crack my skull wide open falling down in the dark in this house. You've got to turn on the lights. And stop talking to yourself like this. Listen to Celia's shrieking that would burst your eardrums and Digna's shrieking you can barely hear. Listen. *(A great hullabaloo of voices. Everything returns to normal.)*

TICO and ANISIA *(without their masks)*: In this house there are two dead people that pretend everybody else is dead.

ALL THE DEMONS: In this house the terrible invisible clocks go *Tick tock, tick tock, tick tock, tick tock, tloc-tloc-tloc-tloc-tloc-tloc-tloc.*

DIGNA *(hopping on one foot)*: *Tick tock tick tock tick tock.*

* *

(Everyone begins going "Tick tock," producing a rhythmic litany that grows louder and louder until it is unbearable. Suddenly, ADOLFINA leaps into the middle of the room and screams. The PRINCES stand back even farther.)

ADOLFINA: There's Fortunato knocking at the door!

(Absolute silence. Everything freezes. THE FOREST takes shape once more, as once again the sound of the "tick tocks" is heard, very softly and far off. DEAD-ESTHER and DEAD-FORTUNATO walk toward center stage. They begin to cross the river.)

ESTHER *(on FORTUNATO's arm)*: . . . All of time. All of time. We have all of time. I knock and I don't knock. We have so much time. I walk, whenever I want to, right on top of the water, and sometimes I console myself by thinking that I might drown . . . But I have to remember that we have all of time. You and I, my dear cousin, have all the time in the world to walk among the memories we've invented. All the time in the world. All of time.

FORTUNATO: And yet there's not a thing we can do with it. Imagine what it is to say, "I am eternal." Imagine what it is to leave this place and go nowhere, and never to have left anywhere, and not to be able ever to hope to get anywhere, either.

ESTHER: Imagine what it is to be always here, listening to each other, looking at each other.

FORTUNATO *(taking a few steps in the water, as though exhibiting his gallantry to ESTHER)*: I get up early early in the morning and I go off to nail little crates together in the factory.

ESTHER *(to FORTUNATO, as though his gallantry found favor)*: I know very well that Baudilio couldn't care less whether I died or went on living.

FORTUNATO *(still more gallantly)*: I get up early in the morning and I feel like I've already lived through everything that's going to happen that day. And so it is. I know I'm going to hammer a nail through my thumb and smash my fingers six or seven times, and that I'm going to suffocate in the heat and sweat like a horse. And I know that Tomasico is going to get mad at me because my crates are so rickety that bars

323

of guava paste spill out of them. And I know I'm going to duck my head and not say anything to defend myself. And I know the other guys are going to laugh at me . . . *(They kiss.)* And that around noon my grandmother will bring me a little milk and a bowl of soup. And I know that as I start to drink the glass of milk I'll say to myself, So this is life. And I know I'll feel a terrible rage building up inside me. And I know I'm going to bite the rim of the glass and want to skin my grandmother alive, although *she's* never done anything to me. *(Embraces* ESTHER *more passionately.)* And I know that I'm going to eat the soup and then go lie down on a sack of crate ends to rest a little. And that then will come the goddamned smell of rotten guavas. And that I'll wash my face and hear the sound of Iluminada's radio, next door, because it's always on full blast. And that then I'll go and pick up the hammer again. *(Hand in hand they now step across the stepping stones.)* I'll fill a can up with tacks. And I'll hammer, while the vats go *Fzzzzz* and my grandmother's voice still cackles in my ears.

THE FOREST *(in a murmur)*: Work, lad, work. Work so you'll be a man someday.

ESTHER *(stopping, and stopping* FORTUNATO*)*: What do you think of Baudilio?

FORTUNATO *(turning and taking her in his arms)*: Really, honestly, I don't know whether this happens to everybody. I don't know whether everybody sees things the way I do. Maybe I'm the only person that feels what I feel. Maybe everybody is *satisfied*. Or is it that they just don't complain? . . . I don't know. I'm a slave that makes crates to put guava paste in. I work from four o'clock in the morning till four o'clock in the afternoon. A thousand crates is two pesos. The slave hammers and hammers and hammers. Not even a slave. An animal. *(They go on, stepping across the stepping stones in the river.)* And Iluminada's radio said it was three o'clock. And the steam from the vats turns into guava paste, and I don't feel like dying anymore. In an hour or so I'll get off work and go home. To go home, all I have to do is take two or three steps. In an hour or so I'll report a thousand crates and I'll go home.

ESTHER: But don't think I care so much about *Baudilio*. The awful thing is that they're all like him. And suffering from him, I'm suffering from them all. The awful thing is that even if Baudilio were another man, he'd still keep being Baudilio. The awful thing is that even if things weren't this way, everything would still go on being this way . . . Don't you feel as though you're always coming to some terrible, abominable place where nobody's waiting for us, or where if they are it's to see what they can take away from us, what fault they can find in us and tell everybody about? Don't you feel the dust, the humidity, the heat, and that horrible blinding-bright sky that disappears, somehow, melts into the land way off on the horizon—that horizon toward which, like it or not, we're always walking? Might that not be the worst thing there is? Or is there something worse? . . . Is that what I really wanted to say? Or is there something more that I can't say, that I suffer but don't know the name for—and which then constitutes my failure?

FORTUNATO: In my house—which is not my house but which anyway is "my house"—Jacinta gives orders, the old man gives orders, Adolfina gives orders, Digna gives orders. And all of them in turn are ordered around by somebody else. And the people that can't give orders are ordered around by *everybody*.

ESTHER: The hills are gray, the rocks are gray; the sky, a metallic gray color, presses down onto the land. Who can be waiting for us on that gray plain? And what—except for the certainty of a gray rain—can we look forward to here?

(Slowly, ESTHER *goes over to become part of the* CHORUS OF WILD BEASTS *which still makes up the landscape. Then is heard the third desperate knocking at the front door, much more loudly than before.* DEAD-FORTUNATO *disappears into the landscape. Everything returns to its normal appearance.)*

JACINTA *(falling to her knees in the middle of the living room)*: My God, it's Fortunato! He's come back! What a blow You give me, Lord!

POLO *(desperate)*: Don't open it! Don't open the door! If they see him come in this house they'll kill us all and burn down my vegetable stand, just like they threatened to do. Watch out if you open that door. Watch out!

CH. OF WILD BEASTS *(hopping all about the room)*: Open it! Don't open it! Ay, don't open it! Ay, open it! Run open that door this second! No! No! No! Don't open it! Open it! No!

JACINTA *(still on her knees)*: Dios te salve, María, full of grace, the Lord is with thee, blessed be the fruit of thy womb. Santa María, madre de Dios. . . . Ay, don't open the door!

TICO and ANISIA *(picking up their masks and shinnying up the rope)*: They're after him. They're right on his heels. Open up. *(They remove their masks.)* Or don't. *(They put on their masks.)* Here you have the big family. *(They furiously throw down their masks.)* Anyway, I'll just practice my eternal, modest part—hangman in a hard time. I mean, of course, any time. *(They solemnly climb down the rope and stand directly under it, examining the end of it.)*

CH. OF WILD BEASTS: I'm at the house. I knock. Nobody comes to the door. They're asleep. But I have to keep knocking. The neighbors have seen me. The police'll know by now, too. If they don't open this door, there'll be no escape for me. They're already out looking for me.

Open up!

Open up!

POLO *(ripping a leg off the table and standing behind the door, brandishing the table leg menacingly as though to say, "I'll brain the first one that takes another step")*: Bananas at three for twenty-five centavos, tomatoes for the best offer, plantains at ten centavos a hundredweight. But I must be crazy—plantains aren't sold by the hundredweight. Meatballs . . . *Meatballs*, did I say? . . . Good lord . . . I won't allow this door to be opened for that halfwit! And anyway, what'll we do with him in the house?

CH. OF DEMONS: He's a halfwit, he's a good boy, he's a worthless no-good, he's a wonderful person, he's hopeless, he's a genius, he's not worth five centavos. Ay, he's such a nice boy. Leave him outside. Save him. Let him die, who cares . . . But what am I saying!

★   ★

(Polo begins to stack furniture against the door.)

DIGNA *(speaking to* ADOLFINA*)*: Moisés hasn't come and I'm still waiting. Moisés is coming, Moisés isn't coming. Will Moisés ever come? Ay, we better open the door, it might be Moisés . . .

*(*ADOLFINA *tries to say something, but the* CHORUS OF PRINCES *and* KNIGHTS IN SHINING ARMOR *suddenly reappears, pre-empting her.)*

CH. OF PRINCES: "Behold, thou art fair, my love; behold, thou art fair; thou hast doves' eyes."

ADOLFINA *(stammering)*: "Behold, thou also art fair, my beloved, yea, pleasant; also our bed is green. The beams of our house are cedar, and our rafters of fir." Open the door! Open the door! Open that door, damn you!

*(*ADOLFINA *runs toward the door, but* POLO *won't let her open it. From outside come the sounds of play—dogs barking, children laughing and shouting.)*

CH. OF PRINCES *(drawing closer to* ADOLFINA, *trying to control her)*: "Behold, thou art fair, my love; behold, thou art fair; thou hast doves' eyes within thy locks; thy hair is as a flock of goats, that appear from Mount Gilead. Thy teeth are like a flock of sheep that are even shorn, which came up from the washing; whereof every one bears twins, and none is barren among them."

ADOLFINA: Open this door, you miserable old coot!

CH. OF PRINCES *(still more quickly and ceremoniously)*: "Thy lips are like a thread of scarlet, and thy speech is comely; thy temples are like a piece of a pomegranate within thy locks. Thy neck is like the tower of David builded for an armory, whereon there hang a thousand bucklers, all shields of mighty men."

CH. OF WILD BEASTS *(walking toward the* CHORUS OF PRINCES*)*: Open that door!

CH. OF PRINCES *(faster)*: "Thy two breasts are like two young roes that are twins, which feed among the lilies."

* *

(ADOLFINA *stops and listens for a moment to the* CHORUS OF
PRINCES, *but then immediately goes back to reality.*)

ADOLFINA: Open the door! Open the door!
JACINTA: Our Father Who art in Heaven.

(*The* CHORUS OF PRINCES *and the* CHORUS OF WILD BEASTS *begin
scuffling with each other.* TICO *and* ANISIA *hang on the end of
the rope and swing all around the living room. As they fly, with
their feet they knock over the remaining vases, kick pictures off
the walls, and topple the armchairs. The* DEMONS *start playing
hopscotch at a sign from* CELIA.)

ANISIA (*greasing the rope and swinging on it*): A woman dancing
    on one toe and pulling out her hair with her teeth.
TICO (*greasing the rope and swinging on it*): Cold, cold—like
    always.

(*At last the* CHORUS OF WILD BEASTS *defeats the* PRINCES *and
clambering over the ruins manages to unbolt the door. Everyone
runs toward the door, while* DEAD-ESTHER *and* DEAD-FORTUNATO
*enter hand in hand from the hallway. The rest of the characters
take on an unreal appearance. They stand immobile with their
backs to us, and start to look like towers, barbicans, posterns,
watchtowers, and so forth—a castle.*)

ESTHER (*standing at the hallway door*): Let's go into this palace.
FORTUNATO: Yes, let's. Let's see whether people still live in it.
ESTHER (*entering on* FORTUNATO'S *arm*): Once upon a time, they
    say, this was the ideal place for dreams.
FORTUNATO (*looking up at the towers*): That's the way it always
    is with places where it's impossible to live.
ESTHER: Once upon a time, they say, there lived a very kind queen
    here who killed her children so as not to see them suffer.
CH. OF WILD BEASTS (*completely motionless, backs to us*): Spi-
    derwebs block their way and everything smells like ancient
    solitude. (*They become spiderwebs.*)
FORTUNATO: But in spite of everything, it still seems as though

I were touching some of the things that will never perish.

ESTHER: You mean—something horrible?

FORTUNATO: I mean something alive.

ESTHER (*affirmatively*): You mean something horrible.

BOTH (*walking on*): Time has stopped, yet we spurn its transitory death.

ESTHER: "It will be the end of the world if we go on."*

FORTUNATO: It's the end of the world if we stay here.

ESTHER: I know that I was here once—a thousand years ago.

CH. OF WILD BEASTS (*still spiderwebs*): A thousand years, a thousand years.

"Adolfina! Adolfina! You've been in that bathroom for five hours! Now I really can't hold it anymore!"

(ONERICA *enters from the hall, dressed entirely in black and banging a drum. Her face is very white. Even her head is swathed in black. For one moment* ONERICA *dances in the middle of the room, banging the drum and walking about with martial steps, giving an unimaginable show.*)

ESTHER (*to* FORTUNATO): There comes your mother.

FORTUNATO: Shh. Don't yell, don't scare her.

ESTHER: Say something to her, go over there and say something.

FORTUNATO (*going over to* ONERICA): Mama, Mama, what are you doing here? Why aren't you up there taking care of other people's shitty screaming kids?

(ONERICA *goes on marching. She exits still banging her drum.*)

ESTHER: She must be dead.

FORTUNATO: Then why didn't she answer me?

ESTHER: She's probably gotten tired of you.

FORTUNATO: Maybe so. But I think she looked at me. And I think

---

* This is a translation, from the Spanish, of Rimbaud's *Les Illuminations*, "Enfance IV," and is probably what RA wants *in meaning*. The French, however, has "Ce ne peut être que la fin du monde, en avançant." Or, in the Fowlie translation—"This must be the end of the world, lying ahead."—Trans.

she wanted to let me know that she recognized me. And I believe she even wanted to cry a little bit and everything. But I think somebody made her keep going and wouldn't let her stop banging that drum.

TICO (*immobile, unreal, a postern*): Was it God?

ANISIA (*immobile, unreal, a watchtower*): Was it the Devil?

ESTHER: But why wouldn't she speak to you?

FORTUNATO: Poor thing. She never spoke. She never said *any-thing*. She never learned how to speak up for herself. Never a squeak. So now, how are we supposed to know what her wishes are?

I DEMON (*coming out from among the towers and hitting* FORTUNATO *repeatedly over the head*): Go find her. Go speak to her. Go on—she's sure to be out behind the house crying somewhere.

3 DEMONS (*appearing among the towers*): Go on, go on, go.

FORTUNATO: I won't go, I won't, I won't. (*Runs out to find her.*)

ESTHER (*walking over to the* CHORUS OF WILD BEASTS, *who turn their backs to her and once more become the towers of the castle*): Touch my hands, they're colder than ice. Touch my hands. Look how cold they are. (*The* CHORUS OF WILD BEASTS, *still posing as a tower, folds its hands. Silence.* ESTHER *is slowly disappearing. Then there is a loud noise of blows, kicks, splintering wood, and empty cans falling. The front door flies wide open and through it bursts* FORTUNATO, *dragging all the junk the old man had been accumulating through the years. Everything returns to normal.*)

CH. OF WILD BEASTS (*as* FORTUNATO *comes into the living room and* POLO *stomps off down the hall, hopping mad, yelling*): I've just come to get the butcher knife. Don't be scared, you silly hens. I've just come for that and then I'll be on my way. The last thing in the world I want is to live with you people again.

JACINTA (*on her knees*): I believe in God the Father Almighty, maker of Heaven and earth, and in Jesus Christ His son Our Lord who . . .

I DEMON (*pulling* JACINTA's *hair*): Old woman, old woman. The time has come for you to take off your mask. Go stick your head out the door a second and you'll see your daughter kissing a Negro.

JACINTA'S VOICE *(offstage)*: Kill that whore, she's no daughter of mine anymore. I won't have her as my daughter. Kill her, kill her right this minute.

ALL THE DEMONS: Old woman. Old woman. Old woman.

ADOLFINA *(running up to* FORTUNATO *and embracing him, as though to say, "You've come back at last; how wonderful that you're here!")*: They're after me. They want to cut off my head because they saw me with that Negro. A Negro. I was desperate. I'm a desperate woman. After I died I didn't know what to do, so I decided to live a little while longer, till I got tired of it. But before that I was with a man. I slept with him. And I got pregnant by the Negro. But thanks to time—and to myself—I died before the child was born. But I was in a man's arms once, and I found out what it was like. And I'll tell you the truth—frankly, I was a little disappointed. Frankly, I'm disappointed now forever. I thought it would be different. I thought . . .

CH. OF PRINCES *(solemnly, as though intoning a hymn)*: "Until the day break, and the shadows flee away, I will get me to the mountain of myrrh, and to the hill of frankincense. Thou art all fair, my love; there is no spot in thee. Come with me from Lebanon, my spouse, with me from Lebanon: look from the top of Amana."

I DEMON: Fry poor Fortunato an egg, he must be starving to death from the distance he's come.

POLO *(entering fearfully, angrily)*: Careful there. Here's the butcher knife. So you've got it. Now you can scat. Scat, you're bad for this house. Ay, go on, go—if the police catch you here they'll burn the whole house down. *(He cries.)* Ay, they'll club me to death. An old man. After working so hard for so many years, for nothing. *(POLO goes on crying.* FORTUNATO *takes the knife and turns to go.)*

ADOLFINA *(holding him back)*: I'm off in the corner and I say to myself, if only someone would come, if only someone would start up a conversation with me. If only somebody would come and even say, "Hope a lightning bolt strikes you." Even if that was all they said, I'd be saved.

FORTUNATO (to POLO): With this knife I'm going to kill a militiaman and take his rifle so I can join the rebels.

DIGNA (dancing with her arms outstretched and one leg straight out): I'm gonna kill me a soldier and take his gun away, and then you'll never see me again.

I WILD BEAST (crying): He's crazy. Poor boy.

TICO and ANISIA (swinging on the rope): Dear son, dear son, dear near-dead son.

ADOLFINA (as the PRINCES sprinkle her with alcohol): I'll go out in the street and start screaming, screaming, screaming. (exits.)

CH. OF PRINCES (behind ADOLFINA): Someone's got to either rescue me or sign my death warrant. Someone's got to bend himself out of shape to give me shape. (They exit also. From the street ADOLFINA's screams can be heard as she begins to burn again. FORTUNATO once more tries to leave.)

CELIA (stopping him): Listen to that cackling. Listen to that interminable singing. I'm the only sane person here, because I'm the only one here that pays any attention to those cries— and they're not even for me. Do you people hear them? (FORTUNATO slips past CELIA.)

DIGNA (stopping him as CELIA had): Son. Son. Baa-aa-aa. (Walks on all fours in front of FORTUNATO.)

I DEMON (jumping up piggyback on FORTUNATO): Son, son, son. (FORTUNATO manages to get to the door, but at that moment ADOLFINA enters, wearing an ermine cape and a crown, though now she is even blacker than before. The PRINCES are trying to extinguish the parts of her still burning with their hands.)

CH. OF PRINCES (waving away the smoke): "Thou hast ravished my heart, my sister, my spouse; thou hast ravished my heart with one of thine eyes, with one chain of thy neck."

ADOLFINA (leading FORTUNATO back into the living room): "I sleep, but my heart waketh; it is the voice of my beloved that knocketh, saying, Open to me, my sister, my love, my dove, my undefiled: for my head is filled with dew, and my locks with the drops of the night."

* *

(FORTUNATO *stands open-mouthed.* ADOLFINA *grabs the knife away and runs into a corner. The* CHORUS OF PRINCES *protects her.*)

CH. OF WILD BEASTS: The knife. Give me that knife.

I DEMON (*making faces, sneering*): Oh, the knife! The big sissy's knife!

POLO (*to* JACINTA): Give that dunce the knife or he'll never leave.

JACINTA (*to* POLO): Give him the knife, you old idiot. Give it to him, go on.

DEAD-ESTHER (*barely visible*): One tiny little push and you're here. One little motion of my nonexistent hands and you'll be with me.

(TICO *and* ANISIA *play with the end of the rope.*)

TICO: As soon as Grandma gets out of the kitchen, I'm going to sneak in there and steal a little sugar to make lemonade with the lemons I swiped from Grandpa when he was asleep with his head propped on the fruit-stand counter. (*Makes a noose with the end of the rope.*)

ANISIA (*tightening the noose*): And all the king's horses and all the king's men!

TICO (*testing the noose around his own neck*): Let's make a king's court out of the bottles today.

ANISIA: And we'll have a party.

TICO (*taking his head out*): And everybody will fall in love.

ANISIA: And there'll be weddings.

TICO (*trying the noose on* ANISIA): And we'll make the married bottles have babies.

ANISIA (*tugging at the knot*): And the ones that aren't married, too.

TICO (*taking off the noose*): And then everybody will die.

ANISIA (*serious, holding the noose*): It has to be that way.

TICO: We could make up another game.

ANISIA: No, if we don't play that one I'm not playing.

TICO: Aren't you tired yet? We've been doing the same thing for so long.

ANISIA: So what else could we do?

TICO: It'll have to stop someday.

ANISIA: Uh-huh, and then start all over again.

JACINTA *(trying to convince* FORTUNATO *to stay)*: Ay, my kidneys. I can't stand this pain anymore. *(Puts her hands on her lower back and begins to howl.)*

ADOLFINA *(to* DIGNA*)*: Enough of your nonsense, you big spoiled baby—go to your room and go to bed. And don't think I'm going to give you the knife, either. You don't know the scare you've put me through.

*(*FORTUNATO *goes off to his bedroom. Suddenly,* ADOLFINA *runs after him and stops him. She gives him the knife. The* PRINCES *follow along disappointedly, whining.)*

ADOLFINA: Go. Go, right now—and don't ever darken our door again. Don't ever come back to this accursed house.

(For one second, FORTUNATO *is disconcerted, but then he snatches the knife and runs over to the* CHORUS OF WILD BEASTS. ADOLFINA, *suddenly having second thoughts about what she has just done, runs after* FORTUNATO *to try to wrestle the knife away from him again. But the* CHORUS OF WILD BEASTS *stops her. And moreover, the* CHORUS OF PRINCES *has surrounded her again.)*

CH. OF PRINCES *(encircling* ADOLFINA*)*: "Who is she that looketh forth as the morning, fair as the moon, clear as the sun, and terrible as an army with banners?"

JACINTA *(banging her fist on the coffee table)*: Adolfina! Adolfina! Aren't you coming out of that bathroom all day! This is too much, woman, what you're doing is laughing at the lot of us. But don't think I'm taking this lying down. I'm going to get the crowbar right this minute and I'm going to break down that door. This has gone too far. And me with my bowels about to burst, with her in there splashing water up her cunt and singing like she was a queen. Ha! I won't stand for this another minute. That great goose is going to drive me CRAZY! But I'm not taking this lying down—I'm going to beat that door down. *(She bangs on the table harder.)*

ADOLFINA *(running to look out the window)*: "The voice of my beloved! Behold, he cometh leaping upon the mountains, skipping upon the hills."

CH. OF PRINCES: "Rise up, my love, my fair one, and come away."

(ADOLFINA *is slowly disappearing into the* CHORUS OF PRINCES. *Meanwhile, the* CHORUS OF WILD BEASTS, *in the living room, becomes a street corner with a lamppost.)*

CH. OF WILD BEASTS *(as the street)*: Now you are out in the street. You've got the knife in your belt. Here comes a militiaman. *(One of the* WILD BEASTS *becomes a militiaman.)* A militiaman has stopped over there on the corner. He's the guard posted on that corner. Your soldier has come. You finger the knife at your belt. The knife is cold. The knife edge is cold. You have to take the knife by the hilt and stab it into that guard's back. That one. That guard. That is your salvation. Over there in the other town they're all waiting for you. The militiaman has a rifle. You—the militiaman—and the rifle. It's easy. Easy.

You just take out the knife. *(*FORTUNATO *takes out the knife.)* You test the blade. *(*FORTUNATO *tests the blade.)* Sharp. Whew, really sharp. Ay, what a sharp edge, what an edgy edge . . . There. Now you've got the knife in your hand. Hide it behind your back, in case the jerk looks around. The corner's darker than a wolf's gullet. Nobody'll see you.

At this moment the world is a militiaman with his rifle, whistling on a corner. The entire world has come to that corner and that corner is the world. And more besides . . . And you are standing on that corner and you try to touch that world. You imagine the shape of that world. You know that there is a world. The world . . . The soldier is scratching his balls. He's seen you, and that's why he's scratching his balls . . . The guard has seen you, and he's scratching his balls, but he hasn't seen the knife. You're a kid about half simpleminded walking along a neighborhood street. Nobody could possibly think you were a rebel. . . . In the house, the demons are jumping around on the chairs till they break their seats. In the house the wild beasts embrace each other, saying, Son. Son. And a huge cockroach climbs up on the bed and starts kissing you on the mouth. Every night this happens, every night. Every night the same thing. That kiss, that kiss you feel this minute. (FORTUNATO *stands now behind the soldier.)*

ADOLFINA *(running out through the ring of* PRINCES*)*: Ay, tie up that boy. Tie that child up.

POLO *(running over to* ADOLFINA *and grabbing her by the neck)*: Shut your mouth, you damned slut. Or do you want us all killed too?

TICO and ANISIA *(caressing the rope)*: Death appears from down the street.

ANISIA: Death, like all the true things of this world, is a whore.

TICO: Death, like all the serious things of this world, makes everything a joke.

BOTH *(inspecting the grease-covered rope)*: Ay, whore, ay whore, ay the greatest whore that ever was.

TICO: You raise your hand. And the butcher knife gleams. And from the lamppost there grows a streetlight. The lamppost is a goddamned plant with one goddamned stalk and on that one stalk there grows a goddamned streetlight.

(The WILD BEAST *who is the lamppost puts out a hand and makes the streetlight.)*

ANISIA: The streetlight is a flower that smells like death. The streetlight throws your shadow in front of the soldier.

I DEMON: The militiaman is whistling. Does he see the shadow? The militiaman stops whistling and scratches, scratches, scratches. Does he see the shadow?

TICO: The tree has no leaves. Just a dried-up stalk a streetlight is growing out of. The tree is cruel, like life itself—not for nothing is it part of life. And all of life is now a dusty tree with an enemy flower that shoots out sparks. (Drags a stool over to FORTUNATO.)

ANISIA *(boosting* FORTUNATO *up onto the stool)*: When we turn into kids again we'll have better aim. When we turn back into kids again we'll throw rocks at that blasted light and bust it. And then you won't have to die this way, so bumblingly.

TICO: *(as he climbs up onto* FORTUNATO's *back and slips the noose around his neck, though* FORTUNATO *is still taking aim at the soldier's back)*: We will never forgive life for the brevity of innocence. That is another thing we will never forgive it for.

ANISIA *(also climbing up onto* FORTUNATO'S *back to inspect the noose)*: We'll never forgive life for our not knowing what our childhood was till we lost it. We will never forgive life for that.

DEAD-ESTHER *(walking out of the living room and standing in the front door, so that all that is seen is her silhouette)*: Everything is so vulgar, so common, that I barely even feel like crying. Everything is so subtle, somehow, so *sneaky*, that when we really come to look, the best part of the best part has already gone by—and there we are, waiting. *(Going back into the living room.)* Really, I don't know what to say. You raise your hand and an angel turns around, the Devil turns around, God turns around—the soldier turns around, in a word, and you stand there with your hand raised and a noose around your neck.

(The soldier slowly turns and faces FORTUNATO, *who raises both his hands as though in surrender. The soldier then once again becomes a* DEMON, *who skips over to the others. The street corner fades and all that is left is* FORTUNATO *standing on a stool with his hands up and a rope around his neck.)*

ALL *(with energy, as* ESTHER *slowly retreats)*: But now we have to give a lesson. An example. Some kid tried to jump the wall with the broken glass on top that went all around the house, and he fell. Hang him from the highest tree, so nobody else will try it. From the highest tree, the one with the most branches and leaves. So that every day, all the people passing by—running away, sweating, bursting inside—who stop in the shade of it a second to catch their breath, they'll all look up and see him—because we've got to set an example.

*(*TICO *and* ANISIA *kick the stool out from under* FORTUNATO, *and it rolls off into a corner of the living room.* FORTUNATO *hangs there twitching, with his tongue out. The* CHORUS OF WILD BEASTS

marches off down the hall, crying. The light grows brighter. ADOLFINA, *who for a second has seemed to react, running over toward* FORTUNATO *to save him, is stopped by the* CHORUS OF PRINCES.)

CH. OF PRINCES *(surrounding* ADOLFINA, *who stands almost underneath* FORTUNATO*)*: "The flowers appear on the earth; the time of the singing of birds is come, and the voice of the turtle is heard in our land. The fig tree putteth forth her green figs, and the vines with the tender grape give a good smell. Arise, my love, my fair one, and come away." *(They lead* ADOLFINA *over to the stool in the corner, set it up, and lift her up onto it, constantly bowing obsequiously and cajoling her.)*

*(*POLO, *looking up at the ceiling, walks over until he is standing practically underneath* FORTUNATO. *At that moment* JACINTA *appears, and she lets out a howl.* POLO *stops.* FORTUNATO *is wildly gesticulating above him.)*

JACINTA: There's your daughter out there, with her two children and a bundle of clothes over her shoulder. Moisés has left her. Go out there and throw a rock at that son of a bitch. You ought to kill that son of a bitch. Ay, go out there and kill him, at least. Get out there and do *something,* because I'm about to bust a gut. And if *you* don't do it, then I'm going out there myself and crack a stalk of plantains over his head. Would you let your wife go out there while you stay cooped up in the house? *(Steps closer to* POLO.*)* Get out there, you old coot, git. Git. *(She embraces him. They exit in an embrace.)*

DIGNA *(picking up and looking under all the chairs)*: I've got to tell somebody that I'm still alive, that I'm waiting, with nothing to wait for. That I'm alive. *(Shouts.)* Here I am—for your entertainment! Here I am, to confound all the people that expected something out of me! With two children, one disgrace behind me and another moving into position right up ahead. *(She discovers* FORTUNATO *hanged, now barely swaying; she goes over, touches him.)* Here I am till the cockroaches decide something different, or I do myself . . . If it weren't that I can't see a thing past my own hard luck, I'd say this is a hanged man I'm standing in front of—and touching. And that this hanged man is my nephew Fortunato. But my own shafting's too terrible to share with just anybody that wants to join in. *(She steps back from the body.)* In a word, all I am is a woman abandoned with two children, and who's fated to spend the rest of her life alone and grieving. And besides, it's *way* too late. *(To* TICO *and* ANISIA.*)* Come on, you kids, it's time for bed.

*(*TICO *and* ANISIA *stop playing with the dead man, pick their masks up off the floor, and hand them to the* DEMONS. TICO *picks up the seashell and the two children listening to the ocean exit with* DIGNA.*)*

ANISIA *(jerking her ear away from the seashell)*: A tongue, growing, growing—a tongue growing out of the bottom of a bottomless well.

TICO *(taking the seashell away from his ear and looking hard at* ANISIA*)*: You're getting warmer. No doubt about that. But you're still cold. *(Goes back to listening to the ocean.)*

DIGNA *(from the hallway)*: Come on, hurry up . . . Good lord, this house is like a cave, it's so dark. And the whole town in the same boat. This is the limit. And the heat on top of all. We're suffocating. And to think this is December . . . Where will this all end if we keep on like we're going now? . . .

*(*CELIA *enters, with* ESTHER *sitting on her shoulders and rhythmically slapping her in the face.)*

CELIA: I'm rummaging around in the highest beams up in the roof, but I get all caught up in a tangle of spiderwebs and there I'm trapped. So then I put out my hands and a drizzle like fine rain starts falling—I can hear my own hands sweating in the dark. Is that drizzle a symbol, Death's latest apparition? *(She stands underneath* FORTUNATO *and looks up.)* Or is it just the dew? Everything is so mysterious that a person comes to doubt any sort of sensation that seems the least bit unreal. Such a constant balancing act between the two abysses just to come finally to *the* abyss. My daughter *(the rate of slapping increases)*—in a fit of ecstasy I will be under the roof, yet above the beams—that's right, neither below nor above. Suspended in the midst of disgrace, misfortune, and loving it. *(The rhythm of the slaps grows faster and more violent.)* . . . Now I begin to hear the music, and the rain falls so heavy that it drowns me almost. And here are the birds. Listen to those birdsongs, people, listen to that singing, listen to that music. *(Goes off as the sound of the beating given her by* ESTHER *grows more and more frenetic, loud, like a marching cadence of drums. They go out of sight down the hall. Immediately, all the* DEMONS *rush to attack* ADOLFINA.)

ALL THE DEMONS *(trying to pull* ADOLFINA *off her stool)*: Ga-ga-boom, ga-ga-boom, ga-ga-boom.

CH. OF PRINCES *(stepping in, soothing* ADOLFINA *with caresses and helping her back up onto her seat)*: "My beloved is white and ruddy, the chiefest among ten thousand. His head is as the most fine gold, his locks are bushy, and black as a raven. His eyes are as the eyes of doves by the rivers of waters, washed with milk, and fitly set. His cheeks are as a bed of spices, as sweet flowers; his lips like lilies, dropping sweet smelling myrrh."

ALL THE DEMONS *(shaking* ADOLFINA *by the shoulders)*: Ga-ga-boom, ga-ga-boom, ga-ga-boom.

CH. OF PRINCES *(quickly forming an obsequious and attentive circle around* ADOLFINA)*: "His cheeks are as a bed of spices, as sweet flowers; his lips like lilies, dropping sweet smelling myrrh. His hands are as gold rings set with the beryl; his belly is as bright ivory overlaid with sapphires."

*(*ADOLFINA *covers her face with her hands and begins wriggling about on the stool.)*

ALL THE DEMONS *(still more violently pulling at* ADOLFINA)*: Ga-ga-boom, ga-ga-boom, ga-ga-boom.

CH. OF PRINCES *(holding* ADOLFINA *and beginning to run their hands over her body more and more frantically and lasciviously)*: "His legs are as pillars of marble, set upon sockets of fine gold; his countenance is as Lebanon, excellent as the cedars."

ALL THE DEMONS (*dragging* ADOLFINA *over to where* FORTUNATO *is hanging*): Ga-ga-*boom*, ga-ga-*boom*, ga-ga-*boom*.

CH. OF PRINCES (*jumping in ahead of her, embracing her, caressing her, attempting to possess her, crying out*): "His mouth is most sweet; yea, he is altogether lovely. This is my beloved, and this is my friend, O daughters of Jerusalem."

(*At this moment* ADOLFINA *bumps into* FORTUNATO's *feet. She looks up. She sees him. She screams. The* CHORUS OF PRINCES *and* KNIGHTS IN SHINING ARMOR *vanishes into thin air. The* DEMONS, *wild with exultance, leap all about the room, destroying any furniture still standing and crying Ga-ga-*boom, *ga-ga-*boom, *ga-ga-*boom. *Then they take up their positions in a classical chorus off to one side of the living room and begin, at the sound of a distant, slow pealing of bells, to intone the ga-ga-*boom *louder and louder, until it finally becomes unbearable.* ADOLFINA *paces all about the room, sticks her head out the window several times, opens and closes the door, and then at last shuts the window for good, runs off to the bathroom, and locks herself in. At that moment the front door bangs open and* JACINTA *stalks in with a crowbar.*)

JACINTA: Adolfina, you're coming out of there this time whether you like it or not. This time I can't take anymore. (*She bangs on the bathroom door as the ga-ga-*boom *grows louder again. From time to time a sound may be heard reminiscent of a great flight of birds trying madly to flee, crashing into trees. The old woman raises the crowbar, gives a great bellow, runs, and knocks down the door.* ADOLFINA *then rushes out, a ball of fire.*)

ADOLFINA (*in flames*): I'll go out into the street, into the street and go to bed with the first man I find.

(ADOLFINA *runs out.* JACINTA *stands there paralyzed for a moment. Then she slowly walks to the center of the living room and kneels down before* FORTUNATO. *Now the ga-ga-*boom *of the*

DEMONS *reaches its peak. It is unbearable. Then it hushes. Long silence.)*

TICO'S VOICE *(offstage)*: You're getting warmer. Yes you are. But you still haven't found the word . . . the exact word.
ANISIA'S VOICE: But I'm not giving up—now less than ever.
TICO'S VOICE: You'll get tired pretty soon, stupid.

*Now Fortunato has taken to hanging himself
early every morning, before the sun
is even up, so every morning we have to get out
of bed and go cut him down.*

THE SIXTH
AGONY

He was about to stab the soldier with the knife. But the soldier turned around. He yelled. And Fortunato froze. The soldier held a gun on him and took his knife away. As soon as he had disarmed him he called out, and at once there were a dozen soldiers surrounding Fortunato, looking at him, laughing at him, and pointing their gleaming submachine guns at him. They led him away to their headquarters. When they arrived, everyone crowded around to look, and to make some comment. So far as they were concerned, he was a cause for laughter, amusement, almost reassurance—a relief. He represented a rest for those young men—fearful, hungry, scared—as well as a chance to brag about their fearlessness and to burn off a little energy, a little pent-up violence. Until the man in charge showed up (a lieutenant apparently) it was just laughter, wisecracks, and a few halfhearted blows, almost accidental, playful, given him with the butt of a rifle or an elbow. Somebody stamped on his foot. But then, at the leader's orders (and how he talked, how he walked, how he held his head and looked and barked out orders), things changed. Now Fortunato was in a small cell (but is there any such thing as a big cell, he wondered) with a tiny window high up in the wall. (But has there ever existed such a thing as a cell with big picture windows?) Apparently Fortunato had taken on the proportions of a rough and ready, subversive, dangerous character in their eyes, for outside, at the door (an iron door, naturally), they had set a guard, rifle in hand. Then the door swung open and the man in charge, the probable lieutenant, entered with a group of

men—his inferiors in rank (and in everything else besides).
For the first time Fortunato was going to be interrogated, for
the first time he was called by name. For the first time in his
life he was a person important enough to be called by first
name, father's last name, and mother's last name, important
enough to merit the gaze, the attention, the work of several
men. The affair was brief. No political questions, no whys or
wherefores. By now that sort of thing was either fatuous or
beside the point. Now the method was simpler. It was now
merely a matter of his telling them who the others were, his
buddies, the guys that he worked with in the underground—
the ones that set off the bombs, tried to kill government
leaders, stole weapons. In short, the names of the people that
aided, abetted, and kept the Revolution alive. That was what
they wanted him to tell them, and quick. After all, this was
mid-1958 . . . At first Fortunato couldn't believe they were
asking him such questions. Couldn't they see he was all by
himself? That he was the only one there was? Didn't they
know that he didn't *know*? That all he wanted to do was just
leave home, get out on his own, because the people, his family, the rats, the sun, the fiber-cement roof, the whole thing.
. . . Couldn't they see that there were no "buddies," no con-
spiracy at all—it was just that there were too many mosquitoes, too little space in too few rooms, too many people, the
noon too hot and glaring. Plus, of course, the smell of rotten
guavas that had permeated the walls and the threat that any
second the ga-ga-*boom* might start up again. *Because you see,
if the bathtub was, were at least separate from the toilet,
then* . . . The first blow stunned him out of his stammering
explanations. It was a terrrible blow—dry, perfectly aimed,
professional. But he still could not remember anything, he
still didn't know what they were asking him, there still were
no names or addresses that came to mind. And the man in
charge, the maybe lieutenant, stared at him, angry no doubt
at having so much of his time wasted. So the second blow,
conferred on Fortunato at the leader's furious nod, made an
even greater impact on him, was even more perfectly cold
and telling. But he still did not remember. He refused, the
son of a bitch, to squeal on his buddies. He thought about

airplanes. Yellow airplanes. And their aviators. And instantly, perhaps by some mechanical, unconscious reflex of the senses, he thought of Aby—the similarity of the sound, it must have been—and then, immediately, his mind jumped to the young men who had always been his companions at Eufrasia's Ball Room. He'd mentioned joining the rebels once to Aby, sure, but that didn't mean he should give them Aby's name. Besides, Aby had refused to join—he'd even told him he'd rather be a steel pot. No, not Aby. Talk, the voice said, and the dry, perfect punch landed in his diaphragm again. But still nothing, still no names came. So that perfect punch had to be repeated—with cold, classic ferocity. There was a window, a high, barred window. Maybe if he kept his eyes up there. There was light. But the perfect punch came again, and with it a flood of insults—reasonable, no doubt, and no doubt justified, for after all, he was wasting these men's time. Yes, if you looked at it from the legal point of view—legal so far as they were concerned—he had no right to waste their time. This was stupid. The natural thing to do, the obvious thing under these circumstances, and what custom and tradition declared proper in these cases, was to confess, tell them who the others were, *where* they were, what their plans were, who were their leaders. "Maybe *you're* one," he heard a voice rasp at the instant someone hit him again, but all it took was the sight of the wry grin on the face of the probable lieutenant for the soldier who'd said it to realize how idiotic such a suspicion was. How could anybody think that this hick, this wet-behind-the-ears kid, with *that* face, with that body all clumsy knees and elbows, could be the leader of a band of rebels? He was one of their gofers, a mule, an errand boy— cannon fodder—sent out to get weapons while the leaders were safe and sound holed up in the mountains somewhere. So they beat him some more, but he remained silent, he never informed on the others. And even the probable lieutenant was surprised and a little irritated by that stubbornness. Because a man didn't have to be a coward, much less a traitor, to confess, to betray his friends, to *act like* a coward under physical pain. The maybe lieutenant knew that. But in spite of everything, even when the beating began again (now in even more strategic, more sensitive, more secret places) and Fortunato said he couldn't give them names because he didn't *know* anybody that worked for the rebels in the city, the soldiers still had more than sufficient reason not to believe him. And yet the blows and punches kept evoking the same useless reply. At last, the man who was surely at least a lieutenant ordered them to try different methods, and he strode from the cell. And seeing the man who had ordered his torture leaving the cell, Fortunato felt real fear for the first time—fear at being alone with the other soldiers. At least the surely lieutenant was *somebody*; he existed, he possessed a certain reality; but *these* men, these other men, were no more than clumsy, stupid machines, unreasoning, passionless animals with no coherent hatred. So it was impossible to reach them with reason, or to insult them. And for one moment he wanted to call out to the no doubt lieutenant, to tell him to stay, to beg him to do the torturing himself, but the man (the only man—tall, firm, cruel, enraged—*real*) had already disappeared down one of the hallways. The cell door closed again, and Fortunato was alone with those impersonal beings before whom one felt totally naked, impotent, and even guilty . . . Now one of them was running his hands with practiced mechanical movements all over Fortunato's body, and that touch from time to time brought back the memory of the touch of other hands. His mother's hand running down his back while he, delighted, thought that at least for today his grandfather had been defeated. But when the hand got to his testicles it stopped, encircled them, took one in its broad cupped palm and squeezed with such violence, with such precision, that even Fortunato was surprised when he heard himself screaming. And he was more surprised, more desolate yet, when he realized that in spite of his screaming, the pain went on. But then the fingers loosened, the pressure relaxed; but all he could do was sob softly—he still could not name (or curse) any names. Then they started giving him tiny knife pricks in his belly; then someone was drilling some red-hot instrument into his neck—a cigarette? a firebrand? a tongue of flame? There were dragons, dragons. He'd seen them somewhere, and now they had returned—look at them. Now they were going away . . . But then, with a strange gleaming object, like a toy for children aged six and under (as some said on their boxes), they began to pry off his toenails. I am joy personified, he thought; I am the great deafening din, he thought. I am the chaste princess who, under an ancient tree, watches troops go by as I sit waving, cheered by all, waiting for my prince. I am the medieval elfin wizard taking shelter from the wilting heat, the fires and spells, lying in the shade of the royal belltower. I am the lord of the wind, the lord of the waters, the ruler of the seasons. And beyond, out there, sometimes, *now*, suddenly he saw himself wrapped in the cloud of wind and water which he himself had unleashed, which he himself was driving, and he was entering a vast garden of high fieldstone walls, to the sound of tambors and flutes, and there were roses, roses in all the beds, and the sun was falling straight down though there was the smell of impending rain. They dragged him out of the cell, down the hall (I am glory, I am joy, I am falling leaves, I am the roar of the sea and tiny ripples of sound, the rustling of the wild coffee bush when you pass your hand over its branches). They threw him into the back of a truck and then dragged him out of it into a field of high grass on the outskirts of the town, near the main highway. But listen, listen, what if at this very minute there were an earthquake, a tremor of the ground, a great flash of light, let us say, and what if it should roll across the earth and make them vanish, and you found yourself all alone, free, in the middle of this wide field—would you know what to do? Would you know what to do with your life then, could you tell me what you would want from life? Jasmine, just jasmine. Near his grandfather's farm there lived some people named Estrada—hardworking people. Even though the land was poor, and pure rocky treeless flatland, the man had made plantains grow; there was him, his wife (Amelia was her name), and seven children, two of them twins, and one was a cripple—and in spite of all the disadvantages of the weather and the land and everything else besides, they had the most lovely hedge of Cape jasmines (which some people called gardenias) that you would ever want to see. Sometimes on Sundays, when it was time to bring the calves in, he would escape instead to the Estradas' place. With the excuse that some animal had strayed, he would run over to that rocky farm where the plantains grew, run to the hedge of Cape jasmines, and simply walk along it—filling his senses with the perfume, the dark green, the milky waxy white. He did not dare touch the flowers (which Amelia sold at two for five centavos), but he almost caressed them with his breath. And that hedge of gardenias sprang up there in that field he was in now, and he began to walk along beside it. But they caught him doing that, and somebody was carrying a rope—he knew he wasn't allowed in that field. Shouts, angry voices, violent shoves, dogs barking, and the suspicion that Amelia had been on the back porch, just waiting for him to break off even one little branch so she could sic the dogs on him, tell his grandpa, rip off his toenails, squeeze his balls. They made him walk now through the high grass, and one of them, the one carrying the rope, started lashing him with it across his back. They saw him as the winner, the victor, the man that had beat the system, who'd gotten away with it—and every blow they landed, every kick, every heavy lash of the rope was evidence of their frustration and rage. Actually, they no longer even felt like beating him. They wanted to get this one over with, they wanted to get back. It had been, all in all, a wasted day. And the way things were . . . Where had he heard that, always? . . . Run, they told him, and (patient, obedient, disciplined, always mindful of the orders older people gave him, carrying them out to the letter while secretly violating them by conceding them no value, no importance, by considering them not even worth saying no to, not even worth not obeying) he ran. They waited for him to get a little way away, and when he had got far enough they shouted for him to halt. They had had the foresight to aim their rifles at him while he was still running, so that before he turned around they could shoot him in the back, thereby justifying (if indeed they were ever called to justify) the death by saying that the prisoner had attempted to escape and had refused to halt when ordered to . . . But hadn't he almost made it to the stand of scrub already? And if he could make it that far, couldn't he hide in among the briars and brambles so nobody would be able to find him, and nobody would bother him anymore? So for the first time in his life he disobeyed the threats, warnings, and orders of those people that were older than him, and he just kept running. So the soldiers could afford the luxury, display the depth of their generosity, so far as to repeat that *Halt!* twice more, and actually open fire justifiably, under the full protection of the law . . . He made it. Even without having to stop to push his way through the fence clogged with briars and prickly wild pineapple plants, he plunged into the scrub, and he saw as he came out into a wide expanse of carefully tended lawn a herd of splendid horses coursing through the dusk, crossing the sky and vanishing—and at that instant he felt a stinging, burning pain pierce him, pass through his body, and he realized that now it was not a question of finding a place to hide in, it was a question of chucking everything and trying to save himself. He ran. He ran wounded through the wide field, and the perfume of the great climbing vine which the air blew in gusts across his path tangled in his feet, and it was hard to free himself from that perfume. But now there was no time for memory, or for sensations, there was only one absolute, hard fact—he did not want to die. He stumbled, fell, and picked himself up again. He shook off that perfume and went on running. But someone was methodically pulling off his toenails again, and now a powerful hand was squeezing one of his testicles again. Now the well-aimed punch to the solar plexus, the blows to his head, the pincers and claws in the most painful and terrifying places. And it was then, as he felt them begin to hold burning brands to his neck again, that he realized that those things simply could not be happening to him. It was impossible. And it was then that he saw (as his neck was attacked by small, sharp teeth, then longer, fatter ones, iron teeth) that he had ceased being *himself* a long time ago, that he had become everyone, all of them. Because he was like a lightning rod for terror, for terror in all its variety, and therefore who better to suffer it. Had he not once been Adolfina, and been able to plumb for himself the rage brought on by abstinence drawn out for a lifetime? Had he not been Digna, and known at first hand a loneliness without the consolation of even one moment of pretense? Had he not been Polo, and experienced for himself frustration in all its degrees? And had it not been he himself who had given voice, the tragic sense, *importance* to those creatures—who, had they spoken for themselves, would have reduced the dimensions of their lives to a brief, almost inaudible death rattle, a common scream lost, drowned, in the tumult of all the world's other insignificant and futile screams. He was the traitor to that silence, the dealer in nightmare, the man chosen, it seemed, to testify, the superior one. Coming undone, being undone, undoing himself, in order to do something. The interpreter—whose task would be finished when he achieved his greatest agony, when he vanished, when the fire's fury had reduced him to ash. So running, panting (yet now serene, happy almost), he realized that only in violence and transfiguration could he find his true being, a justification for his existence, the only self he'd ever have . . . The transfigurations had been achieved, he had been able to achieve them, to undergo them, to *suffer* them, so now all that was left was the violence, and he would reach his absolute apotheosis. Explode. Like a star plunging to earth from its apogee. Be nothing but a million tiny burning particles polluting the earth. Explode. Be nothing but a spurt of blood splattering across the earth. And violently flooding everyplace in it. And go no farther. Not expect that to be a step, a door, a gateway toward the beginning of some new triumph, some new battle, some new hell. Not expect that violent journey, that explosion to ever, ever give meaning to any new development, any new stage of evolution, any new con job. Just simply burst. And splatter walls, trees, empty cans, grass—and vanish completely. He had to go on. He had to exhaust all his energy. He had to waste it all, disperse himself utterly. Until the fall was over . . . There was, in spite of all, a lake—a lake full of floating candles whose flames flickered pale and even guttering, out to the horizon. And he ran toward that expanse so that he could disseminate his particles through all those fires. But when he got there, the candles were gardenias, lilies, floating lotuses, a play of light on the water, windows at dusk, millions of exploding panes of glass, and, at last, a field of shining phalluses—erect or, somewhat pale, beginning to stir upright. Someone was singing, someone was starting to sing that horrible, disgusting song again, the only song he had ever been able to memorize completely. Someone was coming, someone was coming, singing that melody again, and then on his face he saw huge claws descend. It was the fly—which was such a master of histrionic ability that it parodied that old song as it buzzed and fluttered—ceremonious, blue— about his face . . . There was an immense warehouse and it was full of words. What a sight—millions of creatures shoveling, picking through them, digging, trying to choose, hunting, hunting, hunting, as one landslide of words after another crashed down about them—grooved words, short chubby words, unmanageably dense words, sharp words, angular words, restless bouncing words, unbuckled words, words torn, broken, worn out, stinking, toothless, ugly, mutilated, imprisoned, sexless, whining, teary, sticky, prickly—and buried many. And he found himself there in that huge warehouse too, armed only with a small spade, rummaging through all that unspeakable filth desolately, randomly. At last, retching and gagging, he ran out of the huge building. A light rain suddenly began to fall, on him and on the stand of manjack trees at the entrance to the town. And from the warm, slow, heavy drops, Fortunato realized that winter was upon them, that fleeting winter of the tropics with its sticky humidity and that same brutal sun. But then it was the middle of December, so why should this rain surprise him? . . . To refresh himself, to get his breath again so he could run some more, he turned his face to the sky. And then he saw the moon once more, cold, distant, flowing timelessly behind a sheer curtain of translucent clouds. And suddenly it seemed to him the moon didn't look like she was glaring at him in hatred anymore, it looked like she wasn't going to slap him at all— in fact it looked like he had lost all interest for her and that she was going off to new things. And as he shooed off the fly that was buzzing around him once more, it seemed to him that that sallow, pained, bitter face that flowed across the sky was the face of someone he knew, perhaps even someone he loved. But how . . . Who was it? But there was no call to ask himself so many questions. There was no call to lose the thread of his intentions, get all disoriented and off the track, now that he finally knew what those intentions were. There was no call to stop, to waste time there, or anywhere. There was no call to lose sight of the goal. His goal, his *only* goal. Explode. And nothing more. *There* would be his victory. Now, now. And so, snorting, howling, bellowing, swatting at that persistent insect still hovering about his face in the rain, he ran . . . He ran . . . The three men, sheltered under the manjack trees, patiently awaited the end of that race. The man who was carrying the rope made a motion for them to turn off the flashlight. Moonlight flooded the fields. For a moment it stopped raining. And Fortunato, touched by that light, looked up. And he saw her. He saw the moon with that round face of hers, the face of an insulted whore, flowing now through the empty peaceful night. And at last he recognized her, he knew who it was. It was Adolfina scudding through the sky, pale, harried, hurrying, still looking . . .

The Life of the Dead

But when the bullet-riddled, hunted-down, dragged, abused body—the body that would never have to be clothed in rags again, the body that spurred by lord knew what impossible desires would never run him through the night again—when that body condemned to death at last cramps and contracts, is dropped at the end of a rope, and then after a quick snap grows stiff and numb, its last somersault frustrated, then the river of dreams which had seemed infinite stops. The interpreting ceases, the fabulous voyages end, the transfigurations and the imaginings, the invented consolations grow dim and fade away. And all those infinite speculations on death which until one moment ago (this very instant) we were still indulging ourselves in begin to lose their glow; they are discredited, they simply disappear before the evidence (the indisputable evidence) of a weariness, a sleep which cannot be put off, a pain so sharp that it cannot be resolved into images. The river stops, and there end all the invented deaths, all the ends that an unknown but certain death forced us to imagine, however erroneously. The river stops, and with it those wonderful floating lights (like altar lights), the impalpable figures underwater, the trees that never flowered in reality so beautifully as they did in memory, and all the faces we put on things to make our miserable lives livable. The river stops. The great current (down which all possibilities flowed and out of whose constant discontent the shrieks of every day were transformed into song) disappears, becomes a cataract into the void, and its roar dissolves in the sharp burning itch that rises, rises, until it takes body in a stabbing pain in his back. And all the games vanish, and all the flights, all the escapes crash into each other and fuse, burst, and form a hard brick wall. And all the demons submerge. And God turns into a blank movie screen, and a tiny pebble, not brilliant in the least, not polished, hits us in the eyebrow. And all the voices which at one point had ordered us to sing, to rat on our buddies, to run, to halt, to go on, now lose their desperate shrillness, and all noises are now the footsteps of someone coming, to testify no doubt to our death. Closer. The great palace vanishes as eyelashes furiously flutter. Closer. The innumerable pains, the anguish, the misery dissolves as we rush toward that unmoving plane, that blank screen, that brick wall. Closer. And the fire, which we always have in reserve in case there's no other way out, at last makes a tiny circle, a minuscule dot waggling obediently in the fingers of the man who has come to inspect us. The man is here. And the pure one, the poor one, the hero is now but dregs—which still bear the signs of the beating it had suffered.

THE FLY—III

The fly is immune to noise, to bright lights—its buzzing is inalterable. I have seen a fly float, apparently dead, for more than a day in a puddle of water, in hopes that some leaf, some gust of wind, evaporation, will come to its aid. It is cunning—it knows how to tell the feigned breathing of the false sleeper ready to pounce. It is cunning—it can make a clear distinction between the open mouth of a dead man and that of a man merely sleeping. But it is stubborn, persistent, and sometimes it fixes on some trivial object—a lock of hair, the curve of an earlobe, the triangle of a nose, the shine of velvet—and it is capable of following that object for miles, just to prove to itself that it can do it, or perhaps spurred on by rejection, indifference, or the pointlessness of the chase. As it is a being unto itself it is a diabolical being—it knows the secrets of levitation and it can walk upside down on the ceiling. As it is a diabolical being it is eternal—it does not mind living in sewers, in courtrooms, in cracked and broken caskets, in the dark pits of privies. It knows that someday (in the past or in the future or even now perhaps) these customs too will receive their due, for their selfless, noble, heroic nature will be discovered . . . Although apparently up to now the fly (all too attached to life, to nature) has been indifferent to medals and decorations, it goes without saying that someday it will flutter, perhaps out of pure curiosity, above clinking medals, above tall trophies, above noble sashes honoring it . . . On summer afternoons, there often falls a shower. The air becomes transparent, light, full of smells. The fly at such times appears to break with the long-observed tradition according to which it never makes purposeless movements, for it flies up very very high, to make curvets and flourishes in the air. It plays, it buzzes, it bathes in the sunlight filtering through the trees, and then it dies against the screen of the front porch. Out of this agitation, out of that sunbath, out of that playful combination of motion and light, are born the green fly, the red fly, the violet fly—and the archetypal blue fly of the tropics.

356